Romantic Suspense

Danger. Passion. Drama.

Vanished In Texas
Karen Whiddon

Christmas Bodyguard
Katherine Garbera

MILLS & BOON

VANISHED IN TEXAS
© 2024 by Karen Whiddon
Philippine Copyright 2024
Australian Copyright 2024
New Zealand Copyright 2024

First Published 2024
First Australian Paperback Edition 2024
ISBN 978 1 038 91773 7

CHRISTMAS BODYGUARD
© 2024 by Katherine Garbera
Philippine Copyright 2024
Australian Copyright 2024
New Zealand Copyright 2024

First Published 2024
First Australian Paperback Edition 2024
ISBN 978 1 038 91773 7

MIX
Paper | Supporting
responsible forestry
FSC® C001695

Published by
Harlequin Mills & Boon
An imprint of Harlequin Enterprises (Australia) Pty Limited
(ABN 47 001 180 918), a subsidiary of HarperCollins
Publishers Australia Pty Limited
(ABN 36 009 913 517)
Level 19, 201 Elizabeth Street
SYDNEY NSW 2000 AUSTRALIA

Cover art used by arrangement with Harlequin Books S.A.. All rights reserved.

Printed and bound in Australia by McPherson's Printing Group

Vanished In Texas

Karen Whiddon

MILLS & BOON

Karen Whiddon started weaving fanciful tales for her younger brothers at the age of eleven. Amid the gorgeous Catskill Mountains, then the majestic Rocky Mountains, she fueled her imagination with the natural beauty surrounding her. Karen now lives in north Texas, writes full-time and volunteers for a boxer dog rescue. She shares her life with her hero of a husband and four to five dogs, depending on if she is fostering. You can email Karen at kwhiddon1@aol.com. Fans can also check out her website, karenwhiddon.com.

Visit the Author Profile page
at millsandboon.com.au for more titles.

Dear Reader,

I love my little fictional town of Getaway, Texas. The people have become like family to me and it makes me happy to give them brief appearances in every book I set there.

In this story, Willow Allen couldn't wait to get out of small-town west Texas life. She moved to California after college and only returns from time to time to visit her grandmother Isla, who raised her. Rey Johnson also left after high school to join the military. Unlike Willow, he returned to help his father, Carl, run the family ranch along with his younger brother, Sam. He loves his life and can't imagine living anywhere else.

When both Isla and Carl (who have been dating) go missing, Willow rushes home. Rey had been on the road picking up livestock and is concerned to find his father has disappeared. His brother, Sam, claims to have no idea where Carl might have gone.

As Willow and Rey team up to find their missing family members, more and more older people from town are vanishing, and no one seems to know why or where they've gone. The mystery deepens, and Willow and Rey grow closer as they continue to search for clues. Willow knows she cannot return to California until her grandmother is found, and even then, she has her doubts. She hadn't realised how much she'd missed Getaway and her grandmother. Plus, the thought of leaving Rey has become physically painful.

I hope you enjoy reading this suspenseful love story as much as I enjoyed writing it!

Karen Whiddon

DEDICATION

Almost every book I write, I dedicate to my husband,
Lonnie. We've been together for a long time and
seen each other through many ups and downs.
He reads every single book I write once it's
published and that's a lot. He's the model
for every romantic hero! Love you, Lonnie.

Chapter 1

The instant Willow Allen caught sight of her grandmother's white-frame ranch house, something inside her unclenched. West Texas might be flat, the earth dry and desert like, and the weather in July hotter than most people would consider hospitable, but no matter where Willow currently lived, she'd always consider it home.

For the past five years, Willow had lived in California, with its perfect weather, palm trees and beaches. She'd taken a job there right out of college, working as an actuary for a large insurance company. The work was not particularly glamorous, but she'd always loved numbers and considered it a good fit.

But then her grandmama had mentioned going to the hospital with chest pains and, after returning home, had refused to discuss her health further. She'd steadfastly said she was fine, claiming nothing was wrong. Alarmed, Willow had immediately put in for some of her accumulated PTO and made the long drive back to Getaway, Texas. She'd decided not to tell her grandmother, aware Isla would tell her not to come.

She hadn't been home since Christmas. Seven months ago, her grandmother had been just fine. At least, as far as Willow had been able to tell. But Isla lived alone, and despite expressing happiness with her new relationship with a local rancher, Willow worried. The woman she considered her mother had single-handedly raised her and loved her without reservation after Willow's birth mother, Isla's daughter, had died of a drug overdose. She was and would always be the most important person in Willow's life. Willow couldn't wait to surprise her. She planned to wrap her arms around her grandmother's tiny frame, breathe in her unique patchouli scent and spend the next three weeks catching up.

Parking her shiny, new red Ford Bronco in the driveway, Willow got her suitcase out of the back and pulled it up to the front door. She used her own key and entered, calling out to alert her grandmother to her presence.

Nothing but silence answered her. Just her luck. Grandma mustn't be home. She dug out her phone and called her. Immediately, a phone in the master bedroom started ringing.

That was odd, to say the least. Willow hurried over and, sure enough, spotted her grandmother's cell on the nightstand next to the neatly made bed.

Concerned, Willow began searching the house. What if Isla had experienced another chest pain episode and fallen? She might even now be lying unconscious. Heart racing, Willow went through every room, checking in the closet and shower, the kitchen pantry and laundry room and, finally, the garage.

Her grandmother's silver Toyota Corolla still sat parked inside.

What the…? Willow backtracked to the master bedroom and opened the closet. While she wasn't an expert on Isla's wardrobe, it didn't look like much, if anything, was missing.

Maybe her grandma's new beau had picked her up and taken her out somewhere, and she'd simply forgotten her phone. That had to be it. Willow would simply call him, make sure her grandmother was okay and wait for her return.

She grabbed Isla's phone and realized she didn't know the passcode. Despite trying several combinations, from her grandmother's birthday to her own, she couldn't get in. Frustrated, she went back to her own phone and scrolled through the texts between the two of them, trying to find the guy's name. Finally, she located it. Carl. No last name. And while Willow knew most of the families in town, without more information, she had no idea who Carl might be.

Still concerned, she called her friend Amanda. Unlike Willow, Amanda had never left Getaway. After graduating from cosmetology school, Amanda had opened her own beauty salon right on Main Street. No one had better access to the local gossip than the proprietor of Hair Affair. But the receptionist who answered said Amanda was with a client and offered to take a message.

Instead of leaving her name and number, Willow hung up. No way did she intend to sit around aimlessly and wait for Amanda to return her call. Patience had never been one of her virtues.

She grabbed her car keys and decided to head downtown. She might as well ask Amanda in person. That way, she could go directly to this Carl's house and see if her grandmother was there. If not, maybe Carl might know where Isla had gone.

While she hated to take such drastic measures, Willow didn't see how she had a choice. None of this was like her mom. Even if Isla hadn't been aware her daughter was coming to pay her a surprise visit, she had her self-imposed routine. Ever since becoming an empty nester, she'd filled her days with various activities, all scheduled. She attended yoga on Tuesdays, book club on Thursdays, and she volunteered at the local animal shelter on Friday afternoons. She'd taken up knitting and gardening and took great pride in her rose bushes. By her own unvarying schedule, Isla should be home right now, making something for the noon meal.

Pushing away her niggling worry, Willow went back outside to get in her SUV to make the short drive back to town. But before she could even start the engine, a large dually pickup pulled up in front of the house.

Maybe her grandmother had arrived home. Excited, Willow got out of her SUV and started toward the huge truck. As she approached, instead of Isla, a tall man wearing a black cowboy hat got out. He wore well-fitting Wranglers and boots. Ignoring her, he started for the front door.

"Excuse me," she said, causing him to break stride. "No one's home."

This finally caught his attention. He turned, muscles rippling under his tan Western shirt. His handsome, rugged face seemed vaguely familiar, as if she might have seen him on a television show or in a movie.

She froze, her first thought *rodeo cowboy*. But then again, maybe not. He had a strong profile and chiseled features. And he moved with a kind of easy grace that she found somehow sensual. A true West Texas specimen brimming over with masculinity. And absolutely everything that she'd once found unbearably sexy and now abhorred in a man.

Or thought she did, right up until this very moment.

"I'm looking for my father," he said, his husky voice tinged with the familiar West Texas drawl. "Carl Johnson. His, er, lady friend lives in this house."

Crossing her arms, she took a deep breath. "My grandmother lives here. And she's gone. I just arrived in from out of state. I was hoping she was with him."

Now she'd caught his attention. "Gone?" His narrow gaze swept over her. "Where is she?"

"I don't know. Her car is in the garage. And she left her cell phone in her bedroom. I have no idea where she might be. In fact, I was heading into town to see if I could find out where your father lives so I could check there."

"His truck is still at the ranch too," the man mused. "I wonder if they had friends pick them up."

"What about your dad's cell? Did you try calling it?"

Slowly, he nodded. "I did. He left it behind too." Moving a few steps closer, he held out his hand. "Rey Johnson."

"Willow Allen." She took his hand and shook it, hiding her amazement at how easily his large hand engulfed hers. "I need to find my grandmother. And since your father is missing too, maybe we can team up to make the search easier."

"I wouldn't say missing," he began, then shrugged and shook his head. "Though I guess you could call it that."

With that, he turned to go.

"Wait!" Stunned, she rushed after him. "What are we going to do about it? We have to find them."

"We?" He turned and stared.

Deciding to continue pushing, since she had no idea what else to do, she nodded. "Yes, *we.* Two heads are better than one, don't you think? And since our parents are likely together, it only makes sense."

When her plea didn't appear to convince him, she continued. "I grew up here. And while I don't live here now, I know enough about Getaway to know all of us stick together and help each other."

"Did you go to school with my younger brother, Sam?" he asked.

It took her a moment to put the name together. "Sam Johnson?" Stunned, now it was her turn to stare. "I did. I had no idea my grandmother was dating his father."

"Our father," he corrected. "But, yes. The two of them have been seeing each other for several months."

She took a moment to fully digest this. When she and her grandmom had talked on the phone, Isla had been uncharacteristically giddy about her new relationship. Willow had been happy for her. After all, her grandmother had been alone for as long as Willow could remember. She'd dated, certainly. But she'd also cultivated a wide circle of friends, and between social activities and her volunteer work, her life had seemed full.

Until the health scare. The mere fact that Isla refused to talk about it, when she and Willow kept no secrets from one another, had been really concerning. This, more than anything else, had made Willow drive home.

Right now though, she needed to find her grandmother. "What about their other friends? Do you think they might be out somewhere with another couple?"

He shrugged. "I have no idea, but since neither of

them took their own vehicles, that has to be what happened. I just got back from Colorado, where I picked up livestock. Since my dad was really excited about them, and he knew when I'd be back, I was surprised when I couldn't find him. Sam has been busy repairing fence all day, so he didn't know anything."

The undercurrent of worry she thought she heard in his voice gave her pause. "Do you think something might have happened to them?"

When he met her gaze, his brown eyes seemed kind. "Let's not jump to conclusions. I'm sure there's a rational explanation."

She wanted to believe him. Yet she couldn't seem to shake the feeling that something was wrong. "I'm going to go into town and ask around. One lunch at the Tumbleweed Café should catch me up on all the local gossip."

This comment made him laugh. "Truer words have never been spoken."

"What about you? Would you like to join me?" she asked.

"Maybe another time," he replied, holding her gaze. The warmth in his expression made her mouth go dry. "I need to head back to the ranch. How about I give you my number and you can text me so I have yours. That way, if either of us gets any new information, we can let the other know."

She entered his number into her phone contacts and then sent him a text so he'd have hers. Then she watched as he strode to his truck, an unfamiliar ache warring with the worry inside of her.

Just as he reached for his door handle, he stopped and turned. "I changed my mind," he said. "If you still want to, let's go grab lunch. I haven't eaten since sunrise and could go for one of the Tumbleweed's burgers."

"Sounds great." She hurried to join him before he changed his mind.

To her surprise, he went around to the passenger side and opened the door for her. "Thanks," she said, realizing she'd almost forgotten what it was like to live in small-town West Texas.

Buckling up, she waited for him to get in and start the engine. Now she could only hope they'd run into both their parents, so she could put this sense of foreboding behind her.

Damn. Drumming his fingers on the steering wheel as he drove, Rey Johnson tried to reconcile his admittedly vague memories of the teenaged girl who'd hung around with his younger brother with the stunning woman in his passenger seat.

He'd known, of course, that his father's girlfriend had a daughter who lived in California. Sam had mentioned bitterly several times how much he envied Willow for having the courage to get out of West Texas and start a new life somewhere better. For all his talk, Sam seemed awfully content to stick around the family ranch and do the bare minimum to help keep the place running.

Both Rey and their father humored him. Carl because Sam was his youngest son, aka the baby, and Rey because he understood what made his brother tick. While Sam might be a dreamer, he hadn't yet made the connection between dreams and the hard work necessary to accomplish them.

Shaking off these thoughts, Rey glanced at Willow.

"I'm guessing it's been a while since you visited your grandmother?"

"Christmas," she answered, clearly distracted. "Just about seven months ago. I work in LA. I usually save up my vacation days so I can come home. Though my grandmom and I talk on the phone at least once a week. Sometimes more."

"LA?" He could understand why she'd gone to California. Whether her dream had been to model or to become an actor, someone who looked like her would be sure to get noticed. "Do you act?"

"Act?" Frowning, she eyed him as if he'd suggested she'd taken up cliff diving as a hobby. "No. I work in insurance. I'm an actuary. My job is to analyze the financial costs of risk and uncertainty." She took a deep breath and then smiled. "I absolutely love it."

Her smile lit up the inside of his truck and made his heart beat just a little bit faster.

"An actuary," he repeated, trying not to show his surprise. "I take it you must also love math."

"And spreadsheets," she countered, still smiling. "But yes. Math is my jam."

Not sure how to respond, he nodded.

"What about you?" she asked. "Since you're a rancher, I'm guessing you work around the place with your father."

"And brother," he added. "Sam works there too. We raise cattle, though recently we expanded to include bison. That's what I was doing in Colorado."

"Yet neither of you noticed when your dad left? Why wouldn't he have mentioned he was going somewhere?"

"That's just it," he replied, frustrated. "He's been really looking forward to seeing the bison we purchased.

He knew what time I'd be getting back. I actually expected him to be there to help me unload."

Turning onto Main Street, he noticed the way Willow sat up straight. "The Tumbleweed looks busy as always," she said, her lips curving. "I think out of all the places to eat in Getaway, I missed this one the most."

Since he'd never even once wanted to live anywhere else besides the town where he'd grown up, he simply shrugged. "Some things never change."

He found a parking spot close to the entrance. When he and Willow walked in together, several patrons sent interested glances their way. Which meant they'd be talking about him later.

The hostess, a quiet girl named Barbi who looked like a college student, led them to a booth close to a front window. Busy scanning the restaurant, Willow nearly ran her over when she stopped in front of their seats.

"I'm so sorry," Willow said. "I'm just looking for my mother or even some of her friends. Maybe you've seen her? Isla Allen?"

Barbi stared and then shook her head. "I'm new," she replied. "This is only my second day. I'm home from Tech for the summer. So if she's a regular here, I wouldn't know her. I can ask around though, if you want."

"I'd appreciate it." Willow slid into the booth and accepted the menu.

A moment later, Rey did the same. He'd barely glanced at the menu when an older man wearing a Western shirt, Wranglers and boots walked up. "Afternoon, Rey."

Rey pushed to his feet and held out his hand. "Good to see you, Walter. You haven't happened to have seen my father around town today, have you?"

"Nope. I haven't seen much of Carl ever since he went and got himself a lady friend." Walter eyed Willow curiously. "And who's this here pretty young thing?"

"My name is Willow Allen," Willow said, smiling. "I'm Isla Allen's daughter."

Walter's faded blue gaze sharpened. "Nice to see you back in town. I remember when you were just knee high."

"We're looking for them both," Willow continued. "As you seem to know, his father, Carl, and my grandma, Isla, are a couple. We're hoping someone around here might have seen them."

"You can't find them?" Walter asked. "Are you saying they're missing?"

"Not at all," Rey said, aware he needed to step in before Walter started a panic over the gossip grapevine. "Both of us just got back in town—separately—and we're thinking maybe the two of them are out doing something fun together. Willow here wants to surprise her grandmother. That's all."

"Oh." Clearly disappointed, Walter shrugged. "If I happen to see them, I'll let them know you're looking for them." Dipping his chin at Rey, the older man left.

The waitress appeared. "Can I get you something to drink?"

"Iced tea, please," Willow responded. Rey seconded that.

"Are you two ready to order or do you need another minute?"

"I'm ready," Willow said, sliding her menu across the table so the waitress could grab it. "I'll have the mushroom Swiss burger with fries."

"Bacon burger for me, please." Rey handed over his

menu as well. Once the waitress left, he leaned over and spoke quietly so he wouldn't be overheard. "I know you've been gone for a while, but I know you have to remember how quickly the gossip spreads around here."

"I do." She sighed. "And you're right. My grandmom wouldn't be happy if I started rumors about her. I just can't help but be worried. She's never done anything like this before."

"Like what?" he asked. "From what you've told me, she had no idea you were even coming to visit. I really think she and my dad are out somewhere enjoying themselves with friends. They'll show up eventually."

Expression enigmatic, she eyed him. "You sound awfully certain."

"I am." He sat back in his seat to make room for the waitress with their tea. He waited until she'd left before continuing. "Seriously, what are the alternatives?"

She sighed. "You're probably right, but I tend to have an overactive imagination. I worry."

"I get that. But give it until tonight. If she doesn't return home by then, we'll talk again."

Some of the tenseness seemed to leave her expression. Slowly, she nodded. "Sounds like a plan." For a moment, she studied him. "How is it that your dad is around the same age as my granny? You don't seem to be more than a couple of years older than me, and I know Sam and I are the same age."

"Carl is actually my uncle. He and my father ran the ranch together. When my mom died giving birth to Sam, he became like a second father to us." He took a deep breath, since he hated dredging up the painful past. "I was five when my father died during a bull-riding incident out in Cheyenne. He'd taken up rodeo when Sam and I were both toddlers and left us with Carl most of the time. He's Dad to us now and has been for a long time."

Her sweet smile contained a hint of sadness. "Same with my grandmother. She raised me up and is the only mom I ever knew. I don't know what I'd do if something happened to her."

Their food arrived then. Though his burger made his mouth water, he found himself watching as she picked hers up and took a bite. She ate with gusto, which he appreciated, and yet there was somehow something sensual about the way she enjoyed her meal. His body reacted immediately, and he busied himself with eating to get it back under control.

When he looked up again, he realized they'd finished at the same time. Each of them had a few fries remaining, but nothing more.

"You must have been hungry," she said, touching her napkin to the corners of her mouth. "I know I was."

"Starving," he agreed. "Maybe once our folks reappear, we can all go out to dinner together."

"Definitely." Her quick answer made him exhale. "And Sam should come along. He and I have a lot to catch up on."

Since there was no way to counter that suggestion without making himself look bad, he nodded. While he hadn't meant a date, not really, he was actually hoping to get to know her a little better. At least until she went back to California.

Just the thought was enough to put a damper on the moment of brief foolishness he'd allowed himself to entertain. Willow might be beautiful, she might be the most interesting woman he'd met in a long time. Sexy too, he definitely couldn't forget that.

But she wasn't going to stay. Which, in years past, might have made her a perfect woman with whom to indulge in a hot and heavy, no-emotional-baggage relationship. Not anymore. While he loved his life, he'd reached the stage where he thought he might be open to something more.

In addition, her mother and his father wouldn't appreciate their offspring indulging in a no-holds-barred erotic fling. That alone would be enough to counter any temptation.

"Are you okay?" she asked, interrupting his musing.

Blinking, he looked up, glad she couldn't read his mind. "I'm good," he replied, his voice a bit husky. "Lunch is on me."

Just as Willow started to protest, the waitress arrived with the check, as if on cue. They both reached for it at the same time, their fingers colliding. Somehow, Willow managed to come away with it.

"My treat," she insisted. "After all, you drove. And took pity on an exhausted, overly stressed stranger. I appreciate that more than I can say."

Her words touched him. Dipping his chin in a rancher's way of saying thanks, he abandoned any further effort to convince her to let him pay.

"The next one's on me," he said instead.

She considered him for a moment. "Deal."

On their way out, several old-timers stopped them to talk. Unfortunately, none of them had seen his father or her mother in the last couple of days.

He and Willow walked out to his truck without speaking.

After helping her in, he went around to the driver's side and got in. When she looked at him, he swore he could see the worry in her eyes.

"They'll show up soon," he said, feeling quite certain. "And we'll all have a good laugh over this later."

"I hope so." Finally, she sighed. "I'm exhausted. It's a long drive, and now that I've eaten, I can barely keep my eyes open. When I get back to the house, I'm going to take a nap. Hopefully, when I wake up, my mother will be back."

Chapter 2

After Rey drove away, Willow went back inside her mother's house. Despite her overwhelming urge to sleep, she found herself wandering from room to room, hoping she'd see an obvious clue as to her mom's whereabouts.

But the neat and tidy house yielded nothing unusual. Finally, Willow gave up and went into her childhood bedroom, now a guest room, pulled back the covers and climbed into bed.

She must have been more tired than she'd recognized because when she next opened her eyes, she realized she'd slept four hours. A quick glance at the nightstand clock showed it was nearly six, which meant her mother would soon be messing around in the kitchen, making supper.

Except the house remained eerily quiet. With a sense of dread settling in her stomach, she got up and made her way to the kitchen. As she'd guessed, it was empty. Once again, she went through the entire house, almost as if she hoped her mother might simply be hiding. Heck, as weird as that sounded, she'd take her grandmother jumping out to surprise her over this silent disappearance.

Despite knowing better, Willow checked her phone.

While her mom clearly couldn't reply to Willow's texts or phone calls since she didn't have her phone with her, if she'd gotten into some kind of trouble, she might attempt to reach out another way, like through social media. But all three of her mother's online accounts were stagnant, with no new posts at all within the last week. Not even the usual sharing of funny memes, something her mom had taken delight in doing.

Which made Willow wonder how long her mother might have been missing. The last time they'd talked was after Isla had the medical incident that she refused to discuss other than claiming to be fine. To Willow's astonishment, she realized this had been almost a week ago. She'd gotten so busy making sure her work was caught up before she left, she hadn't realized how much time had passed.

What if Isla had been gone all that time? Wouldn't someone have noticed? Her mother lived an active and full life and had many friends. Willow planned to check with them as well. Unfortunately, since she couldn't access her mom's phone, she had no way to contact them. And while Isla had remained friends with a few women whom Willow had known as a child, after Willow had moved away to California, her mom had broadened her interests and circle of friends. Willow didn't know much about them other than their first names.

However, since Getaway wasn't that big of a town, it shouldn't be too difficult to track these people down. Surely one of Isla's friends would know where she'd gone. She'd head into town first thing in the morning and get started. Unless, of course, her mom arrived home before then.

Having a plan of action helped somewhat. Realizing she needed to eat, Willow rummaged in the kitchen looking for something. She found a can of tomato soup and decided to make a comfort meal with that and a grilled cheese sandwich.

After she ate, she found herself roaming the house yet again. What she hated the most was the sense of powerlessness. She ought to be doing *something* to locate her mom instead of sitting around waiting for her to show up. At this point, she realized it was unlikely that Isla would.

For a few minutes, she debated whether it would make sense to go talk to the neighbors. She'd grown up here and knew them all well. While she didn't want to stir up the powerful neighborhood gossip group, who would know more about Isla's comings and goings than the neighbors closest to the house? Only the certainty that her mom would be absolutely horrified to have them involved in her "business" made Willow hesitate.

She decided she'd locate her mom's friends first. Hopefully, doing that would solve the riddle of her mother's whereabouts quietly and without fuss.

After several hours of mindless television, interspersed with pacing the house and checking out the front window for headlights that never pulled into the driveway, she knew she had to go to bed. Despite her exhaustion, she knew she wouldn't sleep well but wanted to try and get some rest so she'd be alert to start her search in the morning.

Though she tossed and turned some, she woke up shortly after sunrise feeling surprisingly refreshed. She checked the entire house again, in case her mom had come home during the night. Unsurprised to see that she hadn't, Willow took a shower, made herself some coffee and a couple of fried eggs with toast and then got ready to go into town.

Before she left, Willow checked her phone several times for a text from Rey but decided against contacting him just yet. She imagined he would be working on his own strategy to find his father and he'd contact her if he learned anything. She'd do the same for him.

Walking out of the house and locking the front door behind her, she got into her Bronco and sat for a moment behind the steering wheel. None of this felt real. Aware she was on the verge of having a panic attack, she concentrated on her breathing. It had taken years of therapy to learn how to train herself away from allowing these to take over. In fact, she hadn't had one in a long time.

And she refused to have one now. Where once she'd believed herself powerless, the focusing techniques she'd learned helped her regain control. Gradually, the tremors subsided, her heart rate slowed and she started the car.

Despite having gone to the Tumbleweed with Rey yesterday, she'd been too preoccupied worrying about her mother and battling her instant attraction to him to really look around.

Today, as she drove, everything came into focus with a sharp clarity. The familiar restored Western storefronts were reminders of how different Getaway was from Southern California.

She found a parking space a few doors down from the hair salon, killed her engine and got out. Her comfy shorts, soft T-shirt and flip-flops had been perfect for her casual life on the West Coast but might look out of place in downtown Getaway.

None of that mattered, she told herself. Growing up here, she'd always dressed how she wanted. Summers were hot, and trying to stay cool could be a challenge.

She just needed to find her mother, make sure she was safe and get in a big hug. After that, the two of them could catch up and have a nice, long visit. Taking a deep breath, she held on to that thought as she headed to the only hair salon in town.

Hair Affair looked busy as always, with every stylist's chair full. The receptionist, a young woman who had spiky purple hair and looked as if she'd recently graduated high school, smiled. "Can I help you?"

"I need to see Amanda," Willow said, smiling back. "Not for hair or anything. I just need a quick word."

Before the receptionist could speak, Amanda came rushing over. "Willow!" she squealed, wrapping Willow up in a tight hug. "I thought I recognized you! What brings you back to our neck of the woods?"

"I'm visiting my mom," Willow replied. "But she's not home." She shrugged, aware she needed to be careful not to add any new information for potential gossip. "She didn't know I was coming, and I want to surprise her. I know she's been seeing someone, and since you do her hair, I thought maybe she might have confided in you about her whereabouts."

Amanda cocked her head. "You mean Carl? Carl Johnson? We went to school with one of his sons. Sam. Remember him?"

"I do. Sam was a lot of fun."

"He still is." Amanda waved one perfectly manicured hand. "But it's his older brother, Rey, who's driving all the single gals crazy."

"Okay." Blinking, Willow debated whether or not to mention that she'd met him. Deciding it didn't matter, she touched Amanda's arm. "I'm assuming they still live out at that ranch near the county line."

"Yep. We were all there once, for Sam's sixteenth birthday."

"I remember." Willow took a deep breath. "Anyway, did Mom mention anything to you about any travel plans?"

Frowning, Amanda shook her head. "No. But she hasn't been in to get her hair done in at least a month. The last time I saw her, she seemed really happy. She couldn't stop talking about how much fun she and Carl were having. I bet she went somewhere with him."

"I'm thinking so too." Careful to keep her voice casual, Willow looked around the packed salon. "Are any of my mother's friends here today? Maybe I can ask them."

Amanda shook her head. "I don't think so. It's a bit early for that group of ladies. You should stop by the yoga studio. They all take a morning class there."

"My mom mentioned that. Where's it located?"

"That's right." With a sigh, Amanda signaled to her client she'd be right there. "It opened up after you moved away. It's on Main, right next to Serenity's. The owner is one of Serenity's sisters, I think. I'm sorry, but I've got to get back to work."

"Thank you." Willow hugged her friend again. "Once all this is settled, you and I will have to catch up over lunch. Right now, I'm going to drive over there and see if I can still surprise my mom. I'm hoping she's there." Even though she knew dang good and well that she wasn't.

"Good luck." Amanda hurried back to her client. "I'll hold you to that lunch," she said over her shoulder.

Back outside in the unrelenting West Texas sun, Willow glanced around before getting into her Bronco. Some things never changed, and downtown Getaway appeared to be one of them. Which she appreciated. Home was like a beacon of stability in an ever-changing world of chaos.

Since Serenity's little shop was only a few blocks away, Willow could have walked. She definitely could use the exercise. Except her time in the temperate climate of California had lowered her tolerance for the heat of Texas in the summer, and she knew she'd be a sweaty mess if she did. So instead, she climbed back into her vehicle and drove the short distance.

There were no parking spots anywhere even remotely close. Which meant the yoga class must have a great turn out. She found a place the next block over and took it. Looked like she'd be walking a little bit after all. At least it wasn't uphill.

In California, Willow had attended a few yoga classes before deciding to learn the moves via an app. She'd practiced it faithfully several mornings a week, since the flexibility she gained helped her surf. But riding the waves had become her true passion, and she'd thrown herself into learning and practicing until she was skilled enough to teach her own beginner class. Surfing had helped her get over her homesickness at first, and then the sport had made her feel connected to the sea.

Shaking off a sudden longing for the Pacific Ocean, Willow opened the door to the yoga studio and stepped inside. She stood in a small foyer with an empty reception desk. In a larger room off to the side, she could see about twenty-five women, all engaged in the same variation of the Bharadvaja's twist pose.

She moved closer, keeping a respectful silence as she scanned the room for any sign of her mom. While she didn't see Isla, she spotted several of her mother's friends. These women appeared to be not only skilled, but completely comfortable.

The instructor noticed Willow watching and acknowledged her with a quick dip of her head. She had her students finish up with several slow stretching moves. Then she announced in a quiet voice that the class had finished and made her way over to Willow.

"Can I help you?" she asked, her expression pleasant. She bore a striking resemblance to Serenity, though instead of flowy, colorful clothes and lots of jewelry, she wore black yoga pants and a pale yellow workout tank. Her shorty, spiky, silver hair wasn't anything like Serenity's long braids, but their facial features were almost identical.

"I'm Willow Allen. My mother, Isla, takes your class."

"She does." Beaming now, the older woman held out one graceful hand. "I'm Velma, by the way."

They shook. Then Velma gestured back at her students, who were now rolling up their mats and chatting. "Is Isla all right? She almost never misses a class, but I haven't seen her for the last three. All her friends have been worried about her too."

Right then and there, Willow's stomach sank. "Actually, that's why I stopped by. I just got in from out of town and was hoping someone might know where she went off to."

Velma's smile dimmed. "Oh. Have you checked with Carl Johnson? He and Isla have been an item for several months now. Maybe they took off together for a bit of a romantic getaway."

"He's missing too, so that's a definite possibility." It took a major effort, but Willow tried to sound upbeat as she thanked Velma and hurried out the door. She made it to her SUV before any of the other women left. Since she had no idea where else to look, she decided she might as well head out to Carl's ranch. Maybe Rey had learned something new.

The Johnson ranch was a good fifteen- to twenty-minute drive from downtown. Willow remembered the way, but only because she and Sam had been good friends back in the day. She'd actually been out to the place more times than she could count. And she figured it, like everything else around here, would look exactly the same.

Fifteen minutes later, she turned her blinker on, waiting to make the turn onto the gravel drive. She could only hope Rey would be home. While she knew she should have texted first, she hadn't taken the time to think. She just needed to talk to someone else who understood how it felt to have a missing parent.

The sound of tires pulling up the gravel drive had Rey's heart skipping a beat. Had his father finally arrived back home?

He hurried over to the window to look. A new Ford Bronco had just parked. The door opened, and Willow Allen got out. She wore flip-flops, a T-shirt and a pair of denim shorts that showed off her long legs. Her long, dark hair swirled around her tanned shoulders.

For a second, he couldn't breathe, couldn't think, could barely move. And then, he rushed to the door and opened it, ridiculously glad to see her. Because he was hopeful she might have some new information, of course. Nothing more.

"Any word?" she asked, by way of greeting. Just like that, she dashed his hopes.

"No. What about you?"

She shifted her weight from foot to foot, drawing attention to her pretty pink painted toenails. "Nothing. My mom didn't come home last night. This morning I stopped by the hair salon and then a place where she takes yoga classes, but no one has seen her. It's looking like she might have gone missing a week ago or more."

"A week ago?" He frowned. "My father was here when I left for Colorado to pick up the bison. That was six days ago."

"Surely someone else was here with him after you left," she said. "What about Sam?"

As if saying his name invoked some sort of magic, Sam appeared, the porch screen door swinging open. "I thought it was you!" he exclaimed. Rushing over, he enveloped Willow in a hug. "How have you been?"

"I'm good." Smiling, she extricated herself. "I'm guessing you were here when Rey left for Colorado?"

He looked to Rey and back to Willow. "I was. Why?"

"Do you have any idea when your father disappeared?" she asked.

Sam groaned. "Not you too. This morning, Rey called every single one of Dad's buddies looking for him."

"I did," Rey said, managing to keep his voice level. "And when the fifth guy acted surprised to hear I was looking for Carl, I gave up. No one has seen hide nor hair of him."

Willow groaned. "This is getting more and more worrisome. I'm thinking it's time to talk to the sheriff."

Crossing his arms, Sam finally appeared to pick up on their concern. "Willow, I know you and your grandmother are close. Don't tell me you haven't heard from her either."

"I haven't," Willow responded. "She's missing too. I came home from Cali to surprise her, but she isn't home. Even though her car is parked in the garage."

"Do you think they're together?" Sam asked Willow.

Rey shook his head, annoyed since he and Sam had already had a similar discussion. "Who else would they be with?" he asked.

Sam barely glanced at his brother, keeping all his attention focused on Willow. "I bet they went on a trip with another couple. Maybe someone from their church."

"I didn't think of that," Willow said. "For as long as I can remember, my grandmother has attended Sunday services at that small, nondenominational church on the south side of town. Straightline Church."

"Yes, that's the one. I remember you went there when we were in high school." Sam smiled. "You even dragged me to a couple of those youth activities back then."

Willow ignored Sam's attempt to reminisce. She turned to look at Rey, her expression hopeful. "That's a great suggestion, don't you think?" she asked. "It's entirely possible a group of them from church went on some kind of outing. I'll run over there and talk to Pastor Clayton."

"I have his number." Keeping his gaze locked on hers, Rey dug out his phone. "Let me just call and ask."

The elderly pastor answered on the second ring. After exchanging a few pleasantries, Rey asked his question.

"Church social events? We don't have anything scheduled until the ice-cream social after services this Sunday. Are you planning to attend?"

"I'm not sure," Rey answered. He took a moment to find the right words before asking his next question. Finally, he decided to just come right out with it. "My father and Isla Allen appear to be missing. You don't happen to have any idea where they might be, do you?"

"Missing? For how long?"

"We're not sure." Catching Willow's eye, Rey slowly shook his head. "I just got back from picking up some livestock in Denver, and he was gone. Sam was here, but he claims he doesn't know."

At this, Sam made a sound of protest. Rey ignored it.

"I had no idea," Pastor Clayton said. "I'll mention this in my sermon on Sunday. Maybe someone in the congregation will know something."

Rey thanked him and ended the call. When he repeated what the elderly man had said, Willow made a face. "Well, that will definitely get the gossip going."

"If it helps find them, it's worth it," Rey replied.

"Come on, you two." Sam rolled his eyes. "I still think you're making too much out of this. Honestly, what do you think happened to them? They're adults. They're fine."

Instead of responding, Willow looked down at her feet. Her worry and anguish seemed palpable, and it was all Rey could do not to reach out and pull her into his arms.

Clearly oblivious, Sam continued. "So, Willow. How long are you in town?"

Willow simply shook her head instead of answering.

"Sam, just stop," Rey warned. As Willow turned blindly to make her way to her vehicle, he took her arm. When she glanced at him as if to thank him, he was unsurprised to see tears in her eyes.

"It's going to be all right," he told her, helping her into her vehicle.

"Is it?" Expression as bleak as her voice, she pressed the button to start her engine. "Please let me know if you hear anything."

He promised he would. Jamming his hands into his pockets, he stood and watched as she drove away.

"What the hell was that?" Sam asked, his voice hard. "Are you seriously trying to make a move on Willow Allen?"

"Make a move?" Rey spun around so fast that Sam had to take a step back. "I don't know what's wrong with you, but you need to stop. She's worried about her mother. I'm concerned about our dad. And you should be too, if you had a lick of sense."

Sam grimaced. "She's not your type, you know."

Gaping at him, Rey took a deep breath. "Who, Sam?"

"Willow."

Sometimes, Rey wondered if he'd ever understand his younger brother. Refusing to dignify that statement with a response, Rey went back inside the house. He wasn't sure how Sam had picked up on Rey's attraction toward Willow, but with their father missing, that would be the last thing Sam needed to focus on.

Because work on a ranch waited for no man, chores

kept Rey busy for the rest of the day. He'd turned the small herd of bison out into one of the larger pastures, keeping them separate from their main herd of cattle. Saddling up Roscoe, he rode out to check on them. Every single time that he stopped, he pulled out his phone and checked it, hoping against hope that his dad would have turned up back home.

But there were no texts. Not from his brother or the pastor or Willow. Finally, after ensuring the bison were doing well and checking on the cattle, he decided the time had come to bring in the sheriff. This, he wanted to do in person. He'd ask Willow if she wanted to meet him there.

Decision made, he rode Roscoe back to the barn, unsaddled him and brushed him down. He noticed Sam's horse's stall was now empty, which meant Sam had finally gotten around to heading out to finish repairing one of the fences. Luckily, they didn't have any livestock in that pasture, but they were due to rotate some of the cattle there within the next few weeks.

Inside the house, he poured himself a glass of iced tea and got out his phone. Willow answered on the second ring.

"I'm about to leave and go into town," he said. "I think we need to bring the sheriff in. Rayna's very thorough, and if anyone can figure this out, she can."

"I agree." Willow hesitated. "Are we going to file missing person reports?"

"I think that would be best. Do you want to meet me there?"

"Yes," Willow replied. "I can leave here in about five minutes."

After ending the call, he called ahead, just to make sure Rayna would have time to talk to them. She agreed to meet with him and Willow. "I've been expecting the two of you to come by," she said. "I'll see you in about twenty minutes."

Hopping into his truck, he drove into town. When he reached the sheriff's office, he waited inside the air-conditioned cab of his truck until he saw Willow's red Bronco pull into the parking lot. Jumping down, he reached her just as she opened her door to get out.

Offering his hand to help her, he couldn't help but smile when she took it. The softness of her skin and the way she gave his hand a quick squeeze before letting go brought a rush of warmth inside him.

"I called ahead to let Rayna know we were coming," he told her, holding the glass door open so she could enter the building before him.

"Thank you." Expression serious, Willow took a deep breath.

Side by side, they made their way through the busy room toward Rayna's space in the back. Several uniformed officers glanced up at them. A few smiled and waved, but no one made any attempt to question or stop them. Which meant, Rey figured, that everyone had known they were coming.

"Come on back." Rayna appeared in her doorway, motioning at them. She went around her desk and pointed to a couple of chairs in front of her. "Have a seat. And go ahead and close the door behind you."

Once they were all situated, Rayna dropped into her own chair and leaned forward. "You're here because Carl Johnson and Isla Allen are missing."

Rey and Willow exchanged a quick glance before they nodded. "Exactly. Both of their vehicles were left at home, as well as their cell phones," Rey said. "This is not like my father at all."

"Or my mom," Willow chimed in. "Granted, she had no idea that I was coming to visit, but she hasn't been to yoga class, and none of her friends have any idea where she might be."

"They aren't the only seniors who have gone missing." Expression serious, Rayna slid a photocopy of a missing poster across her desk toward them. "Do either of you know Ernesto and Yolanda Alvarez?"

Rey stared at the poster. The grainy photo showed a couple of people about the same age as his father. Mid to late sixties or early seventies, the woman appeared to have streaks of silver in her hair. "I don't," Rey answered, glancing at Willow. "How about you?"

"I don't recognize them either." She slid the poster back toward the sheriff. "Do you think there's a chance they all went missing together?"

Chapter 3

Heart pounding, Willow waited to hear what Rayna had to say. The redheaded sheriff took the poster back and considered them both for a moment.

"I don't know yet," she finally said. "Right now, I'd prefer not to speculate. But the Alvarez family reported those two missing yesterday. They had a family reunion scheduled for Saturday, and when everyone arrived, Ernesto and Yolanda were nowhere to be found. Like your folks, both their cars were still at the house, and they left their cell phones. They also didn't leave a note."

Stumped, Willow sat back in her chair. Glancing at Rey, she could tell from his expression that he too had no idea what to make of all this.

"We have no clues as to their whereabouts," Rayna continued. "We've just begun the process of interviewing their friends. So far, they don't appear to have told a single soul where they were going."

Blindly, Willow reached for Rey. He met her halfway, enfolding her hand in his larger one. Though she barely knew him, she found this tremendously comforting.

"I stopped by my grandmother's regular yoga class earlier," Willow offered. "While I didn't speak directly with her friends, the instructor told me they were all wondering where Isla had gone off to. It isn't like her to miss a class."

Rayna nodded, her sharp gaze missing nothing. "I promise to look into this. Will you let me know if you hear anything?"

"Of course," Rey answered for both of them.

"Perfect." Pushing to her feet, Rayna gave them a friendly smile. "And, of course, I'll do the same. Try not to worry, you two. It's entirely possible they got a wild hare and took off on a spontaneous vacation."

"Which isn't likely," Willow pointed out. Rey seconded her comment.

"But you never know." Clearly determined to be positive, Rayna led the way to the door. "I'll be in touch."

Once back outside, Willow had to stop herself from reaching for Rey's hand. While she barely knew this man, his quiet strength gave her sorely needed comfort.

He walked her to her vehicle and waited silently while she unlocked her doors. "Try not to worry," he said. "Rayna's good at what she does."

"I heard she caught a serial killer a while back."

"Two actually." He shrugged. "Hard to believe our little town seemed to be a magnet for them for a little bit. At least it's been quiet since then."

Until now. Though neither of them said the words out loud, she knew they were thinking them.

"I wonder if we should ask Rayna to make sure they're both still locked up and out of commission," she said, getting into her Bronco.

He nodded. "I'm sure she will. But both of them had

specific types, and older couples don't fit those particular profiles."

"That's good." From somewhere, she summoned a smile.

"Stay in touch," he told her, stepping back so she could close her door.

Driving home, she tried to hang on to her composure. The last thing she needed was to break down. Isla would want her to be strong. After all, she'd raised Willow by example.

Back at the house, which felt achingly empty, Willow roamed around. Yet again, she tried to find some clue, some hint, of where her grandmother might have gone. For as long as Willow could remember, Isla had used an old, built-in desk in a corner of the kitchen to pay her bills and to store relevant documents. Willow dropped into the ancient office chair and opened one of the large side drawers. Rows of manila folders filled several hanging files. She went through them. Most of them appeared to be for various bills. Electricity, gas and water were packed full. After that, she found folders for receipts, also neatly labeled. She pulled out one marked Restaurants and began leafing through that. Nothing out of the ordinary jumped out. They were all local eateries here in town.

Putting the file back, she reached for the next one, marked Medical. There she found the discharge notes from her gram's recent hospital stay and a referral to a cardiologist in Midland. As far as Willow could tell, it didn't look like Isla had ever gone. And anything related to a diagnosis had been left out—either stored elsewhere or destroyed. Which made no sense, because Isla had always been a stickler about keeping everything in the right place.

She went through the rest of the medical records and found nothing else related to the ER visit and hospitalization. There'd been the usual routine doctor visits, for physicals and prescription refills. Isla had gotten her annual mammogram in March.

Closing the folder, Willow returned it to its place and sighed. She riffled through a few more, but there wasn't anything out of the ordinary.

A thorough search through the rest of the desk yielded nothing interesting. Which meant she was exactly where she'd started. With nothing.

The flashing light on her grandma's answering machine indicated a message had been left. Since she hadn't even heard the landline ring, this startled Willow. Maybe the call had come in when she'd been out. Heart pounding, she walked over to the outdated piece of equipment and pressed the button to play.

"This is Marlene, the city secretary. I'm calling to let you know that we'll be holding a meeting tonight at the Rattlesnake Pub to discuss recent developments in the disappearance of several of our residents. The meeting will begin at seven, and everyone is welcome. We hope to see you there."

Recent developments? Immediately, she wanted to call Rayna. The sheriff had promised to call her with any news regarding her grandmother. Which likely meant any developments were related to some of the other missing people.

Should she touch base with Rey? Right now, he was the only one she knew who could relate to what was going on. The fact that he was easy on the eyes didn't hurt either. Every time they got together, the physical attraction nearly overwhelmed her. Part of her felt guilty that she could even think of such things when her grandma was missing. But she also realized she was only human. Her body wanted what her body wanted. Since she had zero plans to act on them, she figured she might as well enjoy her little fantasies. Once her grandmother returned, the two of them would have a good chuckle over that.

Returned. For a moment, Willow's breath caught in her throat. Obviously, she couldn't go back to California until Isla had been found. And even then, Willow wasn't sure she'd be able to ever leave her again.

Which meant she had a lot of thinking to do. For now, she'd continue to try and stay anchored in the present. Take things one day at a time.

Until she could come up with something better to do, she decided she'd continue her search of the house. Previously, it had felt too intrusive to do a deep dive through her grandmother's things. Now, Willow didn't see how she had any choice.

She decided to start with the master bedroom, beginning with the main dresser. Once she started opening drawers, she realized that some of Isla's things had to be missing. Though the clothes were still neatly folded, there weren't enough of them for a person to make it through an entire week. Undergarments, pajamas, even socks. Either her grandmother had become seriously minimalistic, or she'd packed some of these things for her trip.

Her trip. The thought made Willow feel better. She

checked the closet out next and once again, she thought some of the clothing had been removed. There were actually empty hangers, which she considered proof.

The shoes, neatly lined up in the bottom of the closet, had a couple of empty spots too. While Willow had no idea where Isla stored her suitcases, she had a feeling one of them had been packed for a getaway.

The next time she talked to Rey, she'd ask him to check out his father's dresser and closet. She'd bet he'd find some indications of packing for a trip there too.

A trip, but to where? And why leave the cell phones behind? And keep the entire thing such a secret, especially from the ones who loved you?

Maybe this topic would be covered at the meeting that evening.

She wondered if she'd see Rey there. Just the thought had her heart skipping a beat. Resisting the urge to text him, she went into her old bedroom and finished unpacking instead.

When she got to the new yellow sundress she'd purchased to wear out to dinner with her grandmother, she found herself blinking back tears. Yellow was Isla's favorite color. The instant Willow had seen the dress in the window of her favorite shop, she'd known she had to have it for her time back home.

She'd wear it to the meeting tonight, she decided. The simple act of having yellow on would help her feel more connected to her missing grandmother.

After she finished unpacking, she rummaged through the refrigerator and made herself a sandwich for lunch. She figured she'd call Rey before the meeting and see if he maybe wanted to grab a drink or something after.

Right now, a nap fit the bill. She turned the TV on low, lay down on the couch and pulled a light blanket over her. Since Isla's disappearance, she hadn't slept well and figured she could use the nap to catch up on some much needed rest.

After a quick lunch, Rey managed to get all his chores done in record time. He planned to take a little of his newly freed up time to do a more thorough search of the house. Hopefully, he could find something that might offer a clue as to where Carl had gone.

When he reached the house, he was surprised to find Sam already there. Since they'd been expecting a hay delivery earlier that day, he'd figured Sam would still be out overseeing the hands as they unloaded and stored it.

"You finished up early," Rey commented, heading to the fridge to pour himself a glass of iced tea.

Sam grunted. "Oh, they're probably still unloading. I didn't see any reason for me to hang around in the heat and watch them. They seem to know what they're doing."

"You didn't help them unload?" Rey asked.

"Heck no. Why would I do that?" Sam scoffed. "We're paying them to unload."

Eyeing his younger brother, Rey couldn't help but think Carl had gone too easy on him. Sam always seemed to do the bare minimum, nothing more. Instead of calloused hands, his were soft. Though to be fair, Sam had never claimed to want the life of a rancher. Unfortunately, he'd never made an effort to do anything else.

Deciding not to say anything, Rey took a long drink from his tea. Sweaty and hot, he needed a shower, but he wanted to rehydrate first.

"There's going to be a town meeting tonight at seven," Sam said, his voice casual. "They left a message on the landline answering machine. I didn't erase it in case you want to replay it."

Rey paused. "Meeting for what? Did they say?"

When Sam turned around, he appeared slightly apprehensive. "Though they only said recent developments, I've heard that another older couple has disappeared. That's up to six people now, three couples. People are starting to freak out."

With his blood running cold, Rey took a second to answer.

"As they should. It scares the hell out of me."

"Did you know?" Sam asked, his voice hard. "Did you know that many people were missing?"

"No. I knew about Dad and Isla, and one other couple. Rayna told us about them when Willow and I went to see her."

"You and Willow?" Sam narrowed his gaze. "Are you still making a play for her? I can't believe you're taking advantage of this situation to hit on her."

Tamping down a flash of anger, Rey clenched his teeth and took a moment before responding. "I'm not sure how meeting her at the sheriff's office to file missing person reports qualifies as hitting on her. But you need to stop. Willow is rightfully concerned about her grandmother. I'm worried about Dad. Nothing more, nothing less."

Instead of appearing appeased, Sam shook his head, his jaw tight. "You know what? I'm going to call her and invite her out to dinner after the meeting. We have a lot to catch up on. I imagine she'll be glad to put aside all the doom and gloom for a minute or two."

"Maybe so," Rey conceded. He refused to even acknowledge the way the idea of her going out with his younger brother made him feel. In fact, now that Sam had announced his plan, Rey wished he'd thought of it. No matter who took her, she deserved to go somewhere nice, to give herself a couple of hours to let her worry and fears take a back seat. Sam was right about that.

"Are you going to the meeting?" Rey asked.

Muttering under his breath and ignoring the question, Sam got out his phone and began scrolling through his contacts. "I know I have her number here somewhere," he mumbled, wandering outside onto the back patio.

Glad he didn't have to offer to give it to him, Rey went over to the desk he and his father shared to begin his search. All the accounting for the ranch was stored there. He hadn't thought to check it before but wanted to go through everything just in case there might be a clue to Carl's whereabouts.

He sat down and pulled out several manila folders, all crammed full of papers. While wading through receipts, he heard Sam come back inside, slamming the door behind him. He glanced up to see Sam scowling.

"She didn't want to go," he said, glaring at Rey as if he thought his brother had something to do with Willow's decision. "Says we can catch up another time, but right now she's putting all of her energy into locating her grandmother."

"Maybe that's how you should have approached it," Rey suggested. "So far, you haven't been very sympathetic, never mind concerned."

Half expecting his brother to explode, Rey exhaled when Sam visibly deflated. "I am worried," he admitted. "Because you're right, none of this is like Dad. I just don't like to dwell on it the way you do. It makes me feel too powerless."

Surprised at Sam's candor, Rey nodded. "I get that. I feel pretty powerless too. When I stop to think about all the possibilities that might have occurred, I can't sleep at night. I'm sure Willow feels the same way."

"That makes sense." Sam grimaced. "I'll give it a few days, and then I'll try again. Maybe Willow will want to meet up if I want to commiserate."

"Maybe so." Rey took a deep breath, about to ask his brother yet again if he planned to attend the meeting. Just then, Rey's phone rang. Glancing at the screen, he saw it was Willow. Luckily, Sam had already lost interest in the conversation and had taken off to his room.

"Afternoon," Rey answered. "How are you holding up?"

"I'm a mess," she admitted. "But I wanted to tell you to go through your dad's dresser drawers and his closet. I just finished looking through my grandmother's, and I feel there's enough missing to prove she did pack for a trip."

"Interesting," he replied. "I've kind of hesitated to do that because I didn't want to be too intrusive, but I guess I'd better."

"I felt the same way, but now that I have, I feel a little better." She took a deep breath before continuing. "I'm sure you've heard about the town meeting tonight."

"I have. I heard another older couple has disappeared."

"What?" She sounded shocked. "My message didn't say anything about that. How many is that now?"

"Six. I definitely hope we're not about to learn there's even more."

"Me too. All of this is seriously freaking me out," she said. "Are you going to the meeting?"

Even though he'd just now heard about it, he said he was. "There's no way I'm missing out on getting more information."

"Same," she replied. "I really need to get out of the house, so I'm glad to have a reason to go into town. Anyway, I'm wondering if you wanted to meet for a drink after."

Deciding not to mention that he knew Sam had just called her and invited her out, he agreed. While he didn't feel hanging out with Willow was like hitting on her, he saw no reason to muddy the waters.

"Perfect," she said, then paused. "Do you want to grab something to eat too? We can go either before or after, though I guess it would depend on how long the meeting runs."

"Before," he answered quickly. "I've been so busy today that I haven't had time to eat lunch. We could eat around five thirty, if that's okay with you."

"Sounds good. I've been craving Tres Corazones. It's been forever since I've had it. California doesn't do good Tex-Mex."

Thinking of his brother, he felt a quick twinge of guilt. But then he wasn't about to turn her down simply because she didn't want to go out with Sam. Their parents were missing. Maybe Sam couldn't focus on that, but Rey could. "That sounds great."

"Perfect. I can meet you there." She waited for him to confirm.

"Sure," he said. "Just remember, the meal is my treat this time."

"As long as any drinks after the meeting are on me," she replied.

That made her go quiet. "We'll see."

After ending the call, he decided not to say anything to Sam. Since he and Willow were meeting up and taking separate vehicles, it wasn't even close to being a date. And if Sam attended the town meeting, maybe after he could join them for drinks to discuss any new information they'd learned.

Since he'd need to clean up early in order to meet Willow at Tres Corazones, he rushed through the remainder of his chores. When he arrived back at the house at four thirty with the intention of taking a shower, he found Sam parked in front of the television, munching on popcorn.

"Did you knock off early today?" Rey asked.

"Did you?" Sam barely looked away from the TV. "I'm assuming you're going to the town meeting?"

For the first time, Rey wondered what he'd do if Sam wanted to go with him. Bring him along to dinner, he supposed. Even if Willow hadn't wanted to go out with Sam by himself, surely she wouldn't object if it was the three of them. "I am. What about you?"

Mouth full of popcorn, Sam shrugged. "I might. And I might not. I figure you'll tell me whatever you hear."

Suppressing a small flare of anger, Rey bit back a retort. "I'm going to take a shower," he said and left the room.

When he emerged later, Sam had shut off the television and left. Since his bedroom door was closed, Rey figured Sam was in there.

A little after five, Rey went out to his truck to make the drive into town. He looked forward to seeing Willow again, even if just to have someone to commiserate with who actually was willing to do whatever it took to help find Carl and Isla.

Even though he arrived early, he spotted Willow's red Bronco already in the parking lot. The restaurant seemed busier than usual at this earlier hour, and he guessed numerous people had decided to grab dinner before the town meeting.

As he parked and got out, Willow emerged from her SUV. She wore a bright yellow sundress, her long hair in a neat braid down her back. The color flattered her skin, and her legs seemed to go on forever. Her beauty had him catching his breath.

"Are you okay?" she asked, making him realize he'd been staring. Without waiting for him to answer, she took his arm. "I wish it wasn't so hot. I love eating outside on the patio."

He recognized the nervousness that underscored her voice. Liking how it felt to have her arm linked in his, he patted her hand. "It's going to be okay."

Her grateful smile made his heart skip a beat.

"Thanks," she said. "I do tend to talk a lot when I'm stressed."

Inside, the hostess greeted them and led them to a small booth near the window. They sat, and she handed them menus and left. Almost instantly, someone else brought them a large basket of warm tortilla chips and two small bowls of salsa.

Rey watched Willow as she studied the menu. With her delicately carved features and lush mouth, she had a kind of sensual beauty of which she appeared completely unaware.

The soft curve of her shoulders captivated him. It might be the worst timing ever, but he ached with desire. As long as she didn't realize how she affected him, he figured he'd be okay.

The waitress arrived and took their drink orders. Willow asked for a small margarita on the rocks, and Rey ordered a Mexican beer with a lime.

While they waited for their food, she told him more about her life in California. Since he'd never been there, he listened closely as she described the beaches and the ocean, enjoying the way her eyes sparkled as she talked.

"You love it there," he observed.

"Not really." She shrugged. "The weather is nicer, but everything is so expensive. I miss Texas sometimes. The ocean is the only thing that makes me feel connected to the earth."

This was something he understood. Something about the wide-open spaces of his home, the way the sky colored orange and yellow and pink at sunrise, tethered him to the ground. "Do you go to the beach often so you can watch the waves?"

Her grin lit up her entire face. "No. I go almost every day so I can surf."

Their food arrived just then, saving him from having to come up with a reasonably intelligent response. What he knew of surfing was next to nothing.

Once the waitress left, he eyed Willow over his fajitas. "Are you any good at it?"

"Surfing?" Her grin widened as she picked up her fork. "I think so. I actually teach beginner surf classes every Saturday."

With that, she dug into her food with gusto, leaving him no choice but to do the same.

"I'm even listed on the surfing school's website," she said, in between bites. "If you do an internet search for my name along with surfing lessons, I'll come up."

He had to fight himself not to reach for his phone to do exactly that. Because now he couldn't get the image of Willow, her sun-kissed skin glistening, riding a surfboard in a bikini.

Pushing the thoughts away, he focused on his meal. By the time he'd finished eating, his arousal had mostly subsided, and he felt normal.

Heaven help him if she ever found out how she affected him.

He paid the check, and she let him, though she apparently couldn't resist telling him the next meal would be on her. She smiled and nodded, giving him hope that there would be a next time.

They walked out to their vehicles.

"I'll follow you," Willow said.

Since the town meeting was being held at the Rattlesnake Pub, which was just down the street from Tres Corazones, Willow and Rey were slightly early. Despite that, the parking lot had begun to fill up, which meant the overflow would spill out onto Main Street.

After getting out of their vehicles, they walked into the pub side by side. The tables had been pushed to one side, and rows of folding chairs had been set up facing a lectern that had been placed on the stage where bands usually played.

Several people greeted him and waved. Rey waved back but didn't stop to talk.

Most of the seats in the first four rows were already occupied. Rey and Willow took chairs near the aisle in row five.

"I recognize so many people," Willow said. "But I'm guessing they forgot what I look like because not one single person has greeted me."

"You can go around and reintroduce yourself after," he said, trying to comfort her.

"Maybe." She shrugged. "I'm not sure I want to, actually."

He guessed that was because she wouldn't be around long enough after her mother was found for it to matter.

By the time seven o'clock arrived, every seat was full and still more people continued to fill the back of the room. Willow kept turning and eyeing the growing crowd. "I had no idea so many people were worried about this," she murmured. "It's now standing room only."

Rey didn't tell her that most of them were there out of a combination of curiosity and boredom.

The sheriff walked in, flanked by several of her deputies. All of them were in full uniform. They took their seats up on the stage, behind the lectern. The meeting was about to begin.

Chapter 4

Bracing herself, Willow reached for Rey's hand without thinking. To her relief, he enveloped her fingers with his larger ones, offering comfort.

Tony Hutchins, the owner of the Rattlesnake Pub and, from what her mom had told her, Getaway's newly elected mayor as of a couple of months ago, made his way through the room. This took him a while as he constantly stopped to talk with people. He finally walked to the center of the stage and eyed the assembled group before tapping on the microphone.

"I need your attention, please." Once the room had gone silent, he continued. "We are all here because we're concerned for one of the most vulnerable groups in our society—our senior citizens. We've recently learned that several of our beloved townsfolk have gone missing."

Murmuring broke out, and for a moment Tony let the sound swell. Then he cleared his throat, tapped the microphone again and, once he had everyone's attention, announced he would be turning things over to Sheriff Coombs.

At this, Willow sat up even straighter. While Rayna had definitely promised to keep her posted, she supposed that meant only regarding information related to Isla and Carl. The other missing couples, while a new development, might not directly impact the case. Either that, or, Willow figured, the sheriff had just been too busy.

"Right now, we've been made aware of six people, all over the age of sixty-five, who have virtually disappeared," Rayna began. "At this time, foul play is not suspected. This means that we have to assume that wherever they went, they went willingly."

Again, people started talking, the swell of voices rising. Standing motionless, Rayna waited this out until eventually everyone quieted and focused again on her.

"We wanted to call this meeting," she continued, "because we need each and every one of you to help. If you have security cameras at your businesses, check your footage. None of these missing individuals took their personal vehicles, which is in itself unusual. We've checked with bus rental and passenger van companies and haven't found anything helpful. But someone in this room might have video of a large van or bus driving by. If you find something like that, I need you to contact me."

"Have you checked with Myrna?" someone shouted. Myrna ran the small travel agency part-time, when she wasn't weaving elaborate shawls and table runners to sell.

"Yes, we did," Rayna answered, her tone level. "None of the missing people booked any kind of trip with her."

Serenity, the self-proclaimed town psychic, who'd attended with her sister, Velma, the yoga instructor, stood. "I have a feeling they are all safe and well."

Since most times her *feelings* turned out to be accurate, no one contradicted her. Not even the sheriff, who, like the rest of the town, knew better.

Even Willow, who wasn't exactly sure how she felt about Serenity's psychic abilities, took comfort from hearing those words.

And then Serenity took a deep breath and continued. "However, just because they don't believe themselves to be in danger at this moment, doesn't mean the threat isn't there. It's just hidden."

She pinned her steady gaze on the sheriff. "This means you have to find them, before trouble manifests itself."

As soon as Serenity sat back down, everyone started talking at once. Again, Rayna stood motionless at the podium, waiting. When the noise finally died down, Rayna asked if anyone had any specific questions. "Bear in mind, we don't know much about this case at the moment. Which means we're extremely limited on answers."

Despite her disclaimer, people began shouting out questions. Most of them, Rayna couldn't answer, and she finally told everyone she would not get into speculation about where the missing people might be. With that, she reminded them to check their video camera footage and then declared the meeting to be over.

Instead of leaving, almost everyone pitched in to help move the tables that had been pushed up against the wall back where they belonged. Tony put country music on over the speakers and announced that the kitchen and bar were now open.

"Do you want to stay and have a drink?" Rey asked. "It looks like that's what most people are doing."

Suddenly, Willow wanted out of there. "I'd rather go somewhere else," she said. "Have you ever been to that place on the other side of town called The Bar?"

"That new place?"

Even though The Bar had opened up a few years ago, everyone still called it new. "Yes," she answered. "I know it's different. Not as down-home and familiar as here, but I'm willing to bet it will be a lot less crowded."

"Sounds good." He held out his arm, and she took it. Together, they wound their way through the crowd toward the door.

Once outside, Willow exhaled in relief. "I'm sorry, but I just don't feel up to any questions. Once everything settled down, I just knew people were going to start figuring out whose family members are among the missing. I don't think we would have gotten a moment of peace."

Gaze steady, he studied her for a moment. "You're probably right. I'll follow you over to The Bar."

"Willow Allen!" a voice called. "I thought that was you."

Slowly turning, Willow tried to summon up a smile and failed. She vaguely recognized the woman hurrying toward them as someone she'd gone to high school with, but couldn't remember her name.

"I'm sorry." Rey took Willow's arm. "We're late for another appointment and have to go. Hopefully you two can catch up another time. Come on, Willow."

More relieved than she could express, Willow allowed him to hustle her over to their vehicles. "Thank you," she muttered, climbing in hers. "I owe you one."

He laughed. "See you in a few."

As she'd expected, only a few cars and pickups were parked in the lot outside. Rey took a spot next to her, and they walked into the place together.

"I haven't ever been here," Rey said, glancing around curiously.

"I've been a few times," she told him. "Though I get why most people go to the Rattlesnake Pub." Gesturing around the smaller, dimly lit space, she made her way to a booth. "This place reminds me of California."

"I take it that's a good thing," he commented, sliding into the booth opposite her.

Before she could answer, a waiter appeared and handed them drink menus. "It's really slow in here tonight," he said. "I'm hoping some of the people who went to the town meeting decide the Rattlesnake is too crowded and come here."

Willow smiled. "I hope so too. That's what we did."

They ordered drinks. Beer for him and a small margarita for her.

Once the waiter left, Willow leaned forward. "I'm not sure what to make of all this. I couldn't help but notice Rayna didn't offer up a hypothesis on where all the missing couples might be."

"Because law enforcement doesn't work with guesses," he replied. "She's just stating the facts. Nothing more, nothing less. I'm sure she's working every angle she can."

She nodded and took a deep breath. "Are you as worried as I am? This is completely out of character for my grandmother."

"Same with my dad," he said. "And if you're like me, you have to stop yourself from coming up with multiple bad scenarios."

"Exactly. I've watched way too many true-crime shows."

Their drinks arrived. The bartender had taken the time to make Willow's margarita look festive. Instead of the usual lime color, hers was gold, shot through with ribbons of pink. "He made you our house specialty," the waiter explained, setting it down in front of her with a flourish. "It's a prickly pear infused with agave. I hope you enjoy it."

Willow took a sip, aware both the waiter and the bartender were watching her from the bar. "Delicious," she said, loud enough for them to hear.

After drinking from his beer, Rey sighed. "While Carl and Isla certainly appear to be enjoying dating each other, neither of them have ever given any indication that they'd do something like this. Which is one of the reasons I'm so worried."

"Same. But tell me something. Why isn't Sam concerned? Every time I talk to him, he acts as if nothing out of the ordinary is going on."

Rey's gaze sharpened. "I don't understand that either. Is that why you turned down his offer to meet you for dinner?"

"He told you about that?" she asked. When Rey nodded, she took another sip of her drink. "I don't want to talk badly about your younger brother, but his determination to pretend everything is normal wears me out. When we were teenagers, Sam and I were good friends."

"And if anyone should understand what it feels like to be worried about a parent, he should," Rey finished for her. "I have a feeling this is his way of coping. If he pretends nothing is wrong, it's easier on him."

The door opened and another couple came in. Willow recognized them as two more who were missing family members. She lifted her hand in a wave.

"Your grandmother is missing, right?" the woman asked. When Willow nodded, the woman held out her hand. "I'm Sofia Alvarez, and this is my brother, Tomas. Our parents, Ernesto and Yolanda, have disappeared too."

"Why don't you join us?" Willow invited. "I'd love to swap details, if you don't mind. There are bound to be some similarities."

Sofia's sad smile touched Willow's heart. "I'd like that," she said, dropping into the seat next to Willow. A moment later, her brother did the same next to Rey.

As it turned out, Sofia's mother and Isla knew each other. They belonged to the same book club. "My mom always talked about her meeting with the book ladies," Sofia said, her gaze sad. "She mentioned Isla Allen more than once."

While Willow and Sofia talked, Tomas sat silent. He barely responded to Rey's attempts to bring him into the conversation. Finally, Tomas pushed to his feet and glared at them. "We shouldn't be talking about this," he said. "That just makes it worse. Come on, Sofia. We need to go by Mom and Dad's house again."

Slugging back the rest of his beer, he slammed his bottle on the table and strode to the door.

Expression apologetic, Sofia stood. "He's having a hard time dealing with all this," she said. "He still lives here in town, just a few blocks away from our parents' place. I think he feels like he should have been able to prevent this from happening."

"I get it." Impulsively, Willow stood too and touched the older woman's hand. "How about we exchange numbers so we can keep in touch if anything changes?"

Sofia got out her phone, and once Willow recited her number, sent her a text. "I'd better go," she said. "Since heart problems apparently run in the family, I don't want anything to happen to Tomas."

With that, she hurried out the door.

Shocked, Willow stared after her. She dropped back into her seat. "Did you hear that?" she asked Rey. "She said heart problems run in the family."

"Okay," Rey replied. "Clearly, I'm missing something."

"My mom had a heart incident. She went to the ER. She kept saying it was nothing, but I don't know for sure. That's the main reason I scheduled PTO and came home."

He eyed her, his expression calm. "And you think there's a connection?"

Just like that, her excitement deflated. "I'm grasping at straws, aren't I?"

"Maybe." He reached across the table and touched her arm. "How about this? Mention it to Rayna. Let her investigate. It might be something, or it might not."

Slowly, she nodded. Taking another drink of her delicious margarita, she realized she wanted to go home. When she told Rey, he nodded. After signaling for the check, he paid the bill and walked her to her Bronco.

Opening Willow's door for her, he nearly leaned in to kiss her. The urge to do so had been strong. If he'd done that, he figured she'd think he was as bad as Sam. Even if she didn't, he knew he would.

Instead, he'd stepped back, plastering what he hoped was a pleasant expression on his face. "Stay in touch," he said.

She nodded, buckled her seat belt and closed her door. He didn't get into his truck until she'd driven away.

Pulling out onto Main Street, he almost stopped back in at the Rattlesnake but decided against it. No one knew anything more than what Rayna had told them, so he'd be wasting his time. He'd done about as much socializing for one day as he could stand.

When he arrived back at the ranch, Sam's pickup was still in the usual spot. Which meant he hadn't gone anywhere, not even a quick stop at the Rattlesnake to hear Rayna speak. Rey supposed he hadn't really expected him to. Still, it would have been nice if he'd shown just a small bit of concern.

Pushing back his irritation, Rey walked inside to find Sam once again lounging in front of the TV. He barely looked up when Rey approached. After standing beside the couch for a minute, Rey finally reached over and grabbed the remote to turn off the television.

"Hey," Sam protested, finally glancing at his brother. "I was watching that."

Rey dropped down onto the cushion next to him. "I thought you might want to hear about the meeting. I take it you didn't go."

"Nope. I figured if anything new happened, you could just tell me. Did you happen to see Willow there?"

At this point, Rey felt like he had nothing to hide. "I did. Willow and I actually grabbed some food before the meeting and went for a drink after. If you'd have come with me, maybe you could have done some of that catching up you claim you want to do."

Sam's expression darkened. "I can't believe you. You're doing what you told me was wrong."

"No, I'm not." Rey kept his voice level. "Willow is worried about her mom, the same way I am about Dad.

That's what we talked about. We sat with each other at the meeting, and then talked to two other people—a brother and a sister—who were worried about their parents."

Narrow-eyed, Sam glared at him, as if trying to ascertain whether or not Rey was telling the truth. "Did Willow ask about me?"

With difficulty, Rey suppressed a groan. "This is not about you, Sam. It's about Isla and Carl. They're missing, remember?"

"How could I forget." Sam pushed to his feet. "You'd never let me." And he stormed into his bedroom, slamming the door behind him.

Some things never changed. Sometimes, Rey thought Sam remained a perennial angry teenager.

Rey picked up the remote and turned the TV back on. If Sam cooled off and wanted to talk, Rey would be there. Otherwise, he didn't have the energy to worry about it.

The next morning, Rey got up before the sun rose and showered and dressed. He made his way into the kitchen for coffee and food. At first light, he intended to head out to check on the cattle, with a stop by the hay barn to make sure all the new bales had been put up.

To his surprise, he'd barely sat down at the table to drink his coffee when a sleepy-eyed Sam stumbled in.

"Mornin'," Sam mumbled. He made himself a cup of coffee and then sat in the chair across from Rey. "Listen, just because I'm not all worried about Dad doesn't mean I don't care. I'm just more optimistic than you. There's nothing wrong with that."

Since Rey didn't want to start something this early in the day, he simply nodded. He could only hope Sam would lose interest if he realized Rey couldn't be provoked.

"I'm sure they're fine," Sam continued. "A group of them probably went away together for a spontaneous trip and didn't want to be disturbed." Sam raised his mug and took a long swig. "You're just being pessimistic for thinking they might be in trouble."

Again, Rey didn't respond. He continued drinking his coffee, hoping Sam would leave him in peace.

Instead, Sam leaned forward. "You never answered my question last night. Did Willow ask about me?"

Rey took a deep breath, barely able to hide his exasperation. "Actually, we didn't discuss you. Last night was all about the missing people."

Eyes narrowed, Sam continued to stare. "I know you're worried, but it seems to me that you're just trying to bond with Willow."

"Come on, Sam." Rey lost the battle to keep his voice level. "How can you not be concerned? There are six people from town who just up and disappeared, leaving their cell phones and vehicles behind. Not a single one left a note. Even if your theory about them all going on vacation were to pan out, you have to admit this is not like Dad. He couldn't wait to see the bison. He must have texted me like twelve times, in between several phone calls. He knew when I'd be back, and he planned to be here to help me unload our new breeding stock. You honestly don't see anything worrisome about the fact that he wasn't? He never goes anywhere without checking in with one of us."

"Okay, okay." Sam shook his head, wincing. "No need to yell. One thing you have to remember is that Dad and Isla are both grown adults. They don't need our permission to go away together. None of those missing people do."

That statement alone meant his younger brother was going to willfully continue to miss the point.

Jaw clenched, Rey knew he had to get out of the house and away from Sam before he said or did something he'd regret later. Even though he hadn't had his breakfast yet, he strode for the back door, yanked it open and left.

"What about breakfast?" Sam called after him.

Rey didn't bother to answer. Sam knew how to cook. He made his way to the barn, headed to Roscoe, the gray gelding he preferred to ride, and saddled him up. Then he rode out, heading down the gravel road for the far pasture. This was one of the places he'd gone as a kid when he needed to think. He still went there every now and then, though less frequently.

Despite Rayna's assurances that she was handling this, with every hour that passed, Rey's worry increased.

What had happened to his dad? Even though he himself had kept reassuring Willow that the two parents would show up, he'd begun to have serious doubts. Carl had never been an impulsive man, and he did everything with a well-thought-out purpose. Running away from not only his responsibilities but also his family without a single word of explanation was the last thing he would do.

All his life, Rey had been what his father called a fixer. He'd always been good at identifying a problem and then finding a solution. But this, he couldn't fix. Not when he had no idea what the problem might be.

He rode for an hour, trying to let the quiet seep inside him. Instead, he found himself imagining various scenarios as to why his father had vanished, none of them good. Even his horse sensed his unsettled mood and acted skittish, shying sideways at shadows.

Since he had work to do, he and Roscoe headed out to check on the herd. Bison weren't like cattle, he realized. They wandered more, and even though some of the terrain where he'd put them to pasture seemed steep, they didn't seem averse to climbing. He'd been advised to keep them separate from the cattle, at least until he could have a vet make sure none were carriers of brucellosis, a deadly livestock disease.

He'd also been told they could be aggressive. While he personally hadn't witnessed that, he made sure to keep his distance so he didn't accidentally provoke them.

After he'd located the herd and done a head count to make sure they were all there, he rode Roscoe down the road a bit to check on cattle in three other pastures. Sam had done recent fence repairs to the second one, which made it even more shocking to see the fence down and two of the groups of cattle in one large herd.

Had Sam forgotten to fix this section of fence? Or had the damage come after that?

Without enlisting the help of his ranch hands, Rey didn't have a prayer of separating out the herd, so he dismounted and made some temporary repairs to the broken section. Without the proper tools and materials, he knew anything he fixed wouldn't last for long. Once again, it seemed he'd be having another talk with Sam. To bolster his case, he snapped some photos with his phone.

About to leave, he spotted another section that appeared to be on the verge of collapse and rode over there. He propped it up as best he could, took a few more pictures and then rode down the rest of the fence line, checking for any more problem spots.

Finally, he'd checked all the fencing in the immediate area. Wondering now if he'd have to check the fencing on the entire ranch, his frustration with his brother threatened to turn to anger. Sam had been given this task for a reason. Once he'd identified problem areas, he had the ability to assemble a crew and materials and get the repairs done as soon as possible. He knew as well as anyone how vital maintaining good fencing was to the safety of the herd.

If he couldn't even handle this simple task, maybe Sam needed to go ahead and get a job in town.

Seething, Rey returned to the barn. After removing the saddle, he brushed Roscoe down. The repetitive motion of currying the horse usually did a lot to soothe him, but not this time.

When he'd gotten Roscoe all brushed, he put his horse back in the stall. Aware he needed to calm down, he slowly made his way back to the main house. On the walk there, he rehearsed what he needed to say several times, hoping he could chastise his younger brother without too much anger. He wanted to be rational and collected. Otherwise, he knew Sam would try to turn the narrative to be about their missing father, rather than his complete and utter dereliction of duty.

But as he got closer, he realized Sam's pickup wasn't there. Sam had left. Which might be a good thing, as that meant Rey would have to wait to talk to him until he returned.

Chapter 5

The morning after the town meeting, Willow woke to the still too silent and empty house with a sinking feeling in the pit of her stomach. She felt like she'd missed something, though she couldn't put her finger on exactly what.

Getting up, she headed straight for the kitchen to grab a cup of coffee and try to think. Hopefully, once she cleared the sleep cobwebs out of her mind, she'd be able to focus and pinpoint what she might have missed.

Sipping her drink, she replayed what Rayna had said at the meeting yesterday, but she kept coming back to Sofia Alvarez's comment about heart issues running in the family. Had one or both of her missing parents struggled with issues similar to what Isla had? If so, what about the other missing people? Had they possibly gone off together for treatment?

Grabbing her phone, she called Rayna. When she got the sheriff on the line, she outlined what she thought.

"Interesting," Rayna commented. "I wasn't aware of that. I'll contact the families of the other missing people and see if they had any heart issues. What I need from you is contact information for your grandmother's doctors. While I know they won't release any personal information, at least I can find out if they recommend any particular heart specialists or facilities."

"Thank you," Willow said. "I'm thinking maybe they went to some sort of inpatient place, like a healing resort."

"This is West Texas, not California," Rayna reminded her. "I can't see someone like Carl Johnson going for something like that."

"Maybe not for himself, but he might for the woman he loved."

"Good point." Rayna sighed. "But even if your theory is valid, how on earth would they get six people to sign up? Places like that are expensive. Not all of the missing individuals would have the funds for a medical retreat or resort."

"I don't know." Deflated, Willow took another sip of coffee. "I was looking for the common denominator. What do these people have in common? Did they disappear together or separately?"

"The timing would seem to suggest together," Rayna said, her tone thoughtful. "And I've got my people looking into any possible connections between the group. By the way, did Isla still attend church?"

"As far as I know, she still went to Straightline Church."

"Well, that eliminates one more possibility," Rayna said. "The Alvarez family went to St. Francis. And the other couple were Baptist. Let me check into the doctor angle, and I'll get back with you."

After ending the call, Willow drank the last of her coffee and made another round of the house. For whatever reason, searching for clues as to Isla's disappearance helped settle her mind.

Her thoughts kept returning to last night. For one,

heart-stopping moment, she'd thought Rey had been about to kiss her. Even worse, she'd longed for the press of his lips on hers.

Was she that desperate for a distraction? Her cheeks warm, she began searching the cabinet under the sink in her grandmother's bathroom. Even though she'd checked it once before, she pulled everything out one at a time, setting them aside until she'd emptied it. Nothing but the usual toiletries.

After she'd put every item back, she did the same to the medicine cabinet above the sink. Here, she hoped to find prescriptions that might give her a clue about her granny's health. But Isla had evidently taken all of that with her, as most people did when traveling.

Instead of starting on the bedroom, which she'd already searched more than once, she decided to jump in the shower and get ready to go into town. She didn't think she could stay alone in the house any longer. Even though she guessed Rayna had already done so, she wanted to stop by her grandmother's church and talk to the pastor and the church secretary in person. Even though Rey had called them, she felt like a visit just to chat might help jog their memories. And she also planned to swing by the bookstore where Isla liked to get her reading material. Then last but not least, Serenity's on Main Street.

Most people in town, even those who considered themselves too hard-nosed realistic to be true psychic believers, respected Serenity and her "visions." After all, she'd been right far more than she'd been wrong. And everyone liked her. Unfailingly kind and supportive, people tended to go to her when they found themselves in need of comfort or wisdom.

Willow could use both right now. Though she hadn't been to her shop since her last time home during the holidays, she knew Serenity would welcome her as if no time had elapsed at all.

In her teens, she had spent quite a few pleasant hours browsing through Serenity's shop. Specifically, the part of the store dedicated to rocks and crystals. Willow had bought her first rock, an inexpensive piece of polished tourmaline, at sixteen. Since then, she'd slowly and steadily added to her collection. She kept them on display in the living room of her apartment.

The heat could be brutal this time of the year, and though she'd normally wear jean shorts, a tank top and flip-flops, this time Willow dressed in a nice pair of khaki shorts, a cap-sleeve blouse and strappy wedge-heeled sandals. She put her long hair up in a high ponytail and grabbed her purse and keys.

Driving into town, she headed for her mom's church first. Willow had grown up attending services there. She'd known Pastor Clayton her entire life. On every visit home, her mother had made sure she got to church on Sunday. Personally, Willow thought it was long past time for the elderly pastor to retire, but he joked that as long as he could stand upright, he planned to preach.

Bertha, the gray-haired church secretary who seemed nearly as old as her boss, looked up from her desk when Willow knocked. Squinting through her glasses, she clearly didn't recognize her guest at first.

"Bertha, it's me. Willow Allen. Isla's daughter," she added for good measure.

The older woman's face creased in a smile. "I thought that was you. Come in, come in. Pastor Clayton will be so happy to see you."

Willow stepped into the small office and went around the desk to give Bertha a quick hug.

"It's a shame about your grandmother," Bertha mused. "We've all been praying for that entire group to be found."

Just then, Pastor Clayton came around the corner. His stooped shoulders and shuffling gait revealed his age. He stopped short when he caught sight of Willow. "My stars!" he exclaimed, clapping his hands together once in excitement. "Willow Allen! To what do I owe the honor of this visit?"

Before she could answer, he took her arm and shepherded her into his office. "Have a seat," he invited. He offered her water, iced tea or coffee, but she declined. She waited until he got settled behind his desk before asking her questions.

"I came to see you about my grandmother," she began. "As her pastor and spiritual advisor, did she come to you with any problems or issues?"

"You should know Ms. Rayna has already been here asking me the same thing," he said, clasping his hands in a steeple on his desk. "And I'll tell you what I told her. If Isla had asked for my counsel on any personal issues, I would not be able to reveal them. However, since she did not, in that respect, there is nothing for you to worry about. In fact, I'm more concerned with the fact that she hasn't attended services in two months."

"What?" Shocked, Willow leaned forward. "She stopped coming to church? That isn't like her."

"I know, I know." He sighed. "I was so worried that I tried calling her and left several messages. When she didn't return my calls, I stopped by her house unannounced."

"When was this?"

"A few weeks ago," he replied, his grave expression matching his tone.

Bracing herself, Willow waited.

"She actually answered the door. Apologized for not inviting me in, but said she had a doctor's appointment. Naturally, I asked after her health, but she waved me away. I never did get a chance to ask her why she'd stopped coming to services."

"How did she look?" Willow asked. "Did she appear to be ill?"

"Not really." He frowned. "Has she been having health issues?"

"I'm not sure," Willow admitted. "She had some sort of heart episode but refused to elaborate. She just said it wasn't anything serious."

"I'm sorry I can't be of more assistance," the pastor said. "I told Rayna the same thing."

Getting up, Willow thanked him for his time. She waved to Bertha on her way out.

When she got into her vehicle, she let the engine run and sat a moment, hoping the AC would cool down the interior. Isla prided herself on being a creature of habit. She liked her routines and seldom, if ever, varied from them. For her to have stopped attending services at Straightline Church and not have mentioned it to Willow set off all kinds of alarms.

Next, she drove to the bookstore. When she parked

and went inside, she didn't recognize the teenager working behind the counter. "Is Mr. Smith in?" she asked, hoping to see the owner.

The kid, a tall, gangly boy with a mullet and wire-rim glasses, looked up at her and blinked. "No," he answered. "He hasn't been here in a few weeks. My older sister Kathy is the manager, and she opens and closes the store. I work here in between my shifts at Pizza Perfect."

Alarmed, Willow swallowed. "Is Mr. Smith all right? He never missed a day coming into his bookstore."

"He never *used* to," the kid corrected. "But he stopped coming in a couple weeks ago. Kathy says she talked to him, and he asked her to keep the place running until he could get back."

She froze. "Got back from where?"

"I have no idea." Clearly losing interest, he looked down at the tablet on the counter in front of him. "If there's something I can help you find, please let me know."

Willow thanked him and left. Had Mr. Smith also disappeared, along with the six others? He was about the same age as her grandmother, late sixties, early seventies. And while she couldn't remember if he was married, she figured she might as well mention him to Rayna, just in case.

The thought that even more older people might have gone missing sent a chill down her spine. Pushing the thought away, she drove the couple blocks north to Serenity's. She parked, took a deep breath and walked inside.

The bells on the door set off a cheerful sound to announce her arrival. Willow took a quick look around. Except for the expansion of the flower shop Serenity ran in conjunction with her metaphysical store, not much had changed since her last visit.

"Willow!" Serenity came from the back, her multitude of bracelets jingling, her colorful skirt making her appear to float. "It's so nice to see you."

She enveloped Willow in a quick hug. When she stepped back, her earlier smile had vanished from her face. "You're worried about your grandmother, aren't you?"

Slowly, Willow nodded. "Very. But I appreciated you letting us know that she and all the others are okay."

Expression distracted, Serenity made a dismissing motion with her hand, which sent the bracelets jingling again. "Come, sit and have a cup of tea. I'll read the leaves after we finish."

Willow followed her through a multicolor beaded curtain to the back. She took a chair at the small, round table and eyed the large crystal ball Serenity kept in a glass case on the counter.

Serenity used an old-fashioned tea kettle on her small, electric stove. When it whistled, she poured the water into two cups that each held a small metal tea diffuser. While the tea steeped, she went to the refrigerator and removed a foil-wrapped pound cake. She didn't bother asking Willow if she wanted a piece. Instead, she sliced off two pieces, put them on saucers and set them on the table.

"My favorite," Willow said, unexpected tears springing to her eyes. Serenity had often served her this dessert when Willow was a teen. She didn't question how the older woman had known to have it on hand.

Bringing over both cups, Serenity smiled. "It's so good to see you again. Yes, the circumstances are terrible, but it hurts nothing to take a few minutes and enjoy each other's company."

She'd just started to relax when Serenity stiffened. "Oh no," the older woman said. "I think someone near Isla might be in trouble."

Though he'd already gone through most of his dad's desk, this time Rey decided to search the entire house. He couldn't shake the feeling that he was missing something. And while he didn't really think it had to do with heart issues or Isla's health like Willow had suggested, at this point, he wasn't willing to rule anything out.

He started in the kitchen. Opening and closing all the cabinets, he saw nothing out of the ordinary. Dishes and glasses, pots and pans. When he reached the junk drawer by the landline, he took the entire drawer out and carried it to the table.

First, he took out every pen and pencil and set them aside. Then he sifted through the rest of the contents, finding nothing of interest. Disappointed, he put everything back and replaced the drawer in its proper spot.

Now what? What should he search next?

The sound of tires on gravel had him looking up. Had Sam finally returned? Pushing to his feet, Rey went to the window to look.

Instead of Sam, he saw Willow's red Ford pulling up.

Just like that, his pulse went into overdrive. He watched as she parked and got out, transfixed by her beauty. Though he knew she'd been born and raised here in Getaway the same as him, she looked like an exotic flower.

Heart in his throat, he hurried for the door. She knocked

just as he reached it. Opening the door, he stepped aside and motioned for her to enter. "Willow! What brings you here?"

As she brushed past him, bringing with her the scent of peaches, he inhaled sharply. She whirled around to face him, her ponytail swinging. Her stormy eyes and troubled expression had him once again yearning to pull her into his arms. Somehow, he managed to resist.

"I just left Serenity's," she said, her voice uneven. "While we were sitting there talking, she suddenly said she thought someone near my grandmother might be in trouble."

Not sure how to react to that, he motioned for her to follow him into the kitchen. While most everyone in town had a healthy respect for Serenity and her prophesies, Rey himself wasn't too sure. Sometimes it seemed she put things in the vaguest terms possible, playing it safe.

Once she'd taken a seat at the farm table, he poured them each a glass of sweet tea and brought them over. "What exactly did she say?"

She sighed. "As usual, she didn't go into any specifics. But we were having cake and tea and chatting when all of a sudden she sat up straight and said she thinks someone near Isla is in trouble."

Near Isla? Like Carl?

"And?" he asked. "Using the word *someone* is pretty darn generic, don't you think?"

"Yes, I agree. If she hadn't followed that up with saying *near Isla*, I wouldn't have paid any attention. But I know Isla and your dad are together, so it worried me." She sighed. "Probably more than it should have."

"Did she say anything else?"

"No. After making that pronouncement, she got very rattled and said I needed to go. I tried to question her, but she refused to say anything else. When I left, I drove right over here."

"I wouldn't put too much stock in that," he said. "Even the words she used—*in trouble*—can mean numerous things."

"True." Visibly trying to relax, Willow blinked rapidly. "I took it to mean in danger, but you're right. It doesn't have to be that."

He tried to think of something else he could say to help her feel better, but short of saying he didn't put any stock in Serenity's so-called prophecies, he hit a wall. "Well, I hope if Serenity *sees* something else, she contacts you."

"Me too." She took a long drink of her tea. "Thank you for this. I didn't realize I was so thirsty."

The back door opened, and Sam breezed inside. He stopped short when he caught sight of Willow. "What are you doing here?" he asked, his gaze going from her to Rey and back again.

"Well, hello to you too," Willow said, raising her brows. Rey half-expected her to jump to her feet and hug his brother, but instead she remained seated, regarding Sam without smiling.

To his credit, her response made Sam grimace. "I'm sorry," he said, his voice sheepish. "It's just you're the last person I expected to find in my kitchen."

"Really? Why is that?" she asked.

Since it seemed Willow might be spoiling for a fight with Sam, Rey figured now might be a good time to excuse himself. He started to get to his feet, planning to claim he needed to go check on something in the barn. But Willow reached out and touched his arm.

"Please wait," she asked, the entreaty in her gaze making him realize he'd do anything for her. "We aren't finished talking, and since Sam here clearly has no interest in the topic we're discussing, we can continue once he's gone."

Ouch. Rey braced himself for his younger brother's response.

"Wow. That's not fair." Expression wounded, Sam went to the fridge to get his own glass of iced tea. Once he'd poured it, he plunked it down on the table and took the seat next to Willow. "We used to be good friends," he said, studying her. "What happened?"

"My grandmother and your father went missing," she said, her voice quiet. "And any time I've tried to talk to you about it, you change the subject. You seem to want to act like everything is normal, that nothing has changed."

Sam took a long drink of his tea, his gaze never leaving her. "I'm well aware of what's going on. I just thought you might want a distraction, that's all."

More than anything, Rey wished he could silently leave the room. But Willow had asked him to stay, so he would. His presence didn't seem to bother Sam, who appeared to be doing his best to pretend he wasn't there.

"You just don't get it." The sadness in Willow's eyes made Rey's chest ache. "I just want to find Isla, to make sure she's safe."

"And Carl," Rey added, earning a sideways glare from Sam. "Actually, all of the missing townspeople," he continued for good measure.

Sam returned his full attention to Willow and nodded. "I'll do better," he said. "What do you need from me?"

She sighed. "Nothing, Sam. Though I do appreciate you offering. Right now, I have zero energy to devote to anything other than searching for our loved ones."

"I can help with that." Sam placed his hand on her arm, which made Rey fight a fierce urge to knock it away. A second later, Willow did it herself.

"Thanks. I've spent several hours talking to people in town to see if they know anything. I need to call Rayna and give her some information that may or may not be relevant." She stood. "Please excuse me."

And she stepped outside to make her call.

Rey and Sam watched her go. Once she'd disappeared from view, Sam turned to eye Rey.

"What is going on here?" Sam asked, his gaze hard. "Willow and I have been friends for years. Why are you trying to ruin that?"

Rey pushed to his feet. "Sam, I'm not sure what you think I've done or what exactly you're trying to say. But not everything is about you."

"Fine." Sam continued to stare. "But I see what you're doing. You're using Dad's disappearance to get close to a hot woman. I get it, because that was my plan, but you beat me to it."

Though he wanted to throttle his brother, Rey took a deep breath and tried to keep his voice level. "That's not what I'm doing, and I'm pretty sure you know that. Willow and I are both trying to find Carl and Isla. I don't think anyone rational could turn a desperate search for loved ones into something else."

Sam put his head down on his arms on the table,

just like he'd done when he'd been a teenager trying to get his way. From experience, Rey knew he could either wait it out or simply walk away. But he didn't want to intrude on Willow's phone call, nor did he want to leave and let her come back and have to be alone in the kitchen with Sam.

Which meant waiting it out would be his choice. He sat back down and took a drink of his tea.

The back door opened, and Willow came inside. Her gaze slid over Sam, still with his head down, and met Rey's. "When I was in town, I stopped at the bookstore. My grandmother is a regular customer there. I learned that Mr. Smith, the owner, hasn't been seen or heard from in a couple of weeks."

Sam raised his head. "What about Mrs. Smith? Did anyone think to ask her?"

Rey and Willow looked at each other, then back to him. "Sam, Mrs. Smith died last year," Rey said. "Mr. Smith has been living alone."

"I didn't know that." Sam shrugged. "Guess I should have gone into the bookstore more often."

"Rayna is going to check on him," Willow continued, ignoring Sam's comment. "He's about the same age as all the others. He might be with them." She sat back down and picked up her drink. "I wonder how many more missing people there might be."

"Just out of curiosity, what do you think happened to them?" Sam looked from one to the other. "Alien abduction? I mean, seriously. What are the actual possibilities?"

"That's just it," Rey answered. "We don't know."

"They might have gone on a trip," Sam said. "Like,

taken a bus somewhere. Maybe Vegas. Old people love to gamble. Or to a spa resort. Who knows? But for this many people to disappear all at the same time, it has to be a coordinated effort."

"That's what worries me." Willow sighed. "Because whatever happened, it was really out of character. Even if you go on vacation, you bring your phone. You tell your family."

"Then what happened?" Clearly frustrated, Sam dragged his fingers through his hair. For once, he appeared to actually be focused on the situation rather than how it affected him.

"That's what we're trying to figure out," Rey said. "Rayna is working on it. She's good. If anyone can get answers, she can."

"I'll start asking around too," Sam promised. "And I'll let you two know if I hear anything."

"Thank you," Willow said, looking at him. "I stopped in at the church my grandmother attends. The pastor said she hasn't been in several weeks. That's not like her."

"Weird," Sam replied. "She even had Carl going to services with her."

Rey noticed she didn't mention her conversation with Serenity. He supposed he couldn't blame her.

"Well, thanks for the tea." Willow stood. "I guess I'd better run. I just wanted to give you an update."

"Do you want to stay for dinner?" Rey asked, giving in to impulse. Sam snapped his head around to stare.

"I might," Willow admitted, her soft gaze locked on his. "Honestly, I dread going back to grandma's empty house. But only if I can help cook."

Rey smiled. "That can be arranged. Most of our meals

are simple, especially in the summer. I usually throw something on the grill. Maybe you can make a side dish."

"I can do that."

In the background, Sam snorted. "We usually just open a can of beans or microwave some frozen vegetables."

Which was only because Sam was in charge of making the sides, though Rey kept that truth to himself.

"Well, I think I can figure out something," Willow said, still smiling. "What are you grilling tonight?"

"Chicken breast," Rey answered.

"Perfect." She glanced at the pantry and fridge. "Do you mind if I take a look and see what you have?"

"Go ahead." Sam smiled. "I can be your assistant while Rey mans the grill."

They ended up having grilled chicken and a delicious corn salad. Even Sam's earlier bad mood appeared to have lifted. He complimented Rey on the chicken, something he never did. Willow's spirits seemed better too. She seemed more relaxed and happy. Rey loved seeing the light in her eyes.

She insisted on helping clean up. Sam, for once, pitched in. Rey went outside to clean his grill. When he'd finished and went back in, Willow thanked him for the meal and headed out.

About to walk her to the door, Rey stopped when Sam stepped in and did it instead. The second he'd closed the door behind her, he turned to Rey and grinned. "I think I'm in love with Willow," he said. "And I'm confident she feels the same way. I think the time has come for me to settle down and start a family."

Chapter 6

A puppy, Willow thought, driving away from the ranch. Sam reminded her of an overeager puppy. Instead of helping as she'd prepared the corn salad, Sam had tripped all over himself and gotten in the way. Even worse, he'd clearly decided she hadn't meant it when she'd told him she wasn't interested. He'd been flirty and had kept touching her. Only when she'd told him sharply to stop had he kept his hands to himself. Which was a good thing, since she'd seriously begun to consider walloping him.

Somehow, even with his interference, she'd managed to whip together her special corn salad. Back in California, she'd prepared this to bring to every beach party and cook out she'd attended, so she knew the ingredients by heart. She could tell it wasn't something Rey and Sam usually ate, so she'd enjoyed watching their reactions when they'd taken their first bite. Especially Rey's.

Despite everything going on, she couldn't seem to stop looking at Rey's handsome face. Oddly enough, he hadn't had this effect on her at all when she'd hung around with Sam as a teenager. But now...

Her breath caught every time their eyes met. She found herself wanting to be closer to him, to touch him.

With Sam's watchful gaze on her every time she looked up, she struggled to act unaffected.

Multiple times during the meal, she found herself about to say something to Rey, but bit back the words due to Sam's presence. Despite his attempt to be empathetic, she knew he still believed Isla, Carl and the rest of the missing people would show up any day. Whether he was overly optimistic or deluded, she wished she could share his belief. With every day that passed with her grandmother gone, her worry grew.

She arrived home and let herself into the house, hoping against hope that Isla would pop out of the kitchen and envelop her in a hug.

But the empty house remained still and quiet. Closing the blinds, she changed into an old T-shirt and soft shorts, poured herself a glass of wine and settled down to watch TV.

Her phone rang. Amanda Epps, her friend who owned the hair salon.

"Hey, girl," Amanda said. "Any luck finding your grandmother?"

Willow told her no.

"Oh. I'm sorry. But listen, I just got off the phone with Sam. It sounds like you and I have something to celebrate, right? I know the timing seems a bit off, but we need to take good news when we can. So congratulations!"

Confused, Willow took a deep breath. "Congratulations on what?"

Amanda went silent. "Oh, dang. I didn't realize…"

"Didn't realize what?"

"That it was supposed to be a secret. You know how

Sam is. He can run on at the mouth. He asked me to organize a get-together for the two of you."

Though she'd begun to feel like a broken record, Willow asked why.

"I don't know," Amanda replied. "All he said was to
celebrate your good news."

Finally, Willow let her exasperation show. "There is
no good news. Please don't plan any sort of gathering or
party, because I won't be attending. Right now, all my
focus is centered on finding my grandmother."

"But Sam said—"

"I don't care what he said. He and I are only friends.
As a matter of fact, I'm going to call him right now and
get this straightened out."

"Oh, wow. I'm so sorry. I thought for sure you two
had gotten engaged," Amanda said.

Engaged? Willow nearly spit out her wine.

"I hope I didn't spoil any surprises," Amanda continued.

After taking a couple of deep breaths, Willow was able
to speak normally. "Don't worry, you didn't. It's all good,
I promise. But I am going to have to let you go now."

As soon as she ended the call, Willow dialed Sam,
simmering. When he didn't pick up, instead of leaving
a message, she phoned Rey. He answered on the second ring.

"What the heck is going on with Sam right now?" she
demanded. "I just got a phone call from Amanda, one
of my high school friends, offering her congratulations
at my and Sam's good news."

"Good news?" Rey sounded carefully noncommittal.
"Are some sort of congratulations in order?"

"Don't you start too!" Frustrated, she took a deep gulp of wine. "Did he say something to you?"

Rey went silent. When he spoke again, the pitch of his low voice sounded intense. "Willow, are you sure you want me involved in whatever you two have got going on?"

Though she rarely, if ever, cursed, Willow did now. "Damn it, Rey. I was just there. You know as well as I do that Sam and I have nothing going on. Now please, tell me what he said. If he's calling people in town and spreading some kind of rumor about me, I need to stop it now."

"I think you should call him."

"I tried to, but he didn't pick up." She could no longer hide her frustration. "Come on, Rey. What's going on?"

"Sam has convinced himself that you are in love," he finally said, reluctance coloring his tone.

"With *him*?" she squeaked. "Are you serious?"

Before he could respond, she heard the sound of Sam's voice in the background. "Is that Sam? Put him on."

"But—"

"Put him on *now*!" she demanded.

"Hold on. Sam, Willow wants to talk to you."

"Tell her I'm not here," Sam said.

"She can hear you," Rey replied. "Here."

He must have handed Sam the phone because a second later Sam greeted her. "Hey, Willow. What's up?"

"What did you say to Amanda?" she asked, not bothering to try and contain her anger. "What celebration are you planning?"

"Oh, geez," Sam said, sounding sheepish. "I was trying to get something set up in advance, that's all. She shouldn't have called you."

"Set up in advance for what?"

"Um, I'd rather not say," he replied.

"Since it involves me, I think you have to. Now, spill."

"Just a sec." Sam sounded weird, like he might choke on his words. "Let me go outside so we can talk in private."

In the background, she heard the sound of a door opening and closing.

"Okay," Sam finally said. "We're alone now."

Silent, she waited. She could hear the nervousness in his voice.

"Willow, I was going to ask you to marry me. That's what the celebration was going to be for. So everyone could share in our happiness."

Dumbfounded, she struggled to find words and failed.

"Willow, are you there?" Sam asked anxiously. "What do you say? Obviously, I haven't got a ring yet or anything, but we could pick out one together."

Though she wanted to ask what planet he lived on, she'd known Sam for years, and if he was serious, she didn't want to break his heart. She thought about playing this off as a joke, giving him an easy way out, but he clearly seemed to think this was an actual possibility. Why, she had no idea.

"Sam, we're not even dating," she said, as gently as she could. "I've made it abundantly clear to you that we are friends, and I'm not interested in anything more."

"But the connection," he said, his tone serious and desperate. "Earlier, when we made that corn salad. Don't tell me you didn't feel it too."

"There was no connection, Sam. We are just two old friends, helping out in the kitchen." Then, just in case she hadn't made it clear enough, she continued. "There will be no celebration, no engagement, heck, no dating. I need you to understand this. Please tell me you do."

Sam was silent for so long, she thought he might have ended the call. "Are you there?" she finally asked.

"I am." He sounded distant now. "I apologize for misunderstanding. Let me take the phone back inside, so you can talk to my brother. Obviously, you've chosen him over me."

"This isn't a competition," she said, but Sam didn't reply.

A moment later, Rey came on. "Willow?" he asked, his voice hesitant. "Are you all right?"

"I'm not sure," she answered honestly. "I have no idea what's going on with Sam. He helped me make the salad tonight for dinner, and somehow he got it into his head that we are a couple."

"He said as much to me," Rey admitted. "I was kind of shocked, but I figured I'd just stay out of it."

"There's nothing to stay out of." She wasn't sure whether to laugh or cry. "This feels almost like a prank. I just wanted to fill you in because your brother is not okay. I'm worried about him."

"I'll talk to him later, once he's calmed down. Maybe Dad being missing has finally hit home with him, and this is his way of dealing with it."

She swallowed. "I think he needs help, Rey. Maybe he should talk to a therapist or a doctor."

"Maybe," Rey agreed. "I promise I'll bring that up too, when the time seems right. To be honest, he's always been a bit immature, but this is next-level stuff. I'm worried about him also."

She wished she were there with him, ached to be able

to take comfort in his strong embrace. Shaking her head at her own untoward thoughts, she took a deep breath.

"I promise I'll talk to him," Rey continued. "Try not to worry. I'll fill you in as soon as I have more answers."

"Thanks." She needed to get off the phone before she said something she'd regret, like how much she needed him. "I'll talk to you later."

"Definitely." Rey hesitated. "And Willow, don't let yourself feel bad about this. None of it's your fault."

The empathy in his voice nearly undid her. Somehow, she managed to hold it together long enough to tell him goodbye.

Putting her phone down on the end table, she knew he was right. She'd done nothing wrong. But now, in addition to battling her overwhelming attraction to Rey, she was honestly concerned about Sam. She might not be romantically interested in him, but he was one of her oldest friends. If he needed help, she would do her best to make sure he got it.

After talking to Willow, Rey went looking for Sam. Sam had been acting erratically, even for him. While Rey wasn't exactly sure what might be going on with his younger brother, he couldn't help but hope Sam might open up to him.

Before he could reach his brother's room, the doorbell rang. That in itself was unusual. Out here at the ranch, visitors were few and far between, and most people let him know in advance they were coming. Frowning, Rey pivoted and headed toward the front door.

He opened it to find a sheriff's deputy in full uniform standing on his porch. Immediately, Rey's heart sank.

"Are you here about my father?" he asked, his voice breaking despite his best efforts.

The man, a deputy Rey didn't recognize, removed his cowboy hat. "I'm sorry, sir. Are you Rey Johnson?"

"I am."

"I'll need you to come with me. Rayna asked me to bring you down to the hospital," the man said.

"The hospital?" Hearing that gave Rey hope. "Can you at least tell me if he's all right?"

"Sir, I've only been instructed to fetch you. I don't know any details."

Which seemed fair. "Just one second," Rey said, calling for Sam. "My brother needs to come too."

When Sam didn't answer, Rey hurried inside to knock on Sam's door. But again, Sam didn't respond. Rey turned the knob and peeked inside. No Sam. Which meant he was somewhere out on the ranch.

Deciding he didn't have time to look for him but would call him on the way to the hospital, Rey hurried out front to rejoin the deputy. He got into the passenger seat at the man's direction.

"I need to make a few calls," Rey said.

"Go ahead, it's a long drive," the deputy said.

"Thanks." Rey punched the contact to make the call. But Sam didn't pick up. Leaving a voice mail, he outlined what he knew and where he was headed. Since he didn't have too much information to go on, he said that too. "Anyway, if you want to head to Midland, that's good. If not, give me a call when you get this. I'll update you when I know more."

Next, he tried Willow. She answered almost immediately. "What's going on?" she asked. "Did you get a chance to talk to Sam?"

"Not yet." He filled her in on what was going on.

She gasped. "Serenity's warning. She said someone with Isla was in trouble."

"She just didn't say who or what kind of trouble," he said, deciding he'd concede this one to Serenity. "I guess we're about to find out."

"Have you called Rayna?" she asked, the tremor in her voice echoing the way he felt inside. "I'm guessing since she only sent for you that my grandmother wasn't found."

"I don't know." His gut twisted. "Let me try her now. If I hear anything new, I'll call you back. If not, I'll update you once I get to the hospital."

But Rayna didn't pick up. Since he really hadn't expected her to, he put his phone away and settled in for the drive to Midland, the location of their closest hospital.

The deputy, whose name Rey still hadn't gotten, wasn't much of a talker. In fact, he barely even glanced at Rey, preferring to keep his focus on the road.

Which suited Rey just fine. He had a million questions, and since this guy clearly had zero answers, he'd make the ride in silence.

Finally, they arrived at the hospital. The deputy parked his cruiser and looked at Rey. "I'll need you to stay with me," he said.

"Fine." Impatience churning inside him, Rey followed the man into the emergency department waiting room, where they were met by another uniformed officer.

"This way, please."

The triage nurse buzzed them back. Down a long hallway past several rooms. Finally, Rey spotted Rayna, sitting in a chair outside a room marked ICU. She jumped up as they approached.

"Is he okay?" Rey asked. "Please tell me he's all right."

"It's not Carl," Rayna said. "When I got the call, the description made it sound like it might be, but when I got here about fifteen minutes ago, they allowed me back to see him. Once I did, I realized it's Floyd Smith. Willow might have told you, but he's been missing too."

Just like that, all the jumbled emotions of hope and fear and relief vanished. "Not Carl," he repeated. Then, realizing they'd recovered at least one of the missing people, he took a deep breath. "Has he been able to tell you where he's been?"

Slowly, the sheriff shook her head. "He's not conscious. In fact, he's in pretty bad shape. Someone found him half naked, wandering a county road out near the edge of Getaway limits. The doctor says he's severely malnourished and dehydrated. I'm hoping they can fix him up quickly so he can give us some information."

Since Rey sensed his legs might give out, he dropped into the chair Rayna had just vacated. "It's not Carl," he repeated, his throat aching as he shook his head. "I honestly thought you'd found my father. I'm not sure whether to be relieved or disappointed."

"I get that, and I'm sorry." Rayna squeezed his shoulder. "I thought, from the description I was given, they'd found your father. Now that we know it's not, we can go from there. Honestly, this is the first real lead we've had in this case. Until now, there's been nothing."

"Nothing?" Rey repeated. "Nothing at all?"

"Yes. No matter how hard we look for evidence, it's like an entire group of people vanished without a trace.

The only thing they have in common is their age. All of them are senior citizens."

Rey took a deep breath, trying to slow his racing pulse.

"So I'm really hopeful once Mr. Smith can tell us where he's been, we'll know where to find the others," Rayna continued. "Assuming they are all together, which seems likely."

Rey nodded. "I need to call Sam and Willow," he said.

"Go right ahead." Rayna moved away to give him some privacy. "I'm going to grab a soft drink from the vending machine. Do you want anything?"

"No thanks." Waiting until Rayna rounded the corner, Rey pulled out his phone. He called Sam first, just in case his brother had jumped into his truck and might be on the way to the hospital. The call went straight to voice mail. Rey went ahead and left a message with all the details he'd just learned from Rayna. "Call me back when you get this," he said.

Next, he phoned Willow. She answered on the first ring, clearly waiting. "The guy isn't Carl," he told her. "Rayna said it's Mr. Smith, the bookstore owner. He's in pretty bad shape and unconscious, so no one has been able to question him to see if he was with the others."

"Oh, that poor man." Willow took a deep breath. "I hope he's going to be all right."

"Me too." He debated whether or not to tell her what Rayna had said about there being no other leads in the case. In the end, he went ahead and passed that on. He didn't want to start hiding things from her.

"No other leads?" She sounded stunned. "She doesn't have anything at all?"

"Unfortunately not."

His answer made her groan. "Great. I really hope Mr. Smith knows something."

"Me too." He found himself wanting to linger on the call. Hearing her voice brought him both comfort and an aching sort of need.

"Please let me know if you learn anything," Willow continued.

He promised he would before saying goodbye. After, he sat and stared at his phone for a moment, wishing he could see her.

Then, shaking his head at his own foolishness, he went to find Rayna.

Walking down the adjacent hall, he located her standing near the vending machine, drinking a cola and talking to one of her deputies. They went silent when he walked up.

"I couldn't reach Sam," he said. "Though, I was able to fill Willow in."

"You might as well go home," Rayna said, her tired smile matching the hint of exhaustion in her eyes. "I'm going to stay here in the hopes that Mr. Smith wakes up. I'll call you once he does."

"Are you sure?" Rey asked, torn between trying to help out and getting the heck out of the hospital. "I'll need to catch a ride back with one of your guys."

"Yes, I'm sure and that's fine. I've got more deputies here too. There's no reason for you to stay."

More relieved than he should have been, Rey thanked her and headed out to the lobby to wait for his ride. Before the deputy got there, he checked his phone just in case Sam had called or texted, but there wasn't anything. Had his brother even gotten his messages?

He tried again, though this time he hung up without

leaving a message. Unsure whether to be angry or just annoyed, he shoved all of that into the back of his mind and greeted the deputy. He wished he could ask to drive. Driving had always been therapeutic for him, so by the time he made it home, he figured he'd have been in a much better frame of mind. Instead, he had no choice but to ride shotgun.

Leaving Midland to head east toward Getaway, the deputy cranked up the radio when an old Brooks & Dunn song came on. By the time the Welcome to Getaway sign came into view, the sunset had turned the sky to purple overlaid with swirls of orange, pink and yellow. In other words, a typical West Texas summer sky.

Once the deputy had dropped him off at the ranch, instead of going inside, he found himself getting in his truck and heading in the opposite direction toward Willow's house. He couldn't articulate why, not even to himself, but he needed to see her. After the emotional upheaval he'd just been through, being with Willow felt like the only thing that could even begin to calm the rawness.

He didn't take the time to think or call her or text her. Instead, he drove with a single-minded intent, focusing only on her.

Finally, after what felt like forever, he turned onto her street and pulled in front of her house. Now that darkness had fallen, the yellow lights she'd turned on inside lit up the front bay window from behind the closed curtains. He sat in his truck for a moment, marveling at the suburban cheeriness of the place, before he turned off the motor. Jumping out, he headed up the sidewalk with a brisk stride. Hoping she'd be as eager to see him as he was her, he took a deep breath and pressed the doorbell.

Chapter 7

When Willow opened her door to find Rey standing there, her pulse went into immediate overdrive. Taking a shaky breath, she stepped aside and motioned him in. He'd barely moved past, brushing lightly against her, when she closed the door and turned to face him. Something intense flared in that instant. The smoldering heat in his gaze made her entire body tingle.

Neither of them spoke. No words were necessary. Instead, they locked gazes and moved toward each other, as if pulled by unseen forces. She couldn't speak, or think. Dizzy with desire, she couldn't look away. Rey took up all her focus.

Claiming her lips with his, the raw hunger in his kiss sent a ripple of excitement through her. She raised herself to meet him, shuddering at the delicious sensation of his kiss. His touch, almost unbearably tender, ignited in her a frenzy of need.

She deepened the kiss, demanding more, craving more. His breath hitched as his tongue met hers. *This*, she thought, her knees trembling. She'd been waiting all her life for *this* man.

On fire, she fumbled with his shirt, needing to feel

the heat of his skin under her fingers. His fingers seared a path across her abdomen as he helped her shed her clothes. Finally, both naked, they came together again, skin to skin. His hardness matched her softness.

Still locked together, they made it to her couch, still kissing as they fell against the cushions.

"Are you sure?" he rasped, lifting his mouth long enough from hers to ask.

This made her chuckle, even as desire thrummed through her blood. "A little late for that, aren't you?" she asked, unable to keep her quivering body from rubbing like a cat against his oh-so-perfect arousal. "And yes, I'm sure. Are you?"

Instead of an answer, he made a low growl deep in his throat. The primal sound sent her already sensitive nerves ablaze.

He lowered his body over hers. She gasped as he entered her, then arched up to meet him, welcoming him into her body.

Moving slowly, he filled her completely before he withdrew and then did it all over again. He intoxicated her, captivated her and drove her utterly mad.

"More," she ordered.

To her surprise and delight, he took her at her word, releasing whatever leash he'd put on his self-control. He took her, fast and deep and hard, driving himself into her with a fury that matched her own frenzied need.

Again and again, each time she met him halfway, nails raking down his skin. Their mutual passion, raw and primal, felt like nothing she'd ever experienced before.

As her climax built, shuddering with tremors that

warned of an impending tsunami, she finally surrendered and gave herself over to an explosion of pure pleasure, sweet and raw. Drowning, she moaned as waves of ecstasy crashed over her, while she rode the crest of the tide.

After, she curled into him, the solid thrum of his heartbeat under her ear. They held on tightly to each other, each reluctant to move away.

For the first time in her life, she allowed a man to sleep beside her in her childhood bed in her mother's house. More than right, or convenient, having Rey there felt necessary.

The next morning, Willow woke before sunrise. Even so, Rey had risen before her. She went into the bathroom and washed her face and brushed her teeth. After dragging a brush through her hair, she followed the smell of coffee to the kitchen, where Rey sat at the table drinking a cup. At the sight of him, her body stirred again.

"I hope you don't mind," he said, gesturing toward her grandmother's old coffeepot. "I need my caffeine, or I'm worthless."

"Of course I don't mind," she replied, aching to kiss him again. "You're up early."

He shrugged. "I always get up at five. Old habits are hard to break."

"I get it. I'm an early riser too." After making her own cup of coffee, she carried it over to the table. "One of my true joys in life is being on the beach when the sun comes up."

"Do you miss it?" he asked. "The ocean, I mean."

"I do," she answered honestly. "But I missed Getaway too. West Texas has a way of getting into your soul and leaving a mark. If I could bring the ocean closer to here, I'd have paradise."

Which would mean she'd stay. She didn't give voice to that thought, which was something that had been rattling around in her head for some time now. Even before her grandmother had disappeared, Willow had missed her. Plus, as Isla grew older, Willow wanted to be around to help her, enjoy her company and learn from her seemingly endless well of wisdom. Now, she had to wonder if she'd ever get the chance again.

Throat aching, she turned her head away to hide the sudden tears in her eyes. But Rey must have noticed. He covered her hand with his. "We're going to find them," he said. "Alive and well."

Slowly, she nodded, grateful for his touch. "I'm going to ask for more time off from my job. I still have vacation days remaining, though I'd planned to use those during the holidays. But there's no way I can leave, not with my grandmother still missing."

Instead of replying, he leaned over and kissed her. Which was much better anyway. When they broke apart, they breathed heavily.

"Do you want to go back to bed?" he asked, the heat in his eyes matching his husky voice.

The thought made her shiver. "I have a better idea," she said. "We both could use a shower. How about you join me?"

Grinning, he got to his feet and pulled her up with him. "You don't need to ask me twice. Let me see if I have one last condom, and I'll meet you there."

The hot shower wasn't as steamy as their lovemaking. Slick, soapy skin, water running down his muscular, hard body. Allowing herself to explore, she loved the way he held perfectly still so she could. Only the immensity of his arousal and the banked heat in his eyes testified how her touch affected him.

Meanwhile, she thought she might melt into a molten puddle. Every nerve ending tingling, her touch became bold, demanding. When he finally gave in, he entered her fiercely, filling her and almost sending her over the edge.

Though they'd spent the night in each other's arms, and their lovemaking had varied from the initial frenzy to a more leisurely pace, this was different. Quick and rough, both standing, when the pleasure overtook her, she let it. Head back, she cried out with wild abandon. A moment later, Rey joined her.

They took turns cleaning each other off. She marveled at his tenderness, giving the same back to him.

She wondered if she'd ever get enough of this man. When around him, her senses heightened. The world looked brighter, sounded softer, and she felt more alive than ever before, except for when riding the crest of a huge wave on the Pacific.

If only Isla, Carl and the others could be found, she thought life would be pretty darn good. Maybe even complete.

Stunned at the turn her thoughts had taken, she grabbed a towel and handed it to him. Then she dried herself off and escaped to her room to compose herself while she got dressed.

When she emerged, dressed but with her hair still damp, she found him fully clothed and waiting. His smile made her catch her breath. "I just talked to Rayna," he said. "There hasn't been any change on Mr. Smith, so he still hasn't regained consciousness. He's still in the ICU."

"I wonder if I should drive out there and see him," she mused. "He was always so kind to me when I stopped in the bookstore."

"Rayna said he isn't allowed any visitors other than immediate family."

"Which means he won't have any." She couldn't keep the sadness from her voice. "Other than his staff and friends, he's completely alone."

He hugged her. "Since he's not conscious yet, I think it'll be all right. If I hear anything else, I'll let you know."

"Thank you."

"I'd better go," he said. "I've got a crew working on fence repair today, and I need to join them."

Since she wasn't sure what to do with herself today, she briefly considered asking if she could join him. But she knew absolutely nothing about fixing fences, and her presence would be more of a hindrance than a help, so she didn't.

Instead, she followed him to the door. Absolutely stunned when he turned to kiss her, she kissed him back and then stood on her front porch to watch him leave.

Rey kissed Willow goodbye and got into his truck to drive home. The familiarity of the simple gesture made his chest ache. Unable to help himself, he glanced back as he pulled away, catching sight of her standing on her doorstep watching him go. Though he didn't want to leave her, work called.

All the way home, he sang along to the radio, his

mood buoyant despite the knowledge that Rayna still hadn't been able to speak to Mr. Smith to get information. If he didn't hear from her by this afternoon, he'd give her another call just to check in. He really hoped Mr. Smith survived and made a full recovery, and not only because everyone wanted to know where he'd been and what had happened to him.

It was still early when he pulled into the ranch drive. His stomach growled, reminding him that he hadn't eaten. He figured he had time enough to make a bowl of oatmeal or something.

"Where were you last night?" Sam demanded, meeting him at the door. "You didn't come home at all. I was worried."

Rey stared, shouldering past his brother. "Do you ever check your text messages or voice mail?" he asked, his voice harsh. "It would have been nice to get some sort of response."

"I checked them." Crossing his arms defensively, Sam continued to give him the stink eye. "You said the guy in the hospital wasn't Dad. I didn't know you wanted me to reply to that. I figured we'd talk about it once you got home. But you didn't come here. I waited up for you too."

Since it clearly hadn't occurred to Sam to pick up the phone and call, Rey wasn't sure he wanted to waste his breath.

Instead, he shrugged and headed to his bedroom to change his clothes before going out to meet his hired hands. "We're repairing more fence today," he called over his shoulder. "Just in case you want to join us and help. There's quite a large section down."

"You still haven't told me where you were. Did you spend the night in town or stay at the hospital?"

Rey turned, eyeing his brother. "I stayed in town. Why didn't you at least call me? I was worried when I didn't hear from you."

"I fell asleep in front of the TV," Sam replied. "By the time I woke up, it was after two a.m., and it was way too late to call."

Exhaling, Rey decided to let it go. Venting frustration had never had any effect on Sam. "It's all good," he said. "Do you want to help with the fence? We can use an extra pair of hands."

"We'll see. You know, you seem awfully happy," Sam mused, following right behind him. "After all the traumatic stuff with the misidentification at the hospital, I'd think you'd be exhausted and crabby."

If Rey felt any exhaustion, it would be due to him and Willow making love several times over the course of the evening. But since he had no intention of mentioning that to his brother, he simply shrugged, went into the bedroom and closed the door behind him. Since he'd indulged in a shower with Willow earlier, he simply needed to change and head out.

By the time he emerged a few minutes later, Sam had disappeared. A quick glance out the window showed he'd taken his truck, which meant he had no intention of working on the ranch.

Figured. Refusing to let his younger brother's antics ruin his mood, Rey went out to the barn to saddle up Roscoe and meet his crew.

He rode over to the same pasture where he'd made temporary fixes the day before. The crew had already arrived, having driven in and parked on the gravel road that abutted the pasture. Rey greeted them and dismounted, tying Roscoe to a low tree branch so he could be in the shade while he worked.

Physical labor turned out to be exactly what he needed. He found himself wishing Sam had shown up because Sam might have benefited from an outlet for whatever was bothering him. Though Rey planned to try to have a sit-down talk with his brother, he knew from past experience that Sam had to be in the mood for a discussion. Otherwise, trying to get him to share anything would only enrage him or cause him to completely shut down.

Finally, the fence repair had been completed. The crew left, and Rey rode Roscoe back to the barn.

When he arrived back at the house, tired and sweaty, he headed straight for the shower. Though Sam's truck once again sat parked in the drive, Rey didn't encounter him on his way to clean up.

His phone rang just as he finished toweling himself off. Though he didn't recognize the number, he answered anyway.

"Rey?" His father's voice, very faint. "Can you hear me?"

"Dad?" Heart racing, Rey gripped the phone. "Where are you? Are you all right?"

Whatever else Carl tried to say broke up, making it unintelligible.

"I can't understand you," Rey said urgently. "Please, just tell me where you are, and I'll come get you."

But only silence greeted his request, indicating the call had dropped.

Immediately, Rey called the number back. It rang

once and then nothing. Not even voice mail or any way to leave a message. He tried again and again, each time with the same result. Then he dialed Rayna.

"Still no change," she said when she answered. "I'm driving home now. I've got men posted to his room around the clock, and someone will call me if and when he's awake and alert."

"That's not why I'm calling." He told her about Carl phoning him and how he hadn't been able to make out what he'd said. "I didn't recognize the number, and I've called it back several times with no luck."

"Text it to me," Rayna ordered. "I'll check it out when I'm back in town."

After ending the call, he did as she asked. Then, just in case he might get lucky, he called the number again. Same result.

"Damn," he said, resisting the urge to hurl his phone at the wall. Next, he dialed Willow. But she didn't answer, so when her voice mail came on, he left her a message to call him when she got a chance.

Once he'd gotten dressed, he went looking for Sam. He found him in the kitchen, eating a sandwich with potato chips.

"I made you one too," Sam said, pointing toward the fridge. "I wasn't sure what time you'd be back, but I figured you'd be hungry."

Not sure what to make of his brother's jovial mood, Rey thanked him before telling him about the phone call.

"He *called* you?" Eyes huge, Sam put his half-eaten sandwich down on the plate. "Can I see your phone? I want to call him back."

"I've already tried that, several times." Rey retrieved

his sandwich from the refrigerator and took the chair opposite Sam. "I've also called Rayna and given her the number. She's going to see what she can find out. I'm hopeful they can ping the location, so we know where to go look for Dad."

Picking up his sandwich again, Sam took a huge bite and chewed before responding. "See? I told you Dad went somewhere on vacation. He's fine. He probably just had bad cell service or something. Since he accidentally left his own phone at home, he probably had to buy one of those cheap, disposable phones."

Not sure what planet his brother might be living on, Rey decided not to reply to that comment. Instead, he concentrated on wolfing down his sandwich, along with a handful of chips. He washed everything down with a diet cola.

"Oh, when I was in town earlier, Gia Barrera asked about you," Sam said, grinning.

Rey didn't recognize the name. "Who?"

"Buddy Barrera's younger sister," Sam said. "The one who used to have a crush on you back in the day?"

Since Rey only vaguely remembered and hadn't seen Buddy in years, he shrugged.

"Don't you want to know what she was asking?"

Eyeing his brother, Rey polished off his sandwich. "Not really. I'm more concerned with figuring out where Dad is and if he's in trouble."

"You should see her now," Sam continued, as if he hadn't spoken. "She's super hot."

"Are you trying to tell me you're going to start dating her?" Rey asked. Maybe a new girlfriend would help get Sam out of whatever rut he'd found himself in.

"Dating her?" Sam laughed. "She's interested in you. I'm just passing on the good news. I told her I'd give you her number." And he slid a piece of paper across the table. "Here you go. Good luck."

Rey didn't even look at the paper. "Thanks, but no thanks. I'm not interested. If you think she's all that great, go ahead and ask her out."

Just then, his phone rang. Willow. His heart skipped a beat. "Hey," he answered, pushing up from the table. "You're not going to believe what just happened."

Though he walked into the living room to continue the conversation, Sam followed. Deciding to ignore Sam's stares, Rey filled Willow in.

"Oh, wow. Did he sound…okay?" Willowed asked, her voice breaking.

"It was hard to tell," he replied, softening his voice. "He kept breaking up. I couldn't even make out any of his words. I tried to call him back several times, but he never picked up. I couldn't leave a message because there was no voice mail."

"But at least you know he's alive," she said, her sniffling letting him know she was on the verge of tears. "I'd give anything to hear my grandmother's voice."

"I know." Lowering his voice again, he glanced up to find Sam not even bothering to pretend to not be eavesdropping. "I've given the information to Rayna, and hopefully she'll be able to get something for us."

"Thank you." She sighed. "I wish you were here. This all gets so discouraging sometimes."

Glancing at his brother again, he decided what the hell. "I can be there in an hour. Would that work for you?"

"Definitely." Her relief seemed palpable. "And bring a change of clothes in case you end up spending the night."

This made him grin. "I'll keep that under consideration. See you soon."

After ending the call, still smiling, Rey turned to go to his room and pack a small bag. Just in case, as she'd said.

"Who was that?" Sam followed him to his room.

Rey turned. Briefly, he considered telling his brother it wasn't any of his business. Then, deciding he had nothing to hide, he shrugged. "Willow. I'm heading over to her place now."

Arms crossed, Sam eyed him. "What for?"

Right then, Rey realized the time had come for them to talk. "Sam, what's going on with you? I know you and Willow were—are—friends, but I'm also aware there's nothing else happening between the two of you."

"There could be," Sam answered sullenly. "If she'd at least give it a chance. But now I know why she won't. Because you're making a play for her."

"Sit down." Rey gestured at his bed. "Please."

Expression hostile, Sam sat. A second later, Rey sat down next to him. "This isn't a competition," he said. "And I think you know that."

"But you're my brother. You're not supposed to go after a girl that I have feelings for."

Rey knew he needed to tread gently. "Sam, talk to me. Willow is a person, not an object you can decide to stake a claim to. You know this. I know you do."

Scowling, Sam considered. "True. But I still don't like the way you're acting, making her be with you."

"We're all adults here. I can't make Willow do anything." Rey took a deep breath. "Now, why don't you tell me what's really going on? You aren't acting like yourself, and it's got me a bit worried."

Sam started to shake his head but then stopped. When he met Rey's gaze, the look of naked vulnerability on his face made him appear much younger. "I don't like change," he finally admitted. "I want things to stay the way they are. First, Dad started dating Isla. That was weird, but kind of nice. I always liked her back when I was in school. But now…"

Sam took a deep breath before continuing. "It's too much, Rey. Like one thing stacked on top of a bunch of others. First, you left to go get bison, leaving me here to try to run things. I'd never tried to manage this place on my own before. Then Dad disappears, and I know you blame me, even if you don't say it. And my old friend Willow comes back. Instead of wanting to hang out with me, the two of you are doing your own thing. Once again, I'm left hanging out here on my own."

Clapping his hand on his brother's shoulder, Rey met and held his gaze. "No one blames you for Dad going missing. How could we? Whatever happened, he made his own choice. I know you were busy because I'm well aware of what it takes to keep this place running."

"Thanks for that," Sam said. "Because I've been feeling pretty guilty. I've been pretty worried about Dad."

"Have you? You sure haven't acted like it."

"It's easier to pretend everything is fine," Sam said, shrugging. "That's what I've been doing. Otherwise, it's way too stressful."

"I know," Rey replied, dropping his hand. "The worry

eats me up sometimes. Willow too. She's quietly trying not to freak out."

They sat in silence for a moment. Then, Sam gestured to Rey's packed bag. "Do you really like her?"

"I do," Rey answered immediately.

Still staring, Sam finally nodded. "You know she lives in California. She'll go back there once Isla is found."

"I know that too." Even if he sometimes had trouble remembering that. "But that doesn't mean we can't spend time together and even enjoy each other's company while she's here." Rey took a deep breath. "Are you going to be okay with that?"

Finally, Sam looked away. When he raised his head again to meet Rey's gaze, a slight smile curved his lips. "Do I have a choice?" he asked. "I mean, it's not like you'd be willing to stop seeing her if I asked, would you?"

"No." Hearing a trace of humor in his brother's voice, Rey chanced a smile back "I like her too much to do that. And I think the feeling might be mutual."

Groaning, Sam rolled his eyes. But when he looked at Rey again, he grinned. "You deserve it, you know. You work harder than anyone I know, and you're always there for me and Dad."

"Thanks." The unexpected praise made Rey's throat ache. "I appreciate you saying that."

Sam stood. "Now all you need to do is find Dad and Isla, and maybe we can all live happily ever after."

Chapter 8

Seeing Rey's truck pull up in front of her house, Willow stood at the window and watched as he strode up her sidewalk. She wondered if she'd ever get used to the way her heartbeat accelerated and her mouth went dry at the first sight of him.

She opened the front door and managed to wait until he'd made it all the way inside before wrapping her arms around him. Despite the fact that they'd spent most of the previous evening making love, she already wanted him again. And judging from his instant bulge of arousal, he felt the same way about her.

Mouths locked together, they stumbled backward toward her couch. But the sound of a ringing phone penetrated her daze of arousal.

"Is that you?" She wrenched her mouth away long enough to ask.

"I…" Fumbling in his pocket, he pulled out his still ringing phone. "It's Rayna," he said, shaking his head as if to clear it. "I think I'd better take this."

Though he was still breathing heavily, he managed to answer. He listened for a second, clearly working at getting himself under control.

"Rayna, I'm going to put the call on speaker," he said, punching the icon to do exactly that. "Willow is here with me, and I know she'd like to hear whatever you have to say." He then placed the phone on the coffee table.

"Sounds good." Rayna's voice sounded clear, though a bit grim. "Theodore Smith is awake. The medical team says he had such severe heatstroke that some of his organs started shutting down. The doctor isn't sure if it caused brain damage or not. But judging from some of the unbelievable things he's saying, I'm afraid it might have."

Willow's heart sank. "I'm sorry to hear that. Were you able to learn anything useful, like if he'd seen Isla, Carl or any of the others?"

"Unfortunately, he's not coherent. He kept saying the same two words, over and over and over. *Prophecy* and *servitude*. And the more we tried to get him to elaborate or explain, the more agitated he became. The nurse finally had to put something in his IV to get him to calm down."

Swallowing back her bitter disappointment, Willow met Rey's gaze. When he moved behind her to put his arms around her, she leaned into the comfort of his embrace.

"Maybe he'll be able to talk more once he's had some rest," Rey said.

"It's possible." Rayna sighed. "I don't know anymore."

"Are you okay?" Willow asked.

"I'm exhausted. I rushed to Midland once my deputy called to tell me Mr. Smith was awake. I'd only just gotten to sleep. Now, I'm going to drive all the way back to Getaway and go home and try to get a few more hours of rest." She took a deep breath. "Rey, I've got people working on trying to figure out where your father called from. So far, they haven't had much success. It's difficult, since he used a burner phone."

Though Rey's expression reflected his disappointment, he didn't comment. Instead, both he and Willow thanked her. Rayna promised to touch base if anything changed and ended the call.

"That was weird," Rey mused, his arms still around her. "Is Mr. Smith super religious?"

She turned to face him. "I don't know. Maybe he became that way once he lost his wife. I guess we could ask some of his employees. They'd know better than anyone."

"True." Brushing his mouth across hers, he kissed her, making her shiver. "I'm sure Rayna will look into that."

Though she welcomed the distraction, something about the information Rayna had relayed about Mr. Smith bothered her. Obviously, Rey could tell that her heart wasn't into it, as he broke away. "What's wrong?" he asked.

"I don't know." Needing to move, she began pacing. "I grew up hanging out in that bookstore. I was around Mr. Smith a lot. He recommended books for me all the time, saying he wanted me to broaden my horizons. Him talking about prophecy and especially about servitude doesn't sound like him."

"Sometimes people turn to religion at times of great need. He'd lost his wife and, from all accounts, was completely alone."

"Maybe so," she allowed, still not entirely convinced. "I've only talked to Pastor Clayton about my grandmother. Tomorrow, I need to stop in at all the other churches in town and see if Mr. Smith attended."

"That's a good plan," he agreed, dropping down onto her sofa and dragging his hand through his hair.

Judging by his pensive expression, he had something to say.

"What's up?" she asked softly, sitting down next to him, close enough that they were hip to hip.

"I talked to Sam before I came over," he said, looking up and meeting her gaze.

She studied him, looking for hints of tension in his eyes or the set of his jaw. She didn't see any. "How'd that go?"

His slight smile caused the corners of his eyes to crinkle. Sexy, sexy man. "Actually, pretty well. He and I sat down like two adults and talked. He and I haven't had that kind of discussion in years."

While she knew she had to choose her words with care, she was also worried about Sam. "Did you mention that he might benefit from talking to a therapist?"

"Not yet." His response came too quickly.

Something must have shown in her face because he reached out and took her hand. "You have to understand. Sam and I haven't always had the greatest relationship. Plus, we come from a long line of stoic ranchers, whose motto has long been to suck it up and bear it. If Sam has something deeper bothering him other than basic immaturity, I can't insist he needs to go to counseling. If I did, even if it had been something he'd previously considered, he'd do the opposite."

He had a point. She'd known Sam for years. "You're probably right," she admitted. "It's just that I'm worried about him. He's always been so happy-go-lucky. But the way he acted the other day has me pretty concerned. Especially when he called my old high school friend to get her to plan a celebration for something that existed only inside his mind."

"I agree." He squeezed her hand. "But I don't think this is the kind of thing that can be rushed. Right now, he seems okay. I'm hoping he and I can keep the lines of communication open and maybe he'll feel comfortable confiding in me if something is wrong."

"Wisdom and good looks, what a combination," she teased, even though she was serious. "You're probably right. Sometimes, I tend to laser focus on what I think is a solution and run roughshod over anything that gets in my way. Sometimes, I have to force myself to stop and take a deep breath." She smiled. "It took more than a few therapy sessions for me to figure that out."

He kissed her then, driving all thoughts of Sam out of her head.

Later, as she got up to make them some microwave popcorn to munch on while they watched a movie, she noticed the light on her grandmother's ancient answering machine flashing. She never remembered to check the thing because most people these days didn't leave messages.

Curious, she pressed the play button, hoping against hope to hear Isla's voice. Instead, a woman said she was calling from a doctor's office. She wanted to remind Isla that she had a follow-up appointment scheduled for this Friday at two o'clock.

Sadder than she should have been, Willow jotted down the office number. She'd call them tomorrow and let them know that her grandmother wouldn't be able to make her appointment. Due to the privacy laws, she figured no one there would be willing to discuss any specifics about Isla's condition, but she might as well try.

Once she'd made the popcorn, she emptied the bag into a large bowl and carried it back to the living room. Rey had the remote and was scrolling through the movie offerings on Netflix.

"Hey." Looking up, he smiled when she approached. "What are you in the mood for?"

"Not rom-com," she said immediately, plopping down next to him. "Action-adventure or horror."

"Horror?" His brows rose. "Like what?"

"I've watched the entire *Halloween* series four or five times," she said proudly. "Same for *Friday the 13th*."

"What about *Texas Chainsaw Massacre*?" he asked.

"Not scary enough," she promptly answered. "But *Nightmare on Elm Street* is good. There are several of those."

"Hard pass." Shaking his head, he looked back at the screen. "I'm not a fan of horror."

She hid her disappointment. "Not many people are. How about action-adventure? Or I can do a Viking movie. I'm not picky. I just don't want to watch anything sappy."

"Sappy?" He turned again to look at her. "Give me some examples of what you consider sappy, please."

Embarrassed now, she grimaced. "I've just never been able to buy into the whole meet-cute movie setup. I'll take things that never happen in real life for ten dollars, please."

"Have you ever even watched one?"

She had to think about that for a moment. "Not for years. And by years, I think I was in middle school." She actually remembered exactly how old she'd been. She and her eighth-grade boyfriend, Tanner, had settled in to watch a movie, and she'd chosen an older romantic comedy. Tanner had spent the entire ninety minutes mocking everything that happened in the movie. When she'd protested, he'd begun ridiculing her too.

Things had gotten heated, and in the end, Tanner had gone home. The next day at school, any time she'd passed one of his buddies, they'd made snide comments. Some of the other girls had joined in. She'd had great difficulty watching another rom-com after that.

"That's terrible," Rey said, after she explained, pulling her close. "I'm sorry that happened to you."

"Thanks." She leaned into him. "It was a long time ago. I was just a teenager, so I probably need to get over it."

"Does that mean you want to try watching a rom-com?" he asked, a teasing note in his voice. "I'll let you choose."

Smiling, she glanced up at him. "I take it you're a huge fan of them?"

"Maybe." He shrugged. "I've been known to watch one or two. Though mostly when on a date." And then he laughed.

She swatted his arm. "Funny. Action-adventure, please. I just need something to get my mind off worrying about my grandmother."

Sometime in the middle of the movie, she must have dozed off. She woke to Rey covering her with a throw blanket. Smiling up at him, she managed to wake up enough to get to her feet and make her way to her bedroom.

Once there, she crawled in beneath her covers, invited him to join her, and promptly fell back asleep.

The next time she opened her eyes, the nightstand clock said 3:15.

She could get used to this, she thought, gazing at the

handsome hunk of man sleeping beside her. The instant that thought occurred to her, panic rose in her throat. She thought of California and her apartment a few blocks from the beach. She could see her surfboard, leaning up against the wall just inside her front door. She'd made a life there, with friends and a job and a sport she'd become really good at. Plus with the surfing classes she taught, she got to spread that love around to others.

Getaway represented her past. While she'd never forgotten where she'd come from, nor would she, the differences between the two places—not just in the landscape, but cultural—sometimes made her feel like they were alternate realities. Still, she'd often found herself yearning for the people and the landscape of home. Not to mention the food. She hadn't been able to find a decent chicken-fried steak or biscuits and gravy anywhere in California.

And to be honest, she'd missed her grandmother. Though she knew Isla had lots of friends and interests and lived a rich and satisfying life, Willow hated living so far away. She'd always felt she should be closer in order to help out when needed.

Now, with her grandmother missing, Willow knew she'd be staying until Isla was found. And even after that, Willow wasn't sure she could return permanently to California ever again. That was even without adding her growing feelings for Rey into the equation.

After waking up late, which felt decadent as hell, Rey shared a leisurely breakfast and coffee with Willow. He liked being with her, probably more than he should. But he'd decided not to worry about a murky future and enjoy the time they had together while he could.

On the way back to the ranch, Rey decided he'd stop off at the bookstore and talk to Mr. Smith's employees. Even though Willow had already gone by, he figured he might as well get their take on their boss's hospitalization. And Willow had made a great point about finding out if Mr. Smith had attended church, and if so, where.

The young kid behind the counter barely glanced up from his phone as Rey approached. Once Rey stopped in front of him at the counter, he reluctantly put his cell away. "Can I help you?"

Rey introduced himself. "I wanted to talk to you about the owner, Theodore Smith."

"He's in the hospital." The young boy swallowed hard. "The sheriff came by and let us know. We had no idea. Several of us are going to carpool to Midland and visit him after closing tonight."

"That's great, but I'd suggest you call first. Last I heard, they were only allowing immediate family in since he's in the ICU," Rey said.

"Oh. Thanks."

Taking a deep breath, Rey continued. "If you don't mind, I wanted to ask you if he's particularly religious?"

"Mr. Smith?" Confusion made the kid frown. "No. Why?"

Keeping his voice casual, Rey shrugged. "I don't know. He was talking about prophecy and stuff like that. I thought I'd see if you knew which church he attends. I wanted to let his pastor know what's happened and see if he might want to visit him."

"Mr. Smith didn't go to church. At least, not as far as I know. He didn't talk much about what he did in his private life. But he sure as heck didn't seem religious.

I know he'd been having some medical issues recently, but he never said what they were. He just went to the doctor a lot."

Now they were getting somewhere. "Do you know what doctor?"

"No." Picking his phone back up, the kid had clearly lost interest. "Let me know if I can help you find anything. A book, that is."

Since he'd been dismissed, Rey turned to go. As he passed a display, a photo book on surfing caught his eye. He picked it up, studying the cover, which showed someone riding the crest of a huge wave. Trying to imagine petite Willow bravely doing something like that, he carried the book over to the counter. "I'll take this," he said, surprising himself and the young clerk.

After making his purchase, he took the bag and his receipt and left. Though he told himself the book had been an impulse purchase, which it had, he also realized he wanted to know more about the things Willow loved.

Once he'd placed the bag on the passenger seat of his truck, he decided he might as well go and see Serenity. She'd told Willow that she'd *seen* someone around Isla was in trouble. He wanted to ask her about Mr. Smith.

Walking into the shop, the nearly overwhelming scent of the incense hit him first. Much stronger than the last time he'd visited. As he moved farther inside, he saw why. In addition to incense, Serenity also had a scented candle burning.

"I've been expecting you for days," Serenity announced, breezing in from the back. Today, instead of her normally vibrant colors, she wore a black-and-gray long, flowing dress. As usual, she had dozens of bracelets on one arm, and large earrings shaped like feathers hung from her ears.

"You look nice," Rey said, deciding not to react to her prediction.

"Do I?" Her smile told him she understood his deflection. "This outfit was a birthday gift from my sister, so I thought I'd better wear it. The dress is lovely, though I would have preferred brighter colors."

"It's a nice change," he said, meaning it. "I came to talk to you about what you told Willow. You said that someone near Isla was in trouble."

Serenity nodded. "Yes. But it wasn't your father. The man who cried out is getting medical help now."

Startled, Rey narrowed his eyes. "Did Rayna tell you?"

"I haven't talked to Rayna in a good while," Serenity replied. "She knows I'll reach out if I get anything concrete."

Rey sighed. He liked Serenity and sure as heck didn't want to offend her, but he couldn't help but speculate that if she had true psychic powers, she should put them to good use and find all the missing people.

"It doesn't work like that," Serenity told him. "And no, I didn't read your mind. You actually said your thoughts out loud."

"Did I?" He wasn't too sure. "Okay then, I'll bite. If it doesn't work like that, can you explain to me how it does?"

"Sure." She smiled. "Do you want to come into the back and have some tea? We can talk there."

Genuinely curious, he followed her through the colorful beaded curtain into the combination stock room, break room and kitchen.

"Sit." Gesturing toward her small table with two

chairs, she continued over to the counter. "I keep this coffeepot full of hot water plugged in so I can make tea anytime I want to."

He took a seat, watching as she made them both cups of hot tea. "Earl Grey," she announced, setting the steaming cup down in front of him. She then took a seat in the other chair, blowing lightly on her tea before taking a tiny sip.

"You're not the first rancher to be sitting in that chair," she said, smiling. "Nor will you be the last. To be honest, sometimes I don't understand how all this works myself. Things come to me. Sometimes in dreams, sometimes in visions. Once in a while, I hear voices."

"Do you see dead people?" he asked, purposely quoting from a movie. "And if so, are there any here right now?"

His question made her chuckle. "Not in the way you mean. Every so often, an entity who has passed has something important to say, and I listen and relay the message. Mostly, I take care not to keep myself open to that kind of thing. If I did, I would be bombarded."

"Okay." He nodded as if he understood, though he really had no idea what she meant. "When you mentioned to Willow that someone with Isla was in danger, how'd you get that message?"

"I didn't say in danger, I said in *trouble*," Serenity clarified. "And I believe the phrase I was told was *near* Isla. Someone near Isla was in trouble."

"Told? By who?"

Taking her time answering, Serenity took another sip of her tea. "Are you going to drink yours?" she asked, inclining her head toward his untouched cup. "It's really good."

Though he preferred his tea over ice, he didn't want to be rude, so he drank some. It tasted different. Trying to identify the taste, he took another sip.

"Oil of bergamot," Serenity said, correctly interpreting his expression. "That's what gives the black tea its unique taste."

"I see," he replied. "But you didn't answer my question. Who told you someone was in trouble?"

"I just *saw* it," she said. "A man, near Isla at first. She tried to help him. He appeared ill. Stumbling, asking for water. I clearly saw Isla get him some. But I got an overwhelmingly strong sense that he was in serious trouble."

"You got that part right." He told her about Mr. Smith and how he'd been found on a back road out in the blazing July sun. "He's still in the ICU. They think he had heatstroke."

She blinked. "Theodore Smith? The owner of the bookstore? That's terrible. I know he's had some health issues recently. And since his wife passed away, he's been completely alone."

Drinking a few more swallows of his tea, he nodded. "I just left the bookstore. His employees are planning to visit him in the hospital after they close for the day."

"That's nice," Serenity said.

"It is, but unless they've moved him out of the ICU, only family is allowed. Plus, I'm not sure if he'll even know they're there. He's not yet fully conscious."

Serenity watched him closely. "Has he said anything yet? Or is he unable to communicate?"

"He's said a couple of words. *Prophecy* and *servitude*."

Frown deepening, she made a clucking sound. "Oh, dear. That doesn't sound like him."

Now it was Rey's turn to watch her closely. "Do you know him well?"

"Not really. I visited him a few times to bring him meals after his wife passed. But he'd stop in occasionally. And we'd talk."

Rey nodded. "Since you said him saying those two words didn't sound like him, I'm guessing he wasn't religious?"

"Correct. He was not religious at all." Serenity sighed. "In fact, he believed there was nothing after death, nothing at all. Until his wife contacted me and asked me to talk to him. That shook him up."

Genuinely curious, Rey eyed her. "How did you prove it was really her?"

"That was easy. She mentioned something that only she could know. At first, he appeared startled. But then the poor man broke down in tears." Misty-eyed herself, she tossed back her drink as if it were whiskey. "I felt so bad for that poor man."

"I take all that to mean you don't think he was attending a church around here?"

Serenity straightened. "I'd be very surprised to learn that he was. Even if hearing from his departed wife shook him, he didn't seem inclined to seek out organized religion. But who knows? All I can tell you is if Theodore Smith did join a church, he didn't share that information with me."

Hiding his disappointment, Rey thanked her. "I'd better go," he said. "Please let me know if you get any other information from any source."

Slowly, the older woman nodded. "Will do."

As he left the shop and walked to his truck, his phone

rang. Seeing the sheriff's number on his caller ID, he answered.

"They've decided to call another town meeting," Rayna said, her tone a mixture of determination and exhaustion. "Not only do we need to provide an update on Theodore Smith, even though there isn't much to report on, but another older couple has gone missing."

Stunned, Rey swallowed. "Who? Do I know them?"

"Maybe," Rayna responded. But he didn't recognize either of the names she mentioned.

"Willow wasn't familiar with them either," Rayna continued. "I talked to her right before I called you."

"I see. And that's what we're going to discuss at this meeting?" He used his key fob to unlock the doors and climbed in behind the wheel.

"I wish that was all. With all of this going on, now we've got a small group of people spouting conspiracy theories. The meeting is mostly because we need to nip this kind of nonsense in the bud."

"What kind of conspiracy theories?" he asked. "I haven't heard any."

Her sigh reverberated over the phone. "Aliens."

It took a moment for her response to register. "Aliens? Are you serious?"

"Unfortunately, I am. This group is telling everyone who will listen that aliens are periodically abducting our elders. They've been lurking on the fringe for years, I'm told. But now, they think they finally have proof that their beliefs are valid. They've actually printed up pamphlets and are going around passing them out."

Rey laughed. "But no one actually gives this theory any credence, right?" he asked.

"There will always be gullible people," she responded. "My office has fielded more than one panicked phone call in the last twenty-four hours."

Dumbfounded, Rey thanked her for calling. When he got off the phone, he drove home. When he got there, he walked into the kitchen to be met by Sam.

"There's another town meeting tonight," Sam told him.

"I heard. I just got off the phone with Rayna. Apparently, there's a small group who believe all the missing people were abducted by aliens." Rey couldn't keep the stunned disbelief from his voice.

"That explains this," Sam said, grabbing a purple pamphlet off the counter and handing it over. "They were walking up and down Main Street and handing them out. Everyone in Rancher's Supply was making fun of them."

"Whoever made these didn't put a lot of time or thought into the design," Rey mused. "One simple fold, and text that appears to be a basic computer font. Not to mention some of the ideas they're presenting as facts are…"

"Out of this world," Sam quipped, then cracked himself up.

About to crumple up the flyer and toss it, Rey set it down on the counter instead. "Rayna also said another senior couple has gone missing."

"Really? Are you going to the meeting?"

"Most definitely. As a matter of fact, I need to call Willow and make sure she knows."

Sam made a face but then, catching Rey watching, shrugged. "Whatever. Do what you have to do. I just want Dad to be found."

Chapter 9

When Rayna had called her to let her know that another older couple had gone missing, Willow asked if
they'd been able to learn anything from Mr. Smith. Unfortunately, the bookstore owner had lapsed into a coma.
His doctors weren't even sure he was going to make it.

This news made Willow feel incredibly sad. Hearing
about more missing senior citizens scared the heck out of
her. When she said as much to the sheriff, Rayna agreed.

"I just don't understand what's going on," Rayna said.
"I've worked other missing person cases in this town,
though they were all young women. Each time, the abductor messed up and left clues. Or people escaped and
were able to tell us what was going on."

Willow latched on to that one word—*abductor*. "Is
that what you think?" she asked, unable to keep the panic
from her voice. "That my grandmother and Rey's father
were *abducted*?"

"Not really. I can't really see why anyone would ab-
duct a bunch of older couples. Though I can't discount
any possibility. Well, except maybe for one," Rayna replied. "But they've called another town meeting for tonight. Same place."

Trying not to hyperventilate, Willow took a deep breath before speaking. "I'm glad people are wanting to work toward a solution."

"Some of our townspeople are definitely trying to help with that, but there are others..." Rayna snorted. "Well, you wouldn't believe it if you heard it elsewhere. So I'm going to tell you. You know how I said I couldn't discount any possible scenario except for one? Well, there's a small but very vocal group claiming that the missing people were abducted by aliens."

"Aliens?" Willow repeated, shocked but somehow not. "Did they happen to say what evidence they're basing this theory on?"

"Nope. Because they're irrational. And people like that don't require proof."

Willow thought for a moment. "If that's all this meeting is going to be about, then I don't see any reason to attend."

"Oh, that's not all," Rayna hastened to reassure her. "I'll let them say their piece, after the main part of the meeting is over. That way, anyone who's feeling uncomfortable or disinterested can simply leave."

"Good thinking," Willow said. "I'll definitely be there."

Rey had called shortly after that, asking if she'd go with him. Of course, she'd agreed.

Now she stood on her front porch, wearing jeans and a T-shirt, impatiently waiting for Rey to pick her up. She didn't know how much more of this uncertainty she could take. All she wanted was to wrap her arms around her grandmother, once she knew Isla was safe. And watch all the other family members reunite with their own loved ones, especially Carl and his sons.

She could only hope that day would come soon. It had to, because she didn't know what she'd do if anything happened to her grandmother.

Rey's truck came around the corner. As always, her stomach did a little flip-flop at the prospect of seeing him. He pulled up in her driveway, and as she started down the sidewalk toward him, he jumped out and opened the passenger door for her. Something guys rarely, if ever, did anymore.

"Thanks," she told him, hopping on up inside. "I appreciate this."

As he got back in on the driver's side, he glanced at her, a half-smile on his handsome face. "No need for gratitude. Naturally, we go together?" he asked. "We're a team, remember?"

Her heart turned over at the warmth in his gaze. For a moment, she thought he might lean over and kiss her, but instead he shifted into Drive and pulled away.

Even though they arrived fifteen minutes early, the Rattlesnake was already packed. Luckily, they found two seats together in the third row. Glancing around, Willow spotted several people she knew. A few waved, a couple of others dipped their chins in acknowledgement, but no one came over and spoke. Which was fine because Willow wasn't in the mood for random chitchat.

At five minutes before seven, a tall, balding man with wire-rimmed glasses jumped up on the makeshift stage and stood behind the lectern. He leaned into the microphone, so close that when he spoke he caused a bunch of feedback. The high-pitched squeal had several people covering their ears. The man shrugged, clearly not embarrassed, and tried again.

"Let's talk about aliens," he said, the enthusiasm in his voice making Willow inwardly wince. "A group of us has been looking into these disappearances, and it seems clear that they've been abducted by extraterrestrial beings. We think they're targeting older individuals as they want to learn from their collective wisdom."

Several people in the audience groaned. Others tossed out disparaging comments. And one man yelled out, "Get off the stage, Ronald. None of us came to hear that kind of nonsense."

"It's not nonsense," Ronald said, his tone offended. The noise level in the room rose immediately. Everyone appeared to be trying to out talk the others.

Rayna chose that moment to stride up to the stage. She thanked Ronald for coming, mentioning that he hadn't been scheduled to speak until after the main part of the meeting. That said, she then asked him to please take a seat so they could start the meeting. She waited until he'd left the stage before turning once again to face the room.

"Moving on," she said, her tone hard. "As you may know, two more senior citizens have turned up missing. We still don't have any leads on where these people might have gone. Instead of discussing aliens, I've been approached by several individuals who would like to organize a search."

Again, everyone started talking at once. Rayna shook her head and held up her hand for silence. "Now, because we have no idea where to even begin, I've got a team of volunteers who are drawing up maps of search areas. We thought we'd begin in the various unfenced fields and pastures on the outskirts of town."

She pointed to three card tables that had been set up in the back of the room, near the bar. "We have sign-up sheets set up back there. Once we have enough people sign up, we'll start. I'm hoping for tomorrow."

Again, the noise level rose. Rayna stood patiently waiting until it died down. "Now these searches aren't going to be looking for the missing individuals, per se. Though it would be awesome to find them. What we will be looking for are clues. Anything, any hints that might explain where these people disappeared to. And even if you can't help with the search, you can help in other ways. Talk to your neighbors."

She scanned the room, which had once again gone quiet. "I know not everyone in town is in attendance. There might even be some people in more remote places nearby, the smaller ranches and such, who aren't even aware that people are missing. Talk to them. Ask questions. Maybe someone, somewhere noticed something out of the ordinary. Whatever it is, no matter how small, please call me. Now, does anyone have any questions?"

Several people raised their hands.

"As long as it's not about aliens," Rayna added. "You first."

After Rayna answered everything, she announced the meeting had ended. People got up and started milling around, some heading for the bar and others for the door. A few people stopped by the table Ronald had set up, accepting his brochures and talking to him.

Though Willow and Rey stood, they stayed near their seats, mutually agreeing to let the crowd thin out before moving.

"I'm not signing up to pair with anyone in the official

search," Willow said. "Mainly because I don't know who I'd end up with. But I do like the idea of going door to door at some of the more remote properties. It's a long shot, but who knows what might turn up."

"I agree," Rey replied. "If you don't mind, I'd like to join you. We can sign up to go as a team." He grinned. "That's becoming one of my favorite words."

"I'd like that." Willow smiled back. She almost told him she thought they made a dang good team in everything, especially the bedroom, but worried someone might overhear. Still, something of her thoughts must have shown in her face because Rey's eyes blazed with a sudden heat. She swayed toward him, entranced despite the fact that they were surrounded by people.

Just then, Sam walked up, accompanied by an attractive woman in a short white dress who looked vaguely familiar. "Hey, you two. I'd like you to meet Gia Barrera. Gia, I think you know my brother, Rey. And this is our friend Willow Allen."

"Pleased to meet you," Gia said, barely glancing at Willow. Instead, she gazed hungrily at Rey.

"I remember you," Willow said, drawing the other woman's attention. "You're Buddy's younger sister."

Gia dipped her chin in acknowledgment. "I am. That's how Rey and I first met." She continued eating Rey up with her eyes. "Do you remember, Rey?"

"I'm not sure." Rey took Willow's arm. "If you'll excuse us. We're making plans to help out with the search."

"I'd like to do that too," Gia exclaimed, batting her false eyelashes. "Rey, maybe you and I could team up."

This comment had Rey frowning. "Willow and I are

already a team. Why don't you and Sam work together?" He glared at his brother.

Then, without waiting for an answer, Rey turned away, taking Willow with him.

She managed to hide her laughter until they were outside. Once they'd stepped into the parking lot, she let it out. Half smiling, Rey watched her. He waited until she'd finally wound down, wiping at her eyes. "What?" he asked.

"As if you don't know." She shook her head. "Little Gia Barrera has the hots for you."

"Sam already told me," he admitted. "And I suggested that he date her."

"Instead, he brought her to the town meeting and came over to you." She shook her head. "I guess he was hoping once you saw her that you'd change your mind."

"Came over to *us*," Rey clarified, grinning. "I'm thinking she probably pressured him into it since I already told Sam that I wasn't interested."

Privately, she figured Sam had likely been all for it too. Despite Rey saying he and Sam had talked heart to heart, she doubted Sam had paid much attention to anything his older brother might have said. Though, she had to admit there might be a chance she was wrong. She'd been gone from Getaway a good while. Sam might have changed.

Rayna exited, waving as she and her deputies got into their sheriff's department vehicle and left.

Just as they turned the corner, Willow's cell phone pinged, announcing a text. She pulled it out and looked, not recognizing the number. Probably spam. But just in case, she clicked on it to open the message.

Help, it read. It's me, Isla. We need…

"Look." Willow tugged on Rey's arm, showing him the text.

His breath caught. "She didn't finish. Needs what?"

"I don't know. She's still typing." Instead of waiting for her grandmother, a notoriously slow typist, to finish, Willow fired off a message.

Where are you? Are you all right? Give me your location so I can come and get you.

The dots that indicated the other person was still typing disappeared. Both Willow and Rey continued to stare at the screen, waiting.

Where are you? Willow tried again. Please tell me.

Nothing. Tears stinging the back of her eyes, Willow fought the urge to throw her phone on the ground.

"Give her another minute," Rey advised. "If she's anything like Carl, it'll take her forever to type something out."

Slowly, Willow nodded. Clutching her phone in a death grip, she stared at the screen, willing more words to appear.

Instead, it remained blank. Willow bit back a cry and swallowed hard.

"Take a screenshot of that number and the messages and send them to Rayna," Rey said, squeezing her shoulder. "Maybe she can trace that number or figure out who it belongs to."

Instantly, she did as he'd suggested. "Hopefully, Rayna will have better luck with this one than she did with the phone call that you got from Carl."

He nodded. "It concerns me that both of them are trying to reach out and ask for help, but something or someone appears to be stopping them."

His words threatened to make her sick. "Do you think they're being held hostage?"

"Let's not jump to conclusions," he said, still squeezing her shoulder. "While it's normal to jump to worst-case scenario, without more information, we have to try and find a more positive possibility."

"Like what?" she snapped. "Because right now, I'm just about out of positivity."

Rey shared Willow's frustration. While he knew Rayna excelled at her job, it rankled that neither she nor any of her deputies had been able to find a single clue as to where those missing might have gone. As far as he could tell, they had these meetings for the sole purpose of appeasing distraught family members. For him, they had the opposite effect.

"Do you want to get out of here?" he asked, not bothering to modify his brusque tone. Then he noticed Willow's bowed head, and the way she seemed deep in thought.

For a moment, she didn't respond. When she raised her head, she simply stared at him, her eyes glistening. "I can't go home right now," she said. "I'd like to get a drink, but I'm not up for the crowd inside the Rattlesnake. Maybe we can go back to The Bar? I can follow you there."

His stomach growled, reminding him that he hadn't eaten. "I have an idea. How about Bob's Burgers? I need food, and they sell beer by the pitcher. A perfect combination, at least as far as I'm concerned."

Looking up from her phone, which still remained blank, she considered. "It's been years since I've had one of their burgers. Sure, I'd like that, though I'm not sure I can eat."

Slowly, he nodded. "Would you rather go home?"

"No," she answered immediately. "I can't handle being alone right now. I just need to talk to my grandmother."

He took her arm and steered her toward his truck. "Maybe you should try to eat something. How long has it been since you had food?"

"I don't know." Shrugging, she stopped. "But what about my SUV? I drove here."

"I can bring you back to it after we eat." He opened his truck door for her.

She thought for a moment and then nodded before she climbed into the passenger seat, still clutching her phone.

It made his chest hurt to watch the sorrow in her expression. He got into the driver's seat and started the engine.

While they drove, she kept sneaking peeks at her phone. Finally, she heaved a big sigh. "Why hasn't she responded? I'm going to try texting her again."

But, still no reply. In the course of the three-minute drive to Bob's, Willow must have checked her phone half a dozen times. She sent a couple more texts, made one phone call that wasn't answered and appeared to be on the verge of a total breakdown.

When they arrived at Bob's, he parked and killed the motor. Turning to her, he cupped her face in his hands.

"It's going to be okay," he said. "I don't know how I know, and I don't have proof, but deep inside I know Carl and Isla will be found."

Gaze locked on his, she swallowed. "But—"

He kissed her then, meaning only a quick press of his mouth to silence her doubts. But the instant their lips met, the usual passion blazed through him. With difficulty, he forced himself to lift his head. "How about we go inside and eat? You can try, and if you still can't, get a to-go box for later."

Slowly, she nodded. "Okay. That way you won't have to sit across from me and devour your burger while I stare at you."

"Exactly!" Smiling, he jumped out and hurried over to open her door. She took his hand and allowed him to help her down. Then, with her hand still clutching his, they walked into the restaurant.

The smell of delicious, all-beef burgers cooking made Rey's stomach growl again, louder this time. Eyes wide, Willow glanced at him. "You really *are* hungry, aren't you?"

He shrugged. "I am."

They were shown to a booth near the back wall with a good view of the front window and each handed laminated menus. "Your server will be with you shortly," the teenaged hostess chirped before flouncing away.

Rey had been here enough times that he didn't need to study the menu. For Willow, it had been a while, so she picked it up and began to peruse the offerings.

When she noticed him watching her, she gave him a small, sad smile. "I have to say, I might be able to eat something. I used to love their mushroom and Swiss burger."

The server came. They ordered their food, and Rey asked for a pitcher of beer. The waitress brought that out first, and Rey poured a glass for Willow and himself. She'd placed her phone faceup on the table and still kept checking it, clearly hoping Isla would try again.

He couldn't blame her. After his father had called, he'd been frantic to hear that beloved voice again. In that moment, he'd have done anything to locate Carl, moved mountains and rivers.

But he hadn't been able to. And somehow, he'd had to make himself accept that. Willow would too, in her own time.

"I wish she would call," Willow said. "Or text. Anything to let me know how to find her."

"I get it, believe me," he told her. "And I hope she does. But I know Isla. She wouldn't want you starving yourself while you wait."

This statement made the corners of her mouth lift. Just a little, but the look in her eyes didn't seem as sad. "Truth. I can hear her now, ordering me to get some food in my belly right this instant."

Since he knew Isla, he had to laugh. "You bet she would."

With that, Willow's mood appeared to lighten. She sipped her beer, and while she kept her phone out on the table, she didn't seem as fixated on it.

They talked about other things. He mentioned he'd picked up a book on surfing, and her face lit up. For the next several minutes, she told him about her adventures learning how to ride the waves and her excitement when she finally mastered it. While he enjoyed seeing the way her eyes glowed as she talked, he realized in that instant he had nothing to offer her that could even remotely compete with that.

When their food arrived, looking as good as it smelled, she eyed her plate and shook her head. "I forgot how huge they are. Good thing they cut it in half."

He grinned and picked his up. Gaze still locked on hers, he took a huge bite. "Mmmmm." The perfection of it made him roll his eyes.

A moment later, she did the same. "Oh, my!" she exclaimed, after chewing and swallowing. She took another bite and then another. Before long, they were both just devouring their meals. She finished her half burger and barely paused before picking up the rest. In between, she dipped her seasoned fries in ketchup and popped them in her mouth.

Initially, he'd slowed down to watch her eat. He found her single-minded intensity sensual. But realizing she didn't intend to stop until she'd completely demolished her meal, he focused on finishing his as well.

When all he had left were a few fries, he glanced up to find her lazily twirling one of her remaining fries in ketchup. "Thank you for getting me to eat," she said. "I feel much better now. Apparently, I needed that more than I realized."

He took a sip of his beer. "Me too."

Though he didn't think he could eat another bite, when Willow asked for the chocolate lava cake and two forks, he didn't say a word. The desert arrived a few minutes later, and she dug in with so much enthusiasm, he could have just sat and watched her.

Except she paused after her third bite, fork halfway to her mouth, and frowned at him. "Are you not going to have some? I can't eat this entire thing all by myself."

Then what could he do but help her finish. He'd never had the lava cake, but it tasted delicious.

Her phone pinged, indicating a text. She jumped, snatched it up off the table and entered her passcode. He knew the moment her face fell that the text wasn't from Isla.

"It's Rayna," she said, the dejection in her voice making his heart squeeze. "Acknowledging she got my screenshots and promising to look into it."

"That's good," he replied. "And she will."

Slowly, she nodded.

The check came, and they both reached for it. She lightly slapped his hand away. "My treat," she insisted. "I wouldn't have eaten at all if you hadn't gotten me to come here."

"Fine," he said. "I'll get the next one."

On the drive back to the Rattlesnake, Willow went quiet. Though she turned her phone over and over in her hands, she no longer seemed to think Isla would be texting again.

"At least we know they're alive," he blurted out, wincing the moment he spoke. "That's what kept going through my head when my dad called. Sure, I'm worried about him. But knowing he was able to reach out gives me hope."

"True. There's that." She sat up straight. "I refuse to allow myself to get worked up worrying about things that may not be true." Glancing at him, her expression determined, she exhaled. "I'm going to try to focus on the positive, like what you just said."

"Good." He turned into the parking lot, which had emptied quite a bit. Pulling up next to her Bronco, he left the engine idling.

Instead of getting out, she turned in the seat to face him. "Do you want to follow me to my place?"

"Any other time, I would. But tonight, I'm going to go on home," he said, as gently as he could. Part of him hoped that she'd ask him to go with her, that she didn't want to be alone. But he knew he couldn't spend every night at her place, and he wanted to have a talk with Sam after that stunt his brother had pulled at the town meeting earlier.

"Okay," she said, leaning over and kissing him. "I'll talk to you tomorrow? I'm planning to start talking to some of the older people who still remain in town. If someone is targeting that age group, surely someone else will have been contacted."

Though he figured Rayna had no doubt already done that, he wasn't sure. "That's a great idea. But I've got a lot to do around the ranch. I've got a couple of buyers coming to look at cattle, and I need to be there. One appointment is in the morning, but the other is early afternoon. I can text you if I get done early, but I'm thinking it's likely to be an all-day thing."

"I understand." Kissing him again, she opened her door and hopped out. "Good luck on the cattle sale. And I promise to keep you posted if I learn anything."

"I'd like that."

She closed her door and walked to her vehicle. He sat and waited until she got in the Bronco, ostensibly to make sure she was safe, but in reality, he didn't want to tear his gaze away.

But finally, he had to drive home. Pulling away, he felt he'd been separated from a part of himself. Too soon, he told himself, gripping the steering wheel. Not just that, but neither of them had ever made the slightest attempt to pretend their relationship was anything permanent. They were enjoying each other's company for as long as they could. But still, he had enough self-awareness to realize he might be in for all kinds of heartache. Hell, if he felt like this now, he couldn't even imagine what it would be like when Willow went back to California and left Getaway and him far behind.

Since the thought didn't bear thinking of, not right now with their parents still missing, he turned up the radio and concentrated on the road.

Chapter 10

Driving away from Rey felt more difficult than it should have. Weird how attached she had gotten to him in such a short amount of time. Somehow, she suspected Isla would approve.

This time, instead of letting thoughts of her grandmother make her sad, she refused to allow her mind to go down that path. Instead, she pulled up into the driveway, parked and went inside.

Isla would be found unharmed and safe. There could be no other alternative.

Going from room to room, turning on all the lights, she realized Rey had been right to go stay at his own home. She missed him, for sure, but they each needed to also have their own alone time. After all, it wasn't as if they were in some kind of long-term, committed relationship.

She washed her face and changed into some comfies. Then she went and got a glass of water, turned on the television and settled onto the couch to catch up on some of the shows she'd been streaming back in California.

Full and oddly content, she dozed off. When she woke, she realized it was nearly three in the morning. She went to her bed, crawled in between the sheets and drifted right back to dreamland again.

In the morning, she felt rejuvenated. She hummed under her breath while she showered and then carried her coffee out to her grandmother's back patio to drink. If things were normal, Isla would be bustling around the kitchen right now, insisting Willow eat a large breakfast in order to start her day right. In days past, Willow would have insisted her grandmother come out and enjoy a few minutes of the quiet morning with her. Most times, Isla would grumble a bit but would finally plop down into the chair next to Willow, mug in hand. Taking a long sip of her coffee, Willow sighed. She would give anything to have her grandmother here right now.

Soon, she reminded herself. Isla was fine and would be found soon, alive and unharmed. Then the two of them would have a heart-to-heart conversation about whatever health issue her grandmother was facing.

She spent the day cleaning the small house from top to bottom. She also did laundry, made a casserole for dinner, and made sure she didn't have a spare moment to think or worry.

When she finally went to bed, she fell into a deep and dreamless sleep.

The sound of someone pounding at her front door startled her awake. Heart racing, she sat up straight in bed and glanced at her nightstand clock. Two a.m.

She grabbed her phone and saw she had several missed calls, all of them from Rey. Since she kept her phone on Do Not Disturb at night, she'd had no idea.

Did that mean Rey was at her front door? If so, that meant something awful must have happened, as in her experience no one ever brought good news at this hour of the morning.

Peering through the peephole before unlocking the door, when she saw Rey standing on her front porch, she unlocked it and yanked the door open. "What's going on?" she asked, stepping back and gesturing for him to come in.

Pushing the door closed, he turned and gripped her arms. Expression intense, he met her gaze and held it. "I want you to stay calm, okay?"

Those words caused her heart to drop all the way to the bottom of her stomach. "Oh no." She swallowed hard. "What's happened? Please, tell me."

"A body has been found," he said. "Rayna is retrieving it and bringing it to the hospital morgue in Midland, until the medical examiner can be here from Abilene or Midland in the morning."

"Male or female?" she managed to ask. Inside, a litany kept running through her head—*Don't let it be Isla. Don't let it be Isla.*

"I don't know," Rey answered. "Rayna just called me and filled me in."

"Did she ask you to go to the hospital?"

"No. All she said was she'd fill me in as soon as she knew anything." He took a deep breath and dropped his hands from her arms. "I decided on my own to come get you."

"Thank you." Spinning around, she grabbed her purse and keys. "Let's go."

Once in his truck, she couldn't stop herself from jiggling her leg. *Please don't let it be Isla. Or Carl*, she amended.

"It's going to be all right," Rey told her. "I can't explain it, but I have a feeling. It's not going to be Carl or Isla."

"I hope you're right," she replied, her voice shaky. "But even if it's not, someone is going to have lost their loved one. It's awful enough that it's looking like Mr. Smith isn't going to make it."

"That's true, but we don't even know if this body is one of the people missing."

Throat tight, she nodded and turned to look out the front window. The flat road stretched out ahead of them, illuminated only by their headlights since there were no streetlights out here in the country. At this time of the morning, full dark with only a sliver of moon, the landscape took on a dystopian feel, which made her shiver.

"There." Rey pointed. "Looks like maybe an ambulance along with the sheriff's department vehicles."

They could see the red-and-blue flashing lights in the distance. Suddenly, Willow's tension returned. Stomach churning, she sat up straight, clenching her hands tightly in her lap.

Rey pulled his truck over to the shoulder behind the sheriff's car. Another one had parked right in front of her. He turned on his flashers and got out, crossing around the back of the vehicle to open the passenger door for Willow. Taking his hand, she jumped down. Then, still holding on to each other, they walked toward the small cluster of people standing a short distance beyond the sheriff's vehicles.

Arms crossed, Rayna watched them as they approached. "Why am I not surprised to see you? I take it you two were together when I called."

Though Willow's cheeks heated, she shook her head. "No, we weren't. Rey came pounding on my door and woke me up."

Meanwhile, Rey appeared to be trying to see past the sheriff.

"I can't let you go any closer," Rayna said, giving him a hard look. "I understand your concern, but I can promise you this isn't Carl or Isla."

"I'd like to see for myself," Rey replied.

"And I understand that, I really do. But I have to respect the family's privacy. Think about how you would feel if that was your loved one lying there. Would you want strangers gawking at their body?"

Willow squeezed Rey's hand. "We would not," she said. "But can you at least tell us who it is?"

"The identity of the victim will be withheld pending notification of their family," Rayna replied in her best law-enforcement-official voice. "And right now, I'm afraid I'm going to have to ask you to leave. This is an official crime scene investigation. I promise to update you both when I can."

That phrasing sent a shudder of dread through Willow. Rey evidently noticed it too because his grip on her hand tightened.

"We'll go," he said, his jaw tense. "But I do expect a full update as soon as possible."

"Definitely," Rayna agreed. "And you know how fast gossip spreads in this town. Pay no attention to anything you hear because all of it will be pure speculation. I'll release an official statement as soon as possible, hopefully by end of day today. Now go. Please. We still have work to do here."

"Thank you," Willow said. Rey echoed her statement. Together, they turned and made their way back to his truck.

They waited until they were inside the cab with the doors closed before turning to each other.

"Crime scene investigation?" Willow asked. "What exactly did she mean by that?"

"I'm guessing it was a clear case of murder." Rey's dark tone echoed Willow's thoughts. "Gunshot wound, run over by a car, a stabbing. Who knows? But apparently, it mustn't have been pretty, otherwise Rayna wouldn't have been working so hard to keep things hidden."

Willow groaned. "I can only imagine what kind of stories will be going around town tomorrow."

"Today," Rey corrected. "Even though the sun won't come up for several hours, it's already tomorrow."

"Thanks for pointing that out." Yawning, she covered her mouth with her hand. "I don't know about you, but I plan on going back to bed as soon as I get home."

"Me too." If he caught her subtle invitation to rest at her house, he didn't let on. "With those cattle buyers coming, I need to at least try and appear well rested."

"I forgot about that," she said, meaning it. "Have you always been the one who sells off your cattle?"

"No. My dad always took care of that. He took a lot of pride in our livestock. He loved to brag and could talk most buyers into almost any price. Since he'd been doing it for years, he knew them well and they knew him. People who buy from us know they're getting quality beef. We have a great reputation. But even so, Dad really enjoyed the whole song and dance."

"And you don't?"

He sighed. "No, not so much. I'm more of a work the land type guy. Not so much a salesman."

"I get that," she said. She thought about asking him if he'd considered having Sam handle it, but decided she already knew the answer. "I'm guessing you don't have much of a choice."

"I don't." His brusque tone told her that he really didn't want to discuss it any further. He started the engine and pulled a U-turn in the middle of the deserted road, and they headed back toward town.

With the mood somber, Willow wondered if she'd have trouble going back to sleep. Despite her exhaustion, her mind wouldn't stop spinning various scenarios as to how the body had gotten there. All of them were gruesome. She'd always had a vivid imagination, and sometimes she wished that she didn't.

Glancing at Rey, who'd turned up the radio in a clear indication he didn't want to talk, she wondered if he might be having similar thoughts. It was a terrible thing to have a loved one missing, with no idea where on earth they might be or if they were safe.

Finally, they turned onto her grandmother's street. When she saw a window lit up yellow in the house, her heart skipped a beat. For one amazing second, she thought Isla might have finally come home. But then she realized she must have left the light on in her hurry to leave earlier.

This made her eyes sting and her throat ache.

Rey pulled up into the driveway and left the engine idling. "I'll walk you to the door," he said.

True to his word, he went with her up the sidewalk, waiting while she fumbled with her key in the lock. Once she had the door open, he pulled her close and gave her a long, lingering kiss.

Returning the kiss, she'd just begun hoping he might change his mind and stay with her when he pulled away.

"I really have to go," he said. "Please try and get some rest. I'll talk to you tomorrow."

"You get some rest too." Hiding her disappointment, she took a step back.

He nodded and turned to make his way back to his truck. Instead of closing the door, she stood and watched him drive away, only going inside once his taillights turned the corner.

Though she'd lived alone in Cali for years, she couldn't get used to the emptiness of staying at her grandmother's house without her.

After dropping Willow off at her house, Rey headed for the ranch. Eyes scratchy, he wondered if he could manage to get a few more hours of sleep before he had to meet the first group of buyers. Since they were due to arrive at nine, he thought that might be doable, especially if he could get Sam to take care of the usual morning ranch chores like feeding and watering the horses. Though those were supposed to be Sam's responsibility, Rey often found himself doing them when Sam randomly disappeared or slept in.

Today though, Rey was really going to need his younger brother's help.

Once inside the dark house, he flipped on the kitchen light. Instead of going directly to his bedroom, he grabbed a pen and pad of paper off the desk and wrote a quick note. In it, he asked Sam to make sure to take care of the horses and the usual household chores since he'd need to sleep in and had cattle buyers coming at nine. He propped that up against the coffee machine. Since Sam always made coffee before doing anything else, that would ensure he would see it.

That done, Rey turned out the light and made his way to his own bed. He undressed in record time, set an alarm for eight on his phone and crawled beneath the sheets. Though he thought he might toss and turn, worrying about today's frightening developments, he didn't.

When his phone alarm woke him, he sat up and stretched before heading directly to the bathroom for a hot shower. The buyers would be here in an hour, which gave him enough time to have coffee and breakfast. Knowing that Sam would have taken care of everything else really helped.

Clean, dressed, and feeling surprisingly well rested, he went to the kitchen. There were breakfast dishes piled up in the sink, still dirty. Moving past, he found himself clenching his jaw and keeping his mouth shut. His note was gone at least, which meant that Sam had seen it.

After making instant oatmeal and a cup of coffee, he ate. From the other room, he heard the sound of the television. Odd, because he doubted Sam would have had enough time to get all the chores done. Unless he'd actually gotten up early for once.

Coffee cup in hand, he wandered into the living room. There, he found Sam kicked back on the couch, watching TV. Squelching a jolt of irritation, he wondered if Sam had been out to the barn to feed the horses. Or if he'd done any of the minor ranching chores essential to the survival of their livestock. He reminded himself not to jump to conclusions. Sam might have gotten everything done earlier and come back to take a break.

"Hey," Rey said, standing near the end of the sofa.

Sam barely glanced away from the TV. "Hey, yourself. I hope you get a good price for those cattle today."

"Thanks." Trying to figure out how to best bring up the subject, Rey decided he might as well be direct. "I appreciate you taking care of the horses this morning."

Now Sam did look up, his expression blank. "What are you talking about?"

"I left you a note," Rey replied, careful to keep his tone level. "I know you saw it."

"Oh, that. I did see it. But then I got busy and forgot about it." Sam turned his attention back to the TV.

Rey checked his fitness watch. "I'm going to need you to turn off the television and get that taken care of. The horses should have been fed and watered long before now. My buyers will be here in twenty minutes, which means I don't have time."

"It shouldn't take more than fifteen minutes," Sam said. "You've got time."

"No. I. Don't." Marching over to his brother, Rey snatched the remote off the coffee table and turned the TV off. "I really needed your help this morning. Actually, I still do," he amended. "Please get the horses taken care of and clean up the kitchen. I've got to meet the buyers and take them down in my truck."

Scowling, Sam pushed to his feet. "I'll do it, but you're wasting a great resource. Me."

Unsure what his brother meant, Rey waited. When Sam simply glowered at him and didn't elaborate, Rey finally asked him to explain.

"I should be the one selling the cattle, not you. Dad always took me with him, and he taught me everything he knows. I could do a great job, and I'd enjoy it. Unlike you, who clearly hates doing it."

"I don't hate…" Starting to explain, Rey let his sentence trail off as he realized his brother was right. Dealing with buyers ranked right up there with mucking out stalls.

"You know if Dad were able to contact us, he'd want me to handle this," Sam continued. "He trained me, after all. He always told me he wanted me to take over for him when he couldn't do it any longer."

"Why didn't you say something sooner?" Rey asked, trying to reconcile the idea of his father trusting Sam with something so important. "And why didn't Dad tell me?"

"Because you made it clear you weren't interested. Even at the dinner table, any time the subject came up, you said you preferred to handle the day-to-day operations and let someone else handle the salesmanship. You know you did."

Rey stared. In that regard, his brother was absolutely correct. "True," Rey admitted.

"Then let me handle this today," Sam pressed. "I know you're doing your best, but you have no idea how to do any of this. The buyers know me. They met me last year when I worked with Dad."

"I don't know." Rey considered. On the one hand, he'd never seen this kind of enthusiasm from his brother. On the other, this was far too important of a transaction to let slide. Sam was the absolute master of flaking out on things.

"You keep saying you want me to help out more." Sam continued. "Well, here's your chance. Give me a shot."

Right then and there, Rey decided to take a leap of faith and trust his younger brother. He could see no reason for Sam to lie about this, and to have him actually volunteer to handle a necessary task that Rey truthfully found burdensome spoke volumes.

"Take my truck," he said, tossing the keys at Sam. "I've got it all clean and ready to meet the buyers."

Though Sam caught the keys, the look on his face told Rey that he'd apparently done something wrong. "Thanks, but I don't need your truck." He tossed them back. "My truck will do just fine. The buyers like to know they're dealing with a real rancher, so the dirtier the truck that meets them, the better. Dad taught me that."

Not sure how to respond, Rey simply nodded.

Grinning, Sam grabbed his cowboy hat, dipped his chin in response and swaggered out the door.

Rey watched him go, hoping his trust was well placed. Either he'd made a huge mistake that he'd pay for later, or he'd done both the ranch and Sam a favor. He really hoped it would turn out to be the latter.

Then, since the horses needed to be fed and numerous other chores waited that Sam had left unattended, Rey got to work. Without the two important meetings hanging over his head, he found his mood lighter. Though the occasional doubt and worry over Sam's ability to sell their livestock at a good price surfaced, he managed to put them from his mind. More than anything else, he hoped that Sam had finally found his niche, an area where he excelled.

Rayna still hadn't called by the time Sam returned from the first meeting, his mood jubilant. "They doubled the usual order," he said. "Even with the increase in price."

"Seriously?" Rey gave his brother a high five. "How'd you know the amount to ask for? I was just going to use what Dad charged last year."

Expression horrified, Sam stopped moving and stared. "If you'd have gone with that strategy, you'd have cost us some serious cash. Dad and I had already discussed our pricing strategy for this year. So that meant I had a great general plan from which to operate."

"Oh." Rey swallowed. "Well, good work. I'm glad you talked me into having you represent our ranch."

"Yeah, you are." Sam practically danced around the room, throwing punches at an invisible foe. "And now that I've clinched this deal, signed paperwork and all, the second group has no choice but to match it."

"Is that how that works?" Rey asked, partly amused but mostly proud. Because once again, he'd have had no idea.

"It is." Sam beamed at him, once again still. "I can't wait to tell Dad!" Then, apparently realizing he wouldn't be able to do that anytime soon, he winced. "I mean, as soon as he gets back home."

Not wanting to kill his brother's mood, Rey decided to wait to tell him about the body that had been found until he'd heard more from Rayna.

"Sit." Rey gestured toward the kitchen. "Let me make us a couple of sandwiches for lunch. You need to eat something before you head out to the second meeting."

"Thanks." Instead of immediately grabbing a chair,

Sam went to the refrigerator and grabbed a couple of cans of Dr. Pepper. "We're celebrating," he said, lifting one can in a salute.

Now Rey grinned. "Sounds good to me. I better up my sandwich-making game."

"Nah." Dropping into a chair, Sam popped open his can and took a drink. "Just ham and cheese with mustard for me."

"Then I'll have the same."

After making the sandwiches, Rey got out some chips, and he and his brother ate lunch together in companionable silence.

When they'd finished, Sam drained the last of his soft drink and pushed to his feet. "I want to get washed up, and then I'm heading out," he said. "I have no doubt that this meeting will go about the same as the first one."

"I'm positive of that." Rey stood too, liking the way Sam carried himself with the new self-confidence.

After Sam left, Rey straightened up the kitchen and then headed out to the barn to clean up a couple of stalls. He usually hired teenagers to help with this, but since it was July, most of them had found summer jobs. If he hadn't heard from Rayna by the time he finished, he figured he'd call Willow and see if she wanted to grab dinner in town. Or maybe he could pick up something and take it to her house.

For the first time since Carl had disappeared, Rey had hope about Sam's role at the ranch. Evidently, Carl had seen something in his youngest son and had been quietly nurturing it.

Damn. Missing his father something fierce, Rey found enough busy work close to the house to clear his mind. When he finished up, tired and sweaty, he headed back with the intention of jumping in the shower.

Sam had already returned, and once again, his mood was jubilant. "I think another celebration is in order," he said the instant Rey walked through the door. "This one went even better than the first sale. I know Dad keeps logs, and this one has to break all records. I'm pumped!"

"Nice job!" Rey wasn't too exhausted to appreciate his brother's excitement. "Seems to me you found your calling."

"You know it. Dad would be so proud." Sam's face fell. "I wish he'd turn up. I really miss him."

"Me too," Rey said. "But I'm really glad you made the ranch a nice profit. That'll help us pay the bills."

"Yeah." Sam shrugged and then grabbed his hat. "You might want to get on that. I'm heading into town to celebrate. Want to go with?"

Looking down at his filthy, sweat-stained clothing, Rey shook his head. "I need to shower. How about if I meet you at the Rattlesnake Pub later?"

"Sounds good." Sam breezed out the door. "Text me."

After a quick shower, Rey decided to take a look at the bills. In the two weeks since Carl had vanished, none of them had been paid. Which made sense, because that had always been one of the things that Carl insisted on doing himself.

Sam had been getting the mail and simply stacking the unopened bills in the inbox on Carl's desk. If he'd noticed the pile growing taller, he clearly hadn't thought about mentioning it to Rey. Until this afternoon.

But Rey couldn't just blame his younger brother. The desk sat in plain sight of the living room and kitchen.

The two of them walked past it multiple times a day. Somehow, Rey had also managed to overlook it.

If he didn't get the bills caught up, they wouldn't be able to buy feed or hay or fencing materials, or any of the other numerous things needed to keep the ranch running.

Pulling out the office chair, Rey opened the middle desk drawer in search of his father's checkbook. When he located it, neatly stowed next to Carl's favorite pen, he opened it to check the most recent entries plus the balance of the ranch account.

Satisfied that everything was as it should be, he grabbed the letter opener and settled in to pay bills.

Thirty minutes later, he'd written all the checks, affixed stamps to the envelopes, meticulously recorded each deduction and then calculated the final balance. Once he'd finished, he decided to take everything to the post office. A few of the bills, like the one to settle their account at the feedstore, he planned to hand deliver while in town.

Feeling a sense of accomplishment after having completed such a small task made him shake his head. He did much more complicated and difficult things on a daily basis, so he wasn't sure why paying bills felt so different. Maybe because he felt like he'd done something to help out his still absent father.

Chapter 11

When Willow next opened her eyes, she was pleasantly surprised to realize she'd slept until nearly noon. Since she considered herself a morning person, this was something she never did. At least, she hadn't since college. But clearly, she'd needed the rest.

Stretching, she pushed back the sheets and hopped out of bed. She felt remarkably better, almost as if she hadn't been running around country roads with Rey in the middle of the night.

Remembering, the thought sobered her. All these people disappearing and then a couple of them turning up under strange and mysterious circumstances. She wondered when Rayna would call with more information, but imagined the sheriff would be busy talking to the family of the deceased person and working with the coroner. That meant she wouldn't be calling anyone who wasn't involved anytime soon.

Frustrated, Willow wanted to do something more to help. Though she'd been born and raised in Getaway, since she'd moved away to California, she knew some people considered her an outsider. Which only lasted until they talked with her and realized she was the same person she'd been before she'd left. You can take the girl out of Texas, but you can't take Texas out of the girl.

Though she hadn't actually joined any of the search teams on the sign-up sheets at the meeting, she wanted to get with Rey and see if he'd join her tackling some of the more remote ranches. While technically these places weren't inside the city limits, their mailing addresses were still Getaway.

Since she knew he would be busy most of today, she figured she'd talk with him about this later. Right now, since she'd had a late start, she might as well tidy up around the house and snoop around some more to see if she could find any hints as to her grandmother's illness or where Isla might have gone.

Already having done a thorough search of obvious places, this time she planned to do a deep dive, no matter how intrusive.

Despite previously going through all of Isla's dresser drawers, this time she removed every single item in each one and felt around for a fake bottom. She found nothing.

Finishing up with both dressers and the nightstands, she moved into the master bedroom walk-in closet. She reached into the pockets of pants, cardigans and skirts. She checked inside every single pair of shoes and boots. And Isla apparently collected purses and wallets. There were quite a few, but Willow looked inside each one.

After going through every article of clothing and finding nothing, she removed all the random items Isla had piled on the top shelf above the hanging rack.

There, she found ski gloves, a knee brace, several pairs of compression hose and several boxes of greeting cards that Isla had received over the years. But nothing referencing her grandmother's medical issues or literature for an upcoming vacation.

The idea made her shake her head. The fact that she could still cling to the possibility that Isla and Carl, along with numerous other people their age, had taken off for some secret getaway without telling a single family member seemed ludicrous.

Once satisfied that she'd checked everywhere in the bedroom, she moved on to the bathroom. Even though she'd checked twice before, she did so again.

Since over an hour had passed and she'd found nothing, Willow decided to get cleaned up and head into town. Back when she'd been a teen, whenever she'd had a problem, she'd gone to Serenity. Talking to the self-proclaimed psychic always made her feel better. Even though she'd stopped by a few days ago, she knew Serenity would always welcome her.

Decision made, she took a quick shower, got dressed and put on her makeup. For convenience's sake, she scarfed down a bowl of cereal for a meal, even though it was afternoon. Then she grabbed her keys.

Driving the familiar route downtown, she thought of how many times she'd traveled this road as a teenager. Back then, she'd owned an old Chevy Impala that Isla had gotten her as a sixteenth birthday gift. It hadn't been a pretty, girly car, but Willow had loved it anyway.

Downtown, she found a parking spot right in front of Serenity's store. Mood improving by the second, she hopped out and headed inside.

Though she'd expected Serenity to come out and greet her, the same way she always did, the empty shop seemed different. For one thing, no incense burned on the counter, filling the air with the thick scent of patchouli. For another, Serenity hadn't turned on her sound system to play the esoteric, heavy-on-harps soothing music that she always played.

Alarmed, Willow hurried toward the back, calling out Serenity's name.

The back area was empty. Since Serenity and Isla were about the same age, for a heart-stopping moment Willow wondered if Serenity too had gone missing.

Then she noticed the closed bathroom door. Taking a deep breath, she knocked, three hard raps of her knuckles against the wood.

"Just a moment!" Serenity shouted. "Please go wait up front. I'll be out to help you in a few minutes."

Though still alarmed, Willow retreated to the store itself. No longer panicked now that she knew Serenity was alive, she still had to wonder if she was all right.

Five minutes later, Serenity emerged, sweeping through her colorful beaded curtain. "Willow!" she gushed. "I'm so sorry you had to wait."

One side of her face looked swollen, and a large bruise purpled under her left eye.

"What happened to you?" Willow asked, once again concerned.

"Oh, this is nothing." Serenity tried to brush her off. "I tripped over my own two feet and fell."

Willow took her arm and steered her toward the back room. "Are you dizzy? Why don't you sit down and tell me all about it."

The older woman allowed herself to be helped over to a chair. "I am a bit off today," she admitted, once she'd taken a seat. "I felt weak and kind of faint this morning, but figured I could press past it. But right after I opened up for the day, I turned too sharply, and my feet got tangled up and I fell." She gave a rueful smile. "I guess I'm just getting old."

"When was the last time you ate something?" Willow asked.

Serenity shrugged. "I'm not sure. Yesterday?"

Opening the small refrigerator, Willow located a cup of Greek yogurt on the shelf. She retrieved a plastic spoon from one of the drawers and set it down in front of the other woman. "Eat this for now. If you'd like, I can run and get you a burger or something."

"I don't eat meat," Serenity said, smiling slightly. "But I'm sure this yogurt will be just fine."

Willow spotted a new coffee machine on the counter. It had the option to make individual cups or a carafe. Knowing Serenity's fondness for tea, she made a pot of hot water.

"Where do you keep your tea bags?" she asked.

Serenity, having finished her yogurt, smiled. "In the cupboard right above you. I'll take oolong, please. You have whatever you'd like."

After making the tea, Willow carried both cups over to the table. She went back for the small container of sugar and a couple of spoons.

"Do you still feel dizzy?" she asked. "That shiner is getting darker. Do you think maybe we should take you in to let Doc Westmoreland look you over?"

"No, no. I'm fine." Serenity waved Willow's concerns away. "I feel better already. Sit, please. We can drink our tea and chat. I want to know all about how you and Rey Johnson are doing."

Startled, though she supposed she shouldn't have been, Willow sat. "We're fine," she said, blowing on her tea before taking a tiny sip. "He's a nice guy."

Serenity snorted. "I saw the way the two of you looked at each other at the town meeting. I thought you both might burst into flames."

Willow's face heated. "Er, thanks?"

"I take it you don't want to discuss that?" Serenity asked, her color improving with every sip of tea.

Just then, Willow's phone rang, saving her. Even though she didn't recognize the number, she answered.

"It's me," a familiar voice whispered hoarsely. "Willow, it's me."

Stricken, Willow's gaze flashed to Serenity, still sitting across from her. "Isla? Where are you?"

"I'm with Carl. I'm really worried about him. We need help." The older woman's voice sounded shaky. "He's sick. I don't know what's wrong."

"Tell me where you are, and I'll come get you." Heart pounding, Willow stood, gripping her phone hard.

"I don't know where we are," Isla whispered, almost in tears. "Someone's ranch maybe? But we're with—"

Just then, the call either dropped or Isla was forced to end it. Despite suspecting the reason Isla had been whispering was that she didn't want to be overheard, Willow immediately called back. But either the phone had been turned off or destroyed, because it simply rang twice and then went silent. No voice mail, nothing.

Knowing it was useless, she still sent a quick text. Nothing, despite staring intently at her screen.

"What happened, honey?" Serenity asked. "Are you all right?"

Still standing, Willow swayed. Fist to mouth, shaking, she tried to speak but couldn't. After a few failed attempts, she managed to dredge the words up from the depths of her throat. "That was my grandmother. She says she's with Carl, and he's sick. But she didn't know where she was, just that it seemed like a ranch."

Serenity immediately pushed herself up out of her chair. Even with her shakiness, she came over and pulled Willow in for a hug. And that simple gesture of kindness allowed the dam of emotions to break.

Head on the older woman's shoulder, Willow sobbed as she hadn't allowed herself to do in the entire time since Isla had gone missing. Silent and supportive, Serenity kept Willow wrapped in her arms.

Finally, Willow's tears eased up. Slightly embarrassed, Willow stepped back. Serenity grabbed a box of tissues and held it out. Accepting this, Willow wiped her eyes, wishing she'd used waterproof mascara. She blew her nose, took a couple of shaky breaths and grabbed her cup off the table and drained her tea.

"Would you like more?" Serenity asked, the gentleness in her gaze bringing a fresh spate of tears to Willow's eyes.

"No thanks, I'm good."

"Your grandmother is going to be all right," Serenity said. "As is Carl. I can see this."

"If you can see that much, why can't you tell me where they are?" Willow asked, struggling to keep all bitterness from her tone.

"I wish I could," Serenity answered softly. "But my gift doesn't work like that. I can't make it show me whatever I want to see. Sometimes I receive impressions, other times I hear voices from spirits telling me things. Believe me, I've tried. Over the years, I've helped out with several police investigations. Not once was I able to determine what information came to me. But I was sent what apparently was needed. So I can tell you that your grandmother is okay, as is Carl Johnson. But little else. I'm sorry."

Immediately, Willow felt terrible. "I'm sorry. I didn't mean to question you."

After turning to get her tea pot, Serenity refilled both their cups, even though Willow had said she didn't want more. "Sit," she said, gesturing toward the chair. "We can talk some more."

Not sure what else to do, Willow sat.

On her way back to her own chair, Serenity staggered. She cried out once before collapsing.

After dropping off most of the envelopes at the post office, Rey stopped at the Rancher's Supply feedstore, since he figured he might as well pick up the bags of grain and horse feed pellets he'd ordered. After having them added to his account, he loaded everything into the bed of his truck. Then he stopped by the back office to say hello to Jason, the manager and part owner. Since Jason appeared busy, Rey didn't stay long. He simply handed his account invoice and the check over, apologized for it being a few days late and left.

Before heading over to the Rattlesnake, Rey sent Sam a quick text to let him know he was on his way. Sam didn't immediately text back, which didn't surprise him since the noise level inside the pub could get quite loud at times. Happy hour would be well underway, and there was a dedicated group of regulars who stopped by on their way home from work.

Before shifting into Drive, Rey called Willow. The call went directly to voice mail. Odd, but maybe she was busy.

Walking into the Rattlesnake, he located Sam seated with a couple of guys at a four top near the bar. From the empty glasses scattered close to the middle of the table, they were each on their second or third beer.

"Hey!" Spotting him, Sam gestured toward the remaining empty chair. "Take a load off and order you a beer."

Rey dropped into his seat. Without him even asking, the waitress brought him his usual light beer in a frosted mug. "Thanks, Cecilia," he said.

Smiling, she blew him a kiss and hurried off.

"Wow," Sam stared. "How the hell do you do that?"

The question made Rey laugh. "I dated her once. We're still friends. She knows what I drink, and whenever I come in, she makes sure and brings me one."

"Oh." Losing interest, Sam turned to his friends and began describing loudly his idea for a side hustle, where he believed he could rake in tons of dough.

Luckily, Rey's phone vibrated in his pocket, which was a good thing since he hadn't heard it ring. Pulling it out, he smiled when he saw Willow's name on the caller ID. He stood, told his brother he needed to take a call and hurried toward the door, answering as he went.

"Just a second," he said, unable to hear her. "I'm at the Rattlesnake. Let me get outside and away from all this noise."

Once the door swung closed behind him, he took a

deep breath. "Sorry about that. I'm glad you called. Did you want to drive over and join us? We're here celebrating Sam's accomplishment getting record prices for the cattle today."

"I'm in Midland. I had to take Serenity to the hospital. I'm not sure what's wrong," she said instead of reacting to his invitation. "She'd apparently fallen before I got there as she has a huge bruise on her face, almost a black eye."

"Is she going to be all right?"

"I hope so. We lucked out as the ER wasn't busy. We didn't have to wait long before they took her back. My cell phone isn't working great inside there, so I came out to the parking lot to call you."

"Do you need me to come out there?" he asked. "I can leave right now and head that way."

"No, it's okay. There's no need for that. I've got to call Serenity's sister, Velma, next. Serenity gave me her number." She took a deep breath. "Oh, and one more thing. I can't believe I almost forgot to tell you this, but with so much going on, I'm a little scattered. My grandmother called right before Serenity fell. She was whispering and sounded frantic. She said she's all right, that she's with Carl, and she's worried about him because he's ill."

Rey froze, his stomach clenching. "What's wrong with him? Did she say where they were?"

"That's just it." Voice shaky, Willow sounded on the verge of tears. "She said she didn't know where she was, but thought it might be someone's ranch. The call dropped or something before she could say anything else."

"Someone's ranch." Rey thought furiously. "That

could be anywhere. There are a hell of a lot of ranches around here."

"I know." Her defeated tone made his chest ache.

"We need to go look," he said, deciding on the spot. "You and I. First thing tomorrow. I'll come pick you up at eight. If you're up to it, that is."

"I am," Willow answered without hesitation. "I need to go call Velma now. I'll talk to you later."

"Stay safe," he said, ending the call. He stood there a moment, shocked that he'd almost told her he loved her.

When had that happened? He couldn't actually say it had snuck up on him, because he'd been battling his feelings for a while now.

Shaking his head at his own foolishness, he turned around and went back inside to join his brother and his friends.

After finishing his beer, Rey declined to join Sam and the others in the back room for a few games of pool. He considered driving out to the hospital, but since Willow had said he didn't need to, he decided to stop by the sheriff's office instead. Rayna hadn't ever called him about the identity of the person they'd found alongside the road.

But the sheriff wasn't in. So Rey drove back to the ranch, stopping at Bob's on the way home for a takeout meal of a burger and fries.

After eating, he went outside and kept himself busy putting up hay. A new shipment had been delivered while he'd been gone, and he needed to move the bales into the covered storage area. Usually, he had a crew meet the hay truck and offload directly into storage, but with everything that had been going on, he'd gotten his wires crossed, which was unusual.

He'd just moved the last bale when his phone rang. Dragging his sleeve across his eyes to clear the sweat, he pulled it out of his pocket and answered.

"I'm heading back to town," Willow said. "Velma made it up to the hospital, and she's going to sit with Serenity. Would you mind if I stopped by? I don't want to go home to my grandmother's empty house right now. I'm still trying to process the fact that I actually talked to her."

"Of course I don't mind," he answered. "I've been working outside, and I'm all grimy, so I'm about to jump in the shower. I'll see you soon."

"Okay. I think I'll stop by Bob's on the way there. Do you want me to bring you a burger or anything?"

He had to laugh. "No thanks. I grabbed something from there a couple of hours ago."

"Great minds think alike." She tried to laugh along with him but failed. "I keep hoping Isla will call again, but she hasn't. I've called several times, sent a few texts, but nothing."

"Which seems to be the pattern," he said. "But at least you got to hear her voice."

"There's that," she agreed, still sounding sad. "Okay, go shower. I'll see you when I get there."

The hot shower felt amazing. After, he dressed in clean clothes and quickly tidied up the house. Sam still hadn't returned from his early celebration in town, so Rey texted him to make sure he had a designated driver. If not, Rey volunteered to pick him up.

Sam texted back that he'd be staying in town for the night, so Rey didn't need to worry. This made Rey feel better, especially since Sam would have only mocked his concern in the past. Maybe, he thought, his little brother was finally growing up.

When Willow arrived, carrying her empty Bob's Burgers bag, he pulled her in for a big hug. She hugged him back, and they stood that way for a few minutes, simply holding on to each other.

Breathing her scent and wondering how she always smelled like peaches, he placed a gentle kiss on her silky hair.

When she finally moved away, she headed directly for the kitchen and tossed her paper bag in the trash. When she turned to face him, her expression serious, he thought she had to be the most beautiful woman he'd ever known.

"I want to search some of the really remote areas tomorrow," she said. "Isla said she thought they were at a ranch. I can't shake the feeling time is running out and we've got to find them as quickly as possible."

"We can definitely do that," he replied. "If you want to stay the night, we can head out in the morning at first light."

"Thank you." She kissed him. He kissed her back. Tangled together, they stumbled over to the couch. As always, passion immediately set him on fire for her.

"What about Sam?" she gasped, her chest heaving. "What if he walks in?"

"He's staying in town tonight," he told her. "He texted."

"Oh, thank goodness."

They lost themselves in each other, tearing off their clothes and making mad, passionate love. As usual, Rey had the presence of mind to put on a condom.

And after, still inside her, he held her close, while

shudders still rocked her body. As they tapered off, she sighed and wiggled out of his embrace. "I need to get cleaned up," she said.

"Me too." He followed her to the bathroom. "Let me. Please."

Once she nodded, he got a clean washcloth. Using warm water, he gently cleaned her. Eyes wide, she watched him. When he finished, he dried her with a soft towel.

"My turn," she said, her voice husky. And she did the same for him.

Once they'd gotten dressed, they turned on the TV to watch the early evening news.

When his phone rang, Rey went ahead and answered even though he didn't recognize the number on the caller ID.

"Hey, Rey, this is Jason from Rancher's Supply. I hate to bother you, but I stopped by the bank after work to deposit some checks, and they wouldn't honor yours."

"What do you mean?" Confused, Rey tried to make sense of the other man's words. "Since we both use the same bank, they shouldn't have a problem. They just transfer the money from our account into yours."

"Yeah." Jason cleared his throat. "That's just it. They said the funds are insufficient to cover the check."

"There must be some sort of error. Let me go in and talk to the bank in the morning, and I'll get back to you. I'm really sorry about this. I'll stop by tomorrow morning. I promise I'll make this right."

"I believe you." Jason sounded more embarrassed than angry. "But I'm afraid I'm also going to have to ask you to pay the returned check fee they charged me."

"No problem." After apologizing again, Rey ended the call. "Something's not right," he told Willow. He recounted what Jason had said. "My dad is very meticulous with that account. I checked the ledger. Every check he'd written had been diligently recorded and subtracted from the balance, which was still substantial. There's no way this account is overdrawn. It's just not possible."

Eyes huge, she simply stared at him. "I'm thinking I need to check my grandmother's bank accounts. I know she has her social security check direct deposited every month. Most of her bills are on auto-pay, so I haven't even thought about dealing with any of that."

It took a moment for her words to register. "You believe this might be tied to them being missing?"

"I don't know. It could be a bank error. But if I check Isla's balance, and it too has been depleted, then we have to assume it's all related. And we'll have to let Rayna know."

"Are you able to check right now?" he asked, his throat suddenly dry.

"Sure." She pulled out her phone. "I have the app. Isla put my name on her bank accounts so I could handle funds if anything happened to her." Immediately, she looked stricken. "I don't think she meant like this. I always assumed she was talking about falling ill."

He waited while she pulled up the app and logged in. After a moment, she squinted at the screen and shook her head. "This can't be right. I don't keep up with my grandmother's finances, but I know she would never let her bank accounts get this low. There's barely a hundred dollars in her checking account. And her social security check doesn't come for another ten days or so."

"Are you able to pull up transactions?" Rey asked.

"I think so." She touched a few things on her screen. "Here we are." A moment later, she gasped. "She transferred nearly twenty-five thousand from her savings and withdrew it just a few days before I arrived. That's a lot of money."

He nodded. "Yes, it is. Does she still have anything in savings?"

Frowning, Willow scrolled. "Yes. There is still a decent amount left. But this concerns me. What did Isla need twenty-five grand in cash for? What did she buy?"

"Or who did she give the money to?" Feeling sick, Rey pushed to his feet and began pacing. "I don't have an app, but I am on the ranch accounts as a co-signer. I need to call the bank in the morning. Actually, I need to stop by."

"Should we call Rayna?"

"Not yet." He took several deep breaths, trying to calm his racing heart. "I need to make sure that the bank didn't make an error. Though I have a sinking feeling they didn't."

Chapter 12

After a restless night with Rey tossing and turning next to her, Willow rose quietly before sunrise. She left Rey still slumbering in his bed. He'd finally fallen asleep sometime around three, and she figured he needed all the rest he could get. Standing at the side of the bed, she gazed at him, admiring his profile and the way his big body relaxed in sleep.

While she'd slept, she'd been plagued by dreams of Isla calling out for help while Willow struggled, unable to reach her. She was glad that they were going to do something and proactively search. Sitting around and doing nothing but worrying wasn't productive. And since no one else seemed to be able to find any clues, she'd look for them herself.

Moving quietly through the dark and silent house, she made a cup of coffee and carried it back into the living room to drink while she scrolled through social media on her phone.

Once she'd finished, she emerged again, noticed his bedroom light was now on, but his door was closed. Deciding to get ready before having more coffee, she headed toward the bathroom. After brushing her teeth, she took a quick shower, managing to locate clean towels. She found herself wishing the bathroom door would open and Rey would join her, but he didn't.

When she emerged twenty minutes later, she opened the door to the smell of bacon frying. She made her way to the kitchen and found Rey cooking. Judging from the food spread out on the counter, he either was expecting a lot of company or doing some sort of breakfast meal prep.

"Good morning," she said, wondering if she ought to mention she would have welcomed him in the shower.

"Mornin'. I made a pot of coffee," he said, turning. With his early morning stubble and mussed hair, he looked good enough to eat. "I used the good coffee, the one Carl always keeps in the freezer for special occasions."

"What's the occasion and how did you do all this in what, twenty minutes?" She gestured at the array of food. Pancakes and scrambled eggs, bacon and sausage, toast and the fixins for biscuits with gravy were all spread out on the kitchen counter. "It looks like you made more than enough to feed a small army. Are we expecting company?"

With a grim smile, he shrugged. "I figured I'd text the ranch hands to stop by and eat on their way out to work the cattle. They should be getting up right about now."

She sipped her coffee and watched while he got out his phone and sent a text. A moment later, his phone pinged in response. "They'll be stopping by shortly." He smiled. "I know you've never met my ranch hands. I think you'll like them."

"I'm sure I will," she responded. "Now tell me, what's really going on? Are we still going out searching some of the more remote areas?"

"We are, but not this morning." He dragged his hand

through his hair, his expression distracted. "I'm sure you noticed how restless I was during the night."

"I did." She ached to kiss his frown away.

"That's why I made all this," he explained. "I had to keep myself busy until the bank opens at nine, and then I want to go into town. The ranch can't exist with no money in our account." He took a deep breath. "I'm sorry, but I don't have a choice. Are you okay with that?"

Slowly, she nodded. She liked that he even asked how the change in plans made her feel. "I get it. We can go search after, right?"

"Sure, as long as it's not too hot. Since temps are supposed to be in the hundreds all week, it might be better if we tried early tomorrow morning."

Though she didn't want to wait, what he said made sense. Plus, with everything else he had going on, the poor guy needed a break.

"I've been wondering what we're going to do if it turns out the ranch bank account has been emptied," he continued. "The only people with access to it are me and my dad. Which makes me wonder. Did my father have some sort of backup plan? It kills me that I don't have any idea."

She watched as he continued to cook, moving with a lot of grace for such a big man. He continued setting everything up on the counter. He put out a container of orange juice and some plastic cups, stacked paper plates and disposable utensils nearby and stepped back. "I think that'll do it."

"Where will everyone sit?" she asked, furiously trying to blink away a sudden haze of desire. Rey eyed her, apparently unaware. Clearly, she didn't have the same effect on him as he did on her.

"Outside at the picnic table." He turned back toward the spread. "Dad always tried to cook for the guys at least once a month, kind of as a treat."

A moment later, the back door opened and six men trooped inside. They greeted Rey enthusiastically, smiled and nodded at Willow, and went immediately to grab a paper plate and pile it high with food.

One by one, after filling their plates, they trooped back outside to eat, murmuring their thanks as they passed.

"Grab you some breakfast," Rey said, nodding toward the spread. "Get some before it's gone. I guarantee you they'll be back for seconds."

They both got food and sat down across from each other to eat. Sure enough, most of the crew came back, and after making sure no one had missed eating, they loaded up again. As they carried their once again heaping plates back outside, Willow saw that they'd demolished the spread.

"That's also an incentive for asking them to start work without me or Sam this morning," Rey said, beginning to clean up. "I'd like to be at the bank as soon as they open."

She got up and started helping him. Since he'd used paper plates, all that needed to be washed were the pots and pans he'd used to cook and the serving bowls.

"Would it be okay if I go to the bank with you?" she asked, bracing herself for him to refuse. "I understand if you'd rather I didn't, since this is intensely personal."

His gaze met hers. "I'd appreciate the support," he answered quietly. "Because I'm still struggling with this. The ranch finances have always been something Carl insisted on handling himself. Now I regret not insisting to be part of it. I just don't see how this could happen."

She touched his hand. "Try not to jump to conclusions until you've talked to the bank. They might be able to clue you in on the full story."

"Maybe so." But he didn't seem convinced. "All that keeps running through my head is that this has to be some sort of ransom payment."

Shocked, she recoiled. "Has anyone made a ransom request?"

"No. But what else would be urgent enough to make my father do something like this?" he asked, the anguish in his voice making her want to comfort him.

"I don't know. But hopefully, we'll find out."

Later, traveling into town, she made small talk as she could tell Rey felt nervous. While he nodded and made one-word responses, she finally gave up and stared out the window until they made it downtown.

When they walked into the bank, Rey asked to speak to a man named William Bates. "He's our personal banker," Rey said. They were shown immediately to a small office, more like a cubicle really. A short, bald man with wire-rimmed glasses stood as they entered and held out his hand.

"Good to see you, Rey," William said as they shook hands. Rey introduced Willow, who vaguely remembered William from somewhere.

The two men made small talk for a minute before Rey got down to business and asked the banker to pull up the ranch account. "I wrote a check at Rancher's Supply yesterday, and for some reason, this bank wouldn't honor my check. My father usually handles the ranch's finances, but as I'm sure you know, he's missing. But he's always been meticulous about keeping accurate records." Rey slid Carl's checkbook across the desk. "As you can see, there should still be substantial funds."

Keying something into his computer, William didn't even glance at the checkbook. He frowned as he read something on the screen and then looked over his glasses at Rey. "There would be, except your father made a large withdrawal roughly two weeks ago that essentially cleaned out the account. He only left one hundred and fifty dollars, just enough to ensure he isn't charged any banking fees."

"Two weeks ago?" Rey met Willow's gaze. She knew exactly what he was thinking. This would have been right about the time Carl Johnson and Isla went missing.

"Did he happen to say why?" Rey asked.

"No, he did not," William answered promptly. "But then, we're not in the habit of asking people what they intend to do with their money."

Rey took a deep breath. "One last question. I'm guessing you personally handled this, since we're your clients, right?"

"Correct." Sitting back in his chair, the banker crossed his arms.

"Then I need to know, if my father came in person to make the withdrawal, which I'm assuming he did, was he alone or did he have someone with him?"

This made William frown. "I believe he came by himself." He glanced at Willow. "Your grandmother wasn't with him, if that's what you mean."

"Okay," Willow replied.

"But that's not what I meant," Rey said. "I wanted to know if anyone might have been with Carl. Someone who made him withdraw all that money."

William puffed up at that. The question clearly offended

him. "I can assure you that your father was not being co-erced by anyone. Rest assured, he came alone." Clearing his throat, the banker stood. "And before you ask, he didn't appear nervous or out of sorts or anything else. He was fine. I'm not sure what you're insinuating, but nothing out of the ordinary occurred with this transaction."

"Thank you." Rey stood also, so Willow did the same. "I appreciate you taking the time to talk to us."

After leaving the bank, Rey went quiet. Willow couldn't blame him. It was bad enough that her grandmother had removed twenty-five thousand from savings, but to have your father empty the ranch's operating account without knowing why...

"You know what," Rey said as they turned into the ranch drive. "It's still early enough that we could cover some ground before it gets too hot. How about we go out for an hour or two? What we don't get to today, we can start with in the morning."

Since anything was better than sitting around wait-ing for something to happen, she agreed. "Let's do it."

Pulling up in front of the house, he killed the engine. "I need a minute to grab some provisions. You can wait here if you'd like."

"I can come help." She followed him into the house, watching as he loaded up a backpack with bottled water, protein bars and other assorted nonperishables. "I thought we were only going out for a couple of hours," she said.

"We are." He zipped the backpack closed. "But where we're going, it's best to be prepared. I learned that the hard way when I was a teen."

They got back in his truck and drove past the barn,

pulling up in front of a metal storage building. "Here we are," he said, hopping out and going around to open her door. Once she'd joined him, he unlocked the building's huge sliding door and pushed it open.

"Our transportation for the next couple of hours." He made a sweeping gesture toward the interior.

She took a couple of steps and peered inside.

"Four-wheelers?" she asked, surprised despite herself. "It's been forever since I drove one of those."

"It's like riding a bicycle," he said. "Once you get back on, it all comes back to you."

"I don't doubt that." She liked the idea. "Two or one? Are you expecting me to ride on the back of one with you, or do I get my own?"

One brow raised, he appeared surprised by her question. "We have two. You'd be driving one. Unless you don't feel up to it."

"Challenge accepted," she promptly responded, making him laugh. "I actually like the idea, but I have to ask why. Is there a reason we can't just take your truck?"

"We could." He shrugged. "But it would take forever, at least to go to the ranches I have in mind. Their land borders ours, but some of them are so huge that their homestead is in the next county."

"So what, you want to cut across pastures? What about fencing?"

"There are gates. Most of them are fairly easy to find. If we did this, we could cut off a lot of distance," he replied.

"Why not just call them? Wouldn't that be an even better time saver?"

He grimaced and shook his head. "I checked Dad's

contact records, and all he has saved are their landline numbers. If they still have landlines, which they probably do, it'd be hard to catch them at home. Unless we called late at night, and even then it's iffy. I don't know any of their cell phone numbers. And, since we also want to look for clues, calling wouldn't help."

Which made sense, sort of. Since she'd never lived on a ranch and had no idea what it entailed, she hadn't even considered how seldom the people living on the ranch were actually inside the house.

"If you'd rather we take the truck, we can," he said.

"No, four-wheelers are fine. If it turns out to be too difficult, we can always come back, right?"

"Of course." He pulled her in for a quick kiss. "And that may be the case. It's been a long time since I've taken these trails to the other ranches. I haven't done it since I was a teenager. They might be more difficult than I remember."

"I guess we'll find out."

Expression thoughtful, he nodded. "We will. Also, there are a couple of remote areas that I want to check out. Over the years, I know some of the ranchers have found squatters living on their land. One time at least, it was long term. As in, they'd built cabins."

"What? How is that possible? Is it really so vast that they can't keep up with what's going on?"

"It is." He handed her a key. "We keep these gassed up and start them at least once a week to make sure they're running. Are you ready?"

"I am." She climbed aboard, inserted the key and started the engine. It came to life immediately.

Rey pulled away first and she followed him, thrilled that she finally might be doing something constructive.

* * *

Though his first thought shouldn't have been how hot Willow looked driving a four-wheeler, Rey had to grin at himself. He couldn't help but admire her courage and readiness to tackle any situation.

They headed north, still on his family's land, toward the location of the first of several gates separating various pastures. The largest part of his ranch lay to the south, and there were two huge neighboring ranches to the north. Since he'd lived here his entire life, he knew exactly where to find those gates.

Finally, they'd passed through the last hundred acres of Johnson land. Pulling up to the final gate, he hopped off, opened it and motioned her through, just as he had with all the others.

"Now we're on Rafferty land," he told Willow. Pointing northwest, toward a visible rise in the land, he showed her where he wanted to go.

They took off. The slight incline made seeing ahead difficult, but he remembered thinking the view from the top was stunning.

However, this time as they crested the hill, an unfamiliar fence blocked the path. The gate had been locked with a chain and padlock, and there were signs posted.

"No Trespassing?" Rey eyed the bright yellow signs and made a gesture around the gently rolling hills. "This is the RF Ranch. It belongs to Don Rafferty, and it's been in their family for generations. We've always had an easement agreement with them. They can move herds through our back pastures, and we can do the same with theirs."

He dug out his phone and scrolled through contacts. "I went to school with Jeremy Rafferty. I think I have his number here somewhere."

Pulling it up, he pushed the button to make the call. A woman answered. After Rey identified himself, she explained that she was Claire, Jeremy's wife. It turned out each Rafferty child had been gifted one thousand acres of the family land, to do with as they pleased. Jeremy had sold his and used the money to buy himself his dream house on the Gulf Coast. They lived there now, and she had to say life had never been better.

"Do you happen to know who the buyer was?" Rey asked. She apologized, but said she didn't. Jeremy had only said it was some corporation and that they'd promised not to develop the land into condos or retail or a housing development.

Since this parcel sat in the middle of nowhere, without access to paved roads, Rey could see why someone would agree to those conditions. "Any idea what they planned to use it for?" he asked.

"We assume a small ranch," Claire replied. "I'm sorry, but did you need me to have Jeremy call you back? I'm late for an appointment."

Rey left his number, even though he figured she'd already have it. After the call ended, he looked up at Willow and explained the situation. "That's why the no trespassing signs. I'm guessing the new owner doesn't want anyone snooping around."

"Guess so," Willow agreed. "You'd think with the way news travels around Getaway that people would have been talking about this."

"I know. But I didn't hear a word. I honestly had no idea that Jeremy Rafferty sold off a thousand acres." Stunned, Rey removed his cowboy hat and dragged his fingers through his hair where the hat had flattened it.

"The fact that they weren't sure what the buyer intended to do with it is the weirdest part of the entire thing."

"What do you mean?" Willow asked. "I mean, if developers bought it, they'd still have to get permits or something, wouldn't they? And have it rezoned, from agricultural to whatever?"

"They would. But sometimes this kind of thing skates by under the radar. Especially if the developer greases the wheels, if you get what I mean."

"I do," she said. "Unfortunately."

He grimaced. "But Jeremy's wife claimed they got an agreement that the land wouldn't be used for retail or a housing development. She said a corporation bought it and plans to use it for a small ranch."

"Which makes sense, since this is a very remote location."

"I agree." Putting his hat back on, he sat back on the four-wheeler. "But what do we do now? With all these no trespassing signs, we can't legally cut across this property. The new owner would be within his or her rights to shoot at us."

"Can we go around?" Willow asked. "While I'm not familiar with the area, I'm guessing you can tell where the property line ends by the lack of those yellow signs."

"We could, but at this point, it would be quicker to make our way to the road." He struggled to contain his frustration. "It looks like we'd have been better off if we'd taken my truck like you suggested."

The wind picked up, and tiny pieces of grit stung his skin. "That's not good," he said. "Wrong time of the year for something like that."

"Look." She pointed west. "I know it's July, but that sure as heck looks like a dust storm on its way."

Turning, he looked where she pointed. "Damn, you're right. We usually get those in March and April. I don't think we've had one in the summer my entire life."

"We need to take shelter." Panic edged her voice. "And I don't see anywhere we can do that. I've only seen these things from the safety of inside my house. You know as well as I what kind of damage they can do."

"It's going to be okay," he said. "I promise. Like I said, I believe in being prepared. We keep emergency provisions in each four-wheeler. One of these has a small tent. We need to find a place to pitch it and crawl inside until the storm is over." He started rummaging in the storage compartment, hoping Sam hadn't taken the tent out for some reason and forgotten to replace it.

"We'd better hurry." Willow began doing the same thing on her vehicle. "Hey, I think I've found it."

Glancing back at the horizon, he decided the best place would be right below a dip in the land, in the middle of a small grove of twisted trees. Just past all the no trespassing signs.

"There." He pointed. "It's on their land, but I think our safety trumps a sign anytime. Hopefully, no one will even notice we were there."

Leaving the four-wheelers, they climbed over the metal gate, which had been padlocked closed. The wind had picked up, and the sky had turned that particular shade of reddish brown that everyone who'd ever lived in West Texas recognized as an ominous forewarning.

Quickly, he glanced around.

"We don't have too long," he shouted as the wind began to howl. Dirt stung their skin and faces, and he could barely see. "Help me get this tent up."

They struggled against the wind, but somehow managed to put up the two-person tent. "Get inside," he ordered, grabbing his backpack while she crawled in.

Following her, he barely got the zipper closed before the full force of the storm was upon them. Though he'd pitched the tent at an angle that should make it more difficult to blow over, he wasn't sure if it would stand. After all, he'd never actually done this before.

"Me neither," she said, making him realize he'd said his thoughts out loud. She scooched over next to him, and he put his arm around her, tugging her close.

The sides of the small tent billowed and danced, but it held. The wind-driven dust pummeled it, and despite the canvas barrier, some dirt made it inside.

Willow coughed, clearly struggling to breathe.

"Cover your mouth and nose with your shirt," Rey suggested. To demonstrate, he pulled up his shirt.

Instead, she turned to face him and buried her face in his chest. He hoped the low rumble of his laughter, felt rather than heard, comforted her.

Holding tight to each other, time slowed to a crawl. The rise and fall of her chest, the way she relaxed into him, made him feel he could conquer the world. He smoothed her hair, resisting the urge to murmur sweet nothings. Meanwhile, as they huddled together, outside the storm raged, doing its best to annihilate them.

Though he suspected only a few minutes passed, in the moment, it felt like eternity.

One minute, they were being buffeted by wind, and the next, it all suddenly…stopped. Just like that, an eerie silence.

Willow raised her head. "Is it over?"

Kissing her on the forehead, Rey nodded. "Sounds like it. Just a sec and let me check outside."

He crawled the few feet to the entrance and quickly unzipped the zipper to poke his head out. "All clear," he said, glancing back at her. "Looks like our four-wheelers got buried. Once we dig them out, we should be able to make our way home."

When he'd emerged from the tent, he held out his hand to help her up. Simply breathing filled his mouth with grit. "One of the joys of living in West Texas," he mused. "But still, I wouldn't live anywhere else."

Her silence reminded him that not only would she live somewhere else, but she actually did. And as soon as their missing family members were found, she'd no doubt return.

In that moment, he understood how badly that would hurt.

"Help me take this tent down and get it packed," he said, glad of the distraction. "We're going to have to dig out the four-wheelers."

Working together, they made short work of it, folding the canvas into the right shape to slip it back into its storage bag. After going back over the gate, they both got to work uncovering their vehicles. Once done, he got the storage bag stowed back on the four-wheeler, grabbed his backpack and handed her a bottled water.

She drank deeply before passing it back to him.

Once he'd gulped down nearly half, he passed it to her to finish. Then he stowed the empty plastic bottle in the backpack. "Are you ready to go?" he asked, climbing onto his machine.

Nodding, she did the same. As she did, the sharp staccato sound of a gunshot rang out. Then another. Someone was shooting at them.

Chapter 13

"Was that…?" Willow asked, swallowing hard. Her heart rate kicked into overdrive.

"Gunshots. We've got to get out of here, now. Go." Rey shouted, pointing back toward home.

Immediately, she gunned the motor and took off. He stayed right behind her. She appreciated the way he at least tried to shield her and offer some protection from the shooter. It brought a new meaning to the phrase *I've got your back*.

As they crested the ridge, leaving the no trespassing signs and the new fence behind them, Rey finally eased back on his speed. Noticing, Willow did the same.

Finally, Rey stopped. Willow circled around and joined him. "What on earth happened?" she asked, her voice shaky. "Were they shooting at us because we were on their land?"

"Apparently so."

"Which means they either had some sort of shelter close by where we pitched the tent, or they were out in the dust storm," she said. "Which makes no sense."

"Unless they were some sort of patrol, guarding the perimeter of the land."

"Out in the middle of nowhere?" she scoffed. "What would they even be guarding against? They had to have heard us coming. These things aren't exactly quiet."

"I don't know," he replied, his voice as grim as his expression. "But we need to tell Rayna anyway."

She nodded. By mutual agreement, they headed back toward the ranch.

Once they reached the storage building and drove the four-wheelers inside, Willow handed Rey her key. "You know, the fact that someone shot at us for taking shelter on their land makes me even more curious as to what they might be trying to hide."

Rey stared at her for a moment. "I agree," he said slowly. "Especially since anyone from around these parts wouldn't begrudge us taking shelter during a monster dust storm. It's not like we cut down their fence and were joyriding our four-wheelers around on their land."

"Exactly. And this might be taking a giant leap, but I think we need to find out what they're hiding. It might have something to do with all the missing people."

Though he didn't respond, she also noticed he didn't contradict her either. Which was fine. She'd give him some time to think about it before bringing up the subject again.

And if in the end, he didn't agree, she'd figure out a way to go back to that place and conduct a search by herself.

They hopped in his truck and drove back to the main house. When they arrived and parked, he turned to her. "I'm assuming you can ride?"

"A horse?"

"Yes." He nodded.

"Sure," she answered easily. "It's been a few years, but I don't think that's something I would forget. Why?"

"Because next time we go out that way, I think we should go on horseback. It's quieter, though slower." He thought for a moment. "Then again, we might not be safe."

"I'm thinking we should go on foot," she said. "Easier to stay hidden once we climb that fence gate."

He narrowed his gaze. "You are aware that there aren't a lot of places to hide in a wide open pasture like that, right?"

"You have a valid point. But—"

"How did I know there would be a *but*?" he asked, smiling slightly.

"At least think about it," she said, deciding she wouldn't tell him if he didn't agree to accompany her, she planned on going alone.

"I will." He got out of the truck and, as usual, hurried over to her side to open the passenger door. The small courtesy still charmed her as much as it had in the beginning. She wondered how she'd ever go back to dating a guy who hopped out of the vehicle and never looked back.

Oddly enough, the idea of even dating anyone else made her queasy. And since her PTO had almost run out, she would need to ask for an extension or, more realistically, an unpaid, indefinite leave of absence. She didn't really think her company would go for that, so she might have to face the possibility that she could end up unemployed.

To her surprise, the thought brought an immediate sense of relief. She couldn't go back to Cali until Isla had been found, but even after that, she wasn't sure she could ever leave her grandmother again. Something to think about, for sure.

Rey held the back door open, and they walked into the kitchen. Without her asking, he went directly to the fridge and got them tall glasses of iced tea.

Accepting hers gratefully, she dropped into a chair, unable to keep from wondering how it would feel to see Rey every single day. The notion made her positively giddy.

"Are you okay?" Rey asked, taking a seat across from her.

Since her thoughts were getting too deep, she took a long breath and nodded, aware she needed to talk about something else. "I was just wondering if they ever made a determination about the body that was found. Like identity, cause of death, any of that."

"I don't know," he replied. "I'm sure Rayna will call us when she can. I imagine she has a lot on her plate right now." He sighed. "I still want to mention to her the huge withdrawal my father made."

"True." Willow remembered the desperation she'd heard in her grandmother's whisper and grimaced. "I want to keep looking. That dust storm put an unexpected wrench in our plans, but I refuse to give up. Our folks are out there somewhere. We've got to get to them before they're found wandering some dark road."

He nodded. "Stay here tonight, and we can leave at first light in the morning."

Meeting his gaze, she thought about it for a minute. "That sounds like a great idea, but what about Sam?" she asked. "Won't that be a bit uncomfortable?"

"I don't think so, but that's definitely up to you. Sam is aware you and I are seeing each other, and he's clearly moved on."

"I'll think about it," she said. "For now, I guess I need to go on home." Since even thinking about that made her sad, she couldn't keep her voice steady.

"How about we drive some back roads in my truck instead?" he suggested, placing his large hand on her shoulder and squeezing lightly.

Grateful, she turned to face him. "Are you able to take the time away from the ranch?"

"I can arrange it. And when Sam shows up, he should be able to help out where needed."

"Then let's do it. I'll feel much better if I'm actually doing something."

"Me too." His phone rang. Digging it out of his pocket, he glanced at the screen. "It's Rayna. I'll put her on speaker."

Once he'd answered and informed Rayna that Willow could also hear, he placed the call on speaker.

"I'm glad I caught you both," Rayna said, her voice grim. "Because I was about to call Willow next. We've identified the deceased individual and spoken with his family. I'm not sure if either of you know him, but it was Alvin Pottsboro. Though we'll need the coroner to confirm, the ER doctor said it appears he died of starvation."

Horrified, Willow gasped. "Starvation?"

"Yes."

"We've got a few things to tell you as well," Rey said. He filled the sheriff in on the ranch bank account, and Willow mentioned the large withdrawal Isla had also made.

"Interesting," Rayna commented. "That's something I definitely want to discuss with the other families. There's so many now that I think we need to all get together as a group."

"One more thing." Rey asked if she'd known about the Raffertys selling off some of their land. The news appeared to surprise her. "They had a ton of no trespassing signs posted, but we were out when that massive dust storm hit, so we had to take shelter on their land. As we were packing up to leave, someone shot at us."

"What?" Rayna cleared her throat. "Are you serious?"

"I am. Now, I know this is ranching county, and it's not uncommon for some trigger-happy fools to take potshots at intruders, but we're locals and we had good reason."

"I agree. That was a hell of a dust storm," Rayna said. "I think it took most everyone by surprise. Wrong season and all. Maybe the weather people forecast something, but I don't know how many people had any idea it was coming."

"We sure as heck didn't," Willow put it. "Luckily, Rey had a pup tent on his four-wheeler, so we were safe."

"No one was hit?" Rayna asked.

"No ma'am." Rey chuckled. "Obviously, they were only trying to scare us off. Either that, or they're really lousy shots."

Rayna's short bark of laughter made Willow smile. She really liked the sheriff. Everyone in town did.

"I'm just glad you're safe. I'll be in touch about the meeting," Rayna said before ending the call.

"Let's go," Rey told her, reaching for her hand. She

threaded her fingers through his, and together they walked out to his truck.

In a few minutes, they were bouncing along a gravel and dirt road that ran the perimeter of the ranch.

"Are there a lot of deer leases out this way?" she asked as a thought occurred to her. "I have a vague memory from when I was a kid. My daddy used to take me hunting at one of his friend's. They had a couple of old campers on the property, and the only way in was by dirt bike or four-wheeler."

"I'm sure there are," Rey answered, his expression surprised. "But it's not deer season until November, so most of them will be sitting empty. I didn't know you ever knew your father."

"I did." She smiled sadly. "My mother passed when I was a toddler, and my dad tried, but he wasn't really present. For as long as I can remember, Isla's been my only family."

"Tell me about your father," he said. "When did he take you hunting?"

"I was probably around seven. I don't remember a whole lot about him. He died right after Christmas that year. I have no idea why I thought of this now, other than the chance that maybe our missing people are holed up at an empty hunting camp."

"That's a possibility," he said. "Except didn't you say your grandmother said she thought she was at a ranch?"

"I'm not sure she'd know the difference," Willow admitted. "Isla preferred town life. She rarely, if ever, ventured into the countryside. Only if she had to."

His gaze met hers. "Out of curiosity, why do you

call her Isla? I know she raised you. Did you ever think of calling her something else besides her first name?"

"Like Mom?" She sighed, a familiar ache inside her. "I tried once when I was in middle school. She sat me down and told me I only had one mother and she was watching over me from heaven. She told me I could call her Isla or grandmother, and I have ever since."

He coasted to a stop and shifted into Park. Then he leaned over and kissed her, a long, lingering kiss that had her craving more. By the time they broke apart, they were breathing hard.

"What was that for?" she asked, smiling.

"Because I wanted to. You're beautiful, Willow. Do you know that?"

The compliment made her laugh. "You're easy on the eyes yourself." Eyeing him, she decided to speak a little of the truth inside her heart. "I like you, Rey Johnson. A lot."

He leaned over and gave her another lingering kiss. "I feel the same way about you."

Then he straightened, shifted into Drive, and they continued on down the road.

As Rey had expected, they didn't see anything out of the ordinary. Just miles and miles of rugged West Texas ranch land. As always, he found the arid landscape beautiful, making him proud to be able to claim he owned a part of it.

Wide-eyed, Willow searched the horizon but didn't say much. He found himself wondering if she felt at home in the wide-open expanses like he did, or if she still yearned for the palm trees and beaches of California.

Finally, he had to turn the truck around and head back toward the ranch.

"Are you sure you don't want to stay the night?" he asked. "It will save you a trip over here at the crack of dawn."

"You know what? I think I will. But I'd like to stop by my house first so I can grab a change of clothes."

Which made perfect sense. He kept going past the ranch and drove them to her grandmother's place.

Once they went inside, instead of going to grab her things, she asked him if he'd consider simply staying here instead.

"Why?" he asked, even though he suspected he knew.

She grimaced. "Honestly, I don't want to have to deal with Sam glaring at me all night."

He started to laugh, but then he realized she was serious. "He won't. I told you, he and I talked. He gets it."

With her arms crossed, she didn't appear convinced. "Okay, then please call him. See how he reacts when you tell him I'll be spending the night."

"Fine." Pulling out his phone, he hit the button to call Sam's number. Naturally, his brother let the call go to voice mail. "He didn't answer," he said. "But if it makes you uncomfortable, I can stay here. We'll just drive out to the ranch at first light or before."

He hated that his brother made her feel uncomfortable. One more thing he'd need to discuss with Sam. But for right now, he'd do whatever Willow wanted.

"Let me think about it for a minute." Back straight, she walked to the kitchen window, where she stood and stared out at the small, neatly kept backyard.

He waited patiently, trying to figure out a way to

undo his invitation and insist they simply stay at her place. Sleeping separately wasn't an option he wanted to consider. Especially since he'd come to realize how transient their time together was.

When she finally turned to face him, she lifted her chin, a determined spark in her gaze.

"On the one hand, I don't want any drama," she said. "Not now or ever. But on the other, I refuse to let Sam's attitude influence any decisions I make about how I live my life. Staying at the ranch is more convenient, so that's what we should do."

He crossed the room in three steps and kissed her. "As long as you're sure."

Pressing her mouth to his in response, she smiled against his lips. "I'm sure. But I can promise you I'm not going to stand for it if Sam starts any nonsense."

He tried unsuccessfully to hide his grin. "Can't say I blame you."

"Right? Do you mind waiting a few minutes so I can pack an overnight bag?" She took off for her bedroom without waiting for him to answer.

Damned if he didn't love that woman.

Deciding not to think too hard or long about the way the sudden rush of emotion made him feel breathless, he made a slow circle of the living room.

On a bookshelf next to a scented candle, he spotted a framed photograph of his father and Isla. Rey picked it up to study it. Beaming at the camera, Carl had his arm around the diminutive woman's shoulders. She gazed up at him with clear adoration. And Carl's expression, Rey thought, radiated happiness. He looked…the way Rey felt inside when he gazed at Willow. In love.

For whatever reason, this hit him hard. He'd known Carl and Isla were a couple. Hell, they'd all had dinner together too many times to count. But he didn't remember ever seeing this look of adoration in his father's eyes when he gazed at Isla. Or vice versa. But then again, Rey guessed he'd never really paid attention.

It made him wonder if he looked at Willow the same way.

A few minutes later, Willow returned, carrying a small overnight bag. She saw him holding the photo and came over, smiling. "They look good together, don't they? I've stared at that picture a lot since I got here."

Throat tight, he nodded and placed the frame back on the shelf. "Are you ready?" he asked, his voice a bit rusty.

"I am." Studying him, she cocked her head. "Are you all right?"

Slowly, he nodded.

"Okay, then." Hefting her bag, she took his arm with her other. "Let's go."

Rayna called just as they made the turn onto the ranch drive. He pulled over so he could give her his full attention.

"Hey, Rayna. I've got Willow with me, and I'm putting you on speaker."

"Sounds good. That will keep me from having to repeat myself." Rayna took a deep breath. "I'm working on nailing down everything for the next meeting. I've got a time and place. All that remains to be done is to let everyone know."

"That was quick," he commented.

"Yeah, I've had my people working on making calls."

She cleared her throat. "But I decided to call you and Willow myself."

"I appreciate that," he said.

Willow echoed his sentiment. "You said this wasn't going to be another gathering with everyone in town, right?"

"Correct. This time, we're only meeting with all the family members whose loved ones are missing," Rayna replied. "Not the entire town. I want to update everyone on what we've learned so far." She took a deep breath. "Is Saturday morning at ten a good time for you?"

"Sure," he responded. Willow agreed. "I'll mention this to Sam as well."

"Great. I'll mark you and Willow both down. Let me know about Sam, or have him call my office." She paused. "If you don't mind, please inform Sam that this is for family members only, so he can't bring a friend or a date."

Rayna definitely had his brother pegged.

"Will do. Where is this being held?" Rey asked.

"Since there are too many to fit comfortably in my office, Pizza Perfect has agreed to let me use one of their meeting rooms. They won't be open yet, but will let everyone in. And there will be pizza, of course."

"Sounds good," Rey said.

"Definitely," Willow added, brushing her long brown hair back over her shoulder.

Unable to help himself, he reached out and touched one silky strand. Distracted, when Rayna spoke again, it startled him.

"Thank you," Rayna said. "Now, I've got quite a few more calls to make, so I'll let you go. See you Saturday at ten."

After ending the call, he turned to Willow. "She's really on top of things."

"She does work fast." Willow shook her head. "I just wish she'd had better luck getting some leads on where all these people might be."

The frustration in her voice matched his own. Since they were parked, he put his arm around her and pulled her close. Despite the console separating them, she put her head on his shoulder. He wished they could stay that way forever.

"It can't be that easy to hide so many older folks," she continued. "Therefore, they've got to be somewhere remote. That's why I still think we should try going back to that land with all the no trespassing signs."

"And get shot at again," he pointed out. "And while it's not real neighborly, they're well within their rights."

The stubborn set of her mouth told him she wasn't in agreement. But instead of arguing, she simply moved completely back into her own seat.

With a quiet sigh, he shifted into Drive.

She waited until they'd nearly reached the ranch house before talking again. "If we're not going to the no-trespassing place, then where are we going in the morning?"

He gestured toward the horizon. "There are thousands of acres of ranch land that we can explore."

They pulled up to the main house and parked. Sam's truck sat in its usual place, which meant his brother was home.

Noticing this too, Willow quietly groaned. "It may be cowardly, but I was really hoping he had other plans tonight."

As they walked into the house, Rey flipped the switch to turn on a light. A disheveled Sam popped up from the couch, red-faced and looking shocked and horribly embarrassed. A second later, a woman did the same, her hair mussed, holding a discarded shirt in front of her.

"Rey! And Willow." Grimacing, he cleared his throat. "Would you two mind giving us a moment of privacy? We can join you in the kitchen in a few minutes."

"No problem." Grabbing Willow's arm, Rey pulled her down the hallway to his bedroom instead. They made it inside, and he managed to get the door closed before Willow dropped down onto his bed and began laughing.

A moment later, he joined her. They laughed so hard that by the time Willow got a grip on herself, she had tears running down her face.

"I guess I was worried for nothing," she managed, wiping at her eyes. "That poor woman. I bet he told her they'd have the house to themselves tonight."

"Obviously." He grabbed a couple of tissues from his bathroom counter and gave them to her. "I just don't understand why they didn't go to his room."

"You don't?" For whatever reason, this brought on another spate of laughter. She shook her head, dabbing at her eyes. "I mean, it's not like you and I have ever done it on the couch, right?"

He conceded her point with a wry smile.

They waited ten minutes before Rey got up, opened his bedroom door and called out to Sam.

There wasn't an answer. Cautiously, Rey ventured down the hallway into the living room. It was empty, as was the kitchen.

It turned out Sam and his lady friend had taken off. They hadn't even left a note.

"So much for worrying about nothing," Willow mused. "I do feel bad for the woman, whoever she is."

Rey shook his head. "I'd hoped to tell Sam about the meeting with Rayna on Saturday. Not that he's ever showed much interest in the investigation, but you never know."

"True." Placing her phone on the coffee table, Willow sighed. "I just keep hoping Isla will call me again. Or, if she can't do that, send a text."

"I'm worried about Carl now," Rey admitted. "He's always been in good health for a man his age, but if he's ill… I have to wonder what's wrong with him. Hopefully, he's not being starved or something like that."

His words made Willow wince. "Why would someone do that to an older person? Any person actually. I still fail to see the common denominator in everyone's disappearance. Apparently, Rayna hasn't come up with one either, or she'd have better leads."

"It has to be money," he said immediately. "I can't see what else someone would have to gain."

Tucking a strand of hair behind one ear, she nodded. "I sure hope we find something tomorrow morning. I'm tired of feeling like this search is in limbo."

"Me too," he said. And then, since they both clearly needed a distraction, he pulled her close for a kiss.

Chapter 14

For most of her life, Willow had never had to use an alarm. She always simply fixed the time she needed to wake in her mind and went to sleep. But tonight, after a second bout of passionate lovemaking with Rey, she stretched languidly and thought she'd better not risk it. They were in his bed, with the bedroom door closed, since they hadn't wanted to risk Sam and his friend walking in on them.

They reclined against propped-up pillows. She'd pulled the sheet up over her chest while he'd done the same, but only up to his waist.

As she got out her phone, Rey watched her. The tenderness she saw in his gaze made her fluttery inside.

"Are you thinking five a.m.?" she asked, making her voice brisk to mask her rush of emotion. "Or should we get up earlier, like four thirty?"

"You don't need an alarm." His warm smile made her melt. Again. "I always wake right before sunrise. I can get you up if you'd like."

Tongue-tied, she simply nodded. When he leaned over to kiss her, she met his lips with more than simply desire. She wanted this, *him*, for the rest of her life with a fierceness that humbled her and shook her to the core.

When they broke apart, he pushed up out of the bed, stepped into his jeans and, barefoot, went to make sure the house was locked up tight.

Unable to keep from watching him walk away, she shook her head. With Isla and Carl still missing, now wasn't the time to even think about any sort of future with Rey. They'd never discussed it, and for good reason.

Rey returned, got into bed and, after kissing her again, turned out the light. He pulled her close and held her while she drifted off to sleep.

The sound of a cell phone ringing startled her awake. Blinking, she sat up. Next to her, Rey did the same.

"It's mine," Rey said, grabbing his phone. "Rayna, what's up?"

Bleary-eyed, Willow watched him, wondering what kind of emergency would have the sheriff calling at—she peered at her watch—four in the morning. Rey wasn't doing much talking, just listening, and Willow couldn't hear enough of the other end of the conversation to figure out what had happened.

"Thanks for letting us know," Rey finally said. "And I'll fill Willow in, so no need to call her."

Ending the call, he shook his head. "I'm guessing she knows I'm usually up around this time. The Lawson house went up in flames a few hours ago. They think some kind of accelerant was used."

"While that's terrible news, why would Rayna feel the need to inform us about that? I mean, it's a tragedy, but still."

"Because Philip Lawson is one of the missing seniors," Rey said, swallowing hard. "And his sister who lives in San Antonio was staying in his house while he's been missing. Rayna said she was killed in the fire."

"What?" Not entirely comprehending, Willow rubbed her eyes. "Someone died?"

"Unfortunately, yes. And right now, it's looking as if she was murdered."

After such devastating news, going back to sleep for thirty minutes was out of the question. By mutual agreement, they got out of bed. After brushing their teeth side by side, which felt way more intimate than she thought it should have, they went to the kitchen to make coffee.

"I'm glad we have something to do this morning," Willow commented. "Sometimes, I feel like keeping busy is the only way to stay sane."

Though he nodded and tried to smile, his troubled expression negated his attempt. "I think Rayna's wanting to move up the meeting. She said she planned to call each of the families and let them know that this, whatever it might be, is escalating."

Willow almost choked on her coffee. "She thinks we might be in danger?"

"She said she has to consider the possibility that any or all of the families of the missing people are at risk. Her words, not mine."

"But why?" Willow asked, bewildered. "What would anyone have to gain by hurting those of us who are missing our loved ones?"

"I don't know. That's something Rayna is going to have to figure out."

She took a long sip of her coffee. "Are we still going to go out on horseback? I'd really like to continue the search. We should at least have a few hours before she can get the meeting organized, right?"

"Probably. But I'm not sure I want to risk it. What if we're way out there and miss her call? Or can't get back in time to make the meeting?"

Though she didn't like it, he had a valid point.

"I need to try and get a hold of Sam," Rey said. "He'll still be asleep, but if I wake him, maybe he'll actually answer his phone. It's worth a shot."

Watching him while he dialed his brother, his handsome face intent, such a swell of love rose inside her that she had to grip the edge of the kitchen table to keep from going to him.

His strategy must have worked because he gave her a quick thumbs-up before speaking into the phone. "No, Sam. Nobody has died, at least not in our immediate family. Rayna just called me, and I wanted to fill you in on what's—"

Listening, he shook his head. "Sam, please. It's important." A moment later, Rey cursed. "He hung up on me," he said. "Told me not to bother him again unless it was serious. I never even got a chance to tell him about the fire or the Lawson woman's death."

"Or the fact that Rayna feels other family members might be in danger," Willow added, furious at Sam. "Let me try," she said. She grabbed her phone, pulled up Sam in her contacts and called him. After two rings, he forwarded her to voice mail.

"That's pretty much what I expected," Rey said when she told him.

Frustrated, she decided to go home. "There's no point in me hanging out here. You're welcome to come to my place with me. You'll be closer in case Rayna calls a meeting."

She loved that he didn't even try to hide his disappointment. "I think I'll just get started on chores," he replied. "Since obviously Sam has no intention of coming back and helping."

She carried her coffee cup with her into the bedroom. As she got dressed, Rey stood in the doorway and watched her. At one point, when she looked up at him, the naked longing in his gaze stopped her in her tracks.

"Don't do that," she told him. "When you look at me like that, it's almost impossible for me to drag myself away."

Her comment made him grin. "Then don't go."

Instead of replying, she simply walked over to him and pulled him down for a long, soulful kiss. "That'll have to hold us both," she said once she'd broken away.

Though he followed her out to her Bronco, he made no other move to try and stop her. "I guess I'll see you at the meeting, whenever that may be."

"Definitely," she said. "I sure hope Rayna holds it at Pizza Perfect like she'd planned for Saturday. I wouldn't mind a slice or two of pizza."

She got into her SUV and left him standing in his driveway watching her go. Part of her felt like she'd left her heart behind her.

Rayna called right after Willow got out of the shower. "Can you make the meeting around one?" the sheriff asked. "Pizza Perfect has agreed to still let us use one of their meeting rooms and also provide lunch."

"I can be there," Willow replied.

"Great. Please let Rey know," Rayna continued, evidently assuming they were still together. "See you there."

Immediately after ending the call, Willow dialed Rey. She gave him the information, and though he offered to pick her up, she told him she'd just meet him there. He said he was still trying to get a hold of Sam, but he'd definitely attend either way.

Wanting to be early, Willow left for the meeting thirty minutes before she had to.

Since she didn't see Rey's truck in the parking lot, she went on inside. The restaurant was still packed from the lunch rush. An employee directed her to a meeting room in the back of the building. The smell of pizza cooking made her mouth water.

There were already about a dozen people gathered inside, even though the meeting didn't start for half an hour. Willow walked over to a group she knew slightly, greeting them with a friendly smile.

"We were just discussing the possibility that the sheriff's office must have gathered some very good leads," a middle-aged woman with salt-and-pepper hair and tired eyes said. "Otherwise, why would Rayna hold a meeting?"

Though Willow had to wonder if she knew about the house fire, she kept her mouth closed and simply nodded.

"Agreed," someone else said. "This is the first time I've felt hopeful in a long while."

"Looks like there's going to be a PowerPoint presentation," the first woman said, gesturing toward the front of the room where a large portable screen had been set up. "That's got to be a good thing, right?"

Several others agreed, including Willow. Privately,

she wondered what kind of slideshow the sheriff planned to have.

Her back to the door, Willow felt the energy in the room change. She glanced over her shoulder, unsurprised to see Rey had arrived. He met her gaze, and she felt that familiar jolt. As he made his way toward her, she realized she saw no sign of Sam. Relieved, despite feeling he needed to be here, she wondered what had happened. Rey had been so convinced that Sam had turned over a new leaf.

"Hey," Rey said, his arm brushing hers. Even that slightest of touches sent a shudder of longing through her.

"Hey, yourself," she said back. "Do you want to go grab a seat?"

"Sure." He followed her over to two unoccupied chairs in the front row. "I'm sure you noticed, but Sam couldn't make it."

Sitting, she waited until he'd settled in beside her, their hips touching. Again, she felt an inner jolt at the contact. "Was there a problem?" she asked.

He grimaced. "He said he didn't feel like sitting through some boring meeting and wasting his day, especially since I could just fill him in on the details."

Despite his even tone, she could sense his frustration. "I'm sorry," she said.

"Thanks. I just don't understand his thinking. Sometimes, it's like he's still a teenager. It bugs me more than it should, especially since he promised to be more invested."

In the short time they'd been there, more people had arrived and were also taking their seats.

Five minutes before the meeting was due to start, Rayna and two of her deputies entered, all in uniform, a sign to Willow they wanted this to be as official as possible.

"Good morning, everyone," Rayna said, her voice carrying. "Why don't the rest of you get seated, and then we can begin."

She waited a moment while the latest arrivals got settled. "Now, as you all know, despite us diligently working on this case, we've had precious few leads. Finding Mr. Smith appeared to be our first big break, but so far we have not been able to talk to him. The doctors have recently informed me that his health has declined, and they don't expect him to survive the day."

Murmurs went through the audience as everyone digested this news. The bookstore owner had been a well-liked and respected part of the community.

Rayna waited patiently until it was quiet again. "Secondly, there was a devastating house fire earlier this morning. Philip Lawson's house burned to the ground. Since he is one of the missing, his sister had come in from out of town and was staying there. Unfortunately, she lost her life in the fire."

Evidently, not everyone had been notified because the room erupted. People stood, shouting out questions, talking with each other and expressing their shock.

Rey wasn't sure why, but in the chaos of rampant emotions, he felt a strong urge to protect Willow. Without caring who saw, he put his arm around her and pulled her close. She glanced up at him, her mouth parted in surprise, but she nestled into his side.

Finally, Rayna tapped a pen on the microphone and asked for silence. Everyone immediately complied.

"I'll try to answer your questions as best I can," Rayna continued. "Yes, we do think the fire was deliberately set. Our volunteer fire department found traces of an accelerant. We do not know why, or if it was tied to the group of missing individuals. However, we've decided to err on the side of caution and warn each of you to stay vigilant."

This time, instead of simultaneous outbursts, several people raised their hands. "What about insurance?" someone asked.

"I'm sure Mr. Lawson had insurance on the home," Rayna said, answering the first question. "But with him missing, since the policy would pay him, I don't see how that would benefit anyone. The same for his sister's death. Even if she carried a substantial life insurance policy, only her beneficiary can claim that money."

Rey and Willow watched and listened as the sheriff patiently and painstakingly answered every single question and concern. He kept his arm around her shoulder, and she stayed as close as she could while remaining in her own chair. He noticed several people glancing their way, but for the most part, everyone seemed too captivated by the situation at hand to pay them any attention.

Once no more questions related to the fire remained, Rayna moved on. "I have some more news, though unfortunately I'm going to have to keep it vague for now. Our volunteer group that has been canvassing the town brought back several interesting pieces of information that may or may not be connected. Since we don't know for sure, we're not going to discuss this yet. Instead, I want to talk about what we do know."

She looked around the crowd, briefly making eye

contact with Rey among numerous others. He appreciated the sheriff's no-nonsense manner and suspected others felt the same.

"What we have learned from talking to you all, as well as friends and neighbors of those missing, is that many of them were facing serious health concerns. Not everyone, but at least one partner in each couple. But not all of the health issues were similar, or even close. We have one person recently diagnosed with ALS, several with various types of cancer, COPD, kidney failure with congestive heart failure, heart blockages, you get the picture."

Rayna paused, letting all this digest. Rey glanced at Willow, since her grandmother had been diagnosed with some sort of heart issue. Carl had been healthy, at least as far as they knew. Though when Isla had called, she'd said Carl had fallen ill. Worry twisted his gut at the thought. He swallowed hard and returned his attention to the sheriff.

"We've been investigating a few possibilities," Rayna continued. "Beginning with any individuals or groups promising miraculous cures. We're looking into each and every one we can, in order to see if our missing senior citizens were lured away by outlandish claims."

Willow shook her head. Around them, Rey noticed several others do the same. "Isla would never allow herself to be conned by a snake-oil salesman," she said out loud. "She was always on the lookout for scammers."

"My mom was too," someone else said. A couple more people echoed this statement.

"Desperate people do unusual things," Rayna cautioned. "But please remember, this is just a theory." She sighed. "Right now, it's one of the best ones we've got to go on."

The meeting ended on that note.

Most everyone stayed after, helping themselves to the pizza buffet that had been set out on the back table. Rey had lost his appetite, but because Willow made it clear she intended to eat, he followed her over. Since he knew his body needed nourishment, he followed Willow's lead and put a couple of slices on his plate.

They ate quickly and with purpose. When he asked Willow if she wanted to go back for seconds, she shook her head.

"I'd like to go check on Serenity," she said. "I've been worried since she had that episode when I visited her store. I checked with the hospital and they said she was discharged."

"Have you tried to call her?" Rey frowned.

"I did, but she hasn't picked up or returned my call. So I want to stop by."

Shocked, since he'd known Serenity his entire life, he eyed Willow. "If they discharged her, she must be okay, right?"

"Maybe. I don't know. She looked really bad." She shook her head. "Right after all that happened, Isla called, and as you know, there's just been a bunch going on. I should have checked on her sooner."

"Do you mind if I go with you?" he asked. "Now I'm a little worried too."

"Of course. I welcome your support. I'd like to try to convince her to go get checked out by a doctor again, just to make sure."

Her compassion for others was one of the things he

loved about her. *Loved.* There it was again, that word, that emotion. Glancing away, he couldn't help but wonder if she suspected, if she knew. And most importantly, if she felt the same way.

Pushing those thoughts from his head, he knew he needed to focus. "I don't know how much assistance I'll be, but I'll definitely try."

"I don't know about that." Willow smiled. "If she actually does need some help, I suspect Serenity might listen to you better than she does to me."

Her large brown eyes sparkled when she smiled. He had to force himself to look away. How he could be so enthralled by someone while in the middle of a monumental crisis, he'd never understand.

And then there was the fact that she hadn't made any secret of her intention to go back to California when all this was over.

"Let's take my Bronco," she said, jumping to her feet. "We can leave your truck here."

"Why?" he asked.

"You always drive." She shrugged. "I'd like to this time."

Beautiful, he thought. His smile widened. "Makes sense to me. Unless you'd like to walk. It's not that far."

"I'd rather drive," she replied. "Let's go."

Once they were in her SUV, she glanced at him. "You know, I've always considered my vehicle roomy, but you barely seem able to fit."

He shrugged. "I have this problem sometimes. I'm a big guy, which is why I drive my truck."

"You do take up a lot of space," she agreed. "You make the front interior seem much too small."

They pulled up to Serenity's, and she managed to snag a parking space right in front. Stepping out before Rey could come around, she stood a moment peering down Main Street.

"So many memories here," she mused when Rey caught up. "Every year for five years, I rode in the Fourth of July parade with the 4-H Club. And for PE in middle school, coach made us run laps around that church and cemetery."

"You had a horse?" Rey asked, surprised. "I thought you always lived with Isla in town."

"I did." With a rueful smile, she sighed. "But my friend Cindy lived in those five-acre ranchettes out by 36th Street. I'd always wanted my own horse. Finally, Isla bought me an older mare when I was thirteen. Cindy had an extra stall in her barn, so we paid to let Luna stay there. I went every morning before school to feed her and after school to ride her."

Somehow, he suspected Willow had been a natural on horseback. Her petite, athletic build would lend itself well to many athletic endeavors, like surfing.

The vision sobered him. Quickly, he collected his thoughts. "What happened to your horse?"

"We had to sell her when I went away to college." Willow blinked. "I almost didn't go because of that."

He nodded. Were those tears in her eyes? "But you did."

"Yes. As much as I loved that horse and this town and my family and friends, I wanted something different. Something *more*."

Her words cut like a knife to his heart. He could only smile like a simpleton while she continued.

"Back then, restlessness burned like a fire in me. I

spent countless hours poring over information about the West Coast versus the East. All I knew was I wanted to live on the coast. I didn't care which one. I'd known I'd move away to one of those places and live near the ocean, but until the job offer had come in from Cali, I hadn't been entirely sure where I'd live."

When she looked up, Rey met her gaze, hoping his impassive expression hid his churning emotions. "And that's why you moved away after you graduated."

"It is." Apparently weary of the subject, she turned to Serenity's shop. "Are you ready to go inside?"

"After you." He opened the door for her, letting her lead the way. Bells tinkled a cheerful welcome.

Rey looked around. The interior of Serenity's appeared normal. Incense burned on the back counter, the usual soothing music played and a small waterfall had been added to a table over by the front window.

The instant the door closed behind them, Serenity sailed through her colorful beaded curtain, smiling broadly. Judging by Willow's earlier description, he saw that her bruises had faded slightly, and she'd clearly tried to cover them with makeup.

"Rey and Willow! Both of you at the same time!" she exclaimed, hugging Rey first and then Willow. When she finally stepped back, she glanced from one to the other. "Are you here to shop or just to visit?"

"I wanted to check on you," Willow admitted. "How have you been? Any more er…incidents?"

Serenity narrowed her eyes. "By incidents, do you mean falls? If so, I haven't fallen again."

"She's just concerned about you," Rey said, keeping his tone gentle. "We both are."

Just like that, Serenity appeared to deflate. "Thank you. Come on into the back and have some tea, and we'll talk."

As they followed her through the beaded curtain, Willow couldn't help but notice the older woman appeared to lean to one side. Her gait seemed unsteady, and she grabbed a hold of one of the chairs around the table for stability.

"Maybe I should get a cane," she said, half smiling. "I admit I've been having a lot of dizzy spells for no reason. I went to see Doc, but he wanted to order an MRI at the hospital in Midland, and there's no way I'm getting into one of those things." She sighed. "Maybe I should go see that faith healer who sent out the flyers. I just can't seem to find anyone who's used him, so I can't be sure if he's legit."

Once again, Rey found himself glancing at Willow. She'd straightened, her expression suddenly intent.

"What faith healer?" she asked, her tone casual. Waiting to hear the older woman's answer, Rey attempted to match her lack of urgency, despite his racing heart.

Suddenly, Serenity seemed to sense their interest. One perfectly arched brow raised, she looked from one to the other. "You know I attend lectures dealing with metaphysical things. The last one I went to was a month ago in Abilene. There was a group there passing out flyers for some faith healer. I only took some to be polite. Actually, I forgot about them until I fell the other day."

"Do you still have them?" Willow asked.

"I'm sure I do, somewhere," Serenity replied. "I'm not sure why you both find this so fascinating, but I can assure you I was only half serious."

"Did you share the flyers with anyone else?" Rey crossed his arms.

"I put a stack of them on the counter for customers to take, if they were so inclined," Serenity said. "You know I'm not the kind to push things on people. And since there aren't any left on the counter, I'd say quite a few folks grabbed one."

For the first time, Rey thought they might have an actual lead. Rayna had even mentioned investigating medical leads earlier in the meeting. "Did you happen to mention any of this to Rayna?"

"No. Why would I?" Again looking from Willow to Rey and back again, after a second, the confusion in Serenity's gaze vanished. "Do you think this might have something to do with all those missing people? Like Isla and Carl?"

"It definitely could," Rey replied. "It just depends on how badly they needed relief. Desperate people will step outside of their comfort zone. Even you just said you might have to try giving that guy a call."

"True, but I'm hesitant," Serenity said. "Even though this sort of thing aligns with some of my belief system, something about it just seems off for some reason. I can't quite put my finger on it, but I don't get a good vibe."

"Why don't you look and see if you can find any remaining flyers?" Willow suggested. "I'd like to bring one to Rayna and let her take a look."

"Sure. Give me a few minutes. Would you two like some tea while you wait?"

Resisting the urge to insist on helping Serenity search, Willow shook her head. "None for me, thank you."

Rey echoed the sentiment.

"Okay, then. Wait here." And Serenity disappeared into the public part of her store.

Again, Willow and Rey exchanged glances. "I don't know about you," Rey said. "But I think this could be the break we've been waiting for."

"I agree." Willow swallowed. "Do you think we should go out there and offer to help her? She seems really unsteady on her feet."

Just then, they heard Serenity cry out, followed by a crash.

Chapter 15

Following the ambulance to the hospital, Willow gripped the steering wheel so hard her knuckles were white. Glancing at Rey, she noticed he appeared to be working on unclenching his jaw.

"I swear I've seen more of this hospital these past few weeks than I have in the last several years," he said.

"Me too." Willow felt glum. "And we need to fill Rayna in on what Serenity said about that faith healer."

"It would be better if she'd found the pamphlet." Though Serenity had regained consciousness after the paramedics arrived, her only request had been to ask them to make sure her store was locked up. Naturally, they'd complied, but that also meant they couldn't go back in later and search for it.

"Maybe we can ask Serenity for a key," Rey suggested when she voiced her thoughts. "I'm sure she'd let us go in and look."

"Let me call Rayna. Maybe she can come up with something." She pulled out her phone and put the call on speaker. Rayna picked up almost immediately. "What's up?" she asked, her voice terse.

"We're on our way to the hospital following an ambulance. Serenity fell, and I'm not sure, but she might have had a seizure or stroke."

Rayna cursed. "Has she been ill?"

"We suspect she has." And Willow filled her in on the rest of it, Serenity's black eye, her unsteadiness and the mention of a faith healer.

"A faith healer?" Rayna asked. "Like one of those old-timey revival things were the preacher goes around laying on hands?"

"We don't know," Rey admitted. "She was trying to find a pamphlet when she passed out and fell. The thing is, she said she had a stack of those flyers in her shop and passed them all out to customers. What if this is the missing link?"

"It's a lead," Rayna said firmly. "We don't ever jump to conclusions in law enforcement. But any lead is better than what we have right now, which is next to nothing. Please tell me you got your hands on that leaflet?"

"We did not. And Serenity made us lock up her shop before she'd let the ambulance take her. So we don't have any way to get back in and search for the darn thing."

"If she's okay, please just ask her for her key," Rayna said. "Because based on what you've told me, I don't have a valid reason to break in there just to search."

Disappointed, Willow said they'd try. Privately, she wasn't sure Serenity would allow them to have her key or look through her shop without being present. She honestly didn't seem to understand the possible connection between the faith healer's flyer and the missing people. Hell, even Rey knew it might be a long shot. But it was a hell of a lot more than what they had right now.

They parked. By the time they'd begun walking into

the ER, the paramedics had already taken Serenity inside. Willow had called Velma right after they'd called 911, and Serenity's sister had ridden with her in the ambulance.

"Unfortunately, we can only allow immediate family to go back right now," the triage nurse said. "But you're welcome to wait out here if you'd like."

Since Velma knew they'd made the trip and Willow had given Serenity's sister her cell number, they took seats in the waiting room.

When Willow turned to meet Rey's gaze, the exhaustion in her eyes made him put his arm around her and pull her close. "You can use my shoulder as a pillow if you want," he offered. "Close your eyes and get some rest. I promise to wake you if anything happens."

She gave him a grateful smile and did exactly that.

An hour later, Velma came out. She smiled, appearing relieved. "She's awake and talking. Trying to get them to let her go home. They want to run some more tests and keep her overnight for evaluation. They think she's having TIA's—transient ischemic attacks."

"Oh, no." Willow gripped Rey's arm. "Is she going to be all right?"

"The doctors don't seem too worried." Velma took a deep breath. "I wish I could say the same. I'll let you know if anything changes."

"Thank you," Willow said. Rey echoed the sentiment.

As Velma walked off, she seemed to suddenly remember something. She paused mid-step and spun back around. "Oh, I almost forgot. Serenity tells me you were asking about the faith healer. What did you need to know?"

Willow's heart skipped a beat. "Have you met with him?"

"Oh, no." Velma shook her head, sending her large, dangly earrings swinging. "I just saw the stack of flyers that Serenity had. I even took some for the front counter of my yoga studio."

"Do you have any left?" Willow asked, trying not to sound too eager.

"I'm sure I do. Most of my clients are pretty fit. I only know of a few who took one of those flyers." She met Rey's gaze first before settling on Willow. "I'm pretty sure that Isla was one of them."

Willow's eyes widened. "Hearing that, as far as I'm concerned, that means this faith healer person needs to be looked into. Do you mind if we stop by your studio and grab a flyer?"

"Not at all. I have classes scheduled for this evening, and one of my other instructors will be there teaching them. You can just drop in and get one off the front desk." Velma smiled, gave a quick wave and hurried back to be with her sister.

Willow glanced at Rey, wondering if he could tell her first impulse was to kiss him. "Are you thinking what I'm thinking?"

He stood. "Yes. Let's go. We'll grab a couple of those flyers and hand deliver one to Rayna."

By the time they got back in Getaway and parked outside the yoga studio, dusk had begun to fall. Inside, class had started. Taking care not to disturb anyone, Rey and Willow went to the front desk, saw the stack of flyers and grabbed three.

Back outside, they carried them out to her Bronco

before taking a look at them. To Willow's surprise, they looked professional, with clean, crisp text and colors. There was even a photograph of the supposed healer, a normal-looking man in a well-fitted, navy suit. His name was Jonathan Longtree.

"These seem fairly tame," Rey mused. "I'm not sure what I expected, but maybe some extreme claims about his healing abilities."

"Me too. I thought for sure I'd see something about him healing the blind." She grimaced. "This is way more professional than I expected. It even has his hourly rates."

"Yeah. But one thing it doesn't have is a business address." Rey turned the flyer over and double-checked the other side. "It just says to contact him for an appointment."

"True. But it does say he offers a senior citizen discount." She sighed. "Which definitely would appeal to the older crowd. Still, it's not as much of a huge lead as I'd hoped for."

"Maybe. Maybe not. But I wouldn't entirely dismiss it. Let's get a copy to Rayna. Then we'll grab dinner and head to the ranch. I'd like to make an early start in the morning."

After dropping off the flyer on Rayna's desk—she'd left for the day—they decided to stop for dinner at the Tumbleweed Café. "It's chicken-fried steak night," Rey said. "That's one of my favorite dinners ever."

"You can't get that in California," Willow commented. As they walked into the restaurant, she thought back to all the special occasions she'd celebrated here.

They were shown to a window booth, one where Willow and Isla had sat together many times. Willow sat down across from Rey and sighed. "I'm really missing my grandmother right now. She loves coming here to eat."

He nodded. "So does Carl. From what I understand, he and Isla had a standing Wednesday night date here."

Gazing at him across the table, she realized she wanted all of that with him. Standing dates, making traditions, sharing a history and making a future. She leaned forward, parted her lips to ask him if he wanted the same things and then gave herself a mental shaking. She couldn't ask him something like that. Not when she hadn't even decided her own future.

Her requested PTO was coming to an end, and she'd been putting off calling her boss. She'd either need to request an extension or put in her notice. And as much as the thought of leaving her job pained her, she refused to leave Getaway until Isla had returned home safe.

In fact, right then and there, she knew she wouldn't be leaving at all.

The waitress came over and took their drink orders. They both asked for sweet tea and took a minute to look at the menu. Though Rey opened his, Willow found herself gazing at him again across the table.

"What?" he asked, noticing. "Do I have something on my face?"

This made her smile. "No, not at all. I'm wondering why you're even looking at the menu since you said you were getting chicken-fried steak."

"True." He put the menu down. A few minutes later, they ordered. She went ahead and got chicken-fried steak too.

When their food arrived, they dug in. After they finished eating, Willow grabbed the check before Rey could. "My turn," she said, even though it wasn't.

Though he started to protest, she quickly silenced that by leaning across the table and giving him a kiss. "No debating. Like you said last time, you can get the next one."

"But that's two," he said.

"So? You can get the next two then."

Smiling, he shook his head but gave in.

As they got up to leave, she reached for his hand. They walked out to her Bronco together. "After we get my truck, do you want to take yours home and then ride out to the ranch with me?"

She thought for a moment. "Does that mean you've reconsidered, and we can go out and look around that area tomorrow?"

"No. It means I want to spend the night with you wrapped up in my arms."

How could she say no to that? "I'd like that," she admitted. "But can we at least mention it to Rayna tomorrow?"

"Sure," he answered easily. "As long as she's available, I'd say that's a definite possibility."

Sam strolled in around ten, when Rey and Willow were cuddled on the sofa in the middle of watching an old Western movie. Immediately, Rey hit Pause on the remote and pushed to his feet.

"About time you showed up," he said, keeping his voice level.

"Did you miss me?" Sam grinned, clearly missing the point. "I'm thinking you two welcomed the time alone together."

"I could have used some help with the chores," Rey pointed out. "With Carl missing and it just being the two of us, it takes both of us to keep the ranch running."

Sam's blank stare meant he either didn't get it or didn't care. Rey was betting on the second.

"Sorry," Sam replied. He dropped down into the armchair and changed the subject. "Any news on Dad?"

Right then and there, Rey decided he wouldn't elaborate on anything until they had something concrete. Sam's self-absorption and lack of effort didn't make Rey inclined to share anything with him. "Nope," he said. Willow raised her eyebrows but didn't comment.

"Oh, okay." Sam eyed the TV. "Do you mind if I change the channel?"

"Yes, we do," Rey and Willow answered at once.

"We're enjoying this movie," Willow said.

Sam frowned. "But it's old."

"So?" Rey challenged.

Looking from one to the other, Sam shook his head. "Never mind," he said, standing. "I'll just go watch something in my room."

Once Sam had closed his bedroom door behind him, Rey took the movie off pause and put his arm around Willow. She laid her head on his shoulder, and they watched the rest in a sort of quiet bliss.

This, Rey thought. This sort of domestic evening had never been something he'd thought he wanted. Until Willow. Now, he couldn't even begin to imagine his life without her.

They'd need to talk, and soon. But he knew a conversation about their futures couldn't happen without Isla, Carl and the others being found. He also knew the very real possibility existed that Willow, once she knew her grandmother was safe, would wave goodbye and head back to her home and job in California.

When the movie ended, Willow turned to him and said she wanted to talk. Since this echoed his thoughts, he hid his surprise and nodded. His heart rate picked up as he wondered if she'd actually broach the subject that had been constantly on his mind. Her leaving. Or alternatively, her staying.

"Sure," he managed to say casually. "What's up?"

She took a deep breath and met his gaze. "That area with the no trespassing signs. I know you want to wait and see what Rayna thinks, but I want to go back."

Damn. Hiding his disappointment, he shook his head. "I don't believe it's safe. We've already agreed to mention it to Rayna tomorrow."

She grimaced, clearly reluctant. "I know we agreed to discuss it with her, but I don't really see a need to. She's got her own leads to follow. Why can't we investigate this on our own? I know you feel it's too dangerous, but we can be careful. If we don't have loud four-wheelers, they won't even know we're there."

Persistent, he'd give her that. "Come on, Willow. They shot at us last time. We've been warned. We can't risk it."

"But what if that's where Isla, Carl and the others are being held? I have to think that's a very real possibility."

"Maybe," he allowed. "But we don't have enough reason to get a search warrant. And without something like that, they're within their rights to shoot at us for coming onto their land. This is Texas. The Castle Doctrine says deadly force is justifiable if they believe it's necessary to protect themselves from the unlawful use of force by an intruder."

"But we're not armed. Just trespassing isn't threatening."

"They could claim they didn't know that. It would have to go trial, and that would be too late if they've already shot us."

Though she narrowed her eyes, she finally nodded in agreement. "Fine. We'll talk to Rayna. Maybe she'll have some ideas."

"I'm sure she will. We can run by the sheriff's department first thing in the morning. If I can get Sam to do his fair share of chores. Which might be more difficult than it should be."

Willow laughed, but seemed appeased.

He kissed her then. When they broke apart, he grinned. "How about we continue this in my bedroom?"

She jumped to her feet and grabbed his arm. "Come on. We don't want Sam to walk in on us."

Needing no second urging, he allowed her to pull him along.

Later, as they held on to each other, sated and happy, he kissed the top of her head. Heart pounding, he decided to take a chance and speak his thoughts out loud.

"I could get used to this," he said, quietly.

When she didn't respond, he glanced down at her and realized she'd fallen asleep.

The next morning, Rey managed to get out of bed without disturbing Willow. He headed to the kitchen, where he found Sam finishing up a bowl of cereal. Surprised, he realized his younger brother was already dressed in jeans, work boots and a long-sleeved shirt.

"You slept in?" Sam drawled, taking a long drink of his coffee.

Rey grinned. "Maybe a little," he allowed. "But I'm still up before the sun."

"Truth. I thought I'd get an early start on the chores this morning."

"Good," Rey replied. "I've got to run Willow into town to have a word with the sheriff."

As usual, Sam appeared completely disinterested. He didn't ask a single question or even acknowledge Rey's statement. Instead, he put his bowl and mug in the sink, grabbed his hat off the counter and strode to the door. "See you later," he said.

Once the door had closed behind him, Rey shook his head and went to make himself and Willow a cup of coffee.

After they'd had their breakfast and showered, they hopped in his truck and made the drive into town to see Rayna. Willow had texted to make sure the sheriff would be available. "She says to come on in."

Downtown Getaway still appeared sleepy in the early morning sun. As they drove past the Tumbleweed Café, the usual pickup trucks filled the parking lot, ranchers there for breakfast before heading out to the fields.

When they reached the sheriff's department building, they parked and hurried inside. Talking to the receptionist at the front desk, Rayna looked up and greeted them with a smile. "Come on back," she said.

Once they were settled in her office with fresh cups of coffee, Rey decided to get right to the point. "Willow wants to go back and try to search that area where we were stuck during the dust storm."

Rayna's brows rose. "Where someone shot at you?"

Rey nodded. "I think it's too dangerous."

"But I feel there's a very real possibility we'll find my grandmother and the others there," Willow interjected.

"Based on what?" Rayna wanted to know. She leaned forward, eyeing Willow intently.

Willow shrugged. "Gut instinct. Intuition. Call it what you will, but I can't shake the feeling that they're there."

"Did you discuss this with Serenity at any point?" Rayna asked.

"No." Willow sighed. "If she wasn't still in the hospital, I'd give her a call."

Since Rey wasn't sure why Rayna even brought up Serenity, unless she actually *believed* in her psychic abilities, he kept his mouth shut.

"Well, even if you could ask her about it, that wouldn't be enough." Tone decisive, Rayna sat back in her chair and took a long drink of coffee. "I want you two to promise me you'll stay away from that land," she continued. "They not only have No Trespassing signs posted, but they fired warning shots. They clearly mean business. It's not safe."

"But how else are we going to know if that's where our parents are?" Willow protested.

The long look Rayna gave her spoke volumes. "We don't have a single reason to believe they're there. If I had one, just one valid reason, I could get a search warrant and go in myself."

"What about a drone?" Rey asked. "Don't you law-enforcement types have access to drones? That would be the safest way to find out what's going on."

"I don't have one," Rayna said thoughtfully. "But

I'm sure I could locate one if I made a few phone calls. That's a really good idea."

Rey smiled. "Thanks."

"But they could shoot that down," Willow pointed out.

"Better a drone than a person," Rayna responded. "Let me get working on that. It may turn out to be nothing, but at least we can say we gave it a shot."

"Or," Rey added, touching Willow's shoulder, "a drone might be able to provide exactly the lead we need to bring Carl, Isla and the others home."

Though Willow's disappointed expression revealed her feelings, she simply sighed. "How soon will you know if a drone is available?" she asked.

Rayna shrugged. "This might take some time, but if I can locate one and talk them into letting me borrow it, I should be able to get it by the end of the week."

"That's not soon enough," Willow protested.

"It's the best I can do," Rayna countered. "Now, I'm sorry, but I'm fresh out of time. I'll be in touch as soon as I have something concrete."

After Rayna walked away, Rey took Willow's arm. He could tell she wasn't happy with the solution the sheriff had come up with, but he honestly felt it was a good one. "This is perfect," he said. "Now I don't have to worry about you getting shot."

"But she said it could take a week," Willow protested. "I think we should go in and look around ourselves. If we take precautions, we should be safe."

"Precautions?" He shook his head. "Like wear cammo and try to blend in with the landscape?"

Crossing her arms, she met his gaze. "Why not? It would work."

"I vote we wait for the drone, as Rayna suggested. Not only will that be safer, but we'll get a much better view. Once we have that, we'll see everything there is to see within a matter of minutes. Those things transmit video in real time. It'll be perfect."

Though her expression remained unconvinced, she finally nodded. "Then I guess I'm going to have to go home," she said. "I'm sure you've got work to do around the ranch."

Ruefully, he acknowledged her words. "There's always something that needs doing."

They walked out to his truck. He waited until they were inside before turning to her. "What about you? Any plans for the rest of today?"

After buckling her seat belt, she shrugged. "I'm thinking I might drive back out to the hospital and see if they'll let me talk to Serenity. I'll probably call first, though, because that's a long drive to make if they won't let her have visitors."

"True." He kissed her one more time before starting the engine. Though he couldn't put his finger on it, something felt off. Maybe it had to do with Sam actually doing the chores earlier, rather than the way Willow appeared to be avoiding meeting his gaze.

Chapter 16

After Rey dropped her off at her house, Willow watched him drive away. She knew what she had to do. If she wanted to check out that area quickly, she was going to have to go it alone. Preferably first thing in the morning. No way did she plan on waiting another week to ten days for drones that may or may not be available.

After calling Velma and learning Serenity remained in the ICU—though Velma hoped her condition would soon be upgraded so she could be moved to a regular room—Willow decided she might as well do some housework. It wouldn't do for Isla to come home to a less than tidy house.

She passed the next couple of hours happily cleaning. When she'd finished, she walked around the sparkling house and smiled, imagining Isla's reaction. Though Willow normally didn't enjoy housework (who did?), showing love for her grandmother this way felt good.

Rey didn't call that afternoon. She guessed he'd gotten busy. While she ached to hear his voice, she also had begun to feel guilty about her solo plans for the morning. While she wasn't exactly lying to him, omitting her plans felt wrong. Except for one thing. She knew he'd try to stop her.

They'd never actually had a disagreement. Part of her wondered how he'd handle attempting to convince her not to go. Since she'd begun thinking long-term relationship with him, she knew this would be something she needed to know.

Just not right now. Another time, when the stakes weren't as high.

Though she and Rey had taken to spending every spare moment together, when he FaceTimed her around dinnertime, she claimed she didn't feel well. Which was true. She'd become a mess of nerves. She told him all she wanted to do was get some rest in her own bed. Alone. Which wasn't true.

The hurt that flashed in Rey's eyes wounded her, but she managed to keep herself from offering comfort. He'd be okay for one night. After all, since they'd never discussed her staying, what did he think would happen once she went back to Cali?

Again, she acknowledged she wouldn't be returning. Once she had Isla back safe and sound, she wasn't taking a chance on missing any more time with her. And since her grandmother was growing older and might be facing some health challenges, Willow planned to be by her side to help guide her through them.

Not only that, but she had to admit she couldn't handle the thought of leaving Rey. While they hadn't discussed the future and certainly hadn't made any promises, she realized she wanted to see if what they had now deepened.

That is, if what she planned to do on her own didn't completely tank things between them.

He called her again shortly after nine to ask if she felt

any better. They stayed on the phone for an hour, each of them equally loath to let go of the sound of the other's voice. A couple of times during their conversation, she almost broke down and gave him notice of her plans, but at the last moment, she reined herself in. When they finally said good-night, she decided to turn in early. She knew she'd have a restless night.

Alone in her double bed, she felt Rey's absence so strongly that she almost reached for her phone to call him. Instead, she forced herself to lie still, going over her plans for the morning instead of thinking about him.

Her nerves kept her tossing and turning, and by the time she pushed back the covers and got out of her bed shortly before five, she had serious doubts about her admittedly half-baked plan. For one thing, how hard would it be to find the area with the No Trespassing signs? She didn't have the same familiarity with the land as Rey. To prepare, she'd done some research on the county appraisal district's website and saved a few maps to her phone.

Beyond that, she intended to drive as close to the area as she could, park on the side of the road and go the rest of the way on foot. She would dress in clothing that would hopefully help her blend into the landscape.

She had no concrete plans other than to take photos with her phone if she discovered anything. Unless she caught sight of Isla or Carl, she didn't intend to try to infiltrate any buildings or even get close enough to place herself in any danger.

If Isla, Carl and the others were there, she wanted them out as soon as possible. And if not, then no one would be any the wiser about her investigation.

The pep talk with herself helped. She found some beige, brown and dark green clothing—the closest thing to camouflage she owned—and got dressed. She pulled her hair back into a ponytail and tucked it up under an old baseball cap she'd found in Isla's closet. She also emptied the backpack she'd brought with her from Cali and, following Rey's example, loaded it up with a couple bottles of water and some nonperishable provisions. Just in case.

Once she'd made a cup of coffee to go, she shouldered her backpack and left, too nervous to eat anything. She'd do that once she returned home.

As she left town behind, her headlights swept the empty roads, once again reinforcing how isolated this area truly was. For the first time, it struck home that there'd be no one to help her if she got in trouble. And if the same people who had Isla, Carl and the others grabbed her, no one would have the slightest idea where she'd gone.

She decided she needed to leave a hint or a clue. But what? For the rest of the drive, she considered her options. She could text Rey, but the effect would be too immediate, and if she knew him, he'd head out right away to try and stop her.

A handwritten note might work, but if she was taken, she suspected they'd also move her car. She went over several possibilities before settling on one.

When she reached her destination, she pulled out her phone and searched for Sam's number. If she knew him, he'd be deeply asleep and wouldn't see a text from her for hours.

Sam, it's Willow. I need you to give Rey a message for me. Tell him I went out on my own to the land with the signs. He'll know what that means. Please pass this on to him as soon as you get it, just in case I find myself in trouble.

She reread it and then pushed Send. Satisfied with her solution, she got out of her Bronco, used the key fob to lock the doors and headed in the direction she hoped would lead to the posted land.

Either luck was on her side or she'd somehow retained a good memory, because she'd only been hiking for thirty minutes when she saw the familiar rise in the land that she and Rey had climbed. The sun had just begun to ascend the horizon, and the sky lit up in rose, orange and gold in a West Texas sunrise.

Instantly going on full alert, she headed up the path. When she reached the top, she kept herself close to the large rock and nearby tree, just in case someone might be on the posted land.

To her relief, she saw no one.

So far, so good. She spotted the fence, the gate and the bright yellow No Trespassing signs. And there was the small group of trees where she and Rey had pitched the tent during the dust storm. This brought another twinge of guilt, since she knew Rey wouldn't be happy with what she was doing. But she'd come this far, too far to back out now, even if she wanted. Which she didn't. If nothing came of this, no harm done. And if she did discover something, then everything would change for the better.

Since the posted land sat behind another rise, with

rocky outcroppings dotting the area, she felt certain she'd have numerous places to hide. If they had some sort of regular patrols, she should be able to take shelter and avoid being spotted.

Heart pounding, she shouldered her backpack and sprinted toward the gate. She made it over without incident and, congratulating herself, headed for the small group of trees.

She kept moving, zigzagging between rocks and trees and otherwise trying to stay low to the ground.

Ahead, she saw another slight rise in the land, with two large rock outcroppings that resembled sentries. Since she'd been steadily climbing, she figured things had to level out soon.

As she approached the space between the rocks, out of an abundance of caution, she once again looked around. So far, so good. If whoever owned this land did do regular patrols, they must start later.

In what felt like a safe space, she stood close to the larger of the two boulders and stared. Below, spread out in an area that encompassed at least a couple of acres, sat a sprawling compound. Odd how that word seemed to best describe these buildings, made from a combination of cinderblock and stucco that had been painted the exact color of sand.

What the heck was it? It didn't look like any ranch she'd ever seen. More like a prison or some sort of top-secret, government facility.

Though she hadn't seen any people yet, this would be the exact type of place where she'd expect someone who'd taken hostages to keep them.

Cautioning herself not to get too excited, she plotted the

best way to get closer to the cluster of buildings. Though she still didn't see any movement of people—whether residents or guards—it now made more sense why whoever owned this place would have patrols.

Every nerve ending alive, she kept herself low and kept moving, only stopping long enough to take brief shelter and quickly reassess any possible danger.

The closer she got to the compound, the more suspicious she became. Still, aware of the danger, she continued to take precautions.

At one point, resting behind the trunk of a bent and twisted oak tree, she forced herself to stop and take stock. Beyond seeing the structure, she didn't have a plan. She sure as heck wasn't going to try and break in, especially since she hadn't seen anything concrete that might indicate that Isla, Carl and the other missing townspeople were inside.

She pulled out her phone and began snapping photos. As soon as she had enough, she decided to turn and retrace her route. Though Rey wouldn't be happy, she figured once she showed the pictures to Rayna, the sheriff would want to open an investigation.

Checking the time, she was relieved to see that only a couple of hours had passed. She should be able to get back to her Bronco and be back at the house by lunchtime. By the time Sam saw the text she'd sent and showed it to Rey, there'd be nothing for Rey to say. And she'd have the pictures.

She gave herself a quiet high five and turned to go. Before taking a single step, she once again scanned the entire area for any signs of a patrol.

This time, what she saw made her freeze in her tracks.

Two men, both carrying high-capacity rifles, stood between her and the way she needed to go.

They hadn't seen her yet. Or so she fervently hoped. Neither appeared to be looking her way. Instead, they stood talking, one of them smoking a cigarette, the other continually scanning the area.

If they looked her way, they'd see her.

She didn't dare move. In fact, she had to work hard to control her breathing. If she started hyperventilating and gasping for air, they'd surely hear her.

Move on, move on, she chanted silently. They had a lot of ground to cover. Once they continued their patrol, she could get out of here.

Except they didn't go anywhere. Almost as if they were toying with her. The breeze ruffled the prairie grass, carrying snatches of their conversation to her. *Coffee*, she heard. And the words *target practice*. That last part made her blood run cold.

Afraid to check her smartwatch, she didn't know how long she'd been crouching there, waiting for them to go. It felt like eternity as her legs started cramping. Even worse, she realized that she needed to empty her bladder, which would not be possible right now.

One of the men suddenly pivoted. As his gaze locked on her, she knew she'd been seen. Though every instinct screamed at her to run, she didn't want to take the chance of getting shot in the back.

"Come out with your hands up," the guard ordered, raising his rifle.

As the other man slowly did the same, Willow complied.

* * *

First thing in the morning after he opened his eyes, Rey battled the urge to call Willow, just to say good morning. Not wanting to risk waking her, he forced himself to get up, make coffee and a bowl of oatmeal and eat. The entire time, he kept his phone out on the kitchen table, just in case she texted or called. But she didn't, and he figured she must be sleeping in. He shoved his phone in his back pocket before getting busy doing the morning chores.

Sam hadn't spent the night at home again, which was starting to become a problem. Rey understood how his younger brother might be distancing himself from the ranch, but his desire to do so didn't mean he could skip out on work. Not if he expected the ranch to continue to support him. He guessed he and Sam would be having yet another heart-to-heart discussion very soon.

In the meantime, chores didn't disappear simply because someone didn't show up to do them. Which meant, in addition to his usual tasks, Rey now had Sam's to contend with.

By late morning, he had almost everything done. Glad he hadn't yet showered, he went back to the house and drank a large glass of ice water. Now, he thought, would be a respectable time to call Willow. He couldn't wait to hear her voice.

But instead, he got her voice mail. Disappointed, he left her a quick message, asking her to call him back once she had a chance.

When his phone rang almost immediately after that, he smiled. *That was quick*, he thought. Maybe Willow had been missing him too.

But Rayna's number showed on the screen instead.

"What's up?" Rey asked.

"We've finished checking out that faith healer guy, Jonathan Longtree," she said. "He's a nurse practitioner. Or was, until his APRN license was suspended."

"That can't be good," Rey commented. "So, is he legally allowed to run his healing center?"

"That's where it gets interesting. He played it smart, by labeling his business as religion rather than medical care. There are little to no regulations on churches."

Startled, Rey wished he had the brochure handy. "Is he operating as a church? I don't remember reading that in the pamphlet."

"He doesn't come right out and say that, but it's alluded to. There are several instances where he asks for donations to *keep God's Work going*," Rayna replied. "When you get a chance, take a look at it again."

"I will."

"I reached out to him with the number on the flyer and left a voice mail asking him to call me. I also sent an email. I have a feeling he isn't going to respond."

"Maybe I should try," Rey suggested. "I'm sure he isn't interested in talking with anyone in law enforcement. I can be a regular citizen seeking healing."

"That might work," Rayna said thoughtfully. "Though, I think it would be better if we could get someone older to help us. If this Longtree is our guy, his target appears to be senior citizens."

Which made perfect sense. "Do you have someone in mind who might be willing to help?"

"I'm working on that," Rayna replied. "And I've also

sent out inquiries about borrowing that drone. I'm hoping to hear something back by this afternoon."

"That would be awesome." Rey found himself itching to tell Willow. In fact, he'd give her a call after he finished talking to the sheriff. "Please keep me posted."

"I will. And if you wouldn't mind, pass this info on to Willow for me. I tried to call her, but she didn't answer."

Rey chuckled. "Will do. I'm planning to talk to her as soon as we hang up."

"Sounds great." And Rayna ended the call.

Immediately, Rey punched the contact for Willow. The call went directly to voice mail. He left a quick message to say he'd just gotten off the phone with Rayna and had some news. He asked Willow to call him back when she could.

That done, he tried to understand why his father would trust anyone claiming to be a faith healer. Carl had never been much for church, though he'd started attending with Isla. A pragmatic man, he believed in a power higher than himself, but had little use for anyone claiming to represent that power. Even Serenity, who made no religious claims whatsoever, had been regarded with barely concealed distrust.

Carl was a man of the land. Grounded, he worked with his hands. He understood animals and nature and other people. He had no use for philosophy or esoteric nonsense, as he liked to call it.

If he'd gone to a faith healer, the only reason would have been for Isla. Whether to take care of her health or, if Carl had developed some sort of illness, to please her in trying to take care of his. After all, Carl would do anything for the people he loved.

Damn, Rey missed him. If this faith healer had any-thing to do with his and the others' disappearance, Rey would be hard pressed not to deck the guy.

Shaking his head, Rey went over a mental list of the remaining tasks that needed to be completed that day. He really should try Sam again and demand his younger brother get his rear home and start pulling his weight.

His phone rang, startling him. *Willow.* The thought of hearing her voice made him smile.

But when he glanced at the caller ID, he saw it was Sam rather than Willow. As if thinking about him had gotten him to call.

Since Sam only phoned when he needed something, Rey took a deep breath. Bracing himself to hear what kind of trouble his brother had gotten into now, he an-swered the call. "What's up?"

"I'm really worried. I think Willow's in trouble," Sam said, his voice so agitated Rey could barely understand him. Sam then said something about getting a text from her, but he wasn't making any sense.

"Slow down, please," Rey ordered, despite his own now accelerated heart rate. "Read it to me, word for word."

Sam, it's Willow. I need you to give Rey a message for me. Tell him I went out on my own to the land with the signs. He'll know what that means. Please pass this on to him as soon as you get it, just in case I find myself in trouble.

Rey felt like the earth had shifted beneath his feet. He cursed. And then cursed again.

"Do you understand what she means?" Sam asked,

the worry in his voice matching the absolute terror in Rey's heart.

"Unfortunately, I do. How far away from here are you?" Rey asked, his voice grim.

"I'm on the other side of town, at Gia's place," Sam replied. "About thirty-five minutes away."

"Get here as soon as you can. I'm going to take Roscoe and ride out to look for Willow. I need you to take care of the ranch until I get back."

"Take care of...?"

"I don't have time to explain everything to you," Rey said, letting his frustration show in his voice. "I did both my chores and yours this morning. I need you to do the same this afternoon."

He ended the call without waiting to hear Sam's response. Then he took off running for the barn. He saddled Roscoe in record time, climbed on and took off for the far pasture.

Sticking closer to the roads this time, his heart sank when he spotted Willow's empty red Bronco, parked in a ditch. Impressed at her ability to get the area right, he rode on past, heading for the hill where the no trespassing signs were easily visible.

Once he'd ridden to the top, he scouted the area below and on all sides, looking for any sign of Willow. A slender ribbon of water, all that remained of the river that had once cut through this craggy land, shone silver in the distance. Twisted trees, bent sideways from the perpetual wind, dotted the space. They provided only a little shade, though he supposed someone on foot might use them as cover.

Despite searching thoroughly, going over each area in

several sweeps, he saw no sign of Willow. This scared the hell out of him. What if she'd been right, and someone had set up camp here and was actually holding a couple dozen senior citizens hostage? If they caught Willow attempting to sneak up on them, they'd grab her too. And who knows what might happen after that.

A shudder of pure terror lanced through him. Though he knew better than to leap to conclusions, he couldn't help but consider the worst-case scenario.

Why hadn't she waited for the drone? Why take this kind of risk? He wished he knew what the hell she'd been thinking.

Quickly, he ran through his options. He could call Rayna. Should call Rayna, actually. Except Willow had trespassed, and while that didn't give them the right to hold her captive, they could call the sheriff's office and press charges.

Which he supposed most normal people would. Unless they had something to hide. And he suspected whoever had posted the no trespassing signs definitely did.

Was Jonathan Longtree, the so-called faith healer, involved in this? Perhaps here, on this remote acreage in between two huge ranches, had been where he'd built his home or office or whatever he called it.

Right now, Rey needed to figure out his next move.

He could turn Roscoe around and ride back home. He was still on the outside of the boundaries marked by the no trespassing signs.

Or he could ride the perimeter, remaining careful not to break any laws, and try not to be seen by the armed men who evidently patrolled the perimeter. As long as he wasn't on their land, they'd have no reason to shoot at him.

If that worked, he could question them. Maybe they'd answer, maybe they wouldn't. But at least he'd hopefully get some sort of idea what the hell was going on.

And if he didn't encounter anyone? He supposed he might be tempted to investigate further, even if he had to trespass on their land in order to do that.

Decision made, he turned Roscoe in the direction of the incline. He rode to the top, where he had a clear view not only of the posted boundaries, but also of the pastures spread below. In the distance, he saw two large mesas that divided the land. In between them, an opening that appeared large enough to drive a truck through. Though this definitely meant he could ride Roscoe through it, he also noted that once through, if it was blocked, leaving could become problematic.

Instead of trying to open the gate, which he knew from last time would be futile, he rode along the fence line. He didn't really want to trespass, not just yet.

The ride seemed to take forever. Fully alert, some of his nerves communicated themselves to Roscoe. The well-trained and well-seasoned horse had gotten used to just about everything, but having his rider on edge put him there as well. Which meant in addition to keeping watch for armed guards, he had to keep Roscoe under control as well.

Fifteen minutes later, he saw them. Two men, on foot, carrying semiautomatic rifles. They watched him, keeping their distance, though they made sure he could see their weapons.

Deciding to pretend ignorance, he urged Roscoe closer

to the fence and began waving at them. "Excuse me," he hollered. "I need to ask you something."

The guards looked at each other. One shrugged, and then they strode toward Rey. They stopped about twenty feet from the fence. "Are you lost?" one man asked, his tone harsh and unwelcoming.

"Not really," Rey responded, keeping his voice light and casual in contrast. "I own one of the ranches nearby. I haven't been out this way in a good while, but I'm curious about all those no trespassing signs. We neighboring ranchers are a friendly bunch, and we've always given each other free access to each other's land. What's up with all this?"

"Private property," the second man said, taking a few steps closer. "The signs are to make sure it stays that way."

"That's not real friendly," Rey commented, scratching his head as if truly perplexed. "Who's the owner? He must be new. Is there any way I could talk to him, since we're practically neighbors?"

"No." The first man joined the second. In unison, they raised their rifles. "I'd suggest you make your way back to wherever you came from."

Though he could have pointed out the fact that he wasn't on their land, Rey decided not to bother. For now, he'd make a show of leaving. Then he'd return, either with or without Rayna. If they had Willow, he'd need to figure out a way to rescue her.

Chapter 17

Though her heart hammered as if it might pound out of her chest and her legs were shaky, Willow managed to walk as directed toward the compound. Having two large rifles aimed directly at her provided an incentive to follow orders.

For the first time in a while, she wanted to curse. Though she'd known her exploration would be dangerous, she'd honestly believed she wouldn't be caught. Now that she had, what the heck was she going to do?

Since, at the moment, she couldn't do anything, she figured she might as well play it casual until she found out what was going on. After all, it was entirely possible she'd been wrong about this place. Perhaps the owners were extremely private people and just wanted privacy. Maybe they were famous. Or über wealthy eccentrics wanting to live off the grid.

If that turned out to be the case, while she might have wasted her time, she'd also be in a much better position to explain why she'd trespassed on their land. If she played up that California accent she'd heard so many times while living there, maybe they'd buy a story about an overly curious tourist who'd wandered too far off the beaten path. Maybe looking for fossils or arrowheads or something like that.

Because honestly, that was all she could come up with to explain why she'd disregarded the bright yellow signs. If she could convince them she was just some sort of empty-headed female, they might be more inclined to let her go.

Unless of course, Isla and the others turned out to be captives here. That would change everything. While she had no idea what course of action she'd take then, she had to hope she'd come up with something.

When they reached the front of the structure, which she could now see appeared to be a tall, concrete-block wall surrounding the large stucco building, her guards took her around to the side. There, they stopped in front of a metal door with an electronic keypad. One man punched in the code while the other kept his weapon pointed at her.

She briefly considered asking them to let her go, but she equally needed to see what was inside this veritable fortress. Pushing her fear aside, she lifted her chin, took a deep breath and waited.

The first guard pushed the door open, and the second guy motioned for her to go inside.

"Where are you taking me?" she asked, managing to keep her voice steady.

"To see Jonathan," they both answered. "Now, move."

Jonathan. She guessed he must be the owner of all this. Wait. Hadn't the faith healer's name been Jonathan? Yes. She believed it had. Jonathan Longtree. Just like that, her heart rate accelerated. Somehow, she'd managed to stumble upon what she knew deep inside had to be the right place.

They led her to a small, windowless room and left, closing and locking the door behind them. The only furniture inside was a scratched and scarred wooden bench that had been pushed up against one wall. Unusual, even ominous, to say the least.

But then again, maybe she'd simply watched too many true-crime dramas. This guy called himself a faith healer, after all. Healers weren't supposed to hurt people. However, they weren't supposed to hold people against their will either.

As time passed and no one came, she realized they hadn't searched her or taken her cell phone. Almost hyperventilating, she shakily pulled it out. She'd call Rey first, and he could call Rayna.

But though she called his number, nothing happened. That was when she realized she had no signal.

What the...? Not believing it, she tried again. The little icon in the top left corner showed No Service.

Dang it. She tried turning her phone off and then back on. Still nothing. Which meant this building had some kind of cell blocking thing going on. No wonder they hadn't taken her phone.

Still, because she'd read somewhere that 911 would work, she tried that. The call dropped. She tried again with the same result.

At least her smartwatch still kept perfect time.

One hour passed. It had nearly reached two when the door creaked open and a slender man with long brown hair and an equally long, well-trimmed beard came in. He peered at her through his silver, wire-rimmed glasses, expression intense. Though he wore khaki pants and a white button-down shirt, he had a kind of otherworldly presence that she suspected he cultivated deliberately.

"Welcome," he said, his voice soft yet commanding. "My name is Jonathan Longtree."

"Willow Allen," she replied, relieved that he appeared to be relatively normal. "I'm sorry that I wandered onto your property. I promise it won't happen again."

"Oh, I know it won't." He flashed a pleasant smile. "Because I'm not going to let you leave."

Her heart dropped straight to her feet. Not sure how to respond, she simply stared at him.

Finally, deciding she had nothing to lose, she told him the truth. "Look, my grandmother is missing. So are several older people from our town. I came out here looking for them. Have you seen them?"

He blinked. "Guard," he called. Immediately, the door opened, and one of the armed men from earlier stepped inside the room.

"Bring her water and something to eat," Jonathan ordered.

As the man went to comply, Willow wondered how on earth she'd manage to choke down food. She understood that she somehow would have to try. Something about the steely glint in Jonathan's eyes warned her not to cross him, even in the smallest of ways.

A moment later, the guard returned. He brought a large glass of water and a paper plate with carrot sticks, celery and a spoonful of dip on it.

When he handed this to Willow, she accepted it. The moment she did, the guard backed out of the room, closing the door behind him.

"We insist on healthy eating here," Jonathan said, smiling. "Part of the mind-body connection."

She nodded and took a small sip of the water. "What is *here*, exactly?"

"This is the Longtree Wellness Center." His smile widened. "And we specialize in healing people in the older demographic."

For a moment, she could only gape at him. "Does that mean…" she asked, once she'd found her voice.

"That the individuals you've been searching for are here?" His smug smile widened. "The answer to that would be yes."

Time stopped. Her heart skipped a beat or two while she struggled to find the right words. "Would it be possible for me to see them?" she asked, her tone as respectful as she could make it.

He stared at her, eyes hard. "You have to earn favors here. Most people pay money. I know your grandmother did. Her boyfriend too. What sort of skills do you bring to the table?"

Not sure what he meant, she wondered if he meant sexually. Though she tried to remain calm, her eyes filled with tears. "I'm not sure what you mean," she managed, squeaking out the words.

Clearly impatient, he huffed. "What are you good at? What do you do for a living? How are you best able to help us here at the center?"

When she couldn't come up with an immediate response, he shook his head and strode to the door. "I'll leave you here to think about that. Next time we speak, I hope you have an answer."

When he closed the door behind him, she heard the unmistakable sound of a lock sliding into place.

Great. Now what? First, she needed to calm herself. She took several deep breaths, working very hard to slow her heart rate. Then, out of habit, she tried her phone once again, even though she'd already confirmed she had no service. Just in case, she tried sending Rayna a text, but got an error message saying it wasn't able to be delivered. Of course not.

She got up and began pacing the small room, trying to think. If this Jonathan Longtree wanted to play games, she'd better come up with something so he'd let her see her grandmother and the others.

Mentally, she ran over a list of her strengths. She suspected being organized and good with numbers wouldn't fly. Ditto with surfing—they were miles from the nearest ocean. Her cooking skills were limited, though she could make a mean enchilada soup. Maybe she should play up that, since it was the lone thing she could think of that might be of benefit to others.

Once that occurred to her, she started thinking of other stuff she could do to help people, more specifically, seniors. When she'd been a teenager, she'd volunteered in a senior living center. She'd been really good at reading them books, taking on the voices of the various characters. She'd always loved making her audience laugh. She decided to use those two when Jonathan came back. She could only hope they'd be enough.

Alone in the small room, minutes dragged into an hour, then two. She had to tamp down her rising impatience. Knowing she was this close to her grandmother only increased the aching need to see her. Right now!

Waiting felt intolerable, though she suspected he was taking as long as possible as a deliberate way to show her who was boss. As if she had any doubt. This man had clearly made it his life's work to prey on the sick and aging. Why he'd chosen the small town of Getaway, she had no idea. Unless it had something to do with the purchase of this land. Remote enough for nefarious purposes, and in a part of the country where folks weren't inclined to pry into each other's business.

Finally, just as she'd checked her watch for maybe the hundredth time, the door opened and Jonathan sauntered in. "Did I give you long enough to reflect?" he asked, his dulcet tone at odds with the cold glint in his eyes.

Not wanting to seem too eager or do anything to put him off, she meekly nodded. She'd make sure he had no idea that she was seething inside.

"Good. Now tell me, what skills do you bring to the table?"

As his gaze swept over her from top to bottom, for the second time it occurred to her that he really might have meant something sexual. She hid the way this thought made her recoil and forced herself to smile sweetly.

"I can cook," she said. "I'm especially good at baking cakes. And I've also been told I do a good job reading out loud to people. I used to volunteer in a nursing home, and the residents looked forward to attending my reading sessions."

When she finished talking, Jonathan considered her words. He once again appeared expressionless, before bowing his head as if praying.

Once again, her nerves took over. Yet, somehow she

managed to sit completely still, her hands folded tightly in her lap.

"I think that will do," he announced, his beatific smile not fooling her for one second. "Come. I will take you to see the others."

Slowly, she got to her feet, unwilling to let him see her eagerness. Though her pulse had kicked up, she stood quietly, waiting for him to either lead the way or to call for an armed man to escort her. Either way would work, as long as she got to see Isla, Carl and the others.

He opened the door and stepped out. "Follow me," he said without looking back.

As she left the room, two men immediately flanked her. They weren't the two guards who'd escorted her here. She noticed they didn't carry large rifles like the others had. Instead, they both wore pistols, holstered but still within reach.

Silent, they all marched down a long, windowless hallway. When they reached a door and stepped outside, she realized they were leaving one building and going to another.

This second structure, made of the same beige stucco, also appeared to be windowless. Willow frowned, realizing it looked a lot like a prison.

When they reached a metal door, Jonathan entered a series of numbers in a keypad mounted in the wall. The lock made a clicking sound, and the door opened. "This way," he ordered. He strode ahead without looking back.

Willow hurried after him. She had to practically jog to keep up with his long-legged stride.

Down another long hallway, a right turn, then a left, and they finally emerged into what she could only describe as a room resembling a high school cafeteria. Inside, men and women sat at long banquet-style tables, eating.

"You're lucky," Jonathan said, swinging around to eye her. "Looks like you made it just in time for a late lunch."

Too busy scanning the room to pay attention to him, Willow let out a little cry when she spotted a familiar face. "Isla!" she cried out. Then, before anyone could stop her, she launched herself across the room, running toward her beloved grandmother.

As soon as he had cell service again, Rey called the sheriff. Using as few words as possible, he told her about Willow's text to Sam and his experience a few minutes before.

"Semiautomatic rifles?" Rayna asked. "To patrol a pasture? What do they think they're going to be fighting against?"

"No idea." Rey took a deep breath, tamping down his frustration. "But I need help figuring out a way to get Willow out of that place."

"Except you don't know she's in there," Rayna pointed out.

"Where else would she be?" Rey countered. "Come on. I'm asking for your assistance here."

"Without a good reason, I can't ask the judge for a search warrant," Rayna said, her voice heavy with regret. "And while we know Willow planned to go explore that area, we have zero reason to believe they captured her or that she's being held prisoner. Just like we don't know for sure that's where we can find the missing people."

While she had a point, Rey felt obliged to mention he

didn't know what else to do. "What you're telling me is if I want to go in there looking for her, I'm on my own."

"Hold up." Rayna's voice turned stern. "The last thing we need is you disappearing too. Don't you dare go near that property."

"But what if Willow is in there?" he protested. "We don't have time to wait on those drones."

"If she is, I'm sure she'll be fine," Rayna replied. "Go on back home and let me see if I can come up with a plan. I'll call you when I do."

She hung up without waiting for an answer.

Rey seethed. He'd never been the type to sit around and wait for help. If something needed to be done, he did it. And this was Willow, damn it. The woman he loved.

If she needed saving, then that was what he'd do. And once he held her in his arms again, he was never going to let her go. Ever.

Pragmatic, Rey knew better than to try to rush in without a plan. Rayna was right about that. After all, clearly that was what Willow had done, and look what had happened.

For now, he decided to take Rayna's advice and go back to the ranch. Surely, something would come to him if he thought hard enough.

Once he reached the barn, he took the saddle off Roscoe and brushed his horse down. While his hands were occupied, he thought long and hard, looking for an actual course of action. But all he could come up with was what he'd started out with. Steal into the place under cover of darkness, locate Willow and extricate her. But that didn't take into account the very real possibility that all the missing townspeople might be there.

Rayna called as he was walking back to the main house. "I've got an idea," she said, her voice vibrating with excitement. "We were able to verify through the county tax office that Jonathan Longtree, aka the faith healer, is the owner of that land. And I've been talking to a few of my colleagues in Lubbock, and someone suggested that he might be marketing his faith healing as an actual medical facility without a license to do that. I'm having one of my deputies look into that now."

"What does that mean?" Rey asked, impatience cutting his words short.

"It means I can get him on that violation. It's a third-degree felony, punishable by two to ten years in prison and a fine of up to $10,000. Which means we can send a team out there to arrest him. That'll actually give us a legal ability to search the place. And if all those missing people are being held there against their will, that will be even more charges against him."

For the first time since he'd learned Willow had decided to pull this crazy stunt, Rey felt hope. "I want to go with them," he said, his voice fierce.

"No," Rayna immediately replied. "You're a civilian. You can't."

Since he'd guessed she would say that, he clenched his jaw tight and didn't argue. "How long until you know something?"

"I should hear within the hour. We're treating this as urgent, since it is."

Rey thanked her and ended the call. He started to ride back to his ranch, but halfway there, he stopped. Shaking his head, he turned around. If Rayna managed to put together a valid reason to legally go onto the ranch, great for her. But right now, the woman he loved might be in danger. No way was he letting her sit there until the sheriff's office raided the place. That situation could go south really quickly, and he didn't want to take even the slightest chance of letting the woman he loved get hurt.

He'd save her himself. Failure wasn't an option.

Since he'd grown up here and had spent years exploring his family's land and everything surrounding it, Rey figured that was one advantage that he had over anyone else. The no trespassing signs were a new addition, and as kids, he and his friends had roamed all over that land. He knew every cliff, every hiding place, and where to avoid so he wouldn't be exposed and vulnerable. While it might have been years since he'd ridden up that way, even if they'd built a house there, the land wouldn't have changed.

He continued moving forward.

When the low-slung, industrial-looking structure came into view, he sucked in his breath. The damn place, which looked a lot like a prison, appeared impenetrable. From his vantage point, he couldn't tell if the windowless wall was actually part of the structure or a kind of fence designed to keep prying eyes away.

He'd bet on the second.

Since a metal door appeared the only point of entry, unless he could grab somebody going in or out, he wouldn't be getting inside there. He'd have to figure out another way in. Which meant he'd need to circle around to the back of the building.

As he carefully made his way, he spotted a lone guard, on foot, armed with a semiautomatic rifle. The man appeared bored, kicking at the ground and occasionally glancing around at the admittedly monotonous landscape. He continued moving toward Rey, seemingly oblivious to the presence of an interloper.

Luckily, if he moved a few feet, Rey could duck behind a tree. He waited until the guard appeared to be focused on something on the horizon and made his move.

Now partially hidden, he didn't dare try to look to see the guard's progress. He could only go by sound. Luckily, the guy didn't even try to move quietly.

The closer he got, the more Rey's heart pounded. It might be desperate—hell, it *was* desperate—but he knew what he had to do.

He waited until the guard had moved just a few feet from him before coming out from behind the tree. Launching himself at the completely surprised man, Rey knocked him down before he could even get his rifle up. Two quick blows rendered the guard unconscious.

Working quickly, while keeping an eye on his surroundings, Rey dragged the man as close to the shelter of the tree as he could. Then, glad they appeared to be of similar size, he stripped the guard's clothing and put it on. He found a key fob inside the man's pocket, which he hoped could be used to unlock the door into the structure.

Once dressed and armed with the rifle, Rey hustled over to the metal door. No one stopped or even noticed him. He lifted the key fob and pressed the button, holding his breath as he hoped it would unlock the door.

To his infinite relief, the keypad beeped and then made a loud click. He tried the handle, and the door opened.

Now what? Stepping inside, he realized he'd have to play it by ear and hope he didn't get caught.

Strangely enough, the place seemed deserted. As he moved down a long, windowless hallway, he didn't encounter anyone else. Which might be a good thing, but where was Willow?

Finally, he reached an exterior door. This one wasn't locked, so he opened it and exited. Outside, he found himself in a small courtyard, facing another building with a similar door. Maybe inside would be where he'd find Willow.

After gaining entry, he finally heard the sound of voices. Keeping his head down, he hoped if he acted casual, no one would notice him. After all, he wore a guard's uniform, so he should be basically invisible to anyone who didn't work with him.

He passed two men talking. Since neither of them wore any kind of uniform, they didn't even look at him. Perfect.

Ahead, he heard the sound of many voices, which meant a larger group of people. Bracing himself, he continued moving forward. Around one more corner, he stepped into a brightly lit room that resembled a gymnasium or cafeteria. In one corner of the large area, he saw a group of maybe twenty people gathered together.

His heart skipped a beat as he spotted Willow. Then Isla and Carl. All the others who'd gone missing from town appeared to be there as well.

He dug out his phone, meaning to send Rayna a text. But the screen said No Service, so he shoved it back into his pocket.

He realized he couldn't let any of them see him, especially Willow or Carl. If they let on that they knew him, the others would figure out he wasn't supposed to be there, and chaos would ensue.

Alternatively, what now? He didn't have a workable plan for getting everyone out safe and unharmed.

A tall man with long, brown hair, a beard and wire-rimmed glasses strode into the room. This must be Jonathan, Rey realized. Clearly, the faith healer put a lot of time and effort into appearing saintly. He even clasped his hands in front of himself like some kind of yogi.

"Greetings, my friends," he said.

None of the gathered people responded in kind. Some glared at him, others appeared to be pretending he didn't exist. Not exactly the kind of response Rey would have expected, especially if they truly believed he could heal them. Maybe the fact that they were being held against their will had a lot of bearing on that.

Three armed men burst into the room. "We have intruders," one shouted. "A bunch of people from the local sheriff's office are here. They claim they have a search warrant. What do you want us to do?"

Rayna. She'd gotten here even faster than he'd thought she would. Grateful, he began edging toward the captives. He wanted to be prepared to defend them if necessary.

"You!" Jonathan pointed to Rey. "Take these people to the storm cellar."

Careful to keep his face down and expressionless, Rey nodded. As he moved toward the group, he saw Willow's beautiful eyes widen when she noticed him. His father, who appeared very ill, sat next to Isla with his head hanging down and didn't realize his son had come to try and save him.

Several people in the group began grumbling. "We're not going," one white-haired man declared. "If the sheriff is here, she'll take us home. And that's where I want to be."

"Me too," someone else echoed.

Before Rey had time to respond, he heard gunfire coming from outside. This instantly quieted everyone.

Jonathan Longtree, his pale face turning red, spun on his heel and headed away from the door. "Come on," he snapped to Rey and several other armed men who were in the room. "Forget about them. It's time to protect me and earn the salary I pay you."

While the other guards obediently trotted after the healer, Rey didn't move. Neither did Willow or the others.

Apparently used to being obeyed, Jonathan didn't even bother to look back to see if Rey had followed or had begun herding the others to the storm cellar, wherever that might be. Which was good, since Rey had no intention of hiding these people away. And he definitely wasn't about to protect the healer.

More gunshots, some shouting, the words undecipherable. The bedraggled cluster of senior citizens drew closer, some of them voicing their fear.

"It's going to be all right," Willow said, her voice clear and calm in the middle of danger. Though she sent Rey a grateful look, she stayed with her grandmother and the others.

The door burst open, and several armed sheriff's deputies came through, weapons drawn, with Rayna right on their heels. Rey immediately put down his rifle, just as a precaution, and raised his hands. He knew how easily things could deteriorate in tense situations.

Rayna spotted him and hurried over. "Where is he?"

"He and several of his armed guards went out that door," he said, pointing.

With a brusque nod, Rayna motioned to her deputies. "Let's go get him."

Once they'd left, he turned to face the woman he loved, her grandmother and his father. *Safe*, he told himself. They were okay. He couldn't ask for any more than that.

"Rey!" Willow cried. She came rushing over and wrapped her arms around him. "Did you see? Isla, Carl and all the others are here. And safe."

All he could do was pull her close and hold on. Now his knees finally buckled. "I love you," he murmured, smoothing her hair away from her face and kissing her cheek. "But don't you ever scare me like that again."

And then he went to check on his father, still sitting in the same spot, all hunched over. Carl raised his head to meet his son's gaze. "Hey, son," he said, one corner of his mouth raised in the beginning of a smile. "Glad you finally got here."

In response, Rey gently hugged him, shocked by his formerly robust father's new frailty. "I got here as soon as I could," he replied.

Later, after Jonathan Longtree had been marched off in handcuffs and paramedics had checked out all the people who'd been held captive, everyone was taken into town via a couple of school buses for a joyful reunion with their family members. Carl, who'd hacked and wheezed and had apparently come down with pneumonia, allowed Rey to drive him to the medical clinic so a doctor could take a look at him. He flat out refused to go to the hospital.

Isla remained by Carl's side, her expression worried. She kept one arm linked through her granddaughter's. Rey, unable to tear his gaze away from Willow, found himself aching to haul her up against him and kiss her until they both couldn't think.

"Willow," Isla finally said, clearly seeing right through him. "I think your young man would like a word with you in private."

Pink-cheeked, Willow met his gaze. "Is that so?"

Heart in his throat, he slowly nodded and held out his hand.

"Go on," Isla urged. "Carl and I will be right here when you get back."

When Willow slipped her slender fingers into his, he felt like he'd already won the jackpot. And yet, he hadn't. He still had something he desperately needed to say and wasn't sure how she'd receive it.

When they walked away from the others, Willow spoke first. "Earlier, you said you loved me. Did you mean that?"

"More than you could ever imagine," he responded. "And I noticed you didn't say you loved me back."

Her gaze flew to his. "I thought I did. But you know I do."

"Maybe," he allowed. "Though I really need to hear you say it."

"I love you," she immediately said. "More than you could ever imagine."

Satisfied, he kissed her again. When they broke apart, he exhaled. "Next, I need to know if you're still planning to go back to California."

Eyes locked on his, she shook her head. "I've been thinking about that for a while. Now that I have my grandmother back, no way am I leaving her again. I'm going to give my boss notice, but I'm hoping he'll let me work remotely."

He kissed her once more, long and deep and passionately, hoping she could feel every bit of the all-encompassing love he had for her.

When they moved apart, he was stunned to see her eyes shiny with tears.

"What's wrong?" he asked, using his thumb to gently wipe them away.

"I love you so much," she said. "I can't imagine living life without you."

Heart full, he pulled her close. "Same here. Now it looks like we won't have to."

Her tremulous smile brought tears to his own eyes. "I see a great future ahead for us," he said, touching his forehead to hers.

"Me too." She sighed. "And now we can go on double dates with Carl and Isla."

He laughed, happier than he'd been in a long, long time. "Yes, we can."

Then, arm in arm, they turned and went back to join the others, ready to start their new life together among family and friends. There might be some loose ends to tie up, but he knew they'd handle it all together.

* * * * *

Christmas Bodyguard

Katherine Garbera

MILLS & BOON

Katherine Garbera is a *USA TODAY* bestselling author of more than one hundred novels, which have been translated into over two dozen languages and sold millions of copies worldwide. She is the mother of two incredibly creative and snarky grown children. Katherine enjoys drinking champagne, reading, walking and travelling with her husband. She lives in Kent, UK, where she is working on her next novel. Visit her on the web at www.katherinegarbera.com.

Visit the Author Profile page
at millsandboon.com.au for more titles.

Dear Reader,

Happy holidays! I'm so excited to bring you the third book in my Price Security series. We are back in Los Angeles this time, and all of the team are involved in helping protect Daphne Amana. She's a human rights lawyer who is working hard to return disputed antiquities to their countries of origin.

I've been obsessed with these stories in the news as well as the lucrative black market art deals and wanted a chance to include both in this book. Kenji and Daphne met when they were too young and too excited about the options in front of them to settle for a relationship. Both of them had a lot to prove to themselves and have managed to do that with long and successful careers.

But life puts them in each other's path again and they are different people now and want that second chance.

I hope you enjoy this book!

Happy reading,

Katherine

DEDICATION

For Rob. Sharing our life together makes
every day an adventure. Love you.

Chapter 1

Daphne Amana was a leading attorney in international rights and criminal law. The company directory at Mitchell and Partners law firm described her as a brilliant mind who handled cases of real international importance. She was pretty sure her boss wouldn't see this as her most brilliant move. But she was out of options, so meeting an informant in a dark alley...well... might not be the safest decision, but it was the only play she had in this case. She was trying to return contested artifacts back to the village of Amba Mariam, the modern home of the Gondar tribe from Ethiopia.

The collection was part of items taken during the 1867 expedition of British and Indian soldiers with the stated aim of freeing British hostages and punishing Emperor Tewodros II and his people. The military assault was a success. Hundreds of items were pillaged by the soldiers, and many were sold at an auction where most of the collection that was housed at the British Museum was acquired. The only rival for its significance was the collection at the Los Angeles Museum of Foreign Cultures, which was donated by the grandson of one of the British soldiers and contained gold and silver regalia, jewelry, weapons and liturgical vessels and crosses from the Ethiopian Orthodox Church.

Daphne became aware of the collection at the Los Angeles Museum of Foreign Cultures when a cultural minister for Ethiopia, Marjorie Wyman, hired her law firm to petition to have the items returned when her discussions with the museum director stalled. Working in international rights gave Daphne a background that made this case one she wanted—no, needed—and she'd asked to be assigned to it. But the director of the Los Angeles Museum of Foreign Cultures, Pierce Lauder, was being difficult, and his attorneys kept asking for postponements of the actual trial that were making the discovery of the items still in the museum's collection difficult.

Daphne had taken the museum to court, gaining a motion to compel them to allow her access to their museum and storerooms, but still they were coming up with excuses for why she couldn't get in to inventory the items. Sure, it was the holiday season. Thanksgiving had been last week, so a lot of people had taken extra time off, herself included, but she could see through the flimsy excuse that Mr. Lauder kept providing.

Especially when the list of items he'd sent over marked several as *missing*. Not stolen or lost, simply missing. She'd gone on a local news show to make the public aware of the contested collection, which had stirred up interest and spawned several public protests, but still, Lauder wasn't returning her calls.

History had always been a passion of hers—the fact that many of the exhibits she'd enjoyed at places like the British Museum were taken as spoils of war had never seemed fair to her. It was part of the reason she'd become an international rights attorney.

The collection was a small one that had come to the Los Angeles Museum of Foreign Cultures by way of Jonathon Hazelton-Measham, who'd been part of the 1867 expeditionary force of British and Indian soldiers led by Sir Robert Napier into Maqdala, an almost impenetrable mountain fortress in northern Ethiopia that was the seat of power for Emperor Tewodros II. Tewodros had established a library and a treasury and dedicated a new church as part of his plan to unite the tribes of Ethiopia and create one united country.

The British had been helping Tewodros, including educating and training his son, when they had a falling out, which resulted in a massive assault on the fortress in 1868. It caused the deaths of hundreds of Tewodros's army with only limited British casualties. After the invasion, there was widespread looting of the fortress and church by soldiers.

Many of the pillaged objects were subsequently reassembled and auctioned. But Jonathon Hazelton-Measham kept the objects he'd collected, which included many items from the new church that had been constructed. The items, or tabots, included a silver censer used to burn incense during mass, a ceremonial cross, two chalices, and processional umbrella tops. He also had several weapons and regalia that were rumored to have come from the fortress. The thirty-nine items that Jonathon looted and brought home with him to England were sold via his descendants to the museum in 1985.

Of the thirty-nine items, the museum claimed that roughly twenty-five were still in their possession. Fourteen items either dropped off their inventory or were currently marked missing.

Her client represented the department of culture for Amba Mariam, the modern day name for Maqdala. The items weren't just in the Los Angeles Museum of Foreign Cultures but also in the British Museum. The bulk of the items still accounted for remained in England at different museums and libraries as well as a museum in Canada, all of which were holding ongoing discussions about their return to Amba Mariam.

Which didn't help Daphne's case. There was no precedent stating that the items should be returned. If the items had been returned in London, that would go a long way to swaying the judge to rule in her client's favor.

However, the recent theft of items by a complicit staff member at the British Museum was helping her with this case. There were only so many places to sell rare antiquities without raising suspicion.

The missing items included one chalice, the silver censer—apparently the brass censer was still in the museum's possession—a piece of regalia not named, two other tabots, and a diptych in a silver case that may have come from a private collection in France, which suggested to Daphne that the thief knew the value of what they were taking. Then there were two manuscripts that were described in the late Hazelton-Measham's will as part of his donation but had been dropped from the museum's inventory in the 2010s before the current director was in place.

It wasn't the monetary value that was at the heart of this case as far as Daphne was concerned. It was the cultural value. Emperor Tewodros II had collected these items from all of the tribes of Ethiopia to unite them into one kingdom.

Apparently there had been flooding at the museum, and some of the pieces had been lost during the evacuation of items. Which wasn't a suitable response as far as Daphne was concerned. Museums were sticklers for cataloging their priceless antiquities. She'd been going round and round with Pierce Lauder and his lawyer, Ben Cross, ever since, trying to figure out what happened to the mysterious missing pieces.

Which was didn't explain why she was sitting in her car at nine p.m., trying to get up the courage to go and meet an anonymous person who had messaged her on WhatsApp, saying that they had information on the missing items.

She'd tried to convince them to come to her office, but they'd been insistent they would only meet her away from both the museum and her offices. She'd suggested a twenty-four-hour coffee shop that she frequented, Zara's Brew on North Hollywood Boulevard. Her informant had agreed to her request, but they wanted to meet behind the shop so they wouldn't be observed.

She was a single woman who could protect herself, but still, this had *bad idea* written all over it. She knew Carl would have forbidden her to do it and probably would have removed her from the case entirely, so she hadn't let anyone know she was here. Which now seemed…well, not like her best idea. So she texted her assistant just to say she was meeting an informant and gave her location. She also held her phone in her hand with 911 ready in case things got dicey.

She left her car and hit the lock button as she walked

toward the coffee shop. The barista on duty had their head down scrolling on their phone, and there were only two diners in the café area. She took a deep breath as she headed around the back of the shop and saw that the alleyway was empty and dimly lit.

Because of course it was. Right?

Pulling the strap of her purse higher on her shoulder, she moved into the alley.

"Hello?" she called.

Stepping further into the alleyway, Daphne cautiously scanned the area. A shot rang out, and she felt the impact of the bullet in her shoulder. There was a sharp burning pain and she bit her lip to keep from crying out. God. That hurt. She hit 911 as she fell to the ground, trying blend with the shadows near the dumpster. She felt woozy and scared, and started the deep breathing exercises she'd learned to keep from passing out because she had a low blood pressure condition that gave her dizzy spells.

"911, what's your emergency?"

She heard the sound of footsteps running away and a thud. Glancing toward the sound, she didn't see anyone.

"I've been shot. I'm behind Zara's Brew. I got hit in the shoulder and am bleeding. I can't see who shot me."

"Stay on the line. I'm dispatching police and ambulance to your location."

Daphne leaned against the dumpster, keeping her legs close to her body, her head tipped back as she held the line. The 911 operator kept talking to her, and Daphne always responded, but she knew she was close to losing the battle to stay conscious. She reached for her purse to get a tissue to apply pressure to her shoulder.

She fumbled when opening it, and some of the contents spilled out on the dirty pavement. After a moment, she found the tissues and pressed one against her shoulder, then put her phone on speaker, setting it on her lap. She glanced around, realizing that her wallet had fallen out.

Placing the bloody tissue on her lap, she reached for the wallet and other items, and she noticed something that looked like a burlap bag with the museum logo on it. She pulled it toward her just as the cops parked at the end of the alley. She shoved the bag into her purse along with her wallet.

"I'm over here," she said.

Two cops came toward her location. One of them was on alert, gun drawn.

"I'm unarmed and injured," she said.

"Don't worry, ma'am, the ambulance will be here in a moment. Where are you hurt?"

"Shoulder," she said. She was starting to slur her words as the pain became too much. Her last conscious thought before she passed out was to draw her purse to her body. "Don't…leave…my…bag…behind."

"I won't. We've got you."

The world faded to black. She was semiconscious of being loaded onto stretcher and transported to the hospital. She was still in pain and still scared, but she knew that whatever was in that burlap museum bag was worth it. After all this time, she might have finally gotten a break in the case that would help her figure out why the museum had stopped talking with her and the cultural minister. What really happened to the missing artifacts?

* * *

Working for Price Security gave Kenji Wada a chance to use the skills he'd honed for nearly a decade in the CIA as a field operative. The job had been exciting, and there had been a few life-and-death moments, which suited Kenji's need for adrenaline rushes. But he'd retired after a case had gone sour. And when Giovanni "Van" Price had offered him a job working as a bodyguard at his elite company, Kenji had said yes.

He was Japanese American, raised by his single American mother. He didn't know much about his Japanese heritage except that his father's family was from a highly traditional background of wealth and status and hadn't approved of her. They hadn't been allowed to marry, so his mom had said deuces to his old man and came back to LA, where she'd raised him. He had been close to his mom from the beginning and had nothing but love and respect for her. But he always had questions about half of his lineage and no one to ask since his mom had died several years ago when he'd been overseas on an assignment. He still missed her.

Something he didn't like to dwell on.

As he waited for the latest briefing at Price to start, he knew that he was going to volunteer for whatever new assignment came up. Didn't matter that it was the start of December. Christmas wasn't his favorite time of year. It had always been a struggle for his mom to buy him presents, pay the bills and keep food on the table. She'd always made the holiday special and since he'd lost her... Christmas just felt empty. If Kenji had his way, he'd work through the holidays. He needed to stay busy and focused on the job. Not his personal life.

The others on the team arrived for the meeting. The Price Security team was small and tight. Van liked to say they were a family, and Kenji did view the other members like siblings. They all got along for the most part but also got on each other's nerves at times.

There were two women on the team. Luna Urban-DeVere was a former MMA fighter, wickedly smart and tough as nails. She was married to multimillionaire Nicholas DeVere, who she met while protecting him. Lee Oscar was the tech genius of their team, and though she had skills with weapons and hand-to-hand combat, most of the time she stayed here in the Price Tower, keeping tabs on the team and providing information to them.

Next was Rick Stone, a former DEA agent who always looked like he was about to fall asleep until there was danger—and then he turned lethal. Then Xander Quentin, a big British bloke who was former SAS and Kenji's best friend. Xander had recently fallen in love with a woman in Florida and was now splitting his time between the East and West Coasts. He had just finished an assignment in New York and was taking time off over the holidays to spend with Obie, his girlfriend.

Last, but certainly not least, there was Van Price. He wasn't that tall, but he was solid. All muscle from the tip of his bald head to his broad shoulders with the tattooed angel wings that peeked out from under his collar.

"We've got a new client. Should be a nine-to-five gig and will be running through the holidays and into January," Van said as he came in. "I know I promised some of you time off, so…"

"I'll do it," Kenji said.

"Mate, I thought you were coming to Florida with me," Xander said as he turned to him. His best friend looked hurt.

Kenji clapped him on the shoulder. "It's more important you go."

Xander bro-hugged him. "Yeah. Thanks for that."

"Depending on where it is, I could do it. Nicholas will be working until Christmas Eve," Luna said.

"I've got this," Kenji said. He needed to be busy, more than anyone else. "Unless I'm not right for the job?"

He looked over at Van, who just gave him that slow smile of his. "You're perfect for it. A local attorney was shot while meeting an informant about a case of potential art theft they're investigating, and her firm wants a bodyguard."

Cakewalk.

"Who is it?"

"Lee? You got the presentation ready?" Van asked.

Lee's fingers moved over the keyboard of the laptop she took everywhere with her, and the presentation flashed up on the screen at the end of the boardroom. But he wasn't listening or paying attention once the photo of the client was shown.

Daphne Amana.

Well, screw him. Of course he'd volunteer to protect the one woman he was pretty damned sure didn't want to see him again. He couldn't tear his eyes away from the screen. She'd matured, of course. It had been nearly twelve years since he'd told her *see ya* and broken up with her.

Her deep brown eyes sparkled with intelligence, and her face was still gorgeous, with high cheekbones and a full mouth. She had long black hair and tanned skin. In the corporate photo, she wore a suit that had been tailored to fit her shape in a way that immediately stirred regrets in him about how he'd walked away from her.

He'd done it because family hadn't been in his plans at twenty-three. He'd known that he wanted the most dangerous assignments the CIA had to offer, and having Daphne in his life would have been a liability. So he'd ended it, never expecting to see her again.

But here she was. Doing the good work she'd always wanted to do and putting herself in danger.

"Kenji?"

"Huh?"

"Mate, you okay?" Xander asked.

No way was he bringing up Daphne. He was the best man to keep her safe. Something Van might not agree with if he was aware of their past.

"Yeah," he said, shaking his head. "I'm good. When does the gig start?"

"Today. Head over to their offices, where you'll meet her and assess the situation," Van said.

"Cool."

The meeting went on with everyone updating the team on their current assignments or being briefed for the next one, but his attention was on his phone, where Lee had sent the case file. Daphne Amana. He wasn't sure this assignment was going to be the distraction he'd wanted. But he couldn't step away now.

Kenji walked back to the elevator to get ready for his assignment. Like there was a way to get ready to see the one woman he'd never really forgotten. He'd had moments when he'd thought of her. Had googled her late at night when he wasn't working or playing *Halo* against Xander online. Despite that, he'd never reached out.

When he walked down the hall, he noticed someone had put Christmas wreaths on his and Xander's doors. Kenji stood there staring at the display of holiday cheer. Christmas was going to be all around him. There was no way around it. At this time of year, he had to just grit his teeth and get through it. Normally work was a good distraction, and one time when X had been off the same time as he was, they'd gone to Aruba, rented a house, and gotten drunk and laid by some gorgeous women at their resort for ten days.

It had been perfect. No sign of Christmas or thoughts of exes or parents—the ones who were around and the one who hadn't ever tried to see him.

He rubbed back of his neck and used the security app on his phone to open the door as he heard the elevator opening. As close as he and X were, he didn't want to talk about Daphne or Christmas.

"Hold up, Kenji," Xander called as he got off the elevator.

"Yeah?"

"Hmm, well, I don't want to overstep, but is something up with you?"

They normally didn't do the intense emotional shit unless they'd both been drinking, when they could pretend that neither of them would remember it. So Kenji knew he must be showing signs of weakness. This was the one time when he shouldn't be.

"Dude," he said. Then realized that he was about to open up big-time, and neither of them wanted that. Also he didn't want to burst X's love bubble. He shook his head and opened his apartment door. He and Xander were the only two with apartments on this floor.

Xander put his hand on Kenji's shoulder and squeezed it. "I'm here if you need anything. Obie's working hard studying for finals, so I'm sort of at loose ends because Van didn't want me to get stuck out on assignment. But…"

Kenji turned and looked at the man who was more like a brother to him than just a friend. Xander was a lot like him. Work kept them grounded. True, Xander had his fiancée now, but that hadn't changed who he was at his core.

"I will. But like Van said, it should be a breeze," Kenji said. Hoping Xander bought it.

His friend just raised both eyebrows. "'Kay, but if it's not, I'm here."

"Thanks."

Chapter 2

Daphne's first day back in the office was three days later, and she was met with lots of sympathy. Carl already had visited her in the hospital and learned she'd been meeting an informant, so he had insisted that they were hiring her a bodyguard. That felt extreme. She was capable of taking care of herself, which she'd pointed out. It was her quick thinking that had kept her alive, even if going at all had been a dangerous idea. But Carl had just looked at her shoulder with a grimace, which was in a sling since the bullet had passed through. She was on strong pain medication, which she was trying to wean herself from because it made her mind foggy.

She'd had a quick look in the burlap sack and immediately recognized it as a censer, but hadn't been left alone long enough to check it against the museum's list of missing items.

She hadn't had a chance to examine the burlap bag and had hoped to today, but she had to be in court at ten and now was going to have a bodyguard with her. Daphne'd tried to argue against it, but Carl had threatened to pull her from the case unless she agreed. So she'd acquiesced.

Carl was fifty-eight but looked more like forty something. His hair had been red when she'd started working for him but now seemed more blond as he'd aged. He had laugh lines around his eyes and was easy to smile and joke with around his staff. Contrasting with his jovial personality, he was surprisingly tall, with broad shoulders and a square jaw. She knew from their annual picnic that he was a pretty decent beach volleyball player. The company game was always highly contested due to the competitive natural of most lawyers.

Back in the day, when he'd still been taking cases to court, he was legendary for his laid-back attitude and easy wit. It was said he could lull the opponent into believing the case would be an easy win. He was also known for charming judges and juries. To be honest, Daphne looked up to Carl and had tried to pick up as many tips from him as she could while she'd been working with him.

He was the main reason she'd accepted the job at Mitchell and Partners. Carl had a strong core of integrity, and his morals were impeccable. He didn't take a case based on how much money a client had or if it would be an easy win the way some firms did. Carl had told every one of his attorneys to only take a case if they were passionate about it.

Which Daphne was about this one. There should never be a world where a country could invade another and just take what they wanted and claim it for their own. There were still so many scars left from the brand of colonialism that scattered these artifacts across the globe. So many wrongs yet to be made right. Daphne worked hard to restore the treasures stolen in those past and forgotten crimes.

She was still ticked about it—her case and her bodyguard—when Kenji Wada walked into her boss's office. Turning away from him to look out the floor-to-ceiling glass windows that lined Carl's corner office, she tried to process this without giving anything away.

Kenji.

He hadn't changed at all based on that one glimpse of him in a fitted black suit, white shirt, skinny tie. He still had that angled jaw and that swoop of black hair that fell over his left eye. The rest of his hair was kept short and neat in the back and on the sides.

"Daphne, this is the bodyguard we've hired from Price Security, Kenji Wada."

She stepped forward, putting on her corporate smile and holding out her right hand. "Nice to see you again."

She wasn't going to pretend they didn't know each other. And as Kenji put his sunglasses in the breast pocket of his suit jacket and took her hand, a shiver of sensual awareness went up her arm and straight to her core. He was still that sexy, hot guy that she'd never really forgotten. But she wasn't twenty-three anymore. Her life was about a lot more than a guy.

"Same."

"Great, you two know each other?"

"Yes, we were in college together," Daphne said.

"Perfect. Then there won't be any awkwardness. I'll let you two get acquainted in your office. Are you still going to court this morning, or are you sending one of your assistants?"

"I'm going. The museum is trying to use my injury

as a reason to delay the evidence hearing, and I'm not letting that happen," she said.

"Of course you aren't," Carl said with a note of pride in his voice.

Daphne walked out of his office, very aware of Kenji following behind her down the hall. When she got to her own office, her assistant wasn't at her desk, but Daphne had asked for some files to be pulled from the archive and suspected that Rae was still down there. Dealing with Kenji alone couldn't be any worse than getting shot. Maybe. She started to go into her office, but Kenji stopped her with his hand on her arm.

She glanced down at the hand and then up into his dark eyes. "Excuse me."

"I have to check the room before you go into it. Stand in the doorway where I can see you," he said as he opened the door and walked into her office, keeping his eye on her as he swept the room.

"This is ridiculous."

"Says the woman with the shoulder injury."

He turned away, and she had to fight the childish urge to give him the finger. She'd gotten in over her head. Knew it even before she'd stepped out of her car to come into work, but this felt…like a punishment. She needed the freedom to go back to the alley and see if more clues had been left behind there.

No one cared about her case as much as she did. It didn't help matters that she was a control freak and really only trusted herself to get things done properly. Not that that belief was remotely true. These cases were the result of a lot of teamwork and expertise, not just her own.

She also really wanted to examine whatever was in the burlap bag and check the inventory of missing items the museum had sent over to see if it was on the list. Having Kenji around would make that nearly impossible. But if she did it right she could go on her own and he'd be close by if she got into trouble…not that she would.

"I'm pretty sure no one is waiting in my own office," she said, leaning against the doorjamb as she watched Kenji move. There had always been a fluidity to his movements. It was hard to keep her eyes off his body and to maintain the façade that she was mad he was making her wait.

The reasons for her anger at him were more than a decade old and very personal. She'd already decided that he was in the past, so she wasn't going to ask him why he'd dumped her the way he had. Even if it would be the perfect time for some karmic retribution. There had been no fights, no waning of the passion between them. Nothing to indicate he'd decided to move on. Just an *I don't think we should see each other anymore* before he packed his things and moved out of their shared apartment.

"I'm going to need to move your desk to that corner, away from the door and window," he said.

"Fine. Do you want some help?"

"I don't think you should strain your shoulder," he said.

She poked her head out of the office and saw one of her new paralegals, Alan Field, walking toward the office. "Can you come help move my desk?"

"Sure." He assisted Kenji with the task. "Glad you're

back. I have some more notes for this morning. I can come back later to discuss them."

"No. Stay. He's just my bodyguard," she said.

Alan paused for a moment then just shrugged. "Okay. Want a coffee before we start?" Alan asked.

"Please. Kenji?"

"Nothing for me," he replied.

Alan left, and she moved into her office. She put her laptop on the work surface while Kenji checked that the plugs were still all working. As she sat down, she wanted to ask him a million questions, but he was treating her like she was a stranger. Probably as he treated all of his clients. Something that she was determined to do, too. She wasn't going to be the one to ask why he'd waited so long to come back into her life.

Luckily she had a case that was way more interesting than Kenji Wada. Or at least, that was what she was going to tell herself. It was only the fact that she'd been shot at in a dark alley that had brought him back into her life. He probably didn't want to be here or see her again.

When Alan came back with Pam, her legal secretary, Kenji stopped them.

"What are you doing?" Daphne asked.

"My job. I need to take photos of everyone who comes into contact with you."

"How is taking photos of my staff your job?" she demanded.

"Someone tried to kill you. I need to rule out suspects and accomplices," he said, keeping it short and succinct.

"Will you back down on this?" she asked, knowing she only had so much energy. This fight wasn't worth it if she couldn't win.

"No."

"Fine, go on with it," she said. "Alan, do you mind being first?"

"Not at all."

The paralegal was young, in his late twenties, and had been on her team only a short time, but he had proved reliable and valuable. He had dark blond hair that he wore short but shaggy on the top, and he always wore a collared shirt and a pair of khaki trousers. Because it was December, he'd started wearing either a hunter green sweater or a Christmas-red one over the shirts.

He also had a short nose and full mouth. He often looked like he was brooding, but Daphne had realized it was just his face. Carl called him the moody one. But Alan's attitude was upbeat and cheery. He'd been the one to bring a Christmas tree into the office, and the day she'd been shot, he'd brought some frosted sugar cookies in the shape of Santa's head in as a treat for them all.

When Kenji asked him to stand against the wall to take his photo, Alan straightened his collar and then looked directly at Kenji. While others might have seemed nervous or unsure, Alan just looked at Kenji as if daring the other man to find something in his background that was less than spotless, which made Daphne want to smile.

But she didn't. The reason he was here was because anyone could be a suspect in her shooting. Kenji as a bodyguard was deadly serious, and she knew that he'd keep her safe, even if some of his methods were a bit extreme.

"If that's all," Alan said to Kenji, who just nodded

and turned to the next person on her team. A line had begun forming outside of her door.

Alan came over to her with that intense expression still on his face. "Daphne, we had pushback from the courts on our request for financial data from the museum. I'm going to spend the morning going through precedent and seeing what I can find. Unless you need me on something else."

"No, that's good. Thanks, Alan."

He nodded and turned away.

She watched him leave and then noticed her legal secretary, Pam Beale, was next. Pam had been with Daphne since she'd come to Mitchell and Partners, starting three months before Daphne herself had been hired, and they'd worked together ever since.

Pam had shoulder-length reddish-brown hair that curled around her heart shaped face. She stood against the office wall, clearly not sure if she was meant to smile or not, her mouth moving in an awkward grin and then quickly dropping back flat.

"You can smile. It's not a driver's license photo, right, Kenji?" Daphne said.

"Yes, smiling is fine…unless you have a booking photo on your record already," Kenji said.

Pam looked horrified. "No. Of course not. I'm not someone who breaks rules."

"He's joking."

Kenji glanced over at Daphne. She just raised both eyebrows at him. As soon as he was done with this, they were going to have a little talk. Being her bodyguard meant he should adapt to her workplace. Not the other way around.

"I am," he agreed. "I'm sure you are a law-abiding citizen."

"Mostly," Pam said worriedly.

Which worried Daphne in turn. "Have you ever broken the law?"

"In eighth grade, I kept a book from my school library, and I still have it at home," Pam said.

Which relieved Daphne. That wasn't a serious crime. "What book?"

"*Forever...* by Judy Blume. My mom wouldn't let me buy it," Pam said. "I did donate to the school library after college."

"I'm not surprised to hear that." Daphne said, holding back a chuckle. "When you get back to your desk, can you please send an email to Marjorie? Let her know that I will be going to the museum tomorrow to compile a list of what they have in their inventory."

"Of course," she said before she left Daphne's office.

Daphne had changed so much, and Kenji didn't allow himself to be distracted by those changes. Instead he focused on the job. Moving her desk was a temporary solution to securing her personal space, but she had people in and out of her office most of the morning. He couldn't do more to protect her until they were alone. Meanwhile, Kenji sent the names and photos of each person who entered to Lee to run a background check on.

She seemed tired and probably in pain, as she'd refused to take her pain medication when her legal secretary, Pam, had reminded her it was time. Was this case personal for her? Was that why she was being so stubborn? He decided he'd do some research into that tonight.

This close, she smelled good, like summer flowers and a hint of spice. Her eyes were dark as she watched him taking photographs, and as always, mysterious. He had never been able to tell what she was thinking. Except when she'd been lying under him after they'd made love.

Then she had relaxed, and he'd seen that wave of love and vulnerability on her face. It had scared him, he admitted, to know that another person cared for him that much. He shook his head to dislodge the thought. Nothing scared him anymore. Nothing.

"I'm done," Kenji said when he'd taken the last photo.

"Great. You need to stop being so brusque. One of the department assistants apparently had an anxiety attack after you took her photo."

"I'd think keeping you safe would be everyone's number one priority."

"Just be nice," she said, turning on her heel and walking back to her desk, where more of staff waited.

Kenji sent more information to Lee. He also pulled Pam to one side and asked her to find a space with no windows for Daphne to use until they found out who had shot her. The other woman agreed. While Daphne went to a meeting with the other attorneys on the Hazelton-Measham collection case, Pam would have Daphne's office moved to the new location.

Daphne wasn't too happy about that as they walked down the hall to the conference room for her meeting. "I understand you're trying to keep me safe, but I would appreciate if you spoke to me next time before having my office moved."

"You have more important things on your mind, and this move is necessary. So an argument with me would have cost you time away from your case and wouldn't have changed the outcome," he pointed out.

She almost smiled. He saw the hint of it in the way the side of her mouth twitched. "Fine."

She started to enter the conference room, but he stopped her. She sighed and leaned against the door, crossing her arms over her middle. "Stay here, right?"

He nodded, trying not to be affected by her full presence. It wasn't just that he was attracted to her—that had been the case since the moment he'd first seen her years ago. It was that he understood her frustration. She was strong and capable, so having someone else direct her moves had to be annoying for her. But Kenji took his job seriously, and he wasn't going to let anything bad happen. Especially to Daphne.

He opened the door and scanned the room from the doorway so that he was next to Daphne. The room was empty of people, with one long table in the middle and chairs on either side. There was a wall of floor-to-ceiling windows, which he'd expected. The room had only one entrance, but was window heavy like most office buildings.

"You should sit here," he said, pointing to the location that he deemed safest and easiest for him to protect. It was at the end of the room with walls on two sides, so that Kenji could see Daphne and the door and watch the windows as well. He couldn't rule out a sniper, even on a higher floor.

"Thanks," she said sarcastically, but then shook her head. "I appreciate what you are doing. I'm just on edge."

"I can tell," he said. "Is this case personal?"

"As much as any of them are. I just hate the sense of entitlement that comes from taking items that have meaning to someone and keeping them for yourself."

"You always did have a thing about stealing," he said.

"Everyone should. If it's not yours, don't touch it," she reminded him.

He smiled then. He had never taken the time to find out why that was a hot-button issue for her. Not that he condoned stealing, but growing up, there were times when he'd been poor enough to contemplate stealing food so that he and his mom would be able to eat. He knew she'd gone hungry to make sure he had meals.

"In a world where things are so uneven, sometimes thievery is a necessity."

"Agreed, but not in this case," she said.

"Can you share the details?" he asked her.

"Maybe later," she said as the door opened.

Two men and a woman walked in, followed by Alan, the paralegal he'd met earlier, and Pam.

"It is so good to see you today," the oldest man said. "We weren't expecting you back in the office so soon."

Kenji lifted his phone to quickly take photos of the new faces. Daphne reached out to stop him, but he stepped aside.

"Forgive the intrusion," Kenji said. "But I need to make sure Daphne stays safe."

"Of course," the man said.

Daphne introduced everyone as he took photos,

which he then sent directly to Lee. The oldest man was Pierce Lauder, the museum director. He looked to be in his early fifties and had probably lived in LA all his life as he was fit and tan and looked really good for his age. The other man was his attorney, Ben Cross, and the woman was their paralegal, Lori. No last name given. But Lee would discover that soon enough.

The meeting started, and Kenji leaned against the corner wall, watching the room and the occupants. He felt the underlying tension in the museum director and suspected the man must be hiding something.

Chapter 3

The pain in Daphne's shoulder was unrelenting, but she was determined to get through the day before she took any more medicine. She needed to be clear-minded for this meeting. Pierce and Ben were being very solicitous, but she couldn't help feeling like they saw her injury as an opportunity to force this case into the new year.

Ben was about ten years older than she was. He'd slowed down the number of cases he took since he'd made partner. His face was slightly fuller with age, but he still had a full head of medium-brown hair that he wore short and spiky. Ben favored dark suits and brightly colored ties.

He was a tough opponent in the courtroom. He seemed to remember every other time he'd been up against her, and he would use anything—especially mistakes she'd made previously—to his advantage. He kept her on her toes normally.

Today, when she was tired and her shoulder still ached, hearing him offer to delay felt like a ploy. She met his blue-green eyes and tried to stare him down to see if he was rattled. Perhaps her injury scared him. He just gave her that tight fake smile that they all seemed to have picked up after years of working in this business as he waited for her answer.

He was from Boston, and rumor had it he'd worked in the district attorney's office before coming to the West Coast. He'd started work at Lawson, Cross and Parker when it was only Lawson and Parker. He'd been hungry to move up, which she could relate to.

That was why she'd taken the appointment at The Hague clerking as one of her first jobs. She'd always had a clear path of where her career would take her. This case was an important next step.

She'd become a lawyer to make the world a more just place, as trite as that might sound. But a case like this one, returning items that had been stolen during colonization, was something that Daphne was passionate about.

So anything that wasn't getting her closer to standing in front of the judge and making her case wasn't on the table, as far as she was concerned.

His client, the Los Angeles Museum of Foreign Cultures, was fighting hard to hold on to the pieces in its collection because they made up the backbone of the museum, which was opened in 1985 after the sale of the Hazelton-Measham collection. Jonathon's descendant, Henry Hazelton-Measham, had donated the entire collection to the museum, and it had drawn a large crowd of people and lots of attention in the press.

Pierce Lauder had a sophisticated look about him, almost like he'd been raised around fine art. She'd had a conversation with Marjorie about him, and she'd mentioned that he was well-traveled and had been to see her at her offices in Amba Mariam more than once.

He understood the global significance of his collection and returning it to Ethiopia, at least from what he said. He wore a tailored suit and always had a tie on when Daphne met with him. His salt-and-pepper hair was cut short and stylish. He always was well put together and his aftershave was subtle, and he had an East Coast accent similar to her mother's. Maybe that was why Daphne always got her back up when he spoke to her. There was something about Lauder that reminded her of her mom and the constant disapproval that she'd always showed toward Daphne.

The deputy director of the museum, Dan Jones, wasn't with Pierce today. The other man was more laid back and easier to handle. If she was being honest, Dan was a lot more malleable. Whenever she called and spoke to Dan, it was a matter of hours before she received the information she requested. With Pierce it could be weeks or months.

There was no way she was agreeing to any delay in this case if Pierce suggested it.

Pierce looked to be about fifteen years older than Daphne was, and she knew that his family had been running the museum since it had opened. It was easy to see that the museum's reputation was closely tied to Lauder's own, or at least, it was in his eyes.

He had other things going on managing his family's money and charitable organizations. But the museum seemed to be at the top of his priority list.

Daphne thought that should have made the other man more willing to work with her and her client. There would be a lot of goodwill generated toward the museum by returning the items to their rightful owners.

Pierce had consistently implied that the collection was safer in Los Angeles. As if the items would be damaged if transferred back to their home country. Something Daphne was determined to avoid at all costs.

"When I heard you'd been shot, my first thought was of concern for you, but also that we should push back the court date and give you time to recover," Ben said.

"I agree with Ben. There's no rush in moving this forward," Pierce seconded. "We can wait until January."

"There is a rush for my client. They have been waiting a long time to bring these important pieces from the Ethiopian Orthodox Church home. You also have ceremonial pieces that they are hopeful to have recovered for Easter next year. I do appreciate your concern for my health, but I don't need a delay," Daphne said. Pam, who sat next to her, smiled.

Her team supported moving ahead with the case. She wasn't going to allow any delays now that she had a piece from the museum. One that she still had to examine. That burlap bag told her something fishy was going on.

"We have already filed with the court to ask for a postponement."

"We will counter-file, insisting things go on as scheduled. To that end, I will be at the museum tomorrow morning at ten to examine the storerooms, as we agreed," Daphne said.

Pierce wrote something on the notepad in front of him, turning it so that Ben could read it. This wasn't the first case of this sort that she'd handled. Most of the time, discussions were enough to ensure that the items were returned to the country they were taken from.

But Pierce had stood his ground, which had forced this case into the court system. Daphne knew that there was more going on than just the museum wanting to keep their display.

To be fair, the exhibit was a rare one in this part of the world. Little was known about the Ethiopian Orthodox Church, and seeing the antiquities on display here was sharing that culture with a wider audience, but it wasn't the museum's culture to share. And Marjorie Wyman had insisted her country wanted their ritual headpieces and altar items retuned.

"I'm not sure I'll be available to show you around," Pierce said.

"That's fine. I have the inventory that Marjorie provided us as well as the records you shared during discovery. The archive numbers should match the boxes in your storeroom, and I need to confirm what items are still in the museum's possession and which ones are missing as you've indicated."

Ben cleared his throat. "The court has given you permission to do so, but we both know this shows a lack of trust in my client. He's been transparent about the items, which he could have listed as stolen. He's not hiding them in the archives."

Daphne wasn't too sure that was the case. It was odd to her that the missing items were ones that had no real pattern. They were all smaller items of the size that would fit in that burlap bag waiting in her shoulder bag back in her office. Some of them had significant monetary value. She hadn't been able to find a pattern in the items listed as missing.

"I never meant to imply that he did. I just need a thorough inventory of what the museum has. Also, several of the items were asked not to be displayed by the cultural minister because of their sacred nature. The tabots from Maqdala are not on public display, so I need to just ascertain their location and condition," Daphne said.

"Of course. As I said, we are happy to accommodate your visit. We do ask that it just be you and not your entire team," Ben said.

Kenji stirred from his position against the wall. "I will accompany Ms. Amana tomorrow."

He wasn't asking, Daphne thought.

"Of course, your safety is important to us," Ben said. "I hope you continue to feel better. I won't be at the museum tomorrow. I'm sure you'll send me your inventory when it's completed."

"Definitely," she said. "Thank you for coming to my offices today and for your good wishes on my health. I'll see you tomorrow, Pierce."

"Indeed."

The meeting ended and the others left the conference room, but Daphne stayed where she was. When she was alone with Kenji, she turned to him.

"What did you think?"

"Lauder isn't being entirely truthful with us. He was nervous, and whenever you weren't looking at him, he sort of glared at you."

"Yeah, he's not happy with me," she said, unable to help the smile on her face. He had been the museum director for over twenty years. From her research, she knew that he'd been successful in keeping most of the contested items in the museum on display and declaring the museum as the owner of them. This wasn't the first attempt at getting them returned. Very few of the exhibits were even on loan. Almost all of them were museum property, which was something that Pierce prided himself on.

"I can see that. The attorney respects you and seems frustrated with the case and maybe your determination."

"Probably. Plus, the last time we went up against each other in court, I won. So there is that," she said. "I'm not sure what I'm looking for, but I just feel like the museum is hiding something."

Kenji nodded. "Tomorrow will hopefully give you some answers."

"Hopefully. I do need a few minutes alone when we get back to my temporary office. Do you think once it's secure you could wait outside?"

She wanted to look into the burlap bag and find out what was in it. She needed to know if she was risking her life for a real clue that could help her find the missing items from the museum's inventory, or if she was just looking for danger where there was none.

"Sure."

Kenji led her back to the new office, which was actually an old storeroom. Daphne didn't mind the smaller space, though. Once she was alone, she gave herself a few minutes to silently cry because of the pain in her shoulder. Then, realizing she didn't have any more meetings for the day, she took her pain medication.

Why was she putting off opening the bag? Was she scared that it would be a stolen object, confirming her suspicions?

But she knew she was. Finally she put it on her desk, positioning her large shoulder bag so that it would block anyone who entered from seeing what was in the burlap sack. She opened it carefully and tipped it until fell out. It was a censer. She recognized it from examining pictures of a similar one that was housed in the British Museum and was also part of a contested collection. This censer had a lid and was made of silver but was smaller than the one in London.

Censers were used for burning incense during liturgical ceremonies. This one was engraved with serpentine motifs, and the main container was engraved with pairs of angels on all four sides.

She touched it carefully. It was exquisite, and she quickly accessed the inventory list on her computer and found that this censer was one of the missing items.

That was it. She had to go back to the alley where she'd been shot. Needed to be sure there weren't more bags like this or maybe some other clue she'd missed. The only problem she saw was getting her bodyguard to agree.

It took her all afternoon to figure out how to do it. Kenji hadn't mentioned their past once, so when it was time to leave, she took a deep breath and turned to him.

"How have you been?"

How had he been? Kenji didn't know where to start, and wasn't even entirely sure what she was asking. She was staring at him, and in this moment, he was very aware that he was her bodyguard and that he probably should clear up anything from the past to ensure this job went more smoothly.

He shook his head, giving a small laugh. "I'm okay."

"You understand what I'm asking, Kenji. I want to

know what you've been up to since we last saw each other," she said.

"I don't think the hallway is a great place for that chat," he said.

"You're right about that. How about we go and get some coffee and talk? It might make the next few days easier."

"Okay," he said.

She started to lead the way, but he pulled her back. "Next to me or behind me."

"This is so hard. I'm not used to following anyone."

Of course she wasn't. As they got to the elevator, he checked the inside and then gestured for her to get on with him. "It is an adjustment. You seem…in less pain. Did you take your medicine?"

"I did," she said. "I'm not just being difficult about that. It clouds my mind, and like I said to you earlier, I suspect Pierce is hiding something."

"I'm glad you were able to take it," he said. He had nothing else to add about Lauder at this moment. He'd asked Lee to do one of her deep-dive background checks on everyone involved in the case. Lee had worked for a government agency on an elite task force. She'd been the computer geek assigned to the team—her words, not his. She was just really good at finding things on the internet that no one wanted found.

"So, I guess you can just follow me in your car," she said.

"Nope."

"Nope? Kenji—"

"I'm your bodyguard, Daphne. That means keeping you safe. I'll drive," he said. "You can pick the coffee shop."

She frowned at him. "I was planning to."

He wasn't going to defend his decision. He suspected she knew that, because although she didn't seem happy about it, she walked beside him and then got into his car when he opened the door.

His car was a special model that everyone at Price Security drove on jobs. It was bulletproof and had GPS tracking and a cache of weapons in the trunk to cover all eventualities. Kenji was used to driving it, so he knew the car like the back of his hand, which would prove useful if he needed to do any defensive driving.

"Where to?" he asked when he got in.

"You've changed a lot," she said instead of giving him an address.

"You have, too," he said.

She gave him the address and then sat back into the leather passenger seat as he drove to the coffee shop she'd selected. The traffic wasn't too bad this time of night, not that it was ever quiet in LA.

Zara's Brew wasn't a place that he was familiar with, so he was on guard as they exited the car and walked into the coffee shop. It was set up like a diner with a bar along one wall and booth tables that ran along the windowed front of the building, with two additional booths in the back. One was near the hallway that led to the bathrooms. The one in the corner would offer Kenji a clear view of the door and hallway.

He selected that table and directed Daphne to it. "What do you want? I'll get it."

"Decaf latte and a muffin," she said.

"What kind?" he asked. What he really wanted to know was when she'd switched to decaf. When they'd been dating she'd drank six cups a day and would hold out her mug in the morning asking for that first cup so she could face the day. Also, why this place? It was large and well-lit. Hard to protect from the inside if her shooter came back. The glass didn't look bulletproof. Which he guessed was a good thing. Maybe crime wasn't that high in this area.

"Whatever they have. I'm not choosy," she said.

He waited until she was seated with her back to the wall and then walked over to the counter to order. He got a black double espresso and then carried their drinks and her snack back to the table.

The booth was a bit of a problem. He wanted to sit next to her to block her from the main room, but he knew he needed to be across from her to see the hallway and front entrance. At least he was a really good shot, so there was a chance he could hit anyone who came at her.

For now, it would have to do. He was on his guard as she took a delicate sip of her latte and then looked up at him.

"So…"

Dammit. She wasn't going to let the past drop. He knew that she had a right to ask questions, and he didn't mind giving her answers. But that didn't mean he wanted to give them right now, when learning about her could rattle him and jeopardize their safety. However, he'd always done what was best for his client, and having Daphne trust him was paramount for her safety. That clearly meant she needed closure about their past.

Chapter 4

The interior of the coffee shop was all paneled light brown wood. It had graffiti art on the far wall that had different coffee sayings from movies. Somehow she'd missed that the last time she'd been here.

Well, to be honest, she hadn't exactly come in. Just glanced into the main restaurant, realizing that they'd been about to close after a late night in the office.

There were the standard espresso and coffee machines behind the counter. A glass cabinet that usually held pastries was empty this time of the day. But the chalkboard behind the counter advertised an array of fresh pastries and sandwiches.

Christmas music played low in the background. "White Christmas" came on, and she grimaced. If there was one song she hated, it was that one. She knew a lot of kids grew up dreaming of a snow-covered holiday, but for her, a snowy Christmas meant she'd be trapped inside with her mom.

Her mom wasn't abusive physically, but she'd been so emotionally withdrawn, and after several days, she would start to get mean toward Daphne. Then Daphne's father would suggest she go visit her grandparents until school started back. Which had been a welcome relief. They'd always been happy to see her and spoil her at their little condo in Boca Raton, Florida. It had been shitty flying alone as a kid just after Christmas, and the airports were a hassle, but when she'd got off the plane, Nanny and Poppa had been waiting.

The only Christmas she'd ever dreamed of was warm and sunny and spent lying on the beach. Sadly her grandparents were both gone, but luckily, in Los Angeles, Christmas wasn't snowy, and her dad came to spend the holiday with her some years. Not this year, though—he'd started dating Carmen, and they were going on a cruise since Daphne had thought her case would keep her busy until New Year's. Carmen was warm and kind and always talked to Daphne and not at her. Which was something she was getting used to. It was also a bit of a shock to see her father smiling as often as he did now.

She'd borne the brunt of her mother's ire, but she'd been unpleasant woman and hadn't made Daphne's dad's life easy either.

The song switched to Mariah Carey's "All I Want for Christmas Is You" just as Kenji had made his way back to her, and her heart beat a little bit faster. It would be a lot easier to deal with her ex back in her life if he'd somehow gotten less attractive to her.

Daphne had to tear her eyes from his lean, muscled frame. She'd seen him in action before. Would he still be as fit as he'd been back then? God, she hoped so. She wasn't sure if she was still in danger or not, but if she was going to be saddled with a bodyguard, he'd better be able to defend her.

How had her mom managed to hate someone as much as she'd hated Daphne? Not that she wanted to be anything like her mom, but it would make life a lot easier if she wasn't so hot for Kenji right now. Hating him would at least keep her focused.

She could tell that he wasn't really interested in telling her much about his past. Even when they first dated, he'd always been the strong, silent type. But he'd agreed to come, and she wanted to know what had happened to the boy-man she'd loved all those years ago. He was still hot as hell, but essentially a stranger. A stranger she was going to have in her back pocket for the foreseeable future. Getting to know him made sense. It would hopefully also give her some ideas on how to slip past her bodyguard when she needed to. More importantly, if he opened up a little, it would let her know if she could trust him with more information about the case.

"Kenji?"

He shrugged, looking down into his double espresso. He'd always been wired and drank massive amounts of caffeine. Interesting to see that hadn't changed.

"I don't know what to tell you."

"Start with the CIA. Did you stay with them?" she asked. They'd met when they'd both been recruited by the CIA after finishing their undergrad. It had been a sunny May day when she'd sat down in the testing room and first noticed him. Kenji had been serious and focused. They'd both gotten top marks, and by the end of the testing day, both had been asked to start in the recruitment program.

Daphne liked analytics, but some of the other training like sharpshooting and hand-to-hand combat wasn't up her alley. After a few weeks, she'd dropped out of the program, she'd gone to law school and eventually started dating Kenji. Until he'd come into their shared apartment six months later and broke up with her, packing his duffel bag and two boxes and leaving.

"Yeah, for almost ten years. I can't share the details of that," he said.

"Was it what you'd hoped it would be?" she asked.

He took a sip of his espresso. "Yeah. What about you? Ten years at this law firm?"

Interesting that he was deflecting, she thought. "Yes. Before that, I had a judicial clerkship at the International Court of Justice. I was offered a position in The Hague working as a judicial assistant, but I turned it down. I missed the US and wanted to come home."

He tipped his head to the side, studying her. She wondered what he was thinking, what he saw when he looked at her. She remembered those long, lazy summer days when they'd first gotten together. They'd spent hours with her reading a book for one of her courses, lying on Kenji's lap, while he played a first-person shooter video game. His hand would drift to her hair as he played.

Mentally she gave herself a hard smack. She needed to stay focused. She had a plan and intended to stick to it. Distract Kenji—not herself!

"What about you?" she asked. "Why did you leave the CIA?"

"I...don't want to sound arrogant, but I did everything I could with them. I'd had a lot of excitement and completed a lot of assignments that I hope made the world safer. But it was starting to feel like a job, and— don't laugh—a boring one at that," he said wryly.

She shook her head, smiling over at him. "One thing you hate is boredom."

"You know it. I was doing some freelance bodyguard and security assignments when Giovanni Price invited me to join his team. I said yes."

"Why?"

"I guess part of it was down to Van. I like the man, and I like the work I do for him. I'm not guessing if my skills are actually helping someone like I used to. I know they are. We have a tight, small team, and it suits me," he said.

She could tell that it did. There was something about him that was more relaxed than it had been back then. He was still tense in a way, but more measured. Kenji had always been on guard, watching everything and everyone. Daphne had believed then that nothing could catch him off guard, and she saw that he'd honed that energy into a solid strength now.

Which made her realize that in this whole time she'd been cataloging Kenji's changes, she was still no closer to figuring out how to get to the alleyway. More questions, she thought. There was a lot more she wanted to know about him.

"Where are you based?"

"LA. Though I do a lot of work overseas," he said. "What about you?"

"Same. I have a house in Bel Air." Being an international lawyer at Mitchell and Partners law firm paid pretty well and she had some family money she'd inherited.

"I know."

"You do? Have you been checking me out, Kenji?"

His face got serious for a moment. "Your address

came with the client profile. But I did look you up when I retired from the CIA."

Surprised, she wasn't sure how to respond to that. "Why didn't you contact me?"

"Your life seemed very focused, and I was proud of the success you'd achieved. I figured the last thing you needed was a man from your past."

"You mean a man who left without an explanation."

He shrugged, looking down at his espresso again. "Maybe."

"Why?"

Damn. She hadn't meant to ask that. To seem so hurt. But she had anyway, and she definitely wanted the answer now that the question was out there. It didn't matter that she'd told herself the personal questions were to distract him. Maybe she subconsciously chose to bring him here, to use this strategy, to ask that very question.

She'd never understood how he'd left. There had been no cooling of the passion, no fights or silences between the two of them. In fact, they'd been getting closer, and she'd thought that they would be partners for life. Until that day.

Her gut had never been so wrong before, and she hadn't really trusted it since.

"That doesn't matter. It won't change the past," he said.

"Of course not. But it might help me trust you," she said, using the same level tone she used when she had a difficult witness on the stand. "You're asking me to trust you with my life. Something that's not an easy ask. I thought I knew you, Kenji, and you walked away like I was nothing to you."

He put his hands on the table and leaned across it, closer to her. "You were never nothing to me."

Knowing she would probably bring this up, he'd rehearsed a few answers in his head, but the truth was, he couldn't tell her why he'd left. He'd been a young man with dreams that hadn't included the way she'd made him feel. He'd never really allowed himself to believe that he'd have a family one day. He'd had his mom, of course, but she'd passed away, and then he had no one. He'd always thought that remaining alone would make life easier. But it hadn't.

The truth of why he'd left the CIA was that he hadn't really liked the man he'd become when he'd worked for them. The longer he stayed, the more of his humanity he willingly gave away. He'd seen the worst side of people, and not just in one country or one people but in all of them. He had become jaded and lifeless.

Working for Price Security had given him back a little part of his soul. His friendships with the team, especially Xander, were strong, and he cared for them. Probably for the first time in his life, he felt like he had a family he could count on and a place where he belonged.

But he definitely wasn't going to tell her that.

"It didn't seem that way," she said. "I'm not going to lie to you. The way you left made me question everything I thought I knew about people."

Her words hurt him, because that hadn't been his intent. He had no way of really telling her that he'd been too excited for the possibility of saving the world. Being a hero, and proving to that faceless man who'd fathered him that he'd made a mistake when he'd walked out of Kenji's life. Stupid, but that was the truth.

As much as he'd cared for Daphne back then, there was no way he was giving up on that drive to prove himself. So talking about this now wasn't going to make her feel better about the past.

"I'm sorry."

"I know you are. You told me before you left. You never meant to hurt me," she reminded him.

"I didn't."

"I guess that's really all there is to say about the matter," she said. "I was surprised to see you today. Was there no one else at your company available?"

"I volunteered," he said.

"Oh. You're confusing me, Kenji…but then, you often did."

"I don't mean to. I was free, and Xander, the other bodyguard available, had planned to go to Florida to spend Christmas with his girlfriend."

"So you made sure he could. That's really nice of you," she said.

There was a distance in her voice that he probably deserved. He wished it was easier to convey that he still cared about her. He wanted to resist the attraction between them but still needed to know as much as he could about her life.

"Once I saw it was you, I wanted the assignment."

"Okay."

"Don't be like that," he said. He knew he hadn't made things better between them. But when had talking ever helped him? He was a man of action. Give him a tense situation and he shone. Guns and evasive maneuvers were easy to control, much easier than figuring out the right thing to say.

Daphne was the opposite. She used words as a weapon and a shield. He'd witnessed her doing just that during her meetings throughout the day. This was an uneven battle. Odd—he hadn't realized that they were adversaries until this moment. He'd thought they were getting reacquainted, but now he could admit that there was more going on here. She wasn't as blasé about him as she'd appeared all day.

He made too many assumptions where she was concerned. Maybe he should have let Xander take this client. Daphne was stirring things in him that he hadn't realized he still felt. God, he truly hated emotions. Why couldn't she just be an ex that he had fond memories of?

But he knew the answer. She'd never been just a woman from his past. He hadn't just looked her up when he'd retired. He'd spent a few weeks shadowing her and checking out her life. Looking for…some way back in. But this urbane, sophisticated woman really didn't need a man like him by her side, something that had been very clear to him.

Which was probably why he'd taken this job, looking for some kind of way out of the unsettling emotions she brought to life in him that he'd never been able to shake.

His phone buzzed in his pocket. Kenji glanced at his watch, which notified him that it was a call from Van. He couldn't ignore it.

"I have to take this call," he said.

"Feel free. I'm going to the bathroom," she said as he answered the call.

He nodded. He could see the hallway from his seat and assumed there wasn't a back exit.

"This is Wada."

"Kenji, my man, how's it going?" Van asked.

"Fine."

"Wanted to let you know that Lee found something but hasn't finished running it down. She wanted me to pass on to you to watch your back and not trust anyone at the law firm."

"Thanks. Anything else?"

"Not now."

"Bye."

He ended the call. A shiver of worry went down his spine. All day today, Daphne had been protective of the people who worked with her. The fact that Lee had something on one of them concerned him. Convincing Daphne to keep her guard up would be hard. She always led with her emotions.

That was part of why he'd left. He hadn't wanted to hurt her with the reality of how people were. She trusted everyone. Life had proven to him that people never lived up to that trust. It had put Daphne at risk.

What was taking her so long?

He got up and walked toward the hall, noticing the emergency exit door.

Dammit.

Had someone been waiting for her?

This was why he shouldn't have been answering personal questions and letting his guard down. He wasn't going to lose Daphne. Not like this.

He pulled his weapon from his shoulder holster as he crept down the hall. He opened the unisex bathroom door, which wasn't locked, and confirmed that Daphne wasn't in there.

They he continued further down the hall, opening the emergency door, which didn't trigger an alarm. The alleyway was dark and full of shadows. He glanced both ways, unable to see Daphne.

Daphne took a deep breath before she stepped out into the alley. The conversation with Kenji had been a double-edged sword, cutting both ways. What had she expected? Relationships had never been easy for her, and the one with Kenji had been more complicated than she should have ever allowed it to be.

But this case had brought him back into her life, and the sooner she had the information she needed on the missing artifacts, the sooner she could put this case before the judge and get him back out of her life.

No more asking personal questions.

As if she would be able to keep from wanting to know more about him and to possibly understand the flaw inside her that had caused him to leave. It wasn't like she was hopelessly flawed in other things. In her work, she thrived. She was sought-after by big clients and countries who knew she'd get justice for them.

Which was what she was determined to do for Marjorie Wyman and her country. Kenji would be dealt with later.

Carefully she opened the door and stepped out into the alleyway. It was a bit earlier than when she'd been here the last time but still shadowy and dark as the nights grew longer. Taking her phone from her pocket, she turned on the flashlight function and stooped down to where she'd found the burlap bag.

She noticed blood spatter on the ground. Hers? She remembered hitting her head on the edge of the large dumpster and seeing some dark blood spatter stains from the bullet that had gone through her shoulder on both the dumpster and the ground.

Moving slowly and being very careful to look at every possible place, she noticed more dark spots on the ground, closer to where the bag had been tucked. Daphne took a night mode photo of the ground with her phone to examine later.

It was growing even darker, and she'd taken another dose of her pain medicine before she'd left work, so her mind wasn't as sharp as it usually was. Maybe that explained her asking Kenji why he'd left her. She shoved that thought out of her head.

She heard something—or someone—at the end of the alley and flicked off the flashlight as she crept around the corner of the dumpster, moving back against the wall.

Holding her breath, she waited to see who was coming. Maybe the person she'd been about to meet was coming back? Whoever had dropped the burlap bag with the censer in it wasn't going to just leave it abandoned here. Not for long. That censer was valuable, and unless Mr. Lauder was going to report it as missing— which he hadn't done so far—the museum was going to need it back in the collection by tomorrow when she came to examine the items.

She peeked around the edge of the dumpster but couldn't see anyone. Daphne stepped further away from the restaurant, focused on the end of the alley where the shot had come from the other night. And where she'd thought she'd heard something a few moments ago.

Her heart was racing, and she was scared, but also angry. Angry at herself for putting herself in danger again, but angry at Kenji for making her not trust him, forcing her hand to do this one on her own.

Doing things on her own was what she did, so she was used to it. But this time it might have been better if she'd been able to trust him and include him on this. Although she didn't really trust anyone except her clients.

Standing, she continued moving carefully as she got closer to the end of the alleyway, where she realized that there was a chain-link fence and no way out. They could have climbed out but would have had to wait until she wasn't looking in that direction. Had the person who shot her watched her on the ground? Had they hoped she'd bleed out before help arrived?

That actually creeped her out a little bit. Believing her assailant had shot her and run had been different than this. This meant he'd been close and hadn't finished her off. Had watched her and possibly had waited until the cops had arrived and then snuck away, as if basking in her suffering. Had she seen him that night and not noticed?

Also, it didn't escape her that she was referring to the assailant as *him*, but it could easily have been a woman. She'd been groggy when the cops arrived, finally feeling safe enough to let herself drift off. Had she missed something?

A hand came down on her good shoulder. She

screamed, hoping Kenji would hear her, and brought her knee up, hoping to hit the person behind her with a solid jab. But as she turned, she saw that thick fall of black bangs and those angled cheekbones.

Kenji.

"What are you doing out here?" he demanded, pushing her back against the wall and using his body as a shield.

"Never mind. I think I heard someone."

He pulled her down, pushing her toward the dumpster again. She was becoming really familiar with this part of the alley.

"Stay low and stay hidden."

He had his weapon secure in one hand as he moved away from her. He made a visual sweep of the area before he shifted down the alleyway, a short distance to the fence she'd noticed earlier, then came back.

"Get up. There's no one here now."

She struggled to stand, probably thanks to her meds and panic. Kenji offered his hand, which she reluctantly took. Once she was on her feet, he boxed her in again with the wall against her back. His hand came up to her jaw, and he turned her face until their eyes met.

"You might not like me, but this was stupid and dangerous. The threat to you is real."

"I know that."

"Sneaking off is a good way to get yourself killed. You're smarter than that. What were you doing?" he demanded.

She swallowed, and the adrenaline that had kept her fear at bay waned. She blinked a bunch of times to keep from crying—not that the danger was over. He clearly

wanted to know what she was doing, but she wasn't ready
to tell him. Not when it could put her case in further
jeopardy.

So instead, she put her hand on his face and then
leaned up, brushing her lips over his and kissing him.

Chapter 5

She tasted better than he remembered. And that was saying something, because when he wasn't working and he let himself remember, he always drifted back to the past and those moments in her arms. There was a familiarity to the way her body fit against his. He held her closer because she'd scared him running off like that, and for the first time on the job, he was very afraid he might not be able to keep her safe.

He deepened the kiss. Because it was Daphne, and he wanted even a small taste of the passion that had always sizzled between them, but then he broke it off as his body started to relax. He stayed vigilant though they were still in unguarded surroundings. The smell of the dumpster next to them was a reminder that he was on the job.

That his client wasn't safe and had done something stupid and risky. He wouldn't compound the problem by letting his hormones take over. Careful of her injured shoulder, fighting to keep his body under control, he put his arm around her and led her back to the emergency entrance of the coffee shop. The door wasn't locked from the outside.

Something he should have checked earlier, but he hadn't anticipated trouble here. Rookie mistake.

Once they were inside, he pulled the door closed and led her out of the coffee shop and back to his car. She was shaking and visibly pale as he came around and got into the car next to her.

"Daphne—"

"I'm sorry. I really didn't think this through. Any of it," she said.

"Tell me what you were doing out there," he demanded. Trying to tell himself she was safe and that he wouldn't fuck up again, but he doubted it. Had his twenty-three-year-old self known this? Had he simply forgotten the effect being around Daphne had on him?

"Well, you know I was meant to meet an informant the other night when I got shot."

He kept his level stare on her, just raised his eyebrows, waiting for her to go on.

"It happened in the alley behind this coffee shop," she said.

"You should have mentioned that," he told her.

"I know." She rubbed her forehead with her injured arm and he saw her fail to hold back a wince.

He knew she was in pain, and he should go harder on her about this. She could have gotten herself killed by running off. She needed to start thinking of the consequences. "It's dangerous for you right now. I'm here to protect you. Not judge you. If you needed to go back for some personal reason, that's fine. Let me check it out and keep you safe."

She nodded. "There's more, but I think I should explain it when we are back at my place."

"Sure," he said. He wasn't certain of what else she had to tell him, but right now, he wanted to get away from this street and the scare they'd both had. He'd gotten lucky that no one had been waiting for her. They both had been lucky.

He followed her directions and drove to her place. The radio quietly played as he navigated the streets of LA, and he heard the first notes of "Thrift Shop" by Macklemore. A throwback. He glanced over at Daphne. A smile played around her lips. This song had been playing on repeat at lunch in the cafeteria when they'd first started hanging out. Even before they'd hooked up, she'd called it their song.

She reached over and turned the volume up, starting to sing along. He sang with her. It was a safe release of tension for them.

Letting someone else watch over her wasn't the solution. He was going to have to man up and put his feelings for her aside. Except when she laughed as the song ended and gave him that soft look, similar to the one on her face when she'd kissed him, he knew that wasn't going to be easy.

He pulled into the drive of her house. "This is a nice place."

"Thanks. I worked hard for it. My dad thinks it's too big for one woman, but I like it."

He had never met her parents. She'd never mentioned them when they were together, and this sudden realization reminded him of how little they actually knew each other. They'd been so young that love and sex had seemed like it would be enough, and when he'd felt the pull of the excitement of being an elite agent for the CIA, he'd left before they could go deeper.

"Never mind what he said. You get to choose how you spend your money."

It was something his mom had said once when he'd felt guilty about buying a new game for his Game Boy. He'd promised to return it so they could use the money to pay for food. She told him it wasn't his responsibility to pay for food for them. Something he hadn't agreed with her on, yet she'd wanted him to have a childhood and not be her mini-man all the time. But that was the past, and he was here with the only other woman he'd ever allowed himself to care for. And she still hadn't told him about everything going on. He needed to rectify that before she pulled him in even further.

"Let's go in so you can tell me *everything*," he said.

"Okay. You said you wouldn't judge," she reminded him as they walked up the paved path to her front door, which was dark.

"You should have a security light that comes on, or leave on the front light if you're coming back late," he said to her.

"I always do."

He stepped around her and moved closer to the entrance, catching that the front door was slightly ajar.

"Go get in the car, lock the doors and call 911."

"What are you doing?"

"Making sure there's no one still inside," he said. "Go."

His adrenaline was pumping, and he was almost hoping there was someone in the house so he could have a fight or at least chase them. He watched Daphne as she went back to the car and waited until she was inside with the doors locked. The car was bulletproof, and unless someone fired at it with multiple automatic weapons, she'd be safe in there until he got back.

Even knowing that Kenji could handle himself in any situation, Daphne was tense the entire time he was in the house. She called 911 and felt a bit foolish doing it again so soon. She'd never had to use the service, and now she was becoming a frequent user. Like did they have a stamp card—every fifth call to 911 got you a special mug? They dispatched police to her house and advised her to get Kenji out of the building and someplace safe.

That wasn't happening. She'd seen the look on his face when he'd realized someone might be inside. There was no making that man stand down, and she knew it in her bones.

Believing in his skills was one thing, but her heart was still pounding until he appeared back in the doorway and returned to his car. He unlocked it as he got close and slid into the driver's side. "It's empty, but someone rifled through your stuff."

"What?"

"Yeah, it's trashed. We'll wait for the cops so they can fill out their report. I need to call my boss and keep him up to date. You good?"

Good?

"No. I'm the opposite of good, Kenji. You scared the crap out of me in the alleyway, which I totally deserved, but still. I was hoping to get home and maybe have a relaxing bath and rest my shoulder after a long day. Instead, my home is…" Her voice cracked, and she stopped talking.

She sounded like she was losing it. She *was* losing

it, she thought. Totally had enough of this day. She was tired and achy and scared and—

Kenji pulled her gently into his arms. Her mind stopped running in circles as she put her head on his shoulder. The familiar scent of his aftershave and the warmth of his body were reassuring in a way that the strong, independent woman she was didn't want to admit, but she soaked up every second of it.

She let herself cry for a minute and then wiped her eyes and sat up. "Thank you."

"It's been a day, hasn't it? I'm sure seeing me wasn't what you were expecting. At least I knew I'd see you," he said.

"Yeah, that was unexpected. I didn't even know you were back in the States, much less in LA."

His face was stone cold, and she couldn't read his expression but she could tell that he was determined.

"Let me check in with my boss," he said again.

He was on his phone talking quietly, and she listened as he related everything that had happened when they got to her house. He left out the coffee shop and their alley encounter. Which she was grateful for. She was scared. Whoever had contacted her had either been setting her up or had been injured or killed and had left the item for her. She still had a lot to figure out.

She was tired, and the effects of her pain meds were wearing off. She really hadn't been kidding about wanting a bath and some time to think. Just to feel safe. Safety was something she'd taken for granted and shouldn't have.

Justice had always been the one thing she put her faith in, and this case was about righting an injustice that had been dragged out for too long. The spoils of colonialism weren't something she took lightly, and if she could continue to make a difference, she would.

She was lucky this was the first time that someone tried to fight back outside the courtroom.

"Okay. Bye," Kenji said.

He pocketed his phone, turning toward her. The play of light and shadows over his face made his cheekbones seem even sharper, and she regretted that she hadn't touched him more during that ill-advised kiss she'd initiated.

"Is there anything you are hiding?"

What? She had mentioned needing to talk to him, but she wondered for a moment if he knew about the small burlap bag in her big purse. God, she hoped not. She wanted to trust him. Had been hoping that she could share the burden of this item she'd found with someone so she could discuss it and figure out how to use it to find the other items missing from the inventory.

She was also very aware that she should have turned the bag over to the authorities days ago. Kenji might question her motives for not doing that.

"Hiding?"

"Don't be cagey. You are too direct to pull it off. You said you had more to tell me, and your house has been broken into…so I'm asking you again if there is anything I should know before the cops get here."

He was so calm about it. "I found something the night I was shot, and I haven't had a chance to disclose it yet."

"What is it?"

Red and blue lights flashed around the car before she

could answer. "Something related to my case. Nothing criminal."

And it wasn't, technically. She'd found the censer, and she definitely planned to turn it over to the cops… once she had a chance to document it. Holding on to it as long as she had might make the cops unhappy, but there was no inherent criminal activity.

"Okay. We'll talk when they leave. For right now, keep that to yourself," he said.

"I was planning to," she said wryly.

"Stay here until I've checked their badges."

Kenji gave her a side-eye look as he opened his door and met the cops. Once he was sure they were legit, Kenji asked her to get out. Together with the cops, they went into her house.

She let out a gasp when she saw the damage to it. Paintings had been ripped from the walls. Cushions had been knifed clean open and stuffing spilled out on the ground. Nothing had been left untouched in her entire home. But oddly, her jewelry had been left behind, and she had some pricey pieces that had been left to her by her paternal grandmother.

Officer Martinez and his partner were very thorough as they searched her house for intruders. Martinez was the lead, she guessed, and the one who talked to her. He was young, in his late twenties, and wore an LAPD uniform. He had kind brown eyes and kept apologizing for asking her questions about what was kept in each of the cabinets, drawers and jewelry boxes that had been turned over.

Daphne struggled to hold her emotions in. Her shoulder still ached, but she wasn't a woman known for crying. Not that there was anything wrong with women's tears. But right now she just wanted to power through her house. Trying to be objective wasn't as easy as she had hoped it might be.

"I know this is a lot. You can write up a detailed list of anything missing and bring it by the station in the next day or so," Martinez said, pocketing the notebook he'd been holding.

"I might do that," she said, but he kept moving into the other rooms of her house. "Is there a reason you're still checking the rooms?"

"Just being thorough. We already made our observations, but you might see something we missed. A detail that might help us find the criminals."

"Like what?"

"A threatening message or something that only you'd recognize," Officer Martinez said. "Sorry to be vague, but usually it's a know-it-when-you-see-it kind of thing."

Daphne understood where he was going with it. Her house was wrecked, and there was no way the cops would know what belonged and what didn't. If there was any clue in this mess, she wanted it in their hands so they could find who did this.

But after continuing through the other rooms, she soon realized there wasn't anything but her belongings treated like trash as they'd been dumped on the floor and trampled on.

"They were looking for something," Kenji said.

"Do you know what?" Officer Martinez asked Daphne.

"I'm not sure. I have two big cases right now, but all of the evidence and files for them are kept at my office," she said.

"It's clear someone believes you have something of value. Hiring a bodyguard was a good idea. Do you have a place to go that isn't widely associated with you?"

"No. I mean, my dad lives in New York," she said. "I can't leave the state right now. Not with my caseload. I'm not willing to be the reason why there is a further delay in this case."

"Of course. There is a concern with this second attack that you are being targeted by someone sympathetic to the defendants in your museum case.

"She will be relocating to Price Tower," Kenji said, and gave the cops the address. "You can reach her through me."

He also provided his contact details. The officers just took his word that she'd go with him. It was almost comical. She was going to because she wasn't an idiot, and putting herself at risk of murder just to stay in her home was ridiculous, but she was also used to making her own choices and decisions.

Irritated at him, and more than likely just at the situation in general, she wanted to lash out at someone. Instead, she found herself standing in the middle of her ruined living room, listening to Kenji talk to the cops.

Officer Martinez left Kenji and the other officer to come over to her. He gave her a kind smile. "It's okay to be overwhelmed. You've been through a lot."

"Thanks."

"You should take a few days off from work. Give us time to find out who broke into your place and shot you."

"Thank you, but I can't."

He reluctantly nodded. "I understand. Do you have the police report for the night you were shot?"

"I do. It's in my purse in the car. I can't remember the name of the officer I spoke to."

"That's understandable. Most people don't. We can get it when we all leave," Officer Martinez said. He turned toward his partner before looking back at her. "Sorry about your Christmas tree, by the way."

She glanced over at the prelit tree lying on its side on the floor. The decorations were shattered, and she'd tried not to look at the mess it had become this whole time. Since she'd been on her own, she attempted to create a kind of Christmas that worked for her every year. Something that would give her a chance to be happy on the holiday without flying to Florida. Cass, her best friend and a fellow lawyer at Mitchell and Partners, had come over with her husband on the Saturday after Thanksgiving this year, and they'd helped her decorate it.

Now it was smashed on the floor, and she was trying not to see that as an omen. But in her heart, she was a fatalist. She saw signs everywhere.

Kenji coming back into her life was certainly one. She'd put herself in a dangerous situation, so that much was on her, not fate. He was only here because of that. No matter what they'd discussed at the coffee shop. Nostalgia could only go so far.

Her life was…well, her *personal* life wasn't much different than this hot mess of her house. She tried to do things that would make that part of her life more normal, but it seemed the harder she tried, the more she failed.

"It's okay," she said, realizing she hadn't responded to Martinez lost in herself.

Then she saw one of the ornaments had rolled close to where she was standing, and she bent to pick it up.

Turning it over, she saw it was a tiny picture frame, one that had a photo of her and her dad. She tucked it into the pocket of her jacket.

"I've spoken to my boss, and he is going to send a team over to clean this up and restore everything," Kenji said.

"I didn't know the bodyguard service covered that," she said.

"It does this time," Kenji said.

"Is it your boss footing the bill or you?" she asked.

"Does it matter?" he countered.

"Kenji."

"It's taken care of. I've never been here before and I am… I don't like seeing your house this way. Having it cleaned won't make this memory go away, but the next time you are here, at least it will all be sorted out."

She reached into her pocket and ran her finger over the ornament that had the photo of her father in it. Kenji's offer was gracious. He seemed more understanding that she had expected.

"Thank you. Make sure to send me the bill."

"Sure," he said, but turned to talk to Martinez, who informed them they could leave the house whenever they were ready.

They walked to Kenji's car, and Daphne took out the incident report from the night she'd been shot and gave the information to Officer Martinez.

Chapter 6

Kenji and Daphne went back into the house after the officers left so she could pack a bag to take with her to Price Tower. She'd seemed like she was going to argue going with him, but he had simply pointed to her ransacked house, and she'd gone to get her suitcase and pack without a word.

"Before we go, let's talk," he said when she was done packing.

She sighed as she sat down on her bed. "I'm not sure how much you heard about my case today, but it involves some contested items from the former city of Maqdala that is now part of modern day Amba Mariam in Ethiopia. The items came to the Los Angeles Museum of Foreign Cultures through a bequest from the grandson of a solider who fought in the major battle of the city and took some items with him as spoils of war.

"The items had been on display in the museum until I filed a case in court to find out if the items legally belonged to the museum or to my client. Once that case was filed, the exhibit was pulled, and several items seem to have gone missing," she said.

"That sounds suspicious."

"Yeah, I know. But the director has insisted they haven't been stolen or moved. They are simply missing during an archival reshuffle. Yet he hasn't given us access, even though the court has compelled them to provide us with entrance to the archives."

She knitted her fingers together and looked down at her hands. It was obvious she was stalling, and he allowed himself to look at the fall of her long, straight black hair over her shoulder, where it partially covered her face. She was so beautiful to him. Then she looked up, and their eyes met.

"The other night, I got a message saying that someone had information regarding the missing items. I tried to get them to come to my office, but they wouldn't so I suggested we meet at Zara's Brew. They insisted we meet behind the coffee shop so they wouldn't be observed."

Kenji made a disapproving sound.

Daphne held her hand up. "I know. Dumb. Dangerous. But I needed a break in this case. Something that I could tie to the museum. So I went."

"And that person shot you?" he asked.

"No. No one was there, like I told the cops. I walked into the alley, and there was a shot. I dropped to the ground and hit my head, and when I turned, I saw…"

She stopped talking, pulled her purse toward her and opened it, taking out a burlap bag with a small logo on the bottom corner. He moved closer and immediately realized it was the logo of the Los Angeles Museum of Foreign Cultures.

"This. I put it into my purse as the cops and EMTs arrived and didn't have a chance to look in it until today," she said.

She opened the bag and carefully removed the silver object inside. Moving closer, he could see the delicate item was engraved. It smelled faintly of incense.

"What is it?"

"It's a censer and part of the tabot used in the Ethiopian Orthodox Church. It's an incense burner used during masses on high holy days."

"How does it tie to your case?" he asked.

She put the item back into the burlap bag and then slipped it into her purse. "It's one of the missing items on the list. I was hoping to find more clues tonight in the alleyway. Maybe something that would lead me to whomever contacted me. I want to talk to the person who left this behind."

"Did you find anything?" he asked, coming to sit down next to her.

"Some blood spatter stains, but those are probably mine. The biggest thing was that the shooter was at the end where that chain-link fence was. I think they stood there and watched me until the cops came," she said, shivering slightly as she did so.

He wanted to put his arm around her but waited because he knew she wasn't done talking.

"When we got here and I realized my house had been broken into... I think whoever shot me knows I have the censer and was trying to get it back. What I don't know is if they work for the museum or not."

"You can't keep this item," he said.

"I know. I need to return it, but I am also meant to go to the museum tomorrow, and I want to bring up this censer and see Lauder's reaction. He's been difficult, but it could just be pride and stubbornness making him that way."

Her plan made a kind of sense given the nature of her work. But the longer she had the censer, the more danger there was to her. "Do you mind if I bring my team in on this?"

"Why?"

"Lee is really good at using the dark web to get information. I think she'll be able to search for black market dealers who would buy or sell items like this. It might help you find a connection between the museum and this item."

She pressed her lips together and then gave a tight nod. "I'm not used to doing this kind of leg work for a case. Any help would be great."

"Good. Ready to go?"

"Maybe."

"Maybe?"

"We never finished our personal discussion."

"And we're not going to here. I need to get you someplace safe. You can relax, I can check in with my boss, and then we can talk if you still want to."

She didn't like it, but she didn't argue either. He was ready to leave her house. Van had promised to have a security team come and secure it after they left. He trusted his boss to help keep Daphne safe while he found the people who were after her.

The Price Security Tower was located in downtown Los Angeles on South Broadway. He took the interstate from Bel Air. The Tower was near the Eastern Columbia Building. The Price Tower was only ten floors high and had an underground parking garage. As they left the 10 and he spotted the Eastern Building, Kenji felt safer. They were almost home, and there was no place he'd rather be right now.

He had to think and start to piece together where the threat to Daphne was coming from. At least now he could do that in the modern building that had been his home since he'd retired from the agency.

The building was steel-reinforced concrete and clad in glossy turquoise terra-cotta trimmed in deep blue and gold to match the Eastern Building. Van had spent about an hour talking about it and its history with Luna's husband, Nick DeVere, during their last get-together. They both loved old Los Angeles, having grown up in the city. But compared to his friends, Kenji was a child of the world, having moved around whenever his mom lost a job and needed a new one. As an adult, his life had followed the same pattern. He'd never really sat in one spot. Instead he was used to moving on.

So, yeah. This place was home.

He glanced at Daphne. Her features were occasionally visible as they passed under the street lamps. She had her arms wrapped around her waist, and she'd changed into a pair of ripped jeans and a form-fitting pink sweater that had a rhinestone reindeer on it. Somewhere along the way, she'd pulled her hair back into a ponytail, and he noticed that she leaned her head against the window almost the whole time as he drove.

It had been a long, tough day for her. And it wasn't more than she could handle. He knew she'd be ready for whatever else this night threw at her. But he was moved that she felt comfortable enough with him to let her guard down for a few moments.

His gut clenched. He wanted to be the man she could be safe with, who would protect her from whatever came at her. She'd been shot at, her home had been burgled, and he wasn't sure what the next attack would be. Whatever it was, he would meet it.

But protecting her from himself…was that also something he needed to be concerned with? He hoped not, but it had been too long since he'd allowed his emotions to leak out like this. Hell, not since the last time he'd been with her.

Even this relocation could be a mistake.

"We're almost here," he said.

"Price Tower is nice," she said. "I didn't realize this is where you lived. You know, the courthouse isn't that far from here."

He did, because he'd sometimes gone down there on his days off to see if he could catch a glimpse of her until he recognized what he'd been doing. That had been years ago, and he hadn't gone back since. Now she was sitting in his car, watching him with those wide brown eyes, and everything masculine in him was satisfied. *Yes*, his primal self thought, *she's mine*. But she wasn't, not really. No one knew that more than he did.

Price Tower housed offices and apartments for the entire staff. It was not too far from Nicholas DeVere's building, which included his penthouse and the nightclub Madness. Kenji's apartment was his private domain, and he seldom had brought any of his clients back to the tower. Usually it was reserved for the team, a place for them to relax.

But he couldn't leave Daphne at her place; it was too big and open for him to protect her alone. Bringing her here was logical. Or at least, that was the story he was sticking with for the time being. Van hadn't raised any objection when Kenji had texted saying he was bringing her here.

"Before I take you to my place, let's put that censer in the safe. We can talk to Lee so she can run a search on the dark web," Kenji said, hitting the button for the fourth floor, which was where the safe and Lee's office were.

"Okay to putting it in the safe, but tomorrow, after we visit the museum, I'm going to report finding it to the cops," Daphne said. "I know you suggested doing this. I don't want to keep it long-term. It might cause the judge to look unfavorably on my client."

"Not a problem," Kenji said.

The elevator opened. They stepped out into the hallway, and the lights clicked on as they did so. A door at the end of the hallway opened, and Van and Lee came out. Both were dressed in jeans and black T-shirts. Kenji didn't know much about the pair. They weren't romantically involved—he did know that much—but both had worked together before, eventually getting soured on working for the government and thus starting their own company.

"Kenji, good to see you," Van said as he came forward. "Ms. Amana, I'm Giovanni Price, and this is Lee Oscar. You're in safe hands with Kenji and in the Tower."

"Thank you, Mr. Price," she said, offering him her hand, which Van took and shook.

"Call me Van."

Daphne nodded.

"We have an item for the safe, and we need you to find out how it came to be in an alleyway behind Zara's Brew the night that Daphne was shot."

"Sounds like my kind of puzzle," Lee said.

Van turned to lead the way back down the hall. They entered a room that was dark and had a wall of monitors on the far side. Lee's desk had four monitors on it and two keyboards. It also had the model of top-of-the-line gaming chair that Kenji was thinking about ordering for his place. He spent a massive amount of his downtime gaming.

Van flicked on a light as he led them to the table in the middle of the room. Daphne had left her suitcase in the hall, and she took off her shoulder bag. She hesitated, and he remembered that she was putting a lot of faith in all of them to handle this potentially stolen artifact.

"It's okay," he said. "We won't take possession of the item, and no one is breaking in to steal it."

"I can personally guarantee that," Van said. "What is the item?"

"It was marked as missing in an inventory from the Los Angeles Museum of Foreign Cultures, among a number of other pieces that have been contested by my client, the cultural minister for Amba Mariam. I only had a chance today to look in the bag that I found the night I was shot. I was surprised to see this item. I specifically asked Mr. Lauder if it had been stolen when I first took the case and noticed its value and the fact that it was missing, and he said no."

"So how'd the item get from the museum to the alleyway?" Van asked.

"Exactly. There are more missing items that might be out there," Daphne said. "Do you think you can help in any way?"

She turned to Lee for the last question. Lee leaned down to inspect the censer and then stood up and nodded. "I'll do my best. The black market is tricky, but I have a few contacts that will give me a good place to start."

"I'd like to keep my name out of it if you can," Daphne said.

"Of course. I saw you on the morning news a week or so ago, so I'll use that to explain my interest," Lee said. "I'll find where this came from."

"Don't overpromise," Van said softly.

"I'm not," Lee said with a cheeky grin before she walked to her workstation. As soon as she sat down, her fingers started flying over one of the keyboards.

Kenji turned back to Van. "Can you keep this in the safe overnight?"

"Of course."

"I want to turn it over to the police tomorrow but would like to keep it quiet," Daphne said. "I don't know many detectives. Is there anyone you trust who can help with that?"

"I know a detective. I'll reach out to her and set something up," Van said. "Will you be here all day tomorrow?"

Kenji shook his head. "We're going to the museum in the morning, and then we can be back—"

"I have other clients, Kenji. I'll have to go by my office and work," Daphne interrupted him.

"Not a problem. I'll have her come after hours," Van

said. "The security team is at your house now, and I'll let you know when they are done."

"Great." There was a pause as she glanced around the room. "Will I be able to go back home soon?" Daphne asked.

"That's up to Kenji," Van said.

Daphne turned to look at him, and he just shrugged. "We'll see how tomorrow goes."

He led her out of the computer room after she watched Van put the censer in the safe with hawk eyes. He allowed her to change the key code, and both Kenji and Van looked away as she set the new code and closed the door. Now she was the only one who could get to the item.

He heard her walking quietly behind him with her wheeled suitcase down the corridor to the elevator. They got off on the floor that was split by a short hallway between his very roomy apartment and Xander's.

Someone had put a Master Chief figure from *Halo* inside the wreath on his door, with a small Santa hat glued onto his helmet. Kenji laughed when he saw it, knowing full well it had to be Xander, who made *Warhammer* figures in his downtime.

"That's…one of a kind," Daphne said.

"Yeah. I'm not much on Christmas, but the team tries to get me into it," he said.

"Who's that?" she asked, pointing to the figure.

"Master Chief from *Halo*. He's the guy that you play as in the game," he said. He really didn't want to talk about gaming, Daphne always seemed too refined for it, but at least it was giving him another moment before he took her into his place.

"Did you play that when we were together?" she asked. "I know you did some shooting games."

"Yeah. It came out in 2001. It's a massive multiplayer game, so I would play it online sometimes."

"Did I ever play it?"

"Maybe. It's set in space, and we fight aliens," he said.

She just shook her head as she removed her pony-tail holder, causing her hair to fall over her shoulder. He reached out and pushed it back behind her ear. He should have been keeping his hands off her, but it was hard.

That one kiss had opened memories he'd shoved deep down and away for a good reason. This was no time to be turned on by her. Her place had been broken into. She had a stolen museum item. Not to mention the fact that he'd been hired to be her bodyguard because she'd been shot at and likely remained at risk.

But he still wanted her. More than he'd expected.

There was no way around that. Standing in front of his home. The one place that he was most himself. And he was about to bring her into it. He felt vulnerable in a way that he seldom admitted.

But with Daphne, he was totally willing to lose his armor, and it was freaking him out. He would stand out here all day talking about *Halo* if it meant he didn't have to take her inside, where there was the biggest chance he'd break the oath he made to himself when he'd first accepted that she was his client.

He wasn't going to sleep with her.

Period.

Not that his body gave a crap about promises. Everything masculine in him was on point and ready to pull her into his arms and see just how much they had changed in the years they'd been apart.

But that wasn't the man he was. Not today, and not when he was working. He knew that. It was just…

"My place isn't much."

She put her hand on his forearm, and he looked down at her long manicured fingers where she touched him. A slow, steady beat had started inside of him.

"I'm sure it's cleaner and safer than mine."

Kenji took a deep breath before he used his key fob to open the door. He'd never blurred the lines between personal and professional before, but from the moment Daphne's name had come up, he'd known there was no way around it this time.

Chapter 7

The apartment was one big open room with en suite bedrooms off to either side. The kitchen was chef-grade and had a large island with two stools at it. Meanwhile, the living room had a huge TV—she'd never seen one that large before—with a console underneath it. There were bookshelves all along one of the walls, floor-to-ceiling and stuffed with books of all kinds. There was a couch in front of the TV and two large leather recliners on either side.

She moved into the room, towing her suitcase behind her. Kenji dropped his keys in a bowl on the table in the entryway and then toed off his shoes. She bent to unzip the boots she was wearing before taking them off.

"Nice place," she said, faintly echoing what he'd said when they'd pulled up to her house.

"I don't know my dad, so I have no idea what he thinks of it," Kenji said with a wry grin. "Your bedroom is on the right. There's a nice-size bath in there if you were serious about wanting one."

"Thanks, I was," she said.

"I'm going to have Xander come and hang in the living room while I shower," he said.

"I thought I was safe here."

"You are, but I don't like to take chances," he said. "I should have checked the alleyway at the coffee shop."

"There was no one out there. The only threat was from me being reckless," she said, walking over to him and putting her hand on his shoulder. "I'm not holding that against you."

"I am," he said.

Kenji held himself to a higher standard than anyone else she knew. That was saying a lot given the demands she put on herself to be the best. She suspected, though they'd never had a chance to talk at length about their parents, that it had something to do with the father he'd never met.

He'd told her that one late night when they'd been studying together. For the life of her, she couldn't understand how someone would just walk away from their own child. She knew everyone followed their own path and had their own reasons. It was really…seeing Kenji and the effect that absent man had on him made her furious. Even without being in his son's life, he'd influenced Kenji's.

"Okay about your friend," she said.

"I wasn't asking permission," he said sardonically.

"I'm the client, right? Doesn't that make me the boss?"

"You are the client, but you are definitely not the boss," he said.

A spark of mischief and excitement went through her. For the first time that evening, she didn't feel tired or scared. Even her shoulder was simply a dull ache and not in real pain. And Kenji was acting like *Kenji* and not like an ultra-efficient bodyguard. That meant more to her than she wanted it to.

"Is that a Daphne rule or every client rule?" she teased.

"Every client, but especially you."

"Why?"

"Clients are reckless, and don't think they can be killed. They take risks that put them in danger, and that's why the bodyguard is always in charge."

"I can't be killed with you watching over me, Kenji. That is one thing I know for certain. And I bet your other clients do as well," she said, then leaned up and kissed him quickly on the lips because she wanted to. Then winked and pivoted away, towing her suitcase toward the room he'd indicated would be hers.

Busy congratulating herself on throwing him off his guard, she completely missed him coming up behind her. He turned her around and pulled her into his arms, being careful of her injured shoulder, and brought his mouth down on hers.

She stopped thinking and almost stopped breathing as her instincts took over. This was what she needed. This moment to feel safe and like a woman, not an international attorney who was working on a case that had turned very dangerous. Just Daphne.

Kenji was probably the one person in the world that she truly had ever let her guard down with. Her parents had always had a high standard that Daphne had never felt like she lived up to.

But until he left, Kenji had made her feel like she was enough.

Shutting down her mind, she put her hands in his hair. It was thick and silky and felt good under her fingers. She angled her head to the side as his tongue slid deeper into her mouth. His hands moved down her back, cupping her butt as he lifted her more fully into contact with his body. She put one hand on his hip, drawing herself closer, lifting one leg over his thigh so that the ridge of his cock rubbed against her center.

He squeezed her butt cheek, and she moaned. As he thrust his hips forward, she shivered with need. She pulled her head back, their eyes met, and she wanted nothing more than to take him to bed and pretend for a brief moment that her life wasn't the mess it had become.

He brushed his thumb over her lower lip, looking as if he were going to say something, when there was a knock on the door.

He stepped back, steadying her as he did so. "That'll be Xander."

"Okay then," she said, continuing to make her way into the bedroom.

As soon as she was there, she closed the door and leaned back against it. She heard the rumble of another voice talking to Kenji but stood there rather than opening the door. It was too soon to show herself to someone else. Her pulse was racing, her body was on fire, and all she could think about was how glad she was that Kenji was here with her.

She might not know the reason why he'd left her, but he was here now. After the night she'd just had, that suited her. If her life was in danger and her current case wasn't turning into a big puzzle, she might feel differently, but it was. These heart-pounding feelings would just have to wait.

* * *

Xander was his best friend, probably the one person he felt most comfortable with. But right now, he could have done without the intrusion, or at least that's how his body felt. His mind was glad X once again had his back. Whether his friend knew it or not.

"Thanks for coming over. We've had a rough night. I need a shower, and I… I just don't trust her to stay put."

Kenji was glad that Daphne hadn't intuited that was the reason he'd asked Xander to cover for him.

"Why not?"

"She's independent and used to doing her own thing. Plus this case means a lot to her," Kenji said. "Which is fine. We can talk more about it, but after I've showered."

"No problem. I've got your back."

"Thanks, man."

Kenji left his friend in the living area and went into his own bedroom. As soon as he closed the door, all of the emotions he'd repressed since the beginning of the day flooded out. He walked to the punching bag in the corner and dropped into a fighting stance, kicking and punching it until he was sweating. Then he shook his head, exhausted but still tense, and went to the shower.

Daphne wasn't what he'd expected. *Duh.* How could a woman who he'd just seen in pictures for almost twelve years be real. She was an amalgam of the girl he'd known and what he'd seen of her that one time he'd almost talked to her after the CIA.

She was smart, flirty, fierce and sassy, all things he remembered. But age had honed those things and made her into a woman who was damned hard for him to resist. He wasn't sure he could trust her to do anything but find evidence to win her case. She wasn't going to put herself first, and he wasn't going to be able to convince her to do otherwise.

Which, as he soaped his body, shouldn't have been as exciting a thought as it was. Yes, it would be difficult, but protecting Daphne was the first case he'd had since he'd left the CIA that made him feel this alive.

Part of it was the sexual attraction. He wasn't going to front and act like that didn't matter. If X hadn't knocked when he had, Kenji would have had her up against the wall next to her bedroom, and he was damned sure that Daphne would have enjoyed it.

But that wasn't why she was here. He had to keep reminding himself. He was supposed to keep her safe, not act out his wild fantasies with her.

So that meant shadowing her every move, having Lee run down where the censer had come from, and keeping his dick in his pants and his hands to himself.

No matter that she'd kissed him first. He had to have better control over himself, and he usually did. For her, he had to be the best version of the bodyguard he always was. Not a man too caught up in his hormones to do his job.

He finished his shower, blow-dried his hair, and then got dressed in some black sweatpants and a matching tee. When he came into the living room, Xander had the Xbox on and was playing *Halo*.

Kenji grabbed a couple of nutritious energy drinks from the fridge and then vaulted over the back of the couch and picked up a controller to join the game.

"Any movement from her room?"

"Nothing. I'll leave after this match," Xander said.

"Obie's got an exam this week, so I'm staying a few extra days. Need me for anything?"

Kenji caught Xander up on the case and the fact that they were trying to figure out if there was a black market art dealer involved. "If Lee finds someone, maybe you could help locate them."

"Yeah. No problem," he said.

They continued playing *Halo* until they won the co-op team match they were on. Xander finished his energy drink and then stood up. "You good?"

"Yeah. See you tomorrow."

Xander left the apartment and Kenji settled in on the couch, knowing that he'd probably stay here all night. He'd get some rest in the leather recliner, but he wanted to keep an eye on Daphne's door.

Meanwhile he played another co-op match, and Xander popped up on the opposite team. He had fun hunting down his friend and killing him in the game since the stakes in their real life were higher and more serious. As the match ended, Daphne's door opened, and she came out into the room.

"Oh, I thought you'd be in bed," she said.

He exited the game, putting down his controller. "Nope. You thinking of running?"

"Not at all. Having my house broken into scared me enough to stay put for now," she said. "I couldn't sleep. I have insomnia, and my sleep therapist advises against doing anything other than sleeping in bed. I thought I'd come and find a book to read."

She wore a pair of red silk pajamas and had bare feet as she moved through the living room toward the bookshelves.

She read a few of the spines while he watched her, and then stopped and turned. "We never got to finish our personal conversation."

"And you want to now?"

She shrugged and pushed her hair behind her ear. "Maybe. I can't help thinking about what happened between us today and in college. I want to separate the two, but it's not that easy. After you, I never really trusted my feelings again."

That was hard to hear, but it was her right to say this to him. "I never meant for that to happen."

"I know, so why'd you leave like that?" she asked. Her voice was strong and didn't waver. She just looked at him, right into his soul, and he knew she deserved the truth no matter how difficult telling it would be for him.

He exhaled long and hard and then rubbed his hand against the back of his neck. "Sit down and I'll tell you."

Sitting curled up in the leather recliner in Kenji's apartment felt like she'd stepped out of her life and into an alternate reality. He hadn't really changed in the years since they'd been together. The kisses they'd shared reminded her that, even now, she still wanted him. Wouldn't it be nice if physical attraction equaled shared feelings on both sides?

Life didn't work that way, something she'd known for a while. There was still a part of her that was desperately trying to figure out why Kenji was the man she could never forget. Why was he the one man she wanted, no matter that he'd hurt her before and he wasn't really in her life?

He made her feel safe. But surely her gut could be… What was her gut even saying?

Kenji had asked her to sit down and then he'd tell her the truth, but he was still struggling to find the words.

He offered her a drink. Asked her if she wanted a blanket. She shook her head to both.

"Just tell me. Was it that you never cared?" she asked. "I think the part I struggle the most with is the fact that I loved you the way I did, and you didn't."

Her dad always said that after midnight, the truth had a way of coming out. He was right. She'd gotten the truth from witnesses and clients after the witching hour, which was great. But her dropping truth bombs on Kenji wasn't exactly what she wanted. It cut them both too deeply. Where was her sense of self-preservation?

Did she really need this lethally sexy bodyguard from her past to affirm that he'd never really cared?

"No, Daph. It was never that. I cared too much," he said.

"Sure."

He shoved his hand through that fall of bangs, and of course it artfully fell right back into place. But she'd rattled him. Which surprised and intrigued her.

"I had an idea of who I was, the kind of man I would be and how I would live my life. That plan didn't include a dark-haired woman who distracted me from that path and showed me an alternative life."

"Distracted you?"

"Yes. You must know I was obsessed with you and the life you gave me a glimpse of. I watched you sleep in my arms, and glimpses of a family and future together teased the edges of my mind," he said. Leaning forward, he put his elbows on his thighs and steepled his fingers together as he stared at the carpet.

She had dreams of a future, too. Why had he left? She'd heard what he said about a different path but still couldn't understand the break he'd made between the two of them. "Why didn't you just say you weren't ready for us?"

"There was no way to walk both paths."

There was a finality to his words that made her heart ache a little bit. "Of course there was. You just didn't see it."

"Perhaps. We were young, and I still had a lot to prove to myself and to the CIA. I wanted the excitement and danger they were promising," he said.

"I know that part," she admitted. He'd been clear about anticipating the missions he'd be sent on with gusto. Kenji and she both had wanted to make the world a better place. He had done it by going on covert missions and doing things that she probably would never know about. She'd done it in the courts, seeking justice a different way, and she was happy with her choice.

Was Kenji?

"Yeah, you do. I never meant to hurt you. I figured…"

"What, that I didn't really love you, so when I begged you not to go and cried my eyes out, you thought I'd be fine the next day?" she asked. For the love of all that was holy, why was her mind not censoring her thoughts?

"No. God, no. I just figured you'd write me off as not worthy."

There it was, she thought. The truth that had been buried in all of Kenji's other explanations. Not being worthy was a big part of who he was. "You were always worthy. I know your mom would have wanted you to know that too. *He* wasn't worthy. It was never about you."

"But it was always about him," Kenji said. "I've been to a therapist in the last few years, so I know what you're saying is right. In my head, it makes perfect sense. Fuck that dude who didn't want to know his son, right?"

"In your heart, it's not that easy."

Logic and emotions worked that way. No matter how many times she told herself it didn't matter that she'd never been close to her mom, that she was lucky to have her relationship with her father, Daphne still longed for that bond. She missed it in a way that had left an emptiness inside of her.

She saw the same emptiness in Kenji. Part of her wondered if that had been what had drawn them together. That need to prove something and to fill that chasm in their hearts and souls with saving the world.

That was something she doubted she'd ever find the answer to.

"No, it's not. But the man I am today wouldn't make that choice, Daphne. If you hear nothing else from me tonight, hear this. I walked away because I knew if I didn't, I'd choose you, and I was afraid I'd end up resenting that choice."

His words didn't fix the past, but she had a better understanding for why he'd left her the way he had. Why he'd felt that the only solution was a clean break. And maybe why she was finding it so hard to resist him now that he was back in her life.

It wasn't just that he had made her feel safe. It wasn't just that he was strong and still so sexy she ached to have him inside of her when they were in the same room. It was that she saw the same lost soul she'd once connected with, and she wanted to connect with him again.

Chapter 8

Raw emotion and the past were two things he'd never been keen to spend much time dwelling on. Right now his skin felt too tight, but inside his stomach, that knot he'd had since she'd first asked him why he'd left her started to loosen. Confession was good for the soul.

Van touted that often, and for the first time, Kenji almost got what his boss had been talking about. Maybe if he'd been honest with her back in the day…but he knew he couldn't have been. He had needed to go on the journey he'd been on to get to the man he was today.

"I needed to hear that," she said. "Thank you."

He nodded, keeping that stoic look on his face even though inside he was a seething storm that was ready for a downpour. He knew that he needed to just ride this out. Let her set the boundaries and he'd respect them.

There was something so mature about the way Daphne handled herself, and he struggled to meet it. He knew part of the reason was that he'd never really trusted anyone. His mom had been his one stalwart during his childhood, and having her die as soon as he went to college had shaken him to his core.

Moving into the Price Tower had forced him to drop

his guard slightly over time, becoming friends with the team. That had been easier because they were all loners who'd been hiding something. Time had made them all relax, and true bonds had been forged between them.

But this was Daphne. The woman he'd known when he'd been that lost boy before he'd become the man he was today. It was harder with her because in his gut, he still wanted to impress her.

He was on a case with probably the one client he most wanted to keep safe. Daphne acting measured and polite was the best outcome he could hope for. So why did it make him want to punch something or maybe go to the shooting range on the third floor and fire his weapon at a target until it passed?

"I know that I should say something, but I have no idea what would help either of us," she said. "Work is what I fall back on when life is like this."

"Of course." Her words made sense. Like his own path, the path she'd chosen was dominated by her job. "Want to strategize for tomorrow when we go to the museum?"

"Yeah, I'd love that. Let me get my notepad. I think better on paper," she said.

He watched her get up and walk back to her room. Her hips swayed with each step she took, and he couldn't tear his eyes from her. His gut ached for something that he could have had. Regret wasn't his deal. But remorse, yeah, he had that.

It had been his decision. He'd chosen to leave something that he was pretty sure he wanted again more than anything and wasn't sure that he would ever have.

She turned and noticed him staring at her. "Kenji?"

Busted. "Nothing. I'll get my tablet. I think better on devices," he said, forcing himself to smile and wink at her.

Which made her raise both eyebrows as she tipped her head to the side. "Is it okay for us to be friendly?"

Yeah, because when was he ever a smiling and winking guy? *Never.*

"Okay how?"

"I mean with you as my bodyguard. In that Whitney Houston movie, it didn't end well for them."

"We're not in a movie, and I think it's going to be hard for us not to be friendly given our past. As long as I don't lose objectivity, we should be good."

"How would that happen?" she asked.

"Depends on you, I guess," he said.

She licked her lips, and he wanted to groan as his eyes tracked the movement. He was definitely biased, but she had the best damned mouth he'd ever seen. Because he'd kissed her, he knew that it was still as soft and welcoming as it had been back in the day.

God, he wanted to kiss her again.

"I'll get my tablet."

He stood and walked to his desk in the corner of the living room and grabbed his tablet. The personal stuff was over. He was going to be the consummate bodyguard when she came back in.

He wouldn't allow his mind to drift to her body and all the ways he'd like to touch her. He wouldn't look at her mouth when she spoke and remember how it felt when he'd kissed her last, hot and addictive. He wouldn't allow his hormones to come into play, even though his blood felt hotter and heavier and his erection stirred when she returned to the living room and sat down on the couch next to him.

She smelled of peaches and cream, and her smile was soft and gentle. Did she know that she was driving him out of his mind? Would it matter if she did? Too much had passed between them for there to be any hope of a new relationship now.

"You used to be a really good judge of people. Are you still?" she asked.

"Usually. Want me to observe?"

"Yes. I'm meant to meet Lauder again and someone from the archives. I imagine there might be a few other museum staff that we will come into contact with," she said.

"Should I photograph them?" The camera often showed things that the naked eye didn't catch.

"No. I think putting my staff on edge is one thing, but this is different. What I want is for you to just observe them and maybe make notes on each person. I need to verify if the items are getting out of the museum some-how, and either Lauder or someone on his staff knows something about it."

He agreed. "Tell me more about the items. Do you have a catalog of them?"

"I have a list with descriptions and item numbers from the museum. The exhibit they held in 1985 when they first received the items was covered by several local newspapers and magazines. But these are the only pho-tos I have."

She air-dropped him some scanned images from her phone along with the inventory PDF. He opened them, scanning the list, and eventually landed on the censer she had found in the alleyway. "How many items besides the censer are missing?"

"Fourteen," she said. Then she took a paper from the folio that had her notepad in it. "But over the last five years, seventeen different items have been marked missing and then returned to the collection. I have subpoenaed the museum's financial records, but the judge hasn't ruled if I can see them and if they are relevant to the case."

"Why do you think they are?"

"I want to see if there is an influx or outflux of cash around the time the items were returned. I have two theories."

"And they are?" He liked watching her mind work, and he imagined this was how she got ready for her court cases. Outlining all the possible ways something could go and then preparing for them.

"One: someone in the museum is selling them, and then the museum is buying them back to hide or cover for the theft and sale." She wriggled her eyebrows at him as she said that.

"Possibly," he said. Waiting to hear her other theory before weighing in on it. He was always better when he could see the entire picture. He'd been working with her for a short while, but already he was starting to form an idea of what was going on here.

Could there be two players instead of one, as Daphne was postulating? It seemed obvious that the attacks on Daphne were tied to her case. But she'd said that the shooter had waited at the end of the alleyway and watched her until she called 911. The cops would have searched the area, but the shooter could have left after they arrived.

Were the attacks on Daphne personal and not related to her case? He wasn't going to mention that to her. Not yet. He needed to hear more of her theory.

"Yeah, I know there are a lot of holes in that one. I mean, why wouldn't the museum just fire the person who is selling them? My second theory is that the museum needs money and is selling the pieces to fund an exhibit or operating costs and then rebuying them. Sort of like putting them in a pawn shop. Which I guess is kind of like theory number one, but instead of personal gain, it's to keep the museum afloat."

Money was a strong motivator, and the way the items were simply missing instead of stolen was interesting. Also, some had been missing and then "found" later. "Do you think the judge will grant your request?"

"I have no idea. She was completely right when she said that money isn't what my case is about. The case is supposed to be about finding out who the items belong to and restoring them to their rightful owner. Money shouldn't be a player in this."

"But it usually is," he said.

"Exactly."

Talking with Kenji eased a lot of the tension in her mind. He asked insightful questions and offered avenues that she hadn't considered. The distraction from the day was helpful, but she still wasn't sure she could sleep. Plus a part of her didn't want to leave Kenji.

He probably needed some rest before tomorrow. If he'd been a stranger, more than likely she wouldn't have been hanging out in the living room with him, trying to find reasons to stay awake. Which was really all the answer she needed. "Am I keeping you up?"

He shook his head as he put his tablet on the coffee table. "No. I was planning to stay out here all night."

Something wasn't adding up. He'd brought her here because her place had been burgled. But was there something about the tower she didn't know? "Why? Aren't we safe here?"

"You totally are," he said, stretching his arm out along the back of the couch. "I just don't like surprises, like the one I got tonight when you slipped away from me."

She blushed when he said it. In retrospect, it had been extremely stupid of her to do that. But she was tired of all the back-and-forth in this case and waiting for a break. Sometimes she knew she had to make one for herself. "Sorry for sneaking out on you. I just wasn't sure you'd be down for going back out there."

He pulled his arm down and leaned toward her. There was so much intensity in his face and the way he held his body.

"I am down for keeping you safe, we clear?" he said, but it was clearly an order, not a question.

She wrinkled her nose at him. "If you didn't phrase that way, then yes."

"When it comes to your safety—"

She cut him off. "I know, you are in charge. But do you have to sound like a bossy douchebag?"

"That's usually the only effective way to make sure a client listens to me. There isn't room to debate when your life is on the line."

She'd forgotten that he wasn't here for her personally.

This was professional. Kenji was a bodyguard and used to putting himself in the line of fire to keep his clients safe. Of course there wasn't room for debate.

"Fair enough. I don't actually think my life is on the line."

Or rather, she didn't want to believe that. The shooter had hit her in the shoulder, and her house had been burgled while she wasn't there. That had to mean they wanted the object and were willing to hurt her, but not kill her. *Right?*

"Maybe, maybe not. But I'm not taking any chances. The fact that both these incidents have happened so close together makes me believe that they will escalate. Unless you want to put the censer back in the alleyway."

"No. It needs to be in police custody so I can track what happens to it," she said.

He held his hands up, and she realized she'd been a bit forceful. "Guess you're not the only bossy douchebag in the room."

"Nice to know I have company," he said with a wry smile.

His smile made her heartbeat speed up, and there she was, thinking of him again. Not as her bodyguard or the man from her past who had her hurt her. But the guy she'd fallen for…the guy she still missed. "Will we be staying here from now on?"

"I guess it depends on what you stir up tomorrow. If I think you will be safe at your home, we can stay there."

"You'll stay with me?" she asked him. The thought of being alone right now was frightening, which she knew was logical given the last few days. But she'd always been a strong woman and had no problem living on her own.

She'd been afraid to have a roommate in case…well, in case there was something about her that was off-putting. Kenji had left her, and before that, her mom had loathed her. Was there something unfavorable about living with her that she was unaware of?

She hadn't wanted to risk it, so she had simply always lived on her own. Now she was afraid to be alone. God, this was a mess. It would have been nice if she had some easy solution that she could just pull out and get the case before the judge and win.

"Until the threat to you is gone," he said.

"So after my case," she said.

"If you're safe," he returned.

"Why wouldn't I be?"

"I don't know yet. But I'm just keeping all avenues open."

"Like what else?"

"That someone doesn't want you around, and it has nothing to do with the case."

"But the missing items…"

"Are missing. You'll figure out if there is a crime there," he said. "I'm going to figure out who's threatening you and neutralize the threat."

That made her feel safe all the way to her core. She knew Carl didn't like it when his attorneys were put in the line of fire. And this case shouldn't have been one to do so. Hiring Price, hiring Kenji, had been the right decision.

"What about Christmas?" she asked.

"What about it?"

"My case will go into January. Will you take the holiday off?"

"If the threat to you has passed," he reiterated.

Would it? Christmas was an odd time of year for her. She liked it, sort of. The way everyone was happier in the office was pleasant. Her dad always sent her a nice gift and some years came out to visit her. But then there was the other side. Remembering the years when her mom had still been alive. They weren't the best memories or the happiest Christmases.

"You okay?" he asked.

"Yeah," she said. She wasn't about to share that part of her life with him. She'd grown up in a very privileged home and had wanted for nothing material. She'd had the nicest clothes, gone to the best schools and been given many advantages. Talking about the fact that her mom hadn't loved her and had resented her wasn't something she was going to bring up.

She dealt with it internally as she always had.

"Christmas isn't really something I celebrate since my mom died," Kenji said. "But if you have traditions or things you want to do, we can do them here. Van always orders trees for all of us."

"All of you?" she asked, seizing on Kenji's holiday spirit instead of her own.

"The entire team has living quarters here. Mostly because our assignments take us out of town for long stretches of time."

"Interesting. How many are there?"

"Just six of us. Well, five now that Luna is living with her husband at his penthouse, but it's not too far from here," he said.

"Xander lives across the hall from you. Where does everyone else live?" she asked.

"Rick and Luna used to share the floor above us. Lee has an apartment on the same level as her computer room, and Van has the top floor to himself. I don't usually decorate the tree or anything, but we could if you wanted to."

Did she want to try to make this Christmas different?

Of course she did. She'd bought some ornaments the year that Kenji had dumped her but had never put them up. This year, with Cass, she had finally started to feel like she had some traditions. Maybe it was time to stop dwelling in that space where she wasn't worthy of the love and joy of the holiday season.

"I'd like that."

"I think I would too," he said. "You should head to bed. I imagine you're an up-early person."

"You know I am."

"I wasn't sure if that had changed," he said.

"It hasn't. I guess you're still a night owl." He'd always been awake long after she drifted off to sleep. He'd come into their bed late at night, make love to her and then crash, which had always felt special and sexy to her

"I am. But the job has made me alert all the time," he said. "Thanks for listening tonight."

"Thanks for opening up. I needed to hear it," she said, gathering her stuff. Then she got up and went into the bedroom he'd assigned her.

Closing the door behind her, she looked at the bed and wished she had the courage to ask him to sleep with her. But she wasn't ready for that. Not tonight. She had too much on her mind. The case, the person or people who'd been in her house, the past with her mom and how she'd felt if she could be perfect, maybe she'd be lovable. And the past with Kenji, when she'd learned that even her version of perfection wasn't enough…

Until tonight, when he'd told her that who she was *had* been enough.

Chapter 9

Dressed and ready for the day, Daphne realized her shoulder was starting to hurt a little bit less, and she'd even managed a few hours of sleep after leaving Kenji. He was dressed in another slim-fitting black suit and tie with a white shirt. He even had on dark sunglasses to combat the sun in LA. Growing up on the East Coast, December had been cold and gray with snow or rain. It hadn't taken her long to adjust to the sunny climate in LA. Though it did get cold, most days even in December saw sun.

She had her sunglasses on as well feeling like they were agents in a thriller. She watched Kenji has he drove. His hands on the wheel were strong, and she had never felt safer in a vehicle, even though he was going a little over the speed limit. The traffic wasn't too heavy since they'd left after rush hour. When he pulled into the parking lot of the Los Angeles Museum of Foreign Cultures, she realized she'd spent most of the drive thinking about him instead of reviewing her day.

Blaming it on the lack of sleep was one thing, but she couldn't let that happen again.

The Los Angeles Museum of Foreign Cultures was

on the stretch of Wilshire Boulevard that extended between Fairfax Avenue and La Brea Avenue, home to the famous tar pits. Her offices were on Wilshire, so it wasn't that far of a drive to get to it. The Los Angeles parks department had been busy putting up the holiday lights for the season, and as they drove by them, she couldn't help but wonder about Kenji and Christmas. It was only a few weeks away, and his apartment didn't show any signs of it. She was tempted to ask him about it, maybe take him up on his offer to decorate, but not today when she had to stay focused on getting answers.

The museum was situated on the end of Museum Row. It was one of the smaller establishments but well-known for its rare antiquities. That was part of the reason that Pierce was so determined to hold on to the collection.

The Maqdala collection that had been donated by Hazelton-Measham was unusual in North America, with the only other items housed in Canada at the Royal Ontario Museum. It gave the Los Angeles Museum of Foreign Cultures some cachet in that regard. Many of the collections at this museum were rare and popular. In the museum world, a collection that was both unique and commercially viable was invaluable.

The museum's building was in itself an architectural masterpiece created by the architect I.M. Pei. Like many of Pei's designs, this one had a modern sensibility that made the most of the outdoor space around it. It felt like it was part of the landscape while standing out and drawing the eye. She'd always liked the building. Daphne understood why the museum was fighting so hard to keep the collection. She understood that this loss might bring more lawsuits to them, but that was something many museums were facing in this day and age.

The parking lot was large and usually full, and there was a banner across the front advertising a *Night at the Museum*–style event for the upcoming Christmas season. Two more banners invited visitors to check out winter traditions from around the world. Leading up to the entrance, there was a reflecting pond in the middle of two long lawns that snaked up to a set of wide concrete stairs. There was a large art installation that spelled out Happy Holidays positioned along one of them, facing the parking lot entrance.

The letters showed celebrations from around the world and used the iconography associated with them, which Daphne had first learned when she'd gone on the news to discuss her case. She knew that many were divided on her case, but the only person who needed to hear her was the judge. Thankfully, Judge Mallon wasn't one to be swayed by public sentiment. The case would be judged on facts and merit.

The most salient fact was that Hazelton-Measham, as a soldier in the British expedition, hadn't been granted the right by anyone to loot the church and the treasury and bring the items home with him. Having donated them to the museum…well, Daphne believed they should be returned to Amba Mariam. She hoped that the judge would see this evidence as critically as she did.

Pulling herself out of her legal haze, she reached for the handle of the front door of the car, but Kenji hit the locks.

She glanced over at him.

"I will get out first and then come around so I'm in position," he said. "Are you taking a bag in with you?"

"Yes. I take this thing everywhere," she said, gesturing to her big Louis Vuitton shoulder bag.

"This parking lot is exposed, and there is no way for me to know if there are shooters—

"Kenji, I'm not worried here. I don't think whoever is behind this is going to attack me here."

"I'm not taking any chances. Keep your bag close, and if I tell you to run, go to the left corner of the entrance that's protected on two sides. Get small behind the trash can," he ordered.

"Okay," she said. His seriousness was making her more aware of her surroundings, and the remaining sleepiness that had been around her like a heavy pashmina dissipated. Kenji got out of the car in one swift motion, and she noticed he'd unbuttoned his jacket. When he moved, his hand was on the holster at his hip.

It made her very aware of the dangerousness of the situation she found herself in. It had been hard to believe the threat to her life was real when she was with Kenji, but now this visit didn't seem like just another morning errand she had to run.

He opened her door and she stepped out, quickly moving to close the door behind her. Kenji put hand at the small of her back and urged her to scurry quickly across the parking lot. Another car pulled in just as they reached the museum entrance. He immediately put his body between her and the vehicle, moving her into the corner that he'd mentioned she should use. The car pulled into a spot, and no one appeared to get out.

"Can we go inside?" she asked.

"Yes, stay in front of me. When we move inside, don't stop until you are at the desk."

She just nodded. The tension in Kenji was palpable. This glimpse of the professional that he'd become was showing her another side to him. As much as she might have wished last night that he'd stayed with her all those years ago, he wouldn't have become this man. And the world needed men like Kenji in it.

People who were willing to put their lives on the line to protect others.

She continued with him as he directed them into the museum. They walked to the reception desk, which was manned by a uniformed security guard and an older woman who smiled as they entered.

The security guard nodded at Kenji as they entered the building. The other man held himself the way Xander did, shoulders back and standing at attention. So Kenji clocked him as ex-military. He wanted to let the security guard know he was carrying his weapon. He also hoped to get some extra information from the man. "Hi there. I'm Kenji Wada with Price Security and the bodyguard for Ms. Amana." Kenji held out his hand.

"Paul Richards. Head of security here at the museum. Pierce let us know about Ms. Amana's attack."

"What did he say?"

"Just that she'd been shot at and that we should be on alert when she came here. Like I'm not always watching everyone who comes in and out of the museum."

Kenji heard the irritation in the other man's voice. He also found it interesting that Lauder had mentioned the incident. "I'm carrying and licensed for concealed.

Other than the cameras and alarms on the pieces, do you have other passive security measures?"

"Yeah. Why?"

"Ms. Amana is trying to find some pieces labeled as missing, and your boss insists they haven't been stolen. I was wondering if there was any security footage to look at," Kenji said, glancing over at Daphne. It was her case, and he was aware that he was probably overstepping, but if he could help her out, he wanted to.

"We do have security footage, but I can't just hand it over," Paul said, rubbing the back of his neck and then running his hand over the top of his head. Almost as if he were nervous.

"Don't worry. I wasn't asking to see it. Ms. Amana will go through the courts to get a look at it," Kenji said before nodding at the guard and heading back over to Daphne.

The receptionist, Laverne, recognized Daphne and greeted her by name. "I'm sorry to say that Mr. Lauder is out sick today. He asked that one of the archivists, Grey Joy, show you around and assist you in your search. I'll let her know you are here."

Laverne had curly red hair that framed her full face. She had on sparkly gold eyeshadow and thick eyelashes that had to be fake. They fell to her cheeks whenever she blinked. She wore a puffy-sleeved top that fell to a deep vee neckline, and when she crossed her arms and leaned forward, the medallion necklace she wore swung forward.

She kept chatting away, and Daphne knew she should be paying attention to what the other woman was saying, but her eyes had caught a note on Laverne's desk. It read *C. 4 pm*. Seemed oddly cryptic for a receptionist's note.

There was also a pamphlet for the museum's Arts of Africa exhibit, which currently had a banner over it that said Temporarily Closed. That was her doing, Daphne thought. She'd filed to have the museum stop profiting off showing the contested goods until the matter was resolved.

Laverne noticed her looking at the pamphlet. "Yeah. That's sort of slowed down foot traffic. We used to get a lot of people who had never seen the Ethiopian Orthodox Church tabots. That collection has really helped to raise awareness here in this area and brought in a lot of researchers who can't get visas to go and visit the sites."

"I'm aware of the cultural significance of it. This case is to return it to the rightful owners, and researchers can always get visas if they follow the proper channels and are honest about what they are in the country for," Daphne pointed out.

Laverne looked like she wanted to argue with Daphne but just smiled at her instead. "I'm sure the courts will figure it all out."

"I am too," Daphne said. She hadn't realized how edgy she was this morning. Maybe it was the lack of sleep, or the fact that someone was after her, but she wasn't herself today.

"Thank you. My bodyguard is with me today, which I believe Mr. Lauder was aware of."

"He was. We were expecting you both," she said. "Would you like any water or coffee while you wait?"

"I'm fine, thank you," she said.

She moved away from the reception desk to the current exhibit behind glass in the foyer. It was a collection of tabots from different churches around the world. She noted that several of them were on loan to the museum, but then she spied that one had been removed for cleaning—and it was one of the items from the Ethiopian Orthodox Church. She had saved the inventory to her phone and quickly found the document and checked the item.

It was on her list, so she'd asked to see it today. She wanted photos of everything that the museum had. There was a chance that more items might go missing, and she wasn't willing to let that happen. This case had been going on for over a year, and because of her caseload—and the museum dragging their feet, in Daphne's opinion—there had been too many delays.

She was ready to wrap this up. Get these objects back in the hands of the people to whom they meant the most.

Kenji came up next to her.

"Lauder is out sick. We're getting a tour by an archivist."

"Name?"

"Grey Joy. Female."

Kenji tapped the earpiece he'd put in that morning before he left. "Lee, museum employees so far are security guard Paul Richards, receptionist Laverne Simpson and archivist Grey Joy."

He then tapped the earpiece again to mute it and turned back to her. "The security guard doesn't know anything about missing pieces and mentioned that the security systems around the museum are top-rate. I've called them and they are sending a rep out to inspect, and my team will find out more."

"Thanks," she said.

Before she could add anything, Grey Joy arrived and led them back to the archives.

Grey had a silver bob that framed her heart-shaped face. Her eyes were wide and large, and she had thick, dark brows. She wore a pair of red-framed glasses and had on a LA Museum of Foreign Cultures collared shirt and a pair of khaki pants. She was shorter than Daphne and wore running shoes that squeaked as they followed her to the back of the archive room.

Daphne looked around as they moved through the large room that was full of floor-to-ceiling shelving units with labeled boxes on them. She wanted to stop and check the boxes, especially when she saw sign on the end of the shelves labeled Ethiopia. She had already asked Pierce if some of the missing items could have been housed incorrectly, which he'd denied.

Maybe Grey would be able to help her in that area. Already Daphne had a list of questions for the other woman. She hoped to get some of the answers about the missing pieces, as well as the piece that she'd found in the alley.

But how was she going to casually bring that up? *So, hey, I found a museum bag behind a coffee shop...any details on how it got there?* Not subtle. Daphne would never be that blunt, because she knew that she had to be careful and have an evidence trail that didn't involve her leading a witness. But she was itching to make her way down the aisle and start opening boxes all the same.

Not that she was going to be able to do that. She paused, taking her phone out of her purse and snapping a photo of the labeling so she could use that in her brief.

They clearly had plenty of other boxes of stored items, and she would like a chance to see what was in them.

"How long have you worked for the museum?" Daphne asked her as they moved into the back rooms. There were floor-to-ceiling metal bookshelves that housed boxes running the length of the room. The floor was corporate tile. There were no windows, which made sense given the items they housed. There were two desks positioned near the front of the room. Both had computer monitors on them and piles of folders as well as coffee mugs.

"For about seven years," Grey said.

Daphne's brow furrowed. "Do you work alone? I notice there are two desks."

"No, there are actually five of us who work down here. But today it's just me, and then Steven will be in later."

"Have we met before?" Daphne asked Grey.

Kenji could tell something was up with the other woman when Grey shook her head vehemently and stepped away from Daphne. "How would we have met?"

"Your voice…you're the one who called me?"

"What? I didn't even know who you were until I was asked to show you around. I think we should focus on that. I've pulled the boxes that we keep the contested items in, and they are on a table back here. Please follow me."

Daphne moved to follow her, but while Grey's back was turned, tapped out a message on her phone and showed it to him.

I think she's the one who I was supposed to meet when I was shot. Should I confront her?

* * *

Kenji wasn't sure what Daphne should do, but this could be the break they were looking for. He scanned the other woman. She was small, so if she was the one who attacked Daphne, he was pretty sure he could subdue her until the authorities arrived.

Daphne raised both eyebrows at him as they reached a table that had several boxes on it. One of them was open. He nodded.

Daphne moved closer to the table, pulling out a burlap bag that matched the one she had found in the alleyway.

"Grey, I believe you are the one who I was meant to meet. You can pretend all you want, but I recognize your voice and this burlap bag."

"I can't talk here."

"Why not? Are you in danger?"

"I just can't—"

Something crashed behind him, and Kenji turned. Seeing something moving out of the corner of his eye, he tackled Daphne to the ground, careful of her injured shoulder and his weight. They lay still as something flew past his head, crashing into the wall behind them, shattering. It looked like one of the mugs that had been on the desks. He put one hand on the floor and shifted to a shooting pose, scanning the area behind them. No one was there, and when he slowly moved to sweep the room, he realized Grey was gone as well.

Daphne was on her feet, running toward the end of the room and the open emergency door. Kenji was right behind in a moment, jogging after her and catching her before she could step through the door.

"No."

"She knows something."

"Someone doesn't want you to talk to her. We'll find her again. We need to secure this room and find out who didn't want you two to talk."

Daphne was pale, and her hands were shaking. "Oh, we are going to get some answers."

"Are you okay?"

"NO! I'm pissed and scared and then pissed that I'm scared. What was that crash, anyway?"

Kenji had her between the wall and his body and looked down into her face, reading the truth of what she was saying. Daphne was a strong woman who could handle herself in any situation, but he felt she was out of patience with this.

"I'm not going to let anything happen to you."

"I know that. But I'd like to get through one day without someone trying to hurt me. I don't believe they were trying to kill me."

"If that mug had connected, you might have gotten a concussion," he said. "But you are right. They seem more intent on injuring you and maybe making you take some time off."

"Well, it's not going to work," she said.

"I believe that," he said, tapping his earpiece. Lee acknowledged him. "We've been attacked in the archives of the museum. Notify the police. I'm going to need everything you can pull on all of the museum employees."

"Are you both okay?"

"We're fine."

"Good. Police on their way. I'll let you know when I have the info you requested."

He tapped his earpiece to mute it. "Cops on their way. I don't want to leave you to go and check the room."

"I have pepper spray."

"Great. I'll wait."

As much as he wanted to find the person who'd attacked Daphne, her safety was his mission. They heard the door that led to the museum open and then footsteps echoing as someone rushed toward them. "Hello?"

"Over here," Kenji said.

"What happened? I'm Dan Jones, the deputy director while Mr. Lauder is out. The emergency door alarm was triggered."

"Someone attacked Daphne and Grey, and Grey ran through the door," Kenji said.

"Who attacked them? I'm so sorry I wasn't here to greet you when you arrived."

"I don't know. I couldn't leave her to go and check. Did you see anyone in the hallway when you came down here?" Kenji asked.

The other man was nervous and kept wringing his hands. "No one. Mr. Lauder is going to be very upset by this. He insisted that your visit go smoothly today, Ms. Amana. Can I get you some tea?"

She shook her head. "No. You can get me all of the items I've requested to see and put them in a secure room for me and my bodyguard to examine. The cops are on their way, and I will be filing a notice with the court that I was attacked while trying to view the evidence in the case."

Dan's eyes went wide, and he used his radio to call for more staff. The room was soon full of people, and Kenji knew he wasn't going to be able to pick up a trail on whomever had attacked them. He wasn't sure that the museum staff were the only ones they should be watching.

"Why weren't you here to greet us?" Kenji asked Dan as they waited.

"Mr. Lauder called in with some last-minute instructions," Dan said.

He wondered if someone had leaked Daphne's schedule. Something he knew she wouldn't take kindly to him bringing up. But he still didn't have all the information on her staff, which was now going to be his top priority.

Chapter 10

Dan was truly the most helpful person in the museum based on her calls and her conversation with Laverne. This was her first time meeting him in person. He wasn't at all what she expected. On the phone, he gave her the impression he was older, taller and bit less nervous than he was right now.

In person, she saw that he was in his late twenties and had thick black hair that curled around his head. He had a thick middle, wore wire-rim glasses, and always seemed easygoing even when she'd talked to him on the phone. So honestly, she was a bit surprised at how young he was.

He wore a suit but no tie and had a lapel pin with the museum's logo on it. He was clearly agitated as he joined them. "Sorry to have kept you waiting."

"That's okay," Daphne said.

"I just spoke to Paul," Kenji said, "and he mentioned you had security footage. I wondered if there was any way that it could be used to see what happened to the missing items."

"Who are you?"

"Kenji Wada, Price Security."

"He's my bodyguard and has been helping out with the different incidents that have been happening to me," Daphne said.

"I'd call being shot at more than an incident," Kenji said.

She just rolled her eyes at him. The last thing she wanted to do was let Dan or anyone else at the museum know she was rattled by all the attacks.

"Paul would know more than me on that. I'm just here to discuss what happened earlier," Dan said. He shoved his hands into his pockets. "I think it would be best if you waited for the police in our offices. Can you follow me?"

Daphne wanted to dig in and keep from leaving the archives. She hadn't really gotten to see anything in the room. Was Grey spooked or had this all been a setup?

Purpose always gave her focus, and she was glad for it as she and Kenji were taken to one of the offices in the museum to await the cops. The office was clearly not used regularly since it only had a pretty standard desk in it, no computer, and only a port for a laptop. The office had one window, which wasn't that large and Kenji immediately moved the desk to the far side of the room away from it.

She was agitated. Not surprising, really, but she'd thought…she'd hoped she would find something in the archives that just neatly pointed to Pierce Lauder as hiding items, and then she'd take that to the courts. Which she knew wasn't realistic, but it would have been nice. Especially after the last few days, she was ready to wrap this case up.

It felt like there was something bigger going on than just these contested items.

She gave her statement to the cops and listened as Kenji gave his. He mentioned to them that she'd been shot four days earlier and that last night someone had broken into her home. Kenji suggested the incidents were all related. The cops took that down before they went to interview the museum staff. Daphne was waiting for the items she'd been meant to view in the archives to be brought to them.

"This attack makes no sense if someone in the museum is involved," Daphne said. "The last thing I would have thought the museum wants is the police here."

"I agree. If the museum or its workers have something to hide, they wouldn't want the cops here. Have you considered that someone might be working on your staff?" he asked.

Daphne closed her eyes and counted to five. She had never had a problem keeping her temper, but she was tired, her shoulder was aching again, no doubt from being dropped to the ground, and her day wasn't going at all to plan. "Stop accusing my staff. I only have people on it who I trust. Why are you so sure it's someone close to me?"

Kenji put his hand up. "I know you trust them, but someone knows where you are going to be before you get there. It makes sense to look at your staff as well as everyone in the museum who you've never met before."

"Don't be sarcastic. It totally doesn't suit you. I know I'm being unreasonable, but honestly, I'm not sure I could handle it if one of my staff is behind this," she said. "I like them. Also, what if I wasn't the target this time? Grey ran as soon as she heard the crash. Maybe the person was after her."

"Possibly."

Kenji said it in a way that made her believe he was trying to pacify her. She knew he was right. At this moment, she couldn't just go around blindly trusting everyone. What was she missing with these items? This case should be straightforward, but when were history and the provenance of taken items ever easy?

The items in this case had been taken by a soldier who had put his life on the line fighting for his country. Maybe they needed to talk to his descendants. She'd received a statement from Henry Hazelton-Measham, but she hadn't talked to him firsthand. "Can I go back to my office?"

"Of course. Once you have finished here, we will go back. I'm going to check in with my team and put your staff's background checks on top priority," he said.

"Great."

The museum staff entered with the boxes, and the acting museum director, Dan Jones, hovered as she carefully examined the items and matched them to her list. None of the missing items were in the boxes, and everything on the inventory matched what she'd been sent.

"I'd go through all of your archives to try to find the missing items."

"I'm not sure—"

"I was just attacked in your museum. I think it might help your case if you make this happen," she said. "Talk to your boss if you need to, and let me know by the end of the day. If I haven't heard back, I'll go through the courts and speak to the press about what happened here today."

Dan stood taller and nodded. "I'll get back with you. Can I see you out now?"

"That would be great. I'd also like to speak to Grey when she returns. Could you ask her to call me?"

"I will," he said, taking Daphne's card.

Kenji moved by her side as they walked through the hallway and out of the museum. The acting director waved them off, and Kenji kept a quick pace as they walked across the parking lot to his car. Once they were inside, he didn't say a word, just put the car in Drive and headed toward her offices.

Putting her mind to sorting through what this latest attack meant kept her composed. Had it even been aimed at her? And like Kenji had suggested, was someone on her team leaking her whereabouts even innocently? Kenji was driving a little faster than usual, and she glanced over at him. He had both hands on the wheel and kept peeking at the review mirror as he wove the car through the traffic.

"Is everything okay?"

"I'm not sure. I think someone is following us," he said.

One of the classes she'd taken when they'd both been at The Farm was in noticing the environment around them and checking for surveillance. It had been years ago, but she did her best to clear her mind of the case and the feeling of insecurity that came from thinking one of staff might not be who they said they were. To dredge up whatever she could remember to help them stay alert.

Kenji drove almost like he was a part of the machine, shifting gears seamlessly as he used the other vehicles around them for cover. "Black Mercedes?" Daphne guessed.

"Yes. Can you read the plate?" he asked.

She couldn't, twisted as she was in her seat. But maybe she'd be able to get a photo of it. She dug her phone out of her bag. Loosening the seat belt, she turned toward the Mercedes.

"Be careful."

"I trust you."

And she totally did. It didn't matter if he annoyed her with his astute observations or that she still wasn't sure about her attraction to him. She knew that he'd die to keep her safe, and there weren't a lot of people she'd say that about. Certainly her mom had never been that dedicated to her. Not sure why that had popped into her head. Except that being around Kenji had always made her feel like she was enough.

Now he wasn't telling her how to take the photo or giving her a lecture on what she should do. He trusted her to get it done. He trusted her—that was the thing that made it easier to be herself. He wasn't looking over at her and trying to see if she was snapping the photo. He knew if it was possible, she'd get one.

She snapped a few, but they were blurry, and finally she got a partial of the plate as Kenji swerved to place them back into the line of traffic from the fast lane. He put his hand in the middle of her back to keep her from flying forward as he hit the brakes to squeeze into the line of cars. There was a blast of horns going off as his maneuver caused others to jack on their brakes.

"Get ready."

Realizing what he was doing, she had the camera on her phone focused as the Mercedes pulled up. Daphne clicked a few times and then hit the photo display to double-check.

"Got it."

As she started to turn, she saw the window on the Mercedes open, a black gloved hand holding a Glock G18 appearing. "He's got a gun."

She doubled her body over to make a small target. Kenji did the same as a bullet hit the driver's-side window. It didn't shatter, and she remembered that he'd told her the car was bulletproof. Lucky break.

The assailant fired again and then stopped as they were in heavier traffic. Daphne looked in her side view mirror. "Shoulder is clear."

Kenji gunned the engine, moving the car off the highway and onto the shoulder. He kept steadily increasing his speed, and she started to turn to check their back tail.

"Don't put yourself in their line of sight. I need you safely in the seat. This is going to be dicey. I can't worry about you," he said.

She put her hands in her lap and sat still and straight. The seat belt was tight and fastened around her body as it should be. Her hands were shaking, so she laced them together. Kenji got to the end of the shoulder as it blended into the exit, cut the car in an impossibly small space, and drove to the shoulder on the opposite side, then continued down the exit ramp and through the red traffic light across several lanes of traffic.

Horns blasted and she heard the squeal of brakes as he got them through the intersection and into the flow of traffic. He continued driving at top speed until they were clear of the area. Then he slowed and started winding through a residential neighborhood. It took a few minutes to realize where they were. He was taking her back to Price Tower.

"We lost them," he said.

"That was some driving," she said. "Thank you."

"You helped by getting the plate," he said. "Thanks for keeping your cool."

She smiled over at him, but he was still watching the road. There was something very sexy about watching Kenji at work. He was so efficient and capable, and he made her feel incredibly safe. Even when he'd been driving fast and making aggressive moves, she'd never once worried he'd allow her to be hurt.

"It reminded me of The Farm a little bit," she said.

"That time we had to try to outmaneuver the instructors. We always made a good team," he said.

They had. "Yeah, we did."

"Why did you quit?" he asked her as they pulled into the underground garage she remembered from the night before.

To be honest, it had been easier to focus on Kenji breaking up with her than her part in the entire situation back then. They had been a good team, the top of their class, and worked well together. But it hadn't taken her long to realize that the life of an operative wasn't for her. When she entered law school and they formally started dating, he never asked her why she made the change. Just said that they'd be a different kind of team. And she'd thought, or rather hoped, that Kenji would continue his work and they'd be able to stay a couple.

Something she knew wasn't realistic, even at the

time. "That work wasn't for me. I was good, but I knew that you were better. And it was changing me... I didn't like it."

The tension didn't really leave his body. It was going to take him a while to come down from that drive. He was still wound up from everything that had happened at the museum. He needed time to think and process what was going on so he could find the patterns of their pursuer and then find whoever was after Daphne.

He'd parked the car, and she sat next to him, her hands held tightly in her lap. Why she'd left the training program that would have seen them both in the CIA hadn't been something he'd ever intended to inquire about, but she had been good. They had been good.

And although he knew he'd broken up with her because of the career he wanted for himself, another part of him knew that seeing her go in another direction had been a piece of it. He wanted to be immersed in the life of a CIA operative, and nothing was going to keep him from achieving that. Not even Daphne.

But all of that was a distraction. He knew what he needed. A fight or some kind of physical release, which just made him think about what she looked like when she came in his arms. And it had been so long that he'd have thought that memory would have faded, but it hadn't.

They were so close in the car, he couldn't breathe without inhaling the spicy sweet scent of her perfume. He undid his seat belt and then forced himself to put his hands back on the steering wheel. If he didn't, he was going to reach for Daphne, and he wasn't going to be able to let her go until he was buried deep inside her body.

Which probably wasn't what she needed right now.

Putting her first allowed him to grapple with his self-control and win for the moment.

"We need to call the cops and report the car tailing us. Also, I think we need to brainstorm about who is after you and start narrowing down the leads. My first priority is your safety, so if you can swing the time away from your office for the rest of the day, I'd like to stay here."

She undid her seat belt and twisted her body to face him. "Back to business."

"Yes. I shouldn't have asked you about why you left. That decision was your own, and you can't have any regrets given the career you've had and the people's lives you've made better."

He didn't want to go back to his own pain when she'd told him she had left the program. The confusion it had caused in him and the feelings of once again being left because of who he was. There wasn't anything healthy about that kind of thinking. Both of them had made choices, and their lives had taken them on their own paths. That was enough for Kenji.

"Sure. But what about us?"

"There would probably not have been an us even if you'd stayed and I hadn't broken up with you. The CIA isn't exactly about building trust in people or about making long-term bonds," he said dryly.

"Yeah. So let me check my schedule, and then I'll let you know about the rest of today," she said.

She pulled her phone out, and he watched her long,

manicured fingers moving on the screen, swiping to check her schedule and then tapping out a message.

"Okay. I've asked for the rest of the day off. Carl wants a call to discuss the latest attack on me. But I told him I needed some time to clean up, and then we could talk. Will that work?"

"Yes. I want to clear your entire staff before we go back to your office. Lee's had a day, so she should have most of them finished," Kenji said.

"A day? Is that long enough?"

They both got out of the car, and as they walked toward the elevator, she noticed Xander from the night before waiting there. The big guy had practically blended into the shadows.

"X, three bullets to the driver's window. I'm not sure if they put a tracer on the car. Lee's electronic security will mute any signal from getting out, but can you check it?" Kenji said, tossing the keys to Xander as they walked by him.

"No prob. You two okay?"

"Yes," Daphne said.

Kenji just nodded as they got on the elevator.

"How did my phone work?" Daphne asked since there was an electronic signal blocker in place.

"Last night, when I gave you access to the Wi-Fi, your device was registered as known, so it isn't blocked."

"Oh, wow. I had no idea something like that existed."

"Lee's got all sorts of tech that you probably don't want to know about," he said. "Do you want to get changed first and then talk to the team?"

"That would be nice," she said.

He noticed the stiff way she held herself with her

arms around her waist, and he hated that. Once again, the tension that he hadn't been able to shake was back. It was all he could do not turn pull her into his arms and hit the elevator stop button. He needed…hell, he was pretty sure he needed Daphne. He needed to hold her and make love to her. Reassure himself that she was safe.

He leaned slightly toward her and she leaned closer to him just as the elevator doors opened.

"Kenji, we need to talk."

Van waited as Kenji turned to him and stepped in front of Daphne.

"Of course. Let me get Daphne into my apartment."

Van just nodded.

"Take your time," Kenji said, opening the door to his apartment and motioning for Daphne to go inside.

Chapter 11

Kissing Kenji would have been a mistake—she knew that—but another part of her had needed it. It wasn't just everything that had happened today. It was everything that was going on in her life right now.

She ran her hands down the sides of her hips and couldn't help but feel dirty from being on the floor of the archives. Inside she was still trembling from the day. A hot shower and maybe a chance to lean against the wall and just let her guard down for a moment would be nice.

Kenji was doing his best to keep her safe, but she was still scared. Days of being attacked were starting to take a toll on her. This case wasn't nearly the most high-profile one she'd ever taken, and yet it was definitely the most dangerous.

She realized she was holding her breath as she walked to her room. Once she was inside it and the door closed behind her, she exhaled and wanted to scream but just quietly cried instead.

Stripping off her clothes, she walked naked to the bathroom and turned on the hot water before getting into the shower. She stood at the back of the cubicle and leaned her forehead against the tiled walls. Tears were easy enough to explain, and they didn't bother her. Men punched things. In her experience, women cried. It was just the way nature had made her, and she wasn't going to beat herself up for a normal reaction.

The tears passed as her mind started to force her to recover. It was something she'd learned to do as a child when she'd thought she'd done something that would impress her mother, but instead had been told to stop bragging about herself. There had been no way to make her mom proud, and Daphne wished she'd learned that at eight instead of ten years after her mom had died.

She tried to use that knowledge about herself in her work and everyday life to avoid repeating mistakes.

She heard the bedroom door open and knew that Kenji was in her room. He rapped on the bathroom door.

"Yes."

"Just wanted to let you know I'm in the apartment."

She opened her mouth to thank him, but instead his name came out.

"Yes?"

"I don't want to be alone," she said.

He didn't say anything, and she shook her head. If she'd learned anything from these last twenty-four hours with Kenji, it was that he wasn't going to compromise the job he'd been hired to do.

But then the door opened, and she saw him standing at the end of the nicely appointed bathroom through the glass wall of the shower cubicle.

He watched her for a minute, and she knew he was waiting for her to invite him further. She pushed the shower head so that it hit the wall and opened the door.

He took his clothes off.

She couldn't tear her eyes away as she watched him shrug out of his suit jacket and then slowly remove his tie. His fingers moved down the buttons of his shirt, and he shrugged out of it, tossing it on top of the growing pile of his clothes on the floor.

He toed off his shoes before he undid his pants and pushed them down his legs along with his underwear. Her breath caught in her throat as she really looked at all of him. His wide shoulders tapered to a lean but muscled chest and then a slim waist. His erection was large and strong.

It was undeniable. He wanted her as much as she wanted him.

Kenji bent to take off his socks and then stood, pushing his bangs back as he walked slowly toward her. She licked her lips as he stepped inside the shower, pulling her into his arms. Her body was wet and his was dry, and her breasts felt slick against the solidness of his chest. His hands were on her waist and then on her butt as he lifted her more fully into his body and lowered his head to kiss her.

His mouth was familiar to her now, his tongue against hers stirring a fire deep inside of her. There was a pulse of feminine heat between her legs as she felt his cock against her stomach. She put her arms around his shoulders and angled her head to deepen their kiss.

He turned so that he leaned against the wall and lifted her up with his hands on her hips. Then she parted her legs, wrapping them around his hips. She felt the tip of his penis first against her clit, which felt nice and sent a ripple through her.

She swallowed hard and shifted her body against

his until she felt him at her entrance. Their eyes met as she put her hands on his shoulders and slid down on his cock. She had missed him more than she'd allowed herself to admit until this moment. He turned so that her back was against the wall. His mouth was on her neck, kissing and sucking at her skin as he drove into her again and again.

She couldn't think of the past or the present. The danger she was in disappeared, and the world become just hers and Kenji's. She drove herself against him and felt that shiver in her center as her body started to tighten, and then her orgasm rushed over her. She bit his shoulder as she shuddered and came in his arms. He braced one hand against the wall by her head and drove up and into her again and again until he cried out her name and she felt his cock swell in her body. Then he came inside of her.

She held him, her head on his shoulder, the water still pounding around them. Neither of them spoke, but words would have only ruined this moment. Instead they washed each other silently and then exited the shower.

Kenji had promised his boss he'd get Daphne to the "war room," as they liked to call the big conference room they used when everyone was involved with one client. But he wasn't rushing this. He also wasn't rushing himself.

He'd waited too long to be back in her life to not take having her in his arms again seriously. He wrapped a towel around her and then pulled her close to him, hugging her, because he knew that this might have been a one-off moment.

She'd had a really rough day, and he wasn't ruling out the fact that she'd turned to him for some human contact and release to deal with the stress and tension.

Her head nestled on his shoulder felt right. Like she belonged back in his arms. Though a part of him wasn't entirely sure he'd be able to keep her there.

"Any regrets, Daph?"

The way he held her, she couldn't see his face, which was what he wanted. He was scared of her answer. Almost as much as he had been worried for her safety when she'd been turned around in the car seat to take photos while he'd been driving over one hundred miles per hour. But this time he had no skills to fall back on, no way of keeping his guard up if she said yes.

"No. You?"

"Definitely not."

He let out a relieved breath, which made her laugh as she stepped back. "Worried, were you?"

"Very. Clients get freaked when they've had a day like yours," he said.

She pulled her towel up higher and took a few more steps away from him. "Is this all part of the Kenji service?"

Fuck.

Of course he'd said the wrong thing. "No. That's not what I meant."

"What did you mean?" she asked, turning to the sink, where she'd left a bathrobe draped on the counter. She pulled it on and then dropped her towel, so he knew he'd hurt her.

God, this was hard. He understood what he had to say. If he wanted a second chance with her, he had to just lay it bare and talk about the emotions he had for her. But he felt raw and hated that.

"I like you. I have never slept with a client. I said that because I know what you're feeling might be motivated by fear and adrenaline. I'm more used to being shot at and chased than you are, and even I'm a little shaken."

She turned then, running her brush through her hair, but he noticed that she wasn't glaring at him anymore.

"*Shaken* is a good word to use. Today has been a lot. But I'm not a woman to just sleep with a man to release tension."

"I shouldn't have worded it the way I did," he said. "I still suck at that."

"You do," she agreed.

He smiled at her. "Truce?"

"Truce."

"I'll leave you to finish up. We can discuss next steps over lunch, and then Van is calling in the available team to strategize in the conference room if you're up for it."

"Yeah, I'll be there. I want to be involved in all discussions and planning," she said.

"I knew you would."

He bent to pick up his clothes from the floor and noticed her watching him in the mirror as he stood back up. But she didn't say anything, and he hesitated for a second before nodding at her and walking out the door.

She had her suitcase on the bed, and he noted she had a journal on her nightstand as well as a book. He couldn't read the title but was curious which book she'd taken from his library. He didn't like dust jackets, so he'd removed them all, and the hardcover was just a brown color.

He would ask her about it later. Hooking up with Daphne had felt right in the moment, but Kenji had realized at the museum and in the car that he wanted more with her than just this assignment. He'd be lying if he said he hadn't from the moment her name had come up in the briefing.

He walked through the living area of his apartment and into his bedroom, putting his clothes in the laundry bag and then quickly getting dressed in another black suit, white shirt and thin black tie. He snapped on his holster, tied his shoes, and went back into the other room as his phone pinged, letting him know that the lunch he'd ordered was being brought up by Van.

His boss was hovering, and Kenji wasn't sure why. Was Kenji giving something away about his feelings for Daphne? Or was it just that this case should have been a lot simpler than it was turning out to be?

He opened the door when Van arrived.

"You're not usually the delivery guy," Kenji said.

"No, I'm not."

"Why?"

Van came into the apartment and put the food on the counter. He leaned against it, his legs crossed at the ankles. So this wasn't going to be a quick convo.

"Just wanted to make sure you both were okay. Those shots in the window were aimed right at your head," Van said.

Kenji hadn't allowed himself to dwell on that. The shooter had meant to kill him, maybe with the intent to kidnap Daphne. Something that Kenji wasn't going to let happen.

"Yeah, that's why I came right here. We need to figure out what's going on."

"I agree. Lee's almost done with all the info you asked her to pull on Daphne's work colleagues. I brought up a file you might want to check out and talk to her about privately."

Great. That meant someone on her staff had raised a red flag.

"Thanks."

Van nodded and then left. Kenji glanced down at the file that Van had handed him and realized it was for the paralegal who'd gotten freaked out on the first day. Alan Field. He was related to Pierce Lauder.

Daphne dried her hair and then got dressed, taking her time with her makeup because she always felt stronger when she looked her best. It was a bit of her faking confidence, but once she had her pantsuit on and her heels, she felt like the successful attorney she was.

Not the woman who'd just cuddled in her lover's arms, trying to recover from one of the hardest days she'd ever experienced. She wasn't about to start unpacking her emotions about what had happened between the two of them. Not now. She wanted to figure out why someone was coming so hard after her.

She needed to return the censer she'd found, which she thought was her top priority. Kenji had mentioned that his boss would have the cops come here to collect it. Maybe having it in police custody would stop the attacks on her.

Maybe wasn't her favorite word because it usually meant no. But this time she wasn't sure. Walking out into the living room, she noticed that Kenji had set up the table and was waiting for her.

"What's for lunch?" she asked.

She wondered why he always wore the black suit. It looked good on him, and maybe he used it like she did as armor for his day. She wasn't going to ask him, but she was curious.

"Cobb salad with blue cheese dressing."

Her favorite. It mattered to her that he'd remember that tiny detail. "Thank you."

He shrugged as if it were nothing, but it wasn't. It showed her that leaving her back then…it almost made her feel better about it. His words had started to heal that broken, hurt part that still lingered inside of her, but this…was helping too.

She sat down, setting her phone and notebook next to her spot. Kenji sat across from her. She started to eat and then noticed he wasn't touching his lunch.

"What is it?"

"There is a connection between one of your paralegals and the museum," Kenji said carefully, then turned the electronic tablet next to his spot toward her.

She put her fork down as she saw that it was Alan. He'd been doing a lot of the leg work on this case for her. He'd been the one to do all of the research for the brief she'd used to ask the judge to compel the museum to give her access to their archives and inventory.

"How is he connected to the museum?"

He could be a donor and maybe have a relative on the board. Maybe it wasn't as bad as her mind was making it.

"He's Pierce Lauder's nephew."

Nope. It was definitely a connection that she couldn't ignore. "Okay. I'll need to speak to him. I know we said I'd stay here today, but I think this can't wait."

"I agree. We can head to your office after lunch," Kenji said.

"Yes. Did your boss talk to the cops about me turning over the censer?" she asked.

"He did, and they will be here around four this afternoon. Originally you were meant to be at your office."

"I know. That's good. I was thinking perhaps the attacks on me might stop if the censer is known to be with the cops," Daphne said.

"That's a nice thought."

"Don't be placating. You sound fake," she said.

He shrugged and tipped his head to the left. "It was meant to be supportive."

She took another bite of her salad, but she wasn't sure she could enjoy it. Her mind was buzzing with the thought that Alan might be feeding Pierce information on their case. She was trying to make a connection to one solid piece of evidence, but nothing was coming to her. She wanted to blame the day and was going to.

Because otherwise it meant that she'd trusted the wrong person. She thought she'd become so much better about that than she apparently had. "I wonder why we didn't catch that when he was hired and assigned to my team."

"Were you representing your client then?" Kenji asked.

"No. In fact, he came on to work on a human rights case. He's been one of my most reliable paralegals," she said.

"He might still be. There's a connection. It might not be more than a blood relation that he never talks to," Kenji said.

He had a point. She could have worked for her mom's rival law firm and nothing would have passed between the two of them. "I just hate that you found anything on the people on my staff."

"I hate it too," he said.

"But you expected it?"

He leaned forward, and that fall of bangs drifted away from his face until he pushed it back up on his head. "I did. Somehow your movements are known to whoever is attacking you."

"They did follow us when we left."

"Yes, which means maybe your paralegal isn't leaking your whereabouts. Or, as you said, they just want the censer back."

She thought about that for a minute, rubbing her shoulder where it still hurt, remembering the soft kisses that Kenji had dropped on it when they'd both been washing. She thought back to the drive to the Price Security building and realized something she'd missed before.

The shots fired at the car had been aimed at Kenji's head. The shooter had been trying to take him out.

Looking up to find him concentrating on her, she cleared her throat. "Do you think they want to kidnap me?"

He rubbed the back of his neck and then looked her straight in the eyes. "It would seem that way based on the car."

"What am I going to do?"

"Exactly what we've discussed. My buddy Xander just got hired on as security in your office building, and he'll make sure your office is secure before I bring you in."

Chapter 12

She wore a slim-fitting black sweater that hugged her curves and drew his eyes to her breasts. It was short-sleeved again, which just showed off her toned arms. The sling and bandage had been removed from her shoulder now, and he saw her move her arm gingerly, testing the movement.

She walked to the table to collect her yellow handbag. It matched the flowers appliqued on her brown knee-length skirt. The large yellow blooms ran down the left side. She had on those high heels again.

"Kenji?"

"Hmm."

"You're staring at my legs."

"Just wondering how you can walk in those heels," he said quickly, tearing his eyes from them and forcing his gaze up to her face. She was clearly amused and saw through his smoke screen.

She winked and said, "Very carefully."

Flirting. She was *flirting* with him, and he wanted to flirt back, but he knew that he was walking a very difficult line. He needed to keep her safe. With each passing day and the time they spent together, it was getting harder and harder for him to do just that.

"I'm impressed," he said, before pivoting away from her and leading the way down to the car.

She was quiet as they drove back to her office in a brand-new vehicle. There hadn't been a tracker on the damaged one. Kenji wasn't really sure if that was a good thing or not. It made him feel like they weren't dealing with a professional. The attacks on Daphne had been sporadic, and they had been more menacing than lethal in his estimation. Not that having her house broken into and ransacked hadn't been harrowing for Daphne, but there didn't seem to be any real skill behind the attacker.

Even the car following them earlier in the day had been too aggressive, not a trained operative. Which worried him. Amateurs made mistakes that professionals didn't. But the shooter had been steady so possibly a pro. Daphne's shoulder injury might have been a warning or just a bad shot. At first he'd thought it was a warning, but the incident in the archives had the feel of someone who was just pissed off rather than any real menace. Though the coffee mug would have concussed Daphne if she'd been hit with it.

"Do you remember where Grey was standing when you two were talking?" he asked.

"What?"

"I'm trying to replay the mug hitting the wall in my head, and it's not clear if the mug was aimed at you or her," Kenji said.

"She was already out the door when the mug came. It was aimed at me," she said. "I looked up at the wall from where you'd pushed me down, and there were fragments in front of my eyes."

Damn.

"So the bookcases that were pushed over might have been a warning to Grey that her partner was there."

"Yes. But why not use a gun?" Daphne asked.

"I'm not sure. Maybe they meant to but didn't have time," he said. "Did it seem that Grey was about to tell you something?"

Kenji had been only half paying attention to the actual conversation. He hadn't liked the room with the tall rows of bookshelves that offered ample hiding places.

"I believe she was," Daphne said.

Which didn't really help him that much. "What if she'd been meant to tell you one thing and instead deviated?"

Daphne closed her eyes, and he had the feeling that she was reliving the moment in her head. "She was nervous and didn't like that I called her out on being the person who'd contacted me. Maybe her partner didn't know that?"

"Yes, and if they overheard your questioning, they'd know that Grey had spoken to you. Maybe the bookcase was to shut her up before she gave you the name?"

Daphne pulled out her notebook and made a few notes. "I think you might be right. Will Lee be able to find her?"

"Even if she goes to ground, Lee will find her. It might take a few days, but she'll get Grey Joy for us."

"Good. I need to talk to her. Now I'm wondering what she was going to tell me about the items. Clearly someone at the museum wanted her to give me information that would help their side of the case."

"How?" Kenji asked.

"I'm not sure. It seems the missing items are the key,

but I do wonder if I should be concentrating on them. The already known items, though, are really not enough to satisfy my client. She wants all of them returned."

Kenji didn't understand the legalities and what the different pieces meant culturally or monetarily to her client. "Do you know the value of the missing pieces?"

"I have the museum's figures, which Marjorie accepted as factual. And there is no pattern to the money. I might try to go talk to the great-grandson of the man who took the items originally. They were labeled spoils of war, so he was able to legally keep them at the time. But the museum has mismatched records on what was donated, and it doesn't line up with what my client believes they have or some photos I saw of an exhibit as recently as 2015."

He liked listening to her talk about the case as she continued telling him about the inconsistencies and how she was going to ferret out the truth. She also stopped looking so white and nervous when she discussed the details of the case and getting justice for her client. He liked the changes he saw in her. The woman he'd known when they'd been in college had this same fire, but it seemed honed now. Her intelligence had always been there, and she used it to make connections and rule out possibilities.

He had the feeling she'd leave no stone unturned to get a winning result for her client. Which he appreciated. "Send me the donor's name if you don't mind. We can run down his information for you."

"I was going to have my team… I guess you're right. Until I talk to Alan and the rest of them, I really don't know who to trust. And I don't want to put anyone else in danger," she said.

He liked that she was thinking now about her safety in a way she hadn't been last night when she'd gone into the alleyway by herself. Once that feeling of security everyone enjoyed had been ripped away from her, she wasn't going to trust again easily.

He hit his earpiece as they pulled into the parking garage for her law firm and let Xander know they were there.

"Garage and elevator secure. Lee is looped in with closed circuit cameras that Rick and I installed. You're clear to Daphne's office," Xander said.

Kenji relayed that to Daphne before they both got out of the car and he escorted her to her temporary office. She put her purse in her desk and then asked to have the paralegal brought in to see her.

"Where do you want me?"

"By the door, I guess. I wish I was in my office. It's more intimidating than this closet you put me in."

"You're plenty intimidating without the big office," he said.

Daphne always tried to approach her work like justice itself. Blind to everything but the facts, and usually she could succeed in keeping her emotions out of it. But there were some cases where it was harder. She usually didn't struggle with that in the workplace, yet there were days.

Today was one of those days. She let Alan sweat as he sat in the guest chair that Kenji had brought in for him. A part of her brain was busy mechanically listing all the reasons why he might have concealed the fact that he was related to Pierce Lauder. The other part of her was too hurt to care.

She trusted everyone on her team to want the same results. A win for their client of course meant prestige within the firm and a chance for promotion or partner, depending on their position, so that was always a factor too. But this was different. Alan should have recused himself the moment he learned that his uncle was a named codefendant in the case.

"I'm not sure why I'm here," Alan said, clearly nervous.

"Alan, I'm going to ask you something, and I want you to be honest," Daphne said, taking her time to make sure she could be calm. Maybe if it didn't feel like a personal betrayal it would have been easier, but it did.

"Of course," Alan said, leaning forward. "Daphne, I wouldn't lie to you about anything."

"Are you related to Pierce Lauder?" she asked. Because that was clearly a lie by omission.

He turned beet-red, licked his lips, then swallowed. "You know I am."

"I do. What I don't know is why you never disclosed that relationship and if you are feeding him information," she said.

"I'd never do that. My uncle and I aren't close. In fact, I haven't seen him since I was twelve. He and my mom had a falling out," Alan said.

Daphne didn't want to hear about his family's drama. Everyone had their own version of it. Someone got upset by someone else, and they didn't talk for years. Or they had her version of family drama. Where one person didn't like another one and ignored them, and the rest of the family ignored it as if they couldn't see the damage. Whoa, she thought. She wasn't unpacking that in the office with Alan and Kenji.

She was tired, which was the only excuse she could come up with for all these memories of her mother. And she'd been alive when Kenji and Daphne had been together the last time. Not that that mattered right now.

"That's your mom's relationship with him. Why didn't you say anything to me?"

He rubbed the back of his neck and then scooted forward in his chair toward her. Kenji moved subtly toward Alan.

But he didn't need to. Alan's face was earnest. "I didn't know how. I took a job here because of men like my uncle who put the reputation of their collection above the rightful owners of the pieces they exhibit. I wanted to work here to help right that wrong. I never expected this case to come to us or that it would be you who got it."

"Fair enough, but once I did, you should have mentioned it," she said.

"I was going to, but you were giving me a lot of work to do. No ego here, but I am really good at research and pulling together precedent. I liked the work. Once you were shot, I knew I had to mention it, but you haven't been available on your own," he said.

"You're good at what you do, and I feel the same way about cases that are handed to me. But I have had to recuse myself from more than one," she said. "I hated to do it, but it was the right thing to do."

She'd recused herself from a case that would have seen her go up against her own mother in court. Daphne had struggled with that decision because there was nothing she wanted more than to beat her mom. But she'd known that she couldn't be unbiased when it came to any case involving her mom. Was it the same for Alan?

She wasn't entirely sure that trusting him was a smart decision, but she also didn't see any malintent in him. Glancing up at Kenji, she saw him shake his head. He wasn't sure she could trust Alan still.

"Where were you today?"

"I've been in the office all morning, working on the case. I talked to the new security guy for a while," Alan said.

"What did you discuss?"

Alan looked sheepish. "*Halo.* We both play it online."

Kenji's face changed, and he gave her a small nod. She guessed that Xander had already been checking Alan out, which she wasn't too pleased with. But it did show her how much her safety meant not just to Kenji but to the entire Price Security team.

"For now I'm going to allow you to remain on the case," Daphne said. "From this point forward, there can be no contact with Pierce Lauder. If he contacts you, let me know immediately."

"Thank you, Daphne. I will. I don't think he'll call me or anything. He doesn't have my number."

"I'm glad to hear that. That's all for now."

Kenji opened the door, and Alan got up and left her office. After the door closed, Kenji leaned back against it, and she remembered how he'd stood in the doorway of the bathroom earlier. A sensual shiver went through her.

Like she needed to be thinking about sex right now.

"So, your buddy checked Alan out?"

"I didn't know that. As soon as we arrived back at the tower, Van let me know about Alan, and I let you know. I assume that Van thought he was a security risk and wanted to check it out before you were back in the office."

"I appreciate it, but next time, I want to be looped in before it happens," she said.

"Yes, ma'am."

He was being all formal and agreeable, but she knew that he'd do whatever he felt was in her best interests, even if it ticked her off.

Daphne had a meeting with her boss that Kenji followed her to, sort of like a silent shadow. That was how he always liked to think of himself when he was on the job. Moving in tandem with his client to keep them safe but not to intrude on their lives. The struggle with Daphne was different than with other clients because he cared about her. Deeply.

But he'd been aware of that when he'd agreed to take the case. He wasn't sure what he'd expected. Getting into his feelings had never been easy for him, and this time wasn't any different. It was harder because the only woman he'd truly ever loved was his mom, and she'd died shortly after he'd gone to college.

Kenji'd reacted with an afternoon of deep grieving and then shoved the rest of his emotions down and kept them locked away. He hadn't known how to process that, and at the time, he hadn't been going to therapy. The sessions he had with his therapist mainly dealt with his father.

"I want you to think seriously of coming off this case,

Daphne. I know you've done all the legwork. At this point, if we let Sam take over, she'll just get it over the finish line for you," Carl said. "Your life means more than this win."

Daphne made herself even stiffer and taller, if that were possible. "I have a bodyguard, and I think stepping back now would just signal that whoever is intimidating me is succeeding. Who's to say Sam would be safe?"

Carl leaned back in the big leather chair that he sat in, glancing over at Kenji. Kenji held himself still in the ready position. Van had worked with Carl before, so the other man knew that Kenji was the best in the business. "What do you think? Can you keep her safe?"

"Yes, sir."

Kenji understood where Carl was coming from. No one wanted to see one of their employees threatened and injured. But the cases that Daphne's firm represented often put them in the line of fire. They were human rights cases that won the hearts of the public but often not those of the defendants on the other side.

"What can I do to help?" he asked.

"I know that Ben Cross has filed a motion to delay the trial again this morning. We've filed a counter-motion, but if you could talk to Judge Mallon's office, it might help," Daphne said. "I feel like all of these attacks must mean that the evidence I've compelled them to present is more damning than they want us to know."

"But we don't know why?" Carl asked.

"Not yet. I'm trying to talk with the man who donated the entire cache that is at the heart of my case. I think there must be a connection I'm just not seeing yet. The missing items on the inventory... I feel like someone, maybe Lauder, knows exactly where they are. The archivist I was speaking to was about to reveal something when we were attacked," Daphne said.

"I trust your instincts, which is why I assigned this case to you. I'll talked to Mallon's office and stressed that we don't want any more delays." Carl turned to him. "Do you believe the threat to Daphne will be lessened after the case goes to court?"

"Oh, definitely. They are trying to keep her from finding out something," Kenji said.

"Good. I'll add that in as well. Maybe see if I can get it moved up," Carl said. "Keep me in the loop with the evidence. Will you be talking to the archivist again?"

"Definitely. I'm waiting to hear back from her," Daphne said.

Kenji knew that was a white lie, but also that his team would find Grey Joy, and Daphne would have the chance to talk to her.

Carl and Daphne wrapped up their conversation, and they left his office. In the hall, as they headed toward the elevator, he was alert, watching for anyone. But knowing that Xander and Rick had installed closed circuit cameras made him less anxious than he had been yesterday when he'd come into her office.

"That went better than expected," Daphne said when they got on the elevator and were alone.

"I always knew you'd get a result," he said.

"You did? How?"

He looked over at her. "You don't fail when you put your mind to something. Ever. Carl was always going to come around to your way of thinking because he knows that as well."

"You make me sound…"

"Awesome," he said simply.

She shook her head. "I'm not, but thank you. Between Carl and Alan, it's been a day, and I still have to hand over the censer to the cops later. I would like to do some work and try again to reach John Hazelton-Measham so that I can set up an appointment, and I need to talk to my team and let them know about Alan."

"Whatever you need," he said. He'd already made sure the conference room where she liked to work with her team was as secure as he could make it. He settled into the corner of the room where he had a clear view of the door and Daphne as she worked.

He noticed how everyone on her team worked at a very high level, which he knew was down to Daphne. She gave her all, so everyone around her did the same.

When they were alone in the conference room as she wrapped up her day, he couldn't help watching her—not as her bodyguard, but as a man observing a woman he cared deeply about. The emotions were there, and he was afraid to name them at this moment, but that didn't mean he wasn't feeling them.

Chapter 13

One last thing, she thought, and then she could lie in her bed and pretend she was going to sleep. When they got back to Price Security, Van let them know that Detective Miller was waiting in the conference room. Daphne retrieved the censer from the safe. Legally she probably should have surrendered this as soon as she was conscious in the hospital, but she hoped the officer would be understanding.

Her shoulder was at a dull ache, but only because she'd forgotten about the injury and slung her work bag over that shoulder. Kenji was taking a break, and his coworker, Luna Urban, was with her as she went to talk to the cop.

Luna had introduced herself earlier but had just quietly stood in the background. Unlike with Kenji, Daphne didn't really notice the woman who was acting as her bodyguard. When they got into the conference room, she did notice that Van Price was in the corner on his device. The muscled bald man looked intimidating to her for the first time. The expression on his face was tense and almost menacing.

But when he heard them enter, he looked up, his face softening into a smile. "Good evening, ladies."

He walked over to them, and she noted the angel wings tattoo on the back of his neck as he gave Luna a one-armed hug. "We don't see this one much anymore."

"That's only because Jaz wanted me on tour again, and Nick missed me while I was gone," Luna said.

The names meant nothing to Daphne, who just smiled and moved toward the cop while the other two caught up.

Detective Miller was short and had brown curly hair streaked with gray. She wore a dark blue suit and a button-down white blouse. She had her badge clipped to her belt and a shoulder holster that Daphne first noticed when she shrugged out of her jacket. Her nails were short and neat on one hand, but the thumbnail on her left hand had been chewed back to the quick.

Daphne guessed her job wasn't without its stresses. She pulled a pair of reading glasses from her shoulder bag and put them on. When she looked up, Daphne realized her eyes were a gorgeous light blue, and she had thick eyelashes.

Her voice when she spoke had an air of authority to it that she'd also noticed in Officer Martinez's voice the other night. Most cops she'd worked with over the years had it. They knew they had to be calm but also project it to the person they were interrogating.

Daphne wasn't planning on being anything but honest with the detective. It wouldn't help Daphne find out how the censer had ended up in an alley if she wasn't honest. Working with the courts, she knew she should have turned it in much sooner, but she wasn't going to fabricate a date when she got it to make herself look better. Right now, the only way she was going to find answers was to be as honest as she could.

And being honest with the detective was easier than being honest with herself about her currently messy feelings where Kenji was concerned.

"Thank you for coming down here," she said after they'd introduced themselves. "I found this the night I was shot and put it in my bag. I was finally able to look at it yesterday. As soon as I did, I recognized it as an item that was marked missing in my current legal case. Things…have been hectic."

"That's putting it mildly. Van caught me up on everything that has happened to you. I'm happy to take your statement and this item into custody," Detective Miller said. "I assume today was the first moment you had to turn it in."

"It was," Daphne said.

"If there is anything to be investigated, we will look into it."

"Sorry. That sounded like I was telling you how to do your job. It's just…never mind. Do you have a statement form for me to fill out?" she asked the detective.

"I do. And I'd also like to record your statement as well. I will notify the museum that we have found an item of theirs."

Daphne gave her story. When they were done recording it and she'd signed her written statement, Daphne lingered.

"Yes?" Detective Miller said.

"The censer is a sacred tabot for the Ethiopian Orthodox Church. I'm not sure of the way it should be handled, but the way I found it shows no respect for the church or its believers."

"I'll see if we can contact someone from the church to make sure it's handled properly."

"Thank you. I know it is the property of the Los Angeles Museum of Foreign Cultures, but it had been marked missing and not stolen as recently as yesterday. Would you mind checking to see if any other items similar to this have been turned in?"

"That's not my job, but I can send you some paperwork to fill out so that the evidence clerk can do a search. I am interested in this idea of missing but not stolen. Are there any stolen items on the list?"

Daphne pulled it out. "No, but one of my paralegals found two of the missing items listed for sale on a black market art website. I think this item that I found might be the key to locating these other ones."

"Were you able to purchase the missing items?" the detective asked.

"No. In fact, we can no longer access the site at all. I have two screen grabs that aren't the highest quality," Daphne said.

"Send them to me and include them in your evidence request. I work in homicide, so I can't take this case, but I'll see it gets to the right hands."

"If you work in homicide, why are you here?" she asked.

"Van asked me, and I owed him a favor," she said. "Where can I reach you?"

Daphne gave the detective her cell phone number, and then the detective left. Van came over to her and sat down next to her. "I overheard you mention the black market. I think Lee can help with that. Do you have the URL for the site?"

"Just from the screen grab," she said. "It's not clear. We had clicked on a photo that matched a description of one of the items."

"Do you have time now?" Van asked. "I'd like to get your entire missing list to Lee so she can start digging around for you. Especially if you think they might be going to auction."

"I do have time." She knew she wasn't going to sleep, and she'd much rather get the answers she needed. If Carl was successful at getting their court date moved up, she'd have something substantial to take into court.

It was beginning to look to her like maybe the reason talks had broken down between her client and the museum was that they were doing something shady with the disputed items. She still wasn't clear what the actual play they were making was, but she felt like she was getting much closer to finding some answers.

She spent the next two hours in the computer room with Lee, impressed by the way the woman pulled information together. She was keenly intelligent, and Daphne would love to have someone like her on her team, which she mentioned.

"I can't leave Price Security, but if you need an assist, I'm always available," she said.

"Thanks." Daphne said goodbye to Lee and walked out of the office to find Kenji waiting for her.

She was happy to see him and started to reach for him to hug him, but he stopped her. He put his hand on the small of her back and directed her toward the elevator at the end of the hall.

* * *

The sun was setting as they walked out of her office to his car. Kenji was on alert. Even knowing that Xander and Rick had installed extra security measures didn't ease the tension in his gut. It was bringing back memories of his last assignment in Afghanistan before he'd retired from the CIA.

All of his instincts told him they were being watched. When they got to the car, instead of opening the door for Daphne, he kept her between his body and the vehicle.

"What is it?" she asked. She held her shoulder bag closer to her body.

"Someone is watching us," he said. "I want you to get in the car, lock the doors. The glass is bulletproof, but if there are shots fired at the car, leave. Drive to Price Security. The garage will open automatically for you."

"I'm not leaving you behind," she said.

"I don't have time to debate this. The light is good for this kind of hunt with the sun almost down. Do what I've asked." He opened the door and all but shoved her inside, tossing his keys on her lap.

She stopped him from closing the door.

He waited.

"Be careful."

He just nodded. He tapped his earpiece and pulled his weapon from his holster as he moved in the direction of one of the side buildings. From an earlier survey, he knew that it was a maintenance shed used by the lawn crew for the property.

"Wada here. I'm on the move. Someone is watching us."

"Got you. Where is Daphne?" Lee responded immediately.

"In the car with orders to go to Price Tower if things get hot," Kenji said. "Going silent."

"Affirmative. Sending backup," Lee said.

Kenji had learned early that missions depended on him. He relied on his team, but he had to be able to handle it by himself. He often thought of those old Western and martial arts movies him mom used to watch where a lone warrior had to defend a small village or town. That was how he saw himself.

He was tired of the game that was being played with Daphne. It was as if whoever was watching her was toying with her. He moved around the outbuilding to a small stand of trees that had been planted and was neatly manicured. He kept low as he ran.

There was a rustle in the leaves behind him. He turned as a man dressed in camo fired three shots in rapid succession at him. Kenji swerved his body to avoid being hit and dropped to the ground when the last one almost grazed his head. He watched as the assailant ran away from the building.

Kenji pushed himself off the ground and took off after him. The landscape in LA was hilly, rough terrain, and this part was no different. Kenji's suit was cut to allow him to pursue anyone. His shoes, though looking like fancy dress shoes, had a solid sole good for running. But the deepening shadows as the sun continued to set made it hard for him to find footing. He pursued the shooter down the side of the hill, and as he was getting close, he heard the sound of a car engine.

He slid to a stop at the edge of a paved road that

looked like it wasn't used frequently as the car pulled away. He got the make and model, but it didn't have a tag.

Kenji started to line up a shot but knew he wouldn't be able to hit it and never wasted bullets, so he reluctantly put his weapon back in the holster.

"Wada here. I pursued a shooter down to… Lee, can you get a GPS fix on my location?"

"Yes. Got it. You need extraction?"

"No, there was a late model Toyota Prius waiting. No tag. Looked like black or a dark blue color."

"I'll put an alert out for it. Xander is with Daphne. Do you want me to send them to you?"

"I need to check the shooter's nest. He wasn't a sniper, so he could have left a clue," Kenji said. "Might take me a few to get back up the hill."

"I'll let Xander know. Confirm when you are there."

Kenji hated that the other person got away. He reviewed his performance, looking for any errors. Today at the museum, after the attack, he'd noticed that his senses had been more attuned to Daphne, and the danger to her was secondary.

Was he putting her at risk by staying on this case?

Should he ask to be removed?

There was no easy answer. He wouldn't let anything happen to her. He knew he'd give his own life before he let her be hurt again. But was he sharp enough?

He had done better this evening, but it had been watching her interrogate Alan that had caused the shift in him. Seeing Daphne's passion and commitment to her case had made him realize that nothing was going to stop her from getting the case to court. That meant Kenji had to find and eliminate the threat to her.

There was no other solution at this point.

He got to the top of the hill and found where the watcher had been. There was an indentation from the body, but nothing else. No trash or cigarette butts.

Xander moved the car over to where Kenji was and got out to help him search.

"Daphne is ticked at you."

"Thanks. Use some of that SAS survival training and make sure I'm not missing anything," Kenji said. "I think he was between your height and mine. With the sun almost down, it was hard to get a look at him as we were running. He wasn't a good shot."

"That's positive. Daphne saw you hit the ground and called Van, and he sent me," Xander said.

"I get it. She's not happy with what I did, but it's my job to keep her safe, not make her feel great," he said.

Xander put his hand on Kenji's shoulder. "I know, mate. I just didn't want you walking in blind."

He took a deep breath, and that coil of tension in his gut was tighter than before. "Thanks."

Watching Kenji hit the ground as he ran across the parking lot wasn't something she could get out of her head. She'd forgotten what his job was and how his life had changed since they'd been together. Sleeping with him had opened up a part of her that she'd thought she'd said goodbye to. The part that wanted a partner and a family. But the reality of what Kenji did had been driven home when he'd locked her in the car and put himself right in the path of danger to protect her.

He was okay. Xander had told her that. He'd been scared when he'd driven into the parking lot at top speed and then expertly swung his vehicle next to hers, a little like he'd seen too many *Fast & Furious* movies. He'd gotten out of the Dodge Charger that was identical to the one she was sitting in. He came over to her, and she scooted to the passenger's side, unlocking the door so he could get in, which he did.

"Where is Kenji?" she asked.

"In pursuit of the shooter. That's all I know," Xander said.

His voice was calm and level with a British accent, which surprised her. She realized she hadn't really spoken to him before this. Just seen him. A big, muscled giant of a man who Kenji counted as a friend. That she did know, because of how Kenji spoke of the other man and how he acted around him.

Her throat felt tight, and she realized she'd much rather be with Kenji than sitting in the car waiting for him to get back. What if he was shot and injured? What if…

"Thanks for coming."

"No problem. The boss said you weren't exactly acting."

"I wasn't. Do you think you should go and help Kenji?" she asked. "I did ask for backup for him. I'm good in this car."

"Nah, he's fine," Xander said. "Actually, he's just checked in."

He caught her up on everything that had happened and told her Kenji would be making his way to their location.

Everyone was so calm. Which she guessed was how they needed to be. It wouldn't do for a security company to panic, but she hated how everyday this was for Xander and Van when she'd spoken to him.

It wasn't helping that she realized how much she cared for Kenji. These last two days had been intense, and she was being shoved into a place where there was no more room for subterfuge and pretending. No place to hide and act like the life she'd created for herself was fulfilling away from work. Or had been until Kenji had walked through the door and made her remember she was a woman and had at one time dreamed of a different life.

But the man Kenji was today…scared her. Or maybe not him, but the world he lived in. The world that would demand he give it his all. That world wasn't one she and he could exist in as a couple.

His reasons for breaking up with her still mattered almost fifteen years later. She'd somehow thought that they had changed. That since he wasn't CIA anymore, his life would be calmer. But tonight had showed her that it wasn't.

And she knew that her own life wasn't calm right now. Someone was threatening her, which was the reason he was in danger. But if he wasn't guarding her, he'd be guarding someone else.

"He's back. I'm going to move the car over so we can provide light for him to search the shooter's nest."

Just like that, he was back. She wasn't entirely sure she was ready to see and talk to him. "I need you to stay in the car. We believe the threat has passed but can't take any chances."

"Sure. I'll sit here while maybe the both of you are in danger."

"That's why your company hired us," Xander said in a very low and patient tone. "He's okay."

"Great."

Xander got out, and she caught her first glimpse of Kenji in the headlights of the car. His suit was dirty, and there was a rip above his right knee. He glanced in her direction and then turned away. Her heart was beating so fast she had to do some deep breathing exercises to calm herself down.

She knew that there was nothing she could do to change Kenji and that if she let herself fall for him again, the danger was going to be part of her life. As if she had any control over who she fell in love with. It was one thing to say that she wasn't going to allow herself to feel anything, but she'd never been one to lie to herself.

Well, there had been the one lie that if she changed everything about herself, her mom would love her. But she'd learned from that. She couldn't change for Kenji, and she'd never ask him to change for her.

He and Xander made a thorough search of the area before they both approached the car. They talked for a few more minutes, and then Xander loped off at a run toward his own Dodge as Kenji opened the door to get behind the wheel.

She had a million things she wanted to say to him. She wanted to yell at him for scaring her. She wanted to demand he tell her what he'd been thinking. Wanted to make him give her all the details and let her know if the danger he'd put himself in was worth it.

But then he turned toward her. Her mind stopped, and her heart took over. She threw herself in his arms, and he hugged her tightly to him. Neither of them saying a word.

Chapter 14

They drove down Wilshire on the way back to Price Tower. It seemed like Christmas as the lights were now out on the light poles. "I'm not ready for Christmas. I don't think my case is going to be done before it."

"I'm not either," Kenji said. "But I'm not really big into it."

"You mentioned that. My dad sends me a present, but we don't always get together," she said, rambling because she was really in her feelings right now, and she didn't like it.

"That's nice," he said.

The conversation felt stilted, like she was working too hard to talk to him. "I can't handle your life, Kenji. I just had no idea about the reality of watching you go after someone. When he fired at you and you hit the ground... I thought you were dead for a second, and a part of me wanted to die too."

He pulled the car off the road in the parking lot of a chain restaurant that was busy, and he drove it into a spot where he could watch the road and the entire lot. "It's not always like that."

She shook her head. "I appreciate what you are saying. But for a minute today, I think I was fooling myself into believing that when my case went to court and there wasn't a need for you to protect me, we might be able to see each other."

He put his hand on the steering wheel and shifted so he faced her. "I want that. Can we talk about this back at the tower? You're not safe here."

"We can talk, but I don't see a way forward for us. You're always going to be looking for danger and putting yourself in front of it. You're a protector, and I get and respect that. It's one of the things I really like about you, but I don't know if I can live with the fear I felt."

"You felt that fear because you're tired, and your own life is in danger. Let's get home, and we can talk about it when I'm not trying to watch the parking lot, okay? Don't write me off yet, Daphne."

"Of course. Let's get back there."

She hadn't meant to bring that up, but the fact was, her mind kept replaying him falling to the ground. She knew he was fine, but what if he hadn't been? The training she'd had was a lifetime ago, and she wasn't sure she could have done anything to help. Work. She needed to focus on the case.

Which she did now. "Do you know if Lee found the address for the donor of the items? My team hasn't found his current address. They think he might be in a care home."

"You don't have to stop talking to me about us," he said.

"There is no us, Kenji, is there? We both had some unresolved stuff from the past, but it's my case that brought you back into my life. So I need to focus on that."

Even as she talked, she knew that she wasn't as clear-headed as she needed to be. This case had been difficult from the beginning. Her client had come to her as a last resort. Marjorie had been working with a number of museums around the world to get the items originally taken during the siege back to her country. And everyone was willing to continue the discussion and was on good terms until recently, when the Los Angeles Museum of Foreign Cultures had started blocking her attempts to see them.

"I'm not done with this discussion. Yes, my job is dangerous, but it's nothing compared to what I used to do. To be fair, this is the first time I've been shot at in like seven months."

Seven months without someone firing at him. "That must feel like forever for you."

"It does. When I was still an operative, it happened a lot more frequently. There were people I couldn't protect, lives that were lost, and this job gives me a chance to save some."

She realized that she'd touched a nerve with her comment and reminded herself she wasn't the only one who had feelings here. "I'm sorry that you lost people."

"It's part of the job, and we all knew the risk. That's why I got out. I want to use the skills I've honed to save lives and keep people safe. I know it sounds trite, but it helps me sleep better at night."

She got it. She realized that what she'd seen tonight wasn't anything to Kenji. He wasn't worried because there had been times when his life had been in jeopardy and he'd been all alone. Her mind and her heart were shifting. This man who looked so calm and unflappable wasn't. She had to trust him to do his job. To keep himself safe as he had proved he could protect her.

"Like you said, we can talk when we get back," she told him. Because he was just becoming more attractive to her. Knowing the sacrifice he had made and was still making. He had a sense of justice that was just as strong as hers. His was a more physical kind, but she understood where he was coming from.

"I shouldn't have brought this up," she said, hoping she hadn't made things worse for him.

"You definitely should have. You matter to me, Daphne, I don't want you to ever be afraid for me. I'm not about to let anything happen to either one of us now that you are back in my life."

His words reassured her like nothing else could. They weren't out of danger, but they were together, and that was all she needed right now. She put her hand on his thigh as he continued to drive, and he put one on top of hers and squeezed.

It seemed to him as if the world was conspiring to keep him from being alone with Daphne. When they got back to Price Tower, Van was waiting and wanted a debrief on everything that had gone down.

"Lee has some information for you on the donor as well as a lead on Grey Joy," Van said, turning to Daphne. "We'll escort you there, and then I'll need to speak to Kenji alone, but Lee is fully trained as a bodyguard—"

"Mr. Price—"

"Van, please."

"Van, I feel safe here. You don't need to reassure me that I am," she said.

Van gave her that slow smile of his. "You are very safe here, but given how unpredictable the other places in your life have become, I thought you'd want to know. Nothing can get you when you're here."

"You're right," Daphne said. "Someone is expecting me to back down, and that's not my way."

"I could tell that from the moment we met," he said.

Kenji listened to his boss and the man who was like a brother to him talking to Daphne and being all calm and shit, but Kenji knew Van was anything but. His shoulders were tense, and he was smiling but it didn't make his eyes crinkle with their usual warmth.

What did Van know that Kenji didn't?

Van led the way to the elevator, and the three of them got on. There was silence as they went up, and Daphne adjusted her bag. "How's your shoulder?"

"Better," she said. "With everything else going on, the slight pain I have from that is hardly worth noticing."

"Indeed," Van said.

They got off on Lee's floor, where the other woman waited for them. "I've got good news for you."

"Great. I'm ready for some good news," Daphne said as she stepped off. She glanced back at him, and he just nodded at her. Not sure what she was trying to glean from him. Perhaps Daphne was waiting for him to make her feel like everything was cool.

She gave him a half smile as the elevator doors closed. Van hit the button for the penthouse…his own private living quarters.

"What's up?"

"I might need to pull you off Daphne," Van said.

"I'm not distracted or compromised," Kenji said.

"No, you're not. But I just got wind of…a connection from your past back in town."

"Who?" Kenji asked as they walked into Van's apartment. It was all modern art on the walls and furniture that Kenji thought of as modern Italian. The edges and angles that the Milan school favored.

There was only one person from his past that would concern Van enough to pull him off Daphne and into a private meeting.

"Kaitlyn Leo."

The Director.

Damn. There was only one reason why she wanted to meet, and it was to bring him back to The Farm and his old life. A life he'd been very clear he'd left behind.

"I am not leaving Daphne, but I can talk to Leo while Daphne is working tomorrow. Her office is secure now, and if she stays put with Xander guarding her, I think it could work." He would never say no to Van, but he wasn't leaving Daphne. Not until she was safe, and then he was going to figure out a way for them to try to be together. Their conversation in the car had clarified that for him.

But he needed to talk to her further and assure himself that she wanted him in her life too. She said she'd been scared, and he hated that for her. But he knew that leaving her again…it wasn't something he was willing to do.

"Kenji—"

"I'm not leaving Price," Kenji said. "This place is… You know I'm not one to talk about my feelings."

"You don't have to. The feeling is mutual. Do you want me to ask Leo to come here?"

Did he? The only benefit would be to Leo. She'd

check out Van's arrangement, and Kenji wasn't certain she wouldn't try to recruit Lee or Luna onto her team. She was smart and lethal and capable of making decisions that not everyone could. More than once she'd made a call that had civilian casualties in order to save many more. He had never really understood how she could do that, and that was why he'd eventually left the CIA.

"No. She'll just gather intel. I'm surprised she didn't just use her sources to get my cell."

"Professional courtesy," Van said.

"What were you before Price Security?" Kenji asked.

"That's a different life and has no bearing on what's happening now. Where do you want to meet?"

"Give me her number and I'll set it up. Thanks for not mentioning this in front of Daphne."

"No problem. Would it have meant anything to her?"

"She was in the same training program I was," Kenji said. "She'd know that if the Director wants to talk, it's not because she's in town and looking up a former colleague."

"Interesting. Let's go talk to Lee. She has found a lot of intel on the museum and the collection at the heart of Daphne's case."

Kenji followed his boss back down to Lee's office after Van had given him the Director's number, which he'd programmed into his phone. He was trying to dwell on why the Director had come to Los Angeles. She wasn't just in town. He wasn't sure if she had a mission for him or if it was something else.

When he walked into the room and saw Daphne, he realized that this meeting with the Director couldn't have come at a better time. There was no choice for him as there once had been between the adventure and excitement the CIA could give him compared a life with Daphne.

He wanted to try to make things work with her. No matter what it took. First, he had to eliminate whoever was threatening her life, and then he had to convince her that he wasn't a danger junkie.

Lee offered her a drink as they sat down at the conference table that had been moved into her office since the last time Daphne had been there. "I'm okay for now. What have you found?"

Lee smiled at her. "I'm going to project the info on the monitor over there so you can see it. No need to take notes. I'll send everything to you. Firstly, the archivist, Grey Joy. She's also a black market dealer of hard-to-find goods. I was able to set up a buy for tomorrow with her. She didn't have any of the items on your missing list, but when I asked around, she has been known to trade in some of the items currently on display in the museum," Lee said.

Daphne was trying to make this new information fit with what she knew of Grey. "Okay, which ones?"

"I've marked them in your file. I also found you someone who can authenticate them so you'll know they aren't replicas."

"Thank you. I've subpoenaed the museum's financial records, and I have to send some documents proving the relevance of this to the case. Can you give me the date when each of the items was sold?"

"I can. I'll add that to your file when we are done," Lee said.

Having a date range instead of just a general cry of "show me all your banking details" was what Daphne had been looking for to begin with, but there hadn't been a way to track the items. "How many items have gone from the black market back to the museum? Could the museum be the buyer?"

"Unlikely. The money seems to be coming from Ethiopia."

That didn't make sense. "Are you saying that someone in the country fighting to get the items returned is buying them and then selling them back to the museum?"

"I don't know that part. And I can't trace it further than a bank in Switzerland. I only got the details I did because I talked to one of the guys, and he let that slip and then shut me down. I don't think I'm going to be able to take that any further. But your client might have more information."

She might. Daphne made a note to call Marjorie as soon as she left Lee's office. This case was getting harder and harder to unravel. Each time she thought she'd won a battle in court and got what she asked for, it seemed to prove fruitless.

Cases were always complex and took time, but this one seemed like there was still so much to uncover. Each win she got led her to another mountain to climb.

"So, what time am I to meet Grey tomorrow?"

Kenji and his boss walked in as she'd asked that. She glanced over at Kenji, but his expression was unreadable. She remembered all they were trying to talk about in the car, and she still wanted to give them a chance to talk as a couple, but right now work was the priority.

"What about Grey?" Kenji asked as he sat down across from Daphne.

"I've set up a buy for tomorrow. I can get Rick to go. He's got four hours in the morning," Lee said.

"I'll do it," Kenji said. "Do you mind if Xander covers for me while you are at the office?"

Daphne definitely did. "I want to go with you."

"She won't talk if you're there."

"She saw you and knows we are working together," Daphne said. "What is this really about?"

As soon as those words left her mouth, she regretted it. "Never mind. Tell us what else you found, Lee. We can work out the details of tomorrow later."

Lee's fingers moved quickly over her keyboard, and the images on the monitor changed, but Daphne's attention was still on Kenji. What was going on? Why did he want to go alone? Was there some danger that she didn't know about?

"The original owner of the entire hoard that was donated to the Los Angeles Museum of Foreign Cultures was Jonathon Hazelton-Measham. The collection had been passed down to his son and then grandson, who sold it to the museum in 1985," Lee said. The amount she mentioned was a nice sum but nothing overly suspicious.

"In 2001, the grandson's son Henry contested the sale and said that his father was manipulated by the museum director, Franklin Lauder—the father of Pierce—into selling. They went to court, but the sale was legal."

"Was every item listed in the collection?" Daphne

asked, already texting her team to have them pull up the court documentation on the case.

"Yes, they were. There are seven items that are part of the case and don't show up anywhere on your inventory but were a part of the Arts of Africa exhibit that was shown in 2018. I've included that brochure in your file."

"Thank you," Daphne said. She had to stop thinking about Kenji. This was the kind of information she had needed to begin with. Now they had an original inventory, something that Lauder hadn't produced. "Were any of the items in the collection sold on the black market?"

"Two of them were, so possibly that's why they aren't in your inventory," Lee said.

Possibly, but Daphne would find out exactly what happened to them. "Is the grandson—what's his name?"

"Thomas Hazelton-Measham. He moved to Florida two years ago. I found an address, but it's a retirement park, and I couldn't find a phone number, but I did find an email. I put it in your file."

She appreciated how thorough Lee was. "This is great. I am going to be very busy tomorrow filing this with the court and getting everything in place. Thank you."

"No problem. It was fun doing this kind of project. Lately all I do is background checks and keep an eye on the crew," Lee said.

Daphne and Kenji went back to his apartment a few minutes later. Her mind was buzzing with all the new information she had to go through, but she wanted to talk to Kenji first.

Chapter 15

"Sorry for almost turning things personal in the meeting. I don't know what's going on with me tonight," Daphne said.

"You're being pushed to the edge, and it's stripping away the façade you use to keep everyone at bay. So you don't have time for anything that isn't real," he said. He'd seen it in clients before. There came a moment in every client where living with a bodyguard changed them. Even his wealthy clients who'd grown up with bodyguards around them developed their own way of dealing with it.

She shrugged and walked to the couch, dropping her bag and kicking off her shoes. "It feels like I'm living in someone else's life. What happened to my nicely ordered world?"

Kenji walked over to join her. His pants were torn from the fall he'd taken in the parking lot earlier that evening, and his jacket smelled like sweat. He shrugged out of it and toed off his shoes before sitting down next to her. "What can I do to help?"

She chewed her lower lip between her teeth. "I wish it were that easy. But you're a part of it too."

He got that. He was back in her life with no warning,

and the two of them were still attracted to each other, but he wasn't sure that was enough for her. He knew it wasn't. She'd told him in the car. That the danger of what he did scared her.

"Should we finish our conversation from the car?" he asked her.

"No. I realize now how silly that was. I like you, Kenji, and even if I never saw you again after my case goes to court, I'm not going to stop liking you or forget you," she said. "I was trying to draw a line in the sand and say I can only let myself have feelings for you if these criteria are met. But affection doesn't work that way."

No, it certainly didn't. It would have been easier for him if, after his clean break from Daphne all those years ago, he'd been able to keep her in the past. But he'd thought of her too often and more than once checked her out online. She'd been a sort of saving grace for him when he'd been deep in the shit in Afghanistan. Making decisions every day that cost lives and saved them. Trusting his gut had become harder and harder as everyone in that area had been so desperate.

"Not sure if this will help or not. But I used to google you after a bad day and just read about how successful you were, and it made me feel better…cleaner."

"Oh, Kenji," she said, leaning over and hugging him. He held himself stiff for a minute and then put his arms around her and drew her closer. The feel of her in his arms always shook him. He wasn't used to touching her, though he should have been.

She smelled of her floral perfume and *Daphne*, and there was so much comfort in the scent and the feel of her in his arms that he wasn't sure he would be able to let her go. He kissed the top of her head because sleeping with her now wasn't something he was sure was in his best interests.

The day had been a lot, and watching someone repeatedly stalking her bothered him. He didn't like that she had a stalker no one could identify. That there was no way to expose what was truly going on at the museum.

She sat back, tucking her legs under her body. "I'm glad I was able to help you."

Really, what else could she say to that? He hated that he was in his feelings and knew that he had to get that under wraps. "About tomorrow. It makes sense for me to talk to Grey. You made her nervous at the museum. I'll get the information."

Daphne tipped her head to the side, and her long black hair slid over her shoulder. "You don't honestly believe you aren't going to make her nervous. You look like a hit man or something lethal. That's not reassuring."

"It's supposed to be menacing. People take you seriously when you dress in a suit. And an all-black one makes them give me a wide berth. Which is what I need when I'm working."

"Only when you're working?" she asked.

"No. I use it when I travel too. Airports are the worst," he said.

"They are," she said. "Fine, you can talk to Grey by yourself. I really want to dig into all the information that Lee uncovered. She's a gem, by the way."

"She's the best," he agreed. "Do you think you can find a connection that will help you with your case?"

"She already has. Items that aren't marked missing

have disappeared from the inventory. Now I just have to take that list and see if they were sold. If they were, then we aren't any closer to finding out what the museum is trying to hide by ending the discussions with Marjorie and delaying this case," she said.

Kenji watched her as she talked about the case, once again struck by how beautiful she was when she was passionate about something. "Marjorie is lucky to have you on her side."

"The people of the Ethiopian Orthodox Church are. Lee also uncovered some black market sales where the buyers were in Ethiopia. So I'm going to have ask Marjorie some uncomfortable questions."

"Would she have hired you to cover her buys?" Kenji asked.

"I don't know. I don't think so, but after the last few days, I'm not really sure who I can trust anymore. My gut is telling me Marjorie isn't doing anything shady, but I thought my team would all come back clean."

She wrapped one arm around her waist and then looked over at him.

"You can trust me."

"I know."

"I have a lot of work to do tomorrow," she said. "I should go to bed."

"I need a shower." Kenji said, very aware that he wanted to keep her in his arms, but with the upcoming meeting with the Director on the horizon, he wasn't going to do anything else with Daphne.

Part of him wanted to discuss it with her, but she had a lot on her mind, and the information Lee had gathered was a lot to go through. He was here for her, not the other way around, he reminded himself.

His mom had taught him to rely on himself, always afraid that she'd die when he was young. It had always just been the two of them. No extended family at all to lean on. And his mom hadn't been someone who made friends easily. He saw that as an adult in a way that he hadn't has a child. He'd just enjoyed his Kenji and Mom time growing up.

He wished she was here to talk to now. She'd never had a chance to meet Daphne, but he thought his mom would say she was too smart for him and tell him he was lucky to have found her.

"Why are you looking at me that way?" she asked.

"How am I looking at you?" he countered.

"Like... I'm not entirely sure. A little bit like you're flirting with me, a little bit like you're happy, and a little bit like you have something to hide," she said.

"I'm a lot a bit of those things," he admitted.

"Flirting I get, and happy makes me feel a lot of joy. I'm going to assume it's because we are here together."

"You don't have to assume. I want to be here with you."

"I want you here too."

"Your life is in danger, and I am known for my skills at keeping people safe," he retorted.

"Humble brag?"

"That was a boast. Did I sound humble?"

She threw her head back and laughed. "No."

He couldn't help that he got hard when she laughed. It was just so nice to see her face relax and the stress and tension she carried with her all the time melt away. He wanted to see her that way more often.

"Good."

She tipped her head to the side as she twirled a strand of her hair around her finger. "That leaves whatever you are hiding."

Yeah, it did.

Was he going to tell her?

"In the car, when you said you didn't like the thought of me in danger, did you mean you were thinking of us a couple?"

She chewed her lower lip for a minute and stopped toying with her hair. "Yes."

Her voice was low and raw, some of the tension returning to her face. Which he hated.

"I have been too. The timing of this sucks because there is so much going on."

"It does. That doesn't mean I regret having you back in my life," she said. "I'm scared for you, and I'm not sure if, once my life goes back to its boring routine, you'll still be interested in me. Pretty much I work, come home and watch anime, and then go to bed to not sleep."

"I've always been interested, Daph. And I am now. Which anime?"

"Old ones. *Howl's Moving Castle* is my comfort watch. When I have a human rights case that is really tough to stomach, I just come home and lie on my couch eating potato chips and watching it. It's so sweet. It soothes me."

Kenji made a mental note of what she liked. He wanted to remember every detail so he could be what she needed from him.

"So, what are you hiding?" she asked again.

He rubbed the back of his neck. "The Director is in town and called Van to set up a meeting with me."

She seemed to sink back into herself as his words registered. Then she shook her head and straightened her spine, sitting taller next to him. "What does she want?"

"I'm not sure. Probably me to come back. The situation in the Ukraine is one that lends itself to my particular wheelhouse."

"How? What did you do for them, Kenji?" she asked.

"I worked with informants and set up strike teams to take down military targets," he said. There was no emotion in his voice because he'd had to shove all his feelings about every mission he'd completed in Afghanistan deep down and lock them away or he'd be sitting in a corner rocking and screaming.

"Are you considering it?" she asked. "Don't lie about this. I need to know the truth."

"I told you, you can trust me," he said. A little ticked she didn't.

"You did, but this…this is the CIA, and you've always loved it more than anything else. So I'm asking you, are you considering it?"

Kenji got where she was coming from and knew that her concerns were valid. He had always put the agency before anything else. It had been his dream to be a hero and to prove to his unknown father and to himself that he was worthy. But that dream had turned into a living nightmare during the war in the Middle East and the atrocities he'd witnessed and committed all in the name of justice and world peace. That dream had become something that Kenji couldn't face or be a part of anymore.

But how did he say that to Daphne without revealing the monster he'd become over there? The monster he still wasn't sure he'd caged. The man that he hoped he'd transformed into was in jeopardy. Kenji knew that more than anyone else.

"I'm not."

"It took you a long time to answer."

"It's complicated, but there is no place for the agency in my life now. I made that break because I knew that my future was somewhere else," he said.

There was more to his time at the agency than Kenji was ever going to share with her, which was totally his right. But he seemed a different man when he'd mentioned the Director, and the way he held himself now told her that he still had something unresolved with the CIA.

Not Daphne's problem.

Right, except it sort of was, because she was falling for him again. It didn't seem smart to continue to indulge her emotions and act like maybe they could have a life after this. No matter the discussion they'd just had. Kenji's life had been on a different path than hers since the moment he'd walked out her door all those years ago. She knew it, and she was pretty sure he did too.

That didn't make her want him any less. Was there a workaround where they could find a path they could walk together?

"Thanks for mentioning it to me," she said.

"I told you I'm not going back, and honestly, my life now isn't dangerous at all," he said.

As if the image of him being shot at and falling to the ground wasn't still etched clearly in her mind. "Try telling me that after you've changed out of your torn suit."

"Daphne."

Just her name. But there was so much emotion in that one word. Longing, she thought. That's what it was.

She longed for him too. Longed for a world where they could just be themselves, and people who took advantage of others didn't exist. Longed a place where they could just be together and the past would disappear.

But she'd never been a daydreamer. She was too practical for that. They'd either figure this out or they wouldn't. Either way, she'd continue living her life and doing her job. She wished she could be that pragmatic, but her heart was already flinching, trying to protect itself in case this didn't work out.

"The last thing I want is to return to that life," he said to her at last. "I...you might not know this about me, but I've always been a loner."

"Yeah, that I knew," she said. He'd stuck to himself during their training classes, and if they hadn't been paired together, she was pretty sure he wouldn't have spoken to her. They hadn't started dating until she left the program.

"Good. Then you'll understand this. Price Security isn't just a job to me. It's...like a family. I have people who I care about and who care about me, and it's not based on the results of my last mission."

He shoved his hand through his hair, and she realized how hard this was for Kenji to tell her. That made some of the tension deep inside of her dissipate.

"I'm glad you have them. But people cared about you before," she pointed out.

"Thanks. I think it's difficult to explain because your office…well, your boss hired us to protect you, and your team, including Alan, want to please you and make you happy. You are surrounded by something that I wasn't until Price."

She got it. One of the reasons she'd left the training program at The Farm was that she didn't want to go through life not really able to trust anyone. She wanted people in her office, even if they were simply being cordial, to act like her life mattered.

"I can tell by the comradery between you all that this is different," she said.

"It is. I can't go back to the man I was before or that life. Even if there was no you, I wouldn't. I can't refuse to meet with her, but I won't be accepting any assignments," Kenji said.

There was a finality to his voice that reassured her as nothing else could. She was happy to hear that resolve in his tone and hoped that it would be easy for him to decline whatever the director offered him. "Okay then. So, should we talk about tomorrow? I have a lot of information to add to the brief I've been working on and need to get it over to the courthouse."

Kenji seemed to relax as she changed the subject, which was good. She pulled her phone out and opened the notepad app so she could review the to-do list she'd already started. She lived by her lists.

"That'll keep you busy for how long?" he asked.

"Most of the morning. I'll send one of the assistants to file it in the afternoon. Hopefully either you'll be back with info on Grey Joy, or we'll have a number for Thomas Hazelton-Measham, and I can debrief him and get a statement," she said. Some of the fatigue she'd been feeling left her as she thought about all the work she needed to get done. It was nice to have something to sink her teeth into, and it felt like finally her case was taking shape.

She wanted to check in with a colleague in London who had worked on the British Museum case last year when thousands of artifacts had been stolen. Those items had made their way onto eBay, which she was going to assign her legal secretary to search tomorrow.

"I'll do my best. I'm going to try to talk to the director while I'm out as well. I don't want her to meet you," Kenji said.

"Why not?"

"You're smart and skilled, and she'll try to recruit you," he said succinctly. "And that's not something I can live with."

Daphne smiled when he said that. "She'd fail. I really love my work."

"Enough to take a bullet for it," he said wryly.

"Indeed," she said. She glanced down at the notepad. This night was made of all the things she liked about Kenji. Work, life and laughter all blending into one thing. It had been a long time since she'd laughed, which she hadn't realized until tonight when Kenji had been teasing her.

She was content with her life, but she was only now realizing how insular she'd made it.

Chapter 16

Kenji's suit was a dark gray today, and he had a floral-printed silk pocket square. His tie matched the suit, and his white shirt was pristine as always. She couldn't help the thrill that went through her as she looked at him. He'd styled his hair with some kind of product, because the fall of bangs that usually dominated his forehead was swept up and back.

He was quiet and contemplative, and given what they'd discussed the night before, she knew he had a lot on his mind.

She couldn't pretend she wasn't worried about him talking to the Director of the CIA. Kenji had said he wasn't interested in going back, but Daphne knew how hard it was to say no to the agency when they came knocking. She'd experienced it herself two years ago.

She'd been in The Hague working on a human rights case when she'd been approached. Even though she'd left the program before becoming an operative, the CIA still kept tabs on her and her movements, and they weren't afraid to ask for favors.

She'd declined because her client needed her full attention, but when the trail had ended, the operative sought her again. Once again, she'd declined, and that hadn't gone well.

How much worse would the pressure be on Kenji? She didn't want to imagine what he was dealing with. She wished she hadn't chickened out last night and had asked him to sleep with her.

She missed being in his arms, and that one quick hookup in the shower had whetted her appetite for him. She wanted more. Work had been the one thing she could count on to keep her distracted from the personal life she'd always wanted but never believed she'd find.

Now there was Kenji.

He'd denied that them having sex had been a reaction to the danger they'd both been in, but she wasn't entirely sure that was true. She was always confident, and had worn her favorite pantsuit today to reinforce that confidence in herself. But it was hard right now. Never had she felt this vulnerable.

She hated it.

"Are you okay?" he asked. There was concern in his tone and in his expression as he looked over at her.

"Yeah. Just…" She wasn't going to tell him she was nervous about his meeting with the Director. She'd never try to influence him in any way.

"It'll be okay," he said gruffly, then pulled her close, hugging her. She wrapped her arms around his body, resting her head on his shoulder. His spicy aftershave comforted her as much as his arms did.

What was she going to do if he left when this case was over? Because no matter how she chose to frame it, she still wanted him in her life. For the first time since she'd given up trying to make her mom love her, she wanted to figure out what she could do to make Kenji love her.

That wasn't a road she wanted to be on, but there she was. She had no way of changing it either. The case was a distraction, but in her heart, she knew that she wanted him to be safe and care about her and stay in her life.

Van waited for her in the garage. He smiled as he led her to a Dodge Charger. Having been in the garage before, she knew they had a fleet of them and two big black Hummer limos. Kenji had been dressed as always in a suit. Today it was gray with a white shirt and thin dark gray tie. She'd wanted to say something to him before he went to meet the Director, but she hadn't found the right thought, so had just waved goodbye to him.

She wanted to move on the brief she was writing and get the request for financial records in at the courthouse today. She'd messaged her team to get in early if they could. Most of them would be, but Janice, a paralegal, had to take her kids to school first. Which was perfectly fine.

Daphne's own mom had acted like Daphne was a stumbling block to her successful career and had often driven like a maniac through traffic and dropped Daphne off before the teachers got to school so she could get into her office early. Her father was an ER surgeon, so he wasn't always available to take her to school.

She shook her head and brought herself back to the present. Who cared? It was in the past, but it was Christmastime, and that always stirred up longings for a childhood that she'd never had and was never going to. Normally she just worked through it and didn't let it bother her.

Having Kenji back in her life was calling up her emotions and making her think of things she'd assumed she'd resolved years ago.

"I'll stay out of your way this morning," Xander said as they got to her office.

"Kenji usually just stands by the door and glares at everyone, but I don't mind if you use one of the guest chairs. My staff and I will probably spend most of our time in the conference room down the hall once they are all in," she said.

"I'm good here," Van said, leaning against the wall. "I'll try not to glare."

"Thanks. That'll be a change for my team," she said.

She went behind her desk and started to go through her emails. One response to the email she'd sent last night before going to bed was from her friend in London. She flagged it and continued to move through the messages.

There was one from Pierce Lauder, apologizing for the attack on her at the museum and telling her that the deputy director should have been with her. He said he'd be back at the museum on Saturday if she wanted to come and look at the collection again.

She flagged that one as well.

Alan walked into her office carrying three to-go coffee cups. He started to hand one to Van, then did a double take. "Sorry. I thought you'd be Kenji. Want a double espresso?"

"No thanks. I take mine with lots of milk and sugar," Van said.

Alan nodded and walked to her desk, handing her a chai latte. "Morning, Boss. I started running through the shared task list this morning. I took the financial brief since I was already working on it. Having the specific date of the one sale will give me a good starting range."

She took the chai from him, smiling. "I thought you might want that one. We can work in the conference room today. I'm going to ask Janice to do the eBay search."

Alan nodded. "I'll let the rest of the team know to meet in the conference room and that you have a new bodyguard."

"Just for this morning," Daphne said. "This is Van Price. Van, this is Alan."

The two men nodded before Alan left her office. She cleared the rest of her emails and then opened the one from her friend.

Several thousand items from the British Museum's collection had been stolen or marked missing or damaged, and it was revealed that a staff worker had been facilitating the theft but hadn't been charged in the burglary. Her friend had sent her some information on his case. He'd represented the whistleblower who had purchased an item off eBay and then realized it was the property of the British Museum.

Interesting. Other than the burlap bag that the censer had been in, she wasn't sure if the items from the Los Angeles Museum of Foreign Cultures were labeled in any way. She hadn't noticed anything as obvious as a tracking number on the censer, but she hadn't really examined it either.

She and her staff spent the morning writing the brief that Alan would take to the court that afternoon. The financial documents request, and now that they had proof of a sale of an item, Daphne felt confident they would be granted something. The other was a detailed request for the discrepancies between the donated items and the current inventory.

Pierce had told them the inventory that he'd provided had all of the items, but now that Lee had pulled the complete donation paperwork, there were differences that needed to be explained.

Van stood quietly in the corner, not glaring as he'd promised, but he was on guard. Daphne couldn't help noticing the differences between him and Kenji. Both of them gave off an aura of, well, *menace* wasn't the right word, but they were definitely not men that anyone would mess with…but they also made her feel safe.

Her staff worked on. They decided to order lunch, which she put on her company card. Finally it seemed like this case was coming together, and Daphne had a call scheduled with Marjorie for later that afternoon in which she'd update her and hopefully ask her to look into bank records in her country. As the cultural minister, maybe she'd have some pull. Daphne certainly hoped so.

Sitting in the Charger next to the park near the Los Angeles Museum of Foreign Cultures, Kenji was on guard. The Director was due to arrive any moment, which he could attribute his edginess to, but it was more than that. There was something building inside him that felt dangerous.

It was tied to Daphne. Talking to her last night had been unexpected and had made him realize how much he wanted things to work out with her. Not just to work out. He needed them to find a way to be together, and keeping her safe was his top priority.

He wanted to question Grey Joy. A part of him knew he'd use whatever methods necessary to get her to talk even if it would be beyond his scope. This was a civil mission, not a CIA one, so those methods weren't acceptable. He knew that, but his gut wasn't hearing him. That made him dangerous to everyone, including Daphne.

It was some kind of screwed-up hamster wheel he was on. Needing to be lethal to protect her, but being lethal would make him into that monster he'd been before he'd retired, and then the monster would put her in danger. Then back to trying to protect her.

He shoved his sunglasses up on his head and rubbed his thumb and forefinger over his eyes. He had a headache from trying to figure this out.

A smart man would ask to be replaced. But Kenji wasn't going to do that. No matter how capable the other members of Price Security were, he had to be the one to watch over Daphne and keep her safe.

He heard a rap on his door. Turning carefully, he saw her standing there. Perfectly coiffed hair and form-fitting black suit.

The Director. He hit the unlock button and gestured for her to get into the car. He had already decided he was going to be in control of this meeting. Or at least pretend he was. He knew that the Director had been in his head since Van had mentioned her name.

She was a tall woman at five foot eight inches and had blond hair she always wore pulled back in a low ponytail. She favored navy suits, and today's version had a gray pinstripe in it. She had on a cream-colored silk shirt underneath and wore a pair of dark aviator-style Ray-Bans. When she got into the car, there was no scent of perfume, just a hint of the cool air from this December Los Angeles day.

She closed the door behind her and turned to look at him.

"Thank you for taking this meeting."

Be cordial he warned himself. "As if I had an option."

Yeah, he wasn't in the mood to play the game today. He wanted her taken care of so he could find Grey Joy and move closer to finding out who had shot at Daphne and was now stalking her.

She gave him a savvy smile. Every nerve in his body tingled, and he felt himself shifting into operative mode. It took a moment for him to pull back and remind himself he was out of that life.

"I've missed your honesty, Wada," she said.

She always referred to him and all of her operatives by their last names.

"Why are we here?" he asked.

"I need you. There's a *delicate* mission that you are perfect for," she said.

He pulled his sunglasses back down as he turned his head so they weren't making eye contact. He was skilled, all right, but not the only one who had his training or his success in missions. "You need a retired agent?"

"I do. Interested?" she asked in that low, modulated tone he knew she used when she was probing. She wanted something from him.

"No." One-word answers were the only way to communicate with her. *Keep it quick and simple and get out of here.*

"Wada, I wouldn't be here if I thought you couldn't handle this."

Flattery. She was stroking him, hoping that it would get him to ask for more. He wished it wasn't working.

He swiveled his head to face her. "I know I can handle it. I just don't want to. I'm happy with my current assignment."

"Protecting a lawyer. You were made for so much more than that."

She'd overplayed her hand, Kenji thought. He wasn't going to agree to anything now that she was insulting the peace he'd found working as a bodyguard. As if this role wasn't as important as the one he'd held at the agency.

"Maybe. But it suits me. I like that I have a life here. I'm not the same man I was before I retired," he told her.

"You've never said no when your country needed you," she said.

"Going for the jugular? If sentiment won't sway, try patriotism." Sure, he wanted to defend his country. The family he'd made for himself all were citizens of it. But he also wasn't blindly going to rush out to destabilize a government or turn someone's wife against them without knowing what was at stake.

She gave him that half smile again. "It was worth a try."

It was definitely worth a try. He hated to say no, but he knew that there was almost always a list of people she would ask. "I'm sure you'll find someone who will say yes."

"I will. But I want you for this," she said.

Oh, no. Now he was curious. Why him? Should he

ask about the details? Fuck no. He wasn't going back. He'd already decided that.

He just shrugged. There was no way he was going to let her get out of the car without telling him the mission. He hated that there was still that part of him drawn to the intrigue the Director always brought with her.

"Don't you want to at least hear the mission parameters before deciding?"

"Sure."

Internally he punched the brick wall that he mentally kept in place for dealing with his frustration. At this moment, he had everything he had been craving for the last few years. His found family, and now Daphne was back in his life.

But one little piece of bait from the Director and he was eyeing it, trying to see if he could get it off the hook and keep his freedom.

He knew the answer to that.

It was no.

There were no half measures with the agency or with her. She wasn't going to give him one little mission for the thrill of it and then let him retire again.

Kenji honestly wasn't sure he'd be able to go back to the old life and then return to Price Security and be content. For him, it was one or the other. The man he'd been on his way to becoming before he'd retired was still there.

The man who was half monster. The man who'd said goodbye to his humanity to achieve results at any cost. That man wasn't one who could hold Daphne in his arms.

Kenji knew it. He also knew his answer had to be no.

"I thought you might. It involves an international illegal art and antiquities operation in LA—"

Was this tied to Daphne's case? He couldn't help but feel that it might be. Not that he was going to let Kaitlyn drag him back into working for her. "Let me stop you there. My days of using local informants are done. The answer is still no."

She took her sunglasses off. "What if the informant I have is your friend's husband, Nicholas DeVere?"

WTF? What was Nick involved in? The billionaire was known for dealing in favors, using his wealth to help out others in order to cultivate relationships.

"I'll speak to him. But you're not using him. I'll pass the information to you, and then you leave him out of it," Kenji said. "I mean it, Kaitlyn. Do you understand me?"

"He came to us."

Kenji didn't give a crap about that. He wasn't letting the Director use Luna's husband. "He doesn't know what you will do to him. He's finally safe after a lifetime of being stalked. You take care of the threat and get it away from him."

"I could if I had my best agent back working for me," she said.

This wasn't something he could just say no to. He needed to talk to Nick, and damn that he was still trying to help Daphne and keep her safe.

"I'm in town for a few more days at a conference. Call me and let me know your answer," she said, getting out of the car and walking away.

Kenji grabbed the steering wheel hard with both hands, wanting to punch something. She'd just made him an offer he couldn't refuse. This might be a lead that could help him find out who was behind the attacks on Daphne. Plus the fact that Nick and Luna were family, and he couldn't allow them to be in danger any more than he could allow Daphne to.

Chapter 17

The morning was intense in the conference room. Everyone on her team was focused on the new briefs they were writing to make sure that everything was in place. Janice had started searching eBay for the items in the inventory, while Alan worked on the financials.

Janice came in in a rush. "Sorry I'm late."

Janice had long blond hair that she habitually wore in a messy bun. Her clothes were clean but older or from the secondhand shop, as most of the money she made went to supporting her family. She'd told Daphne that she and her husband had decided it was worth the sacrifice to send their kids to a private school, so all of the money they both made went toward that.

She worked hard as a paralegal. Daphne was mentoring her and had arranged for a scholarship for Janice to an online school so she could continue her education and keep working. She was one semester away from attaining her law degree and then would sit for the bar exam.

"I've forwarded you an article about the British Museum controversy where items stolen from the museum ended up on eBay. Could you start a search and try to match it against any of the items on our list?"

"Yeah, no problem," Janice said.

"How was the school run?"

"Not bad at all. Abby got all the words on her spelling list, and Umberto sang his solo for me three times," Janice said with a smile.

Daphne often wondered if she'd feel the same way about her children if she risked having them. Or were her maternal instincts the same as her own mother's? Nonexistent. She shook her head. She really didn't want to go down that road. "Sounds like a good morning."

"It has been. I'll get on this right away."

Janice moved to the end of the conference table, took her seat and started working on her laptop. Daphne noticed Van observed everyone in the room and kept his attention moving from person to person.

She felt safe with him, but she missed Kenji's presence. Which wasn't the smartest thing for her to be thinking since he had a meeting with the Director today.

Cass, who'd been on Daphne's team the longest, was back from vacation. When she entered, Daphne signaled her to come to the end of the table so they could work together.

Cass was a willowy blonde, and as soon as they'd spotted each other in the break room, they'd both smiled and become instant friends. That hadn't really happened often with Daphne, and she treasured the bond with Cass.

It was as if they'd known each other all their lives, and there was nothing that Daphne didn't feel comfortable telling the other woman. Cass had been married when they met, so as long as she'd known her, she'd known Gerry. He was easygoing and tended to show up unannounced when they were working late with dinner for the three of them.

The two were like family to Daphne, so the last thing she was going to allow was the trouble dogging her with this case to spill over onto either of them. Or any of her staff, for that matter. She needed to know they were safe.

But sometimes when digging through information, things were revealed that could be dangerous. Daphne always thought it was so interesting the facts that people tried to hide.

Cass laughed at something Janice said as she stopped to talk to the other woman before making her way down the room. Everyone liked Cass. Alan had a crush on her, and Daphne noticed that even Van seemed to turn toward her more often. She was just one of those women who made everyone feel good, so they liked to be around her.

Daphne tried to be that way, but it wasn't always easy. It was hard to fight the memory of being told to leave the room when her mother entered. Or told to not speak. It made her want to be invisible, and her entire adult life after her breakup with Kenji, she'd been forcing herself to be visible.

But sometimes she preferred the shadows, where she could observe and sort through the facts and precedents and figure out a way to win the case.

"I freaked when I heard you were shot, but Gerry insisted you would have texted if you needed me," Cass said when they took a break to stretch their backs and walked to the corner of the room where there were no windows per Van's instructions.

"Yes. I'm sure Gerry would have ordered a hit on me if I interrupted your first real vacation in five years."

"He wouldn't because he'd be afraid of having to investigate himself, but otherwise you're right," Cass said with a laugh. "You haven't said how you are."

"I'm…okay."

"Girl, that doesn't sound convincing."

"I know. It's the best I can do. The other bodyguard… he's the one from my past that I mentioned."

"The total d-bag who dumped you without a reason and walked away?" Cass said.

Hearing her relationship with Kenji summed up like that made her cringe. But late-night drinks with girlfriends were for spilling all the emotional vitriol that was stuck inside.

"He's not a total d-bag. In fact, I'm starting to fall for him again."

Cass put her hand on Daphne's elbow and turned them so their backs were to the room. "For real? Or like Whitney Houston falling for Kevin Costner in *The Bodyguard* and him leaving her at the end?"

"For real," she said. "I was planning to ignore him and the past, but you know how I am."

"You need answers. That's why you're such a good lawyer."

"I know, and so crap at relationships."

"Not all of them. We've been friends for twelve years now."

"We have, but you're a lot like me."

"Totally awesome and kickass is how everyone should be," Cass said.

Daphne hugged her friend. Usually in the office she kept things professional. "I missed you."

"Missed you too. Gerry confiscated my cell as soon as we got to the mountain retreat."

Which made sense given that Cass was a workaholic like her. "Did you have fun?"

"You know what, I did," Cass said. "We hiked and cooked together. And neither of us were called to work. It was nice."

It sounded idyllic. What would it be like if she and Kenji were alone for a week? No phones or threats? She wanted that, she thought. Maybe… She still didn't know what would happen when the case was over.

"Hey, Daphne, we are thinking of ordering in from Burger Boy. You two want something?" Alan asked.

They both turned to face the room.

"Girls night soon," Cass said before looking at Alan. "You know I want a Reuben extra kraut."

"Gross," Daphne said.

Cass just stuck her tongue out at Daphne.

"Italian on rye for me. Thanks," Daphne said.

Alan finished compiling the order. Pam ran out to take a call from her husband as Alan placed it. Van had declined food, saying he'd eat when Kenji got back.

She almost asked if he was on his way but stopped herself, instead turning back to the brief. She'd found a piece from the list of donated items Lee had provided that now belonged to a private collector and was on display in their nightclub, Madness. The name was just N. DeVere.

The billionaire?

She'd never been to Madness but had heard it was unique. The item that N. DeVere had purchased was a shield made for one of their emperors. The hide shield had a pendant made from a lion's mane on the front. The inner shield and handle were covered with red saffron leather while the upper side cover was blue silk studded with bands of silver and other silver gilt. It was a remarkable item and part of the regalia that had made up the Maqdala collection. The shield was now on permanent display behind the bar.

"Alan, can you add this to the financial brief 2015? We need to know when the shield was sold and purchased by N. DeVere."

"DeVere?" Van asked.

"Yes, do you know him?"

"Very well. You think he's connected to this?" Van asked.

"He purchased an item from an online auction, according to the Madness website, but I'll have to talk to him to confirm it," Daphne said.

"I can arrange that," Van offered.

"The sooner I can speak to him the better," Daphne said. She wanted to have some facts from DeVere before she filed this brief.

Van tapped his ear, and Daphne realized he had an earpiece in. "Contact Luna. I need to speak to Nick regarding…"

Van glanced over at Daphne.

"The Tewodros Shield purchased in 2015 for Madness."

Van relayed the information back to Lee and then resumed standing in the corner. Daphne imagined she'd hear from Van or Lee when they had the information.

"Where did you find these guys?" Cass asked under

her breath. "I didn't realize they worked for Nicholas DeVere."

"Carl hired them."

"He must have been scared when you were shot," Cass said, her fingers moving over the keyboard as she ran a search on Price Security. But the website was just their name and the tagline *Security is priceless, and your life is worth the price.*

"How did Carl know about them?" Cass asked.

"He's got connections," Daphne said. "Back to the brief. Pull as much information on the piece as you can. I want to demonstrate that this piece was a key part of the collection and just disappeared. It's on Marjorie's list, and the museum has ignored that it's gone."

"On it."

Daphne had a response from Marjorie, who said she'd talk to the finance minister and see what information she could find. They arranged to have a chat later the next day, and Daphne hoped to be able to tell her about the piece that DeVere now owned. Which would add another complication to her case.

If pieces were in the hands of private collectors, that would make it more complicated. The auction houses were within their rights to list and sell pieces that came from museum collections, and in 2015, the public hadn't been aware that contested items made up the backbone of several museums' collections. This was getting messier and messier.

Kenji moved his car around to the employee parking lot to wait for Grey Joy, and his move paid off. He noted that she arrived in a yellow beater of a Ford. She parked the car and then got out, slinging a big canvas messenger bag over her shoulder. She walked into the museum, and Kenji waited to see who else entered. A few minutes later, the deputy director who he'd met yesterday arrived, along with a few more museum staff.

He hadn't thought about doing a stakeout to watch the museum, but now that he was here, it made sense. He tapped his earpiece and waited for Lee to get back to him.

"Sorry for the delay. Busy morning. What's up?"

"Do we have anyone who could watch the museum back entrance just to track movement? Or could we tap into a security feed?" Kenji asked. "There are a lot of people in and out, and I can't identify them all."

"Let me see what I can do," Lee said. He heard her fingers moving over the keyboard in the background. "They have a security camera set up for the back entrance and the main parts of the museum. Seems like the cameras on the archives and file rooms…aren't working. Hmm…let me see if I can find out who monitors them, and maybe we can make a call and get them fixed. Any areas you want me to watch?"

"All of them," he said dryly. "I'm not sure who is responsible for coming after Daphne, but it's definitely tied to the pieces that are missing. And all of these guys are still suspects."

"All right, I'm on it. Also, just to keep you up to date, Nick has one of the pieces that disappeared from the museum."

Kenji wasn't too pleased to hear Nick's name again. "Why? How?"

"He bought it at auction in 2015. Daphne is trying to get more information, and Luna's gone to help out."

"Thanks for keeping me in the loop," Kenji said. "Can you track a yellow Ford?"

He rattled off the license plate number, and Lee agreed to use an algorithm to track the car's movements through speed cameras and ATMs throughout the city.

"Let Van know I'll go and talk to Nick before heading back to Daphne's office," Kenji said. Now that he had a connection to Daphne's case, Kenji felt fairly certain that he could do that without raising suspicion.

He hated that one discussion with the Director and he was back to keeping secrets. But he wanted to get to the bottom of this. He suspected she'd come to him because the CIA had no purview to operate inside the borders of the United States. So she couldn't work Nick as an informant.

"Will do. When should I tell him to expect you?"

Forty minutes if the traffic was good to get to Nick and maybe twenty minutes to talk to him. "A couple of hours."

"Yeah, traffic is a bitch today. I'll keep you posted with the security company and footage if I can get it. Might need to ask for a tap. I'll contact Detective Miller and see if we can work with the art squad."

"Thanks. Let's keep this between us until we have something. Daphne's got enough to worry about now," Kenji said.

"No problem. Later."

Kenji tapped the earpiece to mute it and then headed toward downtown, where Nicholas DeVere lived and worked in an Art Deco–style building. He'd converted two floors into a nightclub called Madness. A year ago he'd hired Price Security when his lookalike bodyguard had been murdered in his place. So Kenji knew the building pretty well.

A lot of the passive security measures they'd put in place were still there. Including access to the parking garage by Price Security. He parked the car and headed up to Nick's office. Not surprised to find Luna waiting for him at the elevator.

"Lee told me you were on your way. I've already relayed the information about the museum piece to Daphne," Luna said. "But it's always nice to see you."

"I'm glad to hear that. I'm actually here for something else as well," Kenji said.

Luna was like a sister to him, and they were close enough that he didn't want her to be surprised by whatever Nick was involved in. Not that Kenji suspected the other man was doing anything illegal. But Nick thought he was unbreakable and wouldn't worry about danger to himself.

Luna sighed. "What else?"

"I'm not sure, but I need to talk to Nick. My old boss at the CIA asked me to cultivate a local informant who has some information regarding an international art and antiquities smuggling operation."

"And Nick's the informant?"

He nodded. He could tell by her face that it was news to her. "Let's go and see him, shall we?"

Kenji almost felt sorry for Nick, but knew the other man would be able to soothe Luna. He got where Luna was coming from all too well. It was sort of how he'd felt when he realized that Daphne had put herself in danger by going out in the alleyway that first night by herself.

It staggered him as he realized that he'd already been falling back in love with her then. Maybe he'd never fallen out of love with her. And that was why everything felt so intense for him.

Nicholas DeVere smiled at Kenji as they walked into his office. His assistant, Finn Walsh, was at his side. "Hello, Kenji. Long time."

"Good to see you, Finn," he said to the other man.

"Are you here about the piece I purchased?" Nick asked. "Finn is pulling the paperwork as we speak."

"I'm here about something else. My old boss got in touch wanting me to liaise with an informant with a connection to an illegal smuggling ring," Kenji said.

"Hell."

Nick shook his head and immediately turned to face Luna. "I didn't want you to find out."

But Nick wasn't speaking to Kenji. Instead, he spoke to his wife.

"Well, I did. You're not supposed to keep things from me. We can discuss it later. Kenji, what does she want?" Luna asked.

"She wants to use your connection and you," Kenji said. "She needs an in with the smugglers."

"What I got was an offer to attend a private auction. I'm not sure that anyone else can go but me."

"I could," Finn said.

"No," Nick and Kenji both said at once.

"Why not?"

"It's dangerous," Nick said. "You're too valuable, Finn."

"Once the Director has your name, she'll never forget it," Kenji added.

"Would you be willing to RSVP to the event and share the information with me? I'll relay the information to the Director."

"Sure. Will that be enough?"

"It'll have to be. She can stake it out or send her own undercover agent in."

"Or I could go," Finn said.

He walked over to Finn and put his hand on the other man's shoulder, because Finn looked as if he were still considering offering himself to help out. "No matter how enticing she makes the work sound, only say yes if you're willing to give up the life you have here. There's no way to live in both worlds."

Finn's mouth got tight, and he nodded.

"Time for me to head back to Daphne."

"I'll see you out," Luna said.

They had just stepped off the elevator when he got an emergency call to report to Daphne's office.

"Go," Luna said. "I'll talk to Nick and Finn and keep them both safe. Are you going back to the CIA?"

"No," Kenji said.

"I'm glad. I've got this. Go now," Luna said, hugging him as he left her.

He tapped his earpiece. "What's going on?"

"Poison. EMTs are on their way. Van wants backup to question and search the area."

"Daphne."

"Fuck, sorry. She wasn't poisoned. One of her team members…but it was her drink that had the poison in it."

Chapter 18

Daphne freaked out when Cass stopped talking mid-sentence and collapsed next her. Van noticed it and was immediately on his earpiece, calling for the ambulance.

"Does anyone have first aid training?" Van asked.

"I do," Janice said.

Janice rushed over to them. Cass was convulsing, and Daphne held her friend's head so it didn't hit the table. "Clear the table and let's lay her on it."

Everyone worked together to get Cass up on the table. Janice took her pulse and checked for blocked airways. "Does she have any conditions?"

"No. She's usually very healthy. What is going on?" Daphne asked.

The EMTs rushed in and started working on Cass. After asking what had happened before she collapsed, an expert was called and they tested her drink and found it had been contaminated with strychnine.

"What? Someone poisoned her?" Daphne was scared when she heard that. Everyone looked white as a ghost.

"No one leaves this room," Van said as soon as the EMTs took Cass out on a stretcher. "The cops are on their way."

"I don't think anyone in here would hurt Cass," Daphne said. She looked around at her staff. They'd had such a productive and fun morning doing work they all loved and were passionate about.

Alan glanced at the cup that Cass had been drinking from and put his hand on his throat. "I think Cass got your drink, Daphne."

She looked at the table and realized her friend had. The cup was clearly marked with her name and her order. Daphne felt lightheaded and sank to her own chair. Cass and she always shared a drink because the shakes were too decadent for one person. Her hand was shaking as she started to reach for it.

Van stopped her, catching her hand. He stood between her and the rest of the room.

"Alan, you brought the order up, correct?"

"Yes."

"Please sit here so I can watch you. Everyone else can sit at the other end of the table. No texting while we wait for the cops, and no talking."

"Van, this isn't necessary," Daphne said, but she was having a hard time controlling the trembling inside her body. She felt weird like she was about to collapse, which was just her nervous system reacting to what was going on. She knew that. There wasn't anything wrong with her. It was Cass...

"I have to text Gerry and tell him to meet Cass at the hospital," she told Van.

He moved so he could look at her while keeping the entire room in his view. "Who?"

"Her husband. I'm not asking you. I'm just keeping you in the loop," Daphne said. Now that her initial scare was passing, she was getting mad and needed to take some control.

She texted Gerry and gave him the bare bones she knew. Told him she'd stop by the hospital after the cops cleared her to leave the office. Then put her phone back on the table.

"Why is Alan separated?"

"He's the one who brought the food up," Van said in the low rumble of a voice that made her aware he was a dangerous man. The smile he usually had on around her had made her almost forget it. "We need to make sure he's not the poisoner."

"I didn't poison anyone."

"Well, someone did," Van said. "You also suggested the restaurant."

"We always get lunch from there," Janice said. "No one knows the people who work there."

Pam nodded along while looking at Alan, who had gotten more sullen and quiet as time passed. Daphne wasn't sure she blamed him. He'd already answered questions about his connection to Pierce Lauder, yet she wasn't sure that he wasn't working with his uncle. But poisoning her?

He noticed her looking at him and then shook his head. "I've already given you my word that I'm not working with my uncle. Do you really think that I would be complicit in something that would harm you? And if I was, do you think I'm so incompetent that I would put it into a drink I know you and Cass share?"

He had a point. Everyone in this room knew that she and Cass shared the shake. The delivery person or the one who prepared her order wouldn't. "Did you see the delivery guy?"

"Yeah. He had on a Burger Boy uniform and baseball cap," Alan said.

Van watched the play between all of them. He tapped his earpiece as he'd done a few times while the EMTs had been in the building and asked Lee to send Luna to Burger Boy and dispatch Xander and Rick to search for the delivery driver.

Detective Miller arrived a few minutes later, along with two cops and Xander, who informed Van that the building was locked down, but Daphne was afraid it was probably too late to save her friend. The poison was odorless, and it was only Cass's collapse that had brought their attention to it.

"Burger Boy reported their driver as missing," Detective Miller said. "I've put out an APB for his vehicle. We're going to need to take everyone's statement."

"Not a problem," Alan said loudly. "I'll be happy to tell you what I know."

Daphne felt bad that Alan was the target of so much suspicion. But Cass was in the hospital. Gerry had arrived and texted that they had pumped her stomach and were keeping her for observation, but she should be able to go home later that night.

"Cass is going to be okay," Daphne told the team.

"I'm glad to hear that," Alan said.

"Me too," Janice and Pam said.

Individually they were all questioned by the detective, and she called in a forensic team to dust the takeout bags and cups for prints. Daphne kept watching the door, waiting for Kenji, but he didn't arrive.

* * *

Kenji rushed back to the Mitchell and Partners office building. Traffic was heavy, but he used all of his evasive driving skills and a lot of speed and intimidation to get to Wilshire Boulevard. He knew that Daphne hadn't been poisoned, but the fact that someone on her staff had been was worrying.

Whoever was threatening Daphne was stepping up their attacks. He almost wondered if they should pretend she had been poisoned to shake them out, but he heard via his earpiece that the cops had already been there and reported that a woman named Cass Smith had been the victim.

It was strychnine, which was odorless, so the fact that the woman had collapsed was the only way they had been able to identify it. Kenji pulled into a parking space just as Rick walked out of the building.

"What's going on?" Kenji asked.

"The restaurant reported that their driver hasn't reported back to work. Detective Miller put out an APB on the car. I'm going to check the parking lot to see if I can find him."

Rick caught him up on all the details and then turned to check out the parking lot for the driver. There was a chance he might have been knocked unconscious or worse.

"Want some help?" Kenji asked.

He knew that Van was keeping Daphne safe, and Kenji needed a few moments to get himself under control. To figure out how to be cool when he saw Daphne. But he wasn't going to be cool. He couldn't be. Not with her.

He was still agitated from his meeting with the Director, where she'd in essence threatened his family, and now his woman had almost been poisoned. Kenji was on edge in a way that he hadn't been since…well, since Afghanistan. He didn't like the emotions that rolled around inside of him, and he was certain he couldn't control them.

"Yeah. Left?"

Kenji nodded and started sweeping to the left of the parking lot. He tapped his earpiece to unmute it as he walked, looking for any signs. "Do we know how anyone would have been sure the food was meant for Daphne?"

"She used her credit card to pay for it," Van said. "Lee, can someone monitor her cards?"

"They could, but it's a better bet that someone inside is a mole."

"Yeah, Detective Miller is going hard on Field," Van said.

The one connected to the museum director. "Anyone else acting odd?"

"The legal secretary keeps crying," Van said. "I think she's scared, and rightly so."

"Pam Beale?"

"Yes, why?"

"She said something odd when I took her picture and almost broke down," Kenji said. "Lee?"

"On it. I'll dig around and see if there's something we missed," Lee said.

Kenji kept walking and noticed one of the hedges along the side of the building had been crumpled like by a foot or something. He moved closer and noticed a man's leg. A guy in jeans and a Burger Boy T-shirt was collapsed on the ground. Kenji knelt to check his pulse, which was low but there.

He unmuted his earpiece. "Found the driver. Southeast corner of the building. Unconscious. Low pulse."

"I'll call for an ambulance," Lee said.

"I've alerted Miller, and Officer Jones is on his way down. Rick?" Van asked.

"On my way, Boss," Rick answered.

Kenji glanced up as his coworker jogged over to his location. There was blood oozing from a wound at the back of the delivery man's neck as well as what looked like a Taser wound on his chest. The burn marks were left on the T-shirt.

"This guy's going to have one hell of headache," Rick said dryly.

"He's lucky that's all he's going to have," Kenji said.

Rick snorted. Kenji glanced up and saw a hint of a smile on Rick's face. "This is turning into something bigger."

"I agree, but what? I can see wanting her out of the picture, but Mitchell will just assign another lawyer to the case," Kenji said.

"Maybe they have a lawyer they want to replace her," Rick said. "Makes sense with all the attacks."

"Yeah, but first they wanted the censer she found," Kenji said.

"Cop incoming," Rick said, walking over to greet the officer as Kenji stood up and turned to do the same.

"We'll take it from here," the officer said. Kenji and Rick walked back toward the main entrance.

"God, I wish I still smoked," Rick said.

Kenji just clapped his friend on the shoulder and offered him a pack of gum. Rick took it, unwrapped two pieces and shoved them into his mouth. "Thanks."

"Rick, head over to Topanga. The APB came back, and the driver's car was abandoned. Miller is sending some beat cops, but maybe you can talk to the locals and get a description of the driver," Van said.

"On it, Boss," Rick said, giving Kenji a little salute before he walked toward his car.

Kenji continued into the building. The two large Christmas trees that flanked the reception desk looked out of place and too damned cheery given that a woman had been poisoned.

But Kenji knew better than most that the holiday season didn't mean everyone was going to play nice. Crime still happened, and criminals like the one who was after Daphne weren't going to take a few weeks off.

This latest attack was like Rick and he had discussed: designed to take Daphne out of the picture. Perhaps now that the museum had learned the censer had been returned, they worried what else Daphne would find out.

Was she closer to uncovering what was really going on than either of them realized?

He wasn't too sure. But he was going to keep her by his side from now on. He had a good lead on Grey Joy, and Kenji wasn't above using whatever means necessary to get information from her.

If she was the one who'd called Daphne to the alleyway, she probably knew who the mole was at Mitchell and Partners and who was threatening Daphne.

Xander snagged him as he walked to the elevator. "Hey, got a minute? You're better with security footage than I am."

"Sure. I guess Lee's not available," Kenji said as he followed his friend into the security offices, where everyone was tense.

The head security guard stood over another man leaning in to try to see the screen better. This was a big screwup on their home turf, and he could tell just by glancing at all the men and women in the room that they were ticked off it had happened.

"I floated the theory that the delivery driver had to know where the cameras were," Xander said. "Hammond over there agrees, but most of them are hidden, so unless someone told him where they are…"

"Someone more than likely did. Let's see the hand-off," Kenji said, knowing that Alan Field was the top suspect as an insider working for whoever was after Daphne. Or, let's face it, the museum. That was his connection.

Part of that bothered Kenji, because the museum had been the scene of another incident. So it added something to investigate as far as Kenji was concerned. There was no way to rule out someone in Lauder's office as the suspect any more than they could rule out Field.

He leaned in closer to watch the high-quality black-and-white footage and noticed that Alan hardly glanced at the driver. Instead he was talking to a woman who stood just past the driver. The woman's face wasn't visible, but she had on a skirt and some chunky boots.

"Who's that?" Kenji asked, reaching over the video operator's shoulder and hitting Pause.

"Who?" Hammond, the security director, leaned in. "Oh, he's talking to someone else."

"Yes, any ideas who?" Xander asked him. "Those boots seem pretty distinctive."

"They do. Most of the staff here doesn't wear boots," Hammond said. "Run the tape back and see if we can identify her before the driver comes in."

Kenji stepped away from the security team while they were running the tape and tapped his earpiece.

"Van, anyone up there wearing chunky boots?"

"Give me a minute," Van said.

Kenji watched the tape from his position, hoping for a glimpse of someone he recognized from his days of watching over Daphne. He'd come into contact with a lot of people. When she walked into the frame, he caught the swing of her hair and realized she was Carl Mitchell's assistant.

Kenji was searching through his mind for her name. "Carl's assistant."

"Yes. That is Leanna," Hammond said.

"Why is she in the lobby?"

They rolled the tape forward, waiting, and saw her talk to the delivery guy and hand him something before he walked out of the building.

"We need to talk to her," Kenji said.

"I can take you to her office," Hammond said.

"I'll stay here and keep trying to identify the driver. It looks like he might have a tattoo under his left ear," Xander was saying as Kenji followed Hammond out the door.

"How long has Leanna worked for the company?" he asked the security guard.

"I couldn't tell you. I'm not entirely sure she wasn't checking on her own order," Hammond said.

"Do a lot of you order from Burger Boy?" Kenji asked.

"Yes. On Thursdays they offer the building a discount, so pretty much everyone places an order with them," Hammond said.

"Did your team?"

"Sure did. In fact, finance had a large order that came in right after the one for the fourth-floor team," Hammond said.

Kenji realized that Daphne's team was identified simply by the floor by security. "How would someone have known what cup was for Daphne?"

"They label them with our names," Hammond said. "Burgers and drinks. Fries are generic since they only serve crinkle cut."

"But everything else can be personalized?"

"Yeah. Dude, haven't you ever had Burger Boy?"

"No," he said. He wasn't much on fatty foods, plus he was usually working or enjoying his downtime in his apartment, where he ate salads and burritos.

Hammond shrugged as they got on the elevator to go to Mitchell's office. "Do the elevators have cameras?"

"They do," Hammond said.

Kenji unmuted his earpiece. "Xander, check the elevators to see if Field messed with the food on his way up."

"Will do. The delivery guy has a tattoo of a hawk below his left ear, Lee. Can you run a check for priors?"

"With that detailed description?" Lee fired back.

"Well, that's all I have. The guy is good at not being seen," Xander said.

Kenji muted the discussion and turned back to Hammond. "Do you usually have the same delivery person?"

"We have some regulars, but there is always someone new. On Thursdays, with so many orders, we just look for the Burger Boy hat and tee, and of course if they have food. No one is allowed up into the offices or even out of the main lobby," Hammond said. "I can't believe this slipped by us."

"This was well-planned. I should have thought ahead and not allowed outside food," Kenji said. Was it just the distraction of being around Daphne, or had he gotten lax? The fact was, he knew that whoever was after her was stepping up the intensity of their attacks. He should have anticipated this.

"Thanks for that. Still don't like it when someone gets injured on my watch," Hammond said.

"Me either."

Hammond led the way into Mitchell's office, and it was clear from the moment they spoke to Leanna that she was rattled and unsettled. Which didn't mean she'd helped whoever had attempted to poison Daphne. But it didn't clear her either.

From what Kenji observed, everyone in Mitchell and Partners was rattled. And given that a lot of the cases the firm represented were high-profile and sometimes controversial, he understood why everyone would be tense.

Which made it harder to figure out who was working with someone on the outside to silence Daphne.

Chapter 19

Daphne looked at the door each time it opened, waiting for Kenji. Finally, after she gave her statement to Detective Miller, he was there. She took half a step toward him before realizing what she was doing.

He was her bodyguard, not her boyfriend. She had to lace her hands together to keep from reaching for him. Kenji came over to her and put his hand on her shoulder. Their eyes met, and she knew—knew—that he wanted to touch her too.

"Are you okay?"

"Yes. Cass is the one who drank the poison," Daphne said. "I want to go and see her. Can you take me to the hospital?"

He nodded. "Let me speak to Van. Get your stuff together."

She made sure to stay in his line of sight as she walked to the end of the conference room table past Alan, who was slumped into himself. It was disheartening to see him this way. And she wanted to believe it was simply coincidence that he'd been the one to place and collect the order.

But Cass was in the hospital, and this was no game that whoever was after her was playing. It was time to stop worrying about everyone else and put her security at the top of the list.

"I thought you trusted me," Alan said.

She turned to face him and realized he'd been watching her the entire time. "This is more than trust. Cass was poisoned."

"I know that. Do you honestly think I would do it?" he asked her.

"Someone did. That's all I know. Since it was my cup, I know I didn't do it, and everyone else was in here. You have a right to be upset about being questioned, but anyone who'd collected the order would be in your shoes. It's not about you."

Justice and the law weren't perfect, but she had always tried to be impartial, and she knew that the cops were too. The only reason Alan was acting like this was…well, she wasn't one hundred percent, but she figured he was upset because she knew he had a connection to Lauder and the museum. When last she'd spoken to him, she'd been satisfied with his answers, but today had changed things.

Had she been kidding herself that Alan was like her and wanted to ensure that antiquities that had been seized or stolen were returned to their proper owners?

"I get that. I do. But it feels personal."

"I think everyone is scared right now. We order from Burger Boy all the time," Daphne said.

"Yeah."

"I think we shouldn't order in anymore," Pam said, coming over to sit down next to Alan. "I mean, I don't want to."

"Yeah, I think I'll be bringing my own food until this case goes before the judge," Daphne said.

She moved on, leaving the two of them chatting. Kenji came over to her. "Want any help?"

"No. I like to put files in my bag a certain way. I'll need to pack up Cass's stuff too," Daphne said.

"Take your time," he said when he noticed her trembling hands.

"I can't. I want to get to Cass and see that she's okay for myself. And…" She scanned the room to make sure no one was looking at them or could hear her. "I want to be alone with you. I need a hug."

"I need to hug you," Kenji said. "Let me help. You can sort your files later."

She nodded. His hand brushed hers, and a shiver of awareness went through her. She needed more than comfort at this moment. She needed more than safety. What she needed was Kenji. Holding her, making love to her, reassuring her that she was alive and that he was going to keep her that way.

Working quickly, they packed up both bags, and Daphne slung Cass's purse over her shoulder with her own. Kenji carried both of the work bags as Daphne turned to the room. Her staff were still in standby mode, some of them giving statements to the cops.

"I wish I could give everyone the afternoon off, but we need to keep working. You can do it from home if you'd rather. Send me whatever you find by the end of the day. I'm going to see Cass. I'll let you know if she wants visitors."

Everyone on her team hugged her on the way out, even Alan, but that just made her more uneasy. Someone had alerted the person who was trying to stop her about the order. That meant if it wasn't Alan, then someone else on her team was leaking information about her.

But who?

As hard as it had been to suspect Alan, he was the newest member of her team. The others had worked with her for years, and Daphne considered them friends. She wanted to believe there was nothing that would allow them to betray her.

Since Cass had been poisoned, she knew that someone had.

As soon as they were in the elevator by themselves, Kenji brushed his hand against the back of hers. She started to turn toward him. He gripped her hand hard.

"There are cameras."

He said it without moving his lips. She'd forgotten about them. She turned her hand and squeezed his before rubbing it on her skirt.

As soon as they were outside, she wanted to throw herself into his arms, but they were still in public. It wasn't that she cared about what other people thought of their relationship, but she didn't want to give them anything else to talk about.

Once they were at his car, the black Dodge Charger that she'd spent too much time in, he finally leaned over and pulled her into his arms. She hugged him tightly, putting her head on his shoulder and letting her guard down.

"I was talking to Cass when she collapsed. Why would someone do that to her?"

"They wanted to do it to you."

It seemed impossible that he'd forgotten how striking Daphne was in person, but on the drive back to her office, somehow he had. The thought of losing her had him seeing her again for the first time.

She had thick black eyebrows that framed her intelligent brown eyes. She had long, straight hair that hung halfway down her back. Though she had a reputation for being tough as nails, she always looked so ladylike and feminine. Today she had her hair pulled back, revealing the delicate shells of her ears and pearl earrings he knew her father had given her when she graduated from high school.

She never really spoke of her mom, which Kenji hadn't questioned. Their relationship had been full of passion and burned fast. There hadn't been time to dig deep into either of their pasts, something he knew appealed to him.

Today she wore a gorgeous light yellow sheath dress that went well with her coloring. It had leather at the collar and as a cuff on the short sleeves. Then a leather accent that ran across her chest. She had on hose because they was something she always wore and a pair of black leather heels that looked impossibly high and difficult to walk in but made her long legs seem even longer.

Her mouth was full, and she wore a shade of reddish-brown lipstick that he knew was close to her natural lip color. She watched him as if she wasn't sure how to react, and he didn't blame her. She had to be shocked to see him.

Actually, on second glance, he saw the signs of fatigue and pain on her face. Something fierce and primitive stirred in him. He wanted to find the person who shot at them and mete out the kind of justice he knew that Daphne would frown on.

She licked her lips, and his eyes tracked the motion. Another primitive emotion stirred in him. He still found her attractive, which wasn't a shock at all. The intensity of that desire was.

Knowing how close someone had come to poisoning her made him scared.

"We have so much to discuss," she said, shifting back to her seat. "Did you see the Director?"

That she was worried about that meeting made him realize he wasn't the only one catching feels. It was reassuring but at the same time heightened his awareness that he had to do everything in his power to protect her. He put the car in gear and started driving toward the hospital.

"I did. She wanted me to work a contact that turned out to be Nick. It involves an illegal art ring who contacted him, maybe because of the piece he purchased legally that's from the Maqdala collection? Anyway, I went to see Nick and instead suggested the agency send an operative in his place."

"What if it is connected to my case? Will the Director be able to tell us what's up for auction?" Daphne asked.

"I'm not sure. But I can ask her. I don't want to get sucked into that world."

"That's easier said than done," Daphne said. "When I was at The Hague, I was approached."

"You were?" he asked, not really surprised. She'd been a candidate they'd recruited and wanted, so even though she'd walked away, the CIA would have kept their eye on her.

"Yeah, I said no. But it was hard," she said.

"I said no. It wasn't hard for me. I won't let her manipulate me into doing anything," he said.

"You know it doesn't work like that," she said. "What if you go and I went with you."

"Are you kidding me? Someone is actively trying to kill you. Plus you're not exactly unknown to that world. I don't want you in any more jeopardy."

"I won't be with you by my side. Just think about it."

He clenched his jaw and kept his eyes forward. "I have. The answer is no."

He wasn't going to think about it more. Not for a single second. He didn't want anyone he cared for in danger. He certainly wasn't going to bring Daphne along on a mission.

They pulled into the hospital parking lot where Daphne's friend had been taken. She had been texting with her friend. When he put the car in Park and turned to her, she stopped him before they could get out.

"Cass's husband, Gerry, is up there with her. I'm here as her friend, so no pictures or the third degree. Got it?"

"Fine. But I'm going to memorize their features so I can have Lee run them.".

"I mean it, Kenji. It's bad enough that she drank the poison meant for me. These people are my closest friends, and I don't want to do anything else to make this day harder."

"I'll be on my best behavior."

"That's all I ask," she said.

Kenji got out of the car first, happy that Daphne waited for him to come and get her door. When she stepped out, he took a moment to look around the parking lot. There were too many people going in and out for him to feel safe, so he hurried her inside and up to the room where her friend waited.

Daphne's worry was clear on her face when they walked into the room. The husband rushed over to hug Daphne and then offered his hand to Kenji. "She's sleeping but doing much better."

"I'm so sorry, Gerry."

"It's not your fault. Cass has said that every time she wakes up. 'Make sure D knows it wasn't her fault.'"

"Of course she'd say that. But I'm the one whose life has been threatened. I should have thought ahead and not ordered food or shared it with her."

Kenji realized how hard Daphne was taking this. "You couldn't have known. Van is the best in the business, and even he didn't raise a flag when you ordered."

He could tell that Daphne still hadn't forgiven herself. They stayed until Cass woke up, and the two women talked and cried and hugged each other. Seeing them together made Kenji realize that it was time they stopped playing defense. It was time to go on the offense.

When they got back to Price Tower, both of them changed, and Kenji was waiting for her when she came out of the bedroom. "I have an idea, and I'm not sure if you're going to like it."

"I wish I had one. Carl asked to have the court date moved up, and I should hear something tomorrow. Which reminds me. when I was talking to Laverne at the museum, I noticed a note that said *C. 4 pm*. Did we check Carl?"

"Your boss?" Kenji asked. "I believe so. Let me ping Lee about it."

Kenji sent Lee a message and then put his phone on the table, leaning toward her. "I found Grey Joy today."

"Great. I want to talk to her. She's the person who called me and set up the meeting where I got shot," Daphne said. "I've gone over her voice and everything that happened at the archives in my head, and I'm sure of it."

"She's definitely not telling us something, and questioning her should be our next move," Kenji said. "I'd like to do it in a public place and set up a sting. See if she's working with the shooter. It would mean putting you in what seems like a very open situation."

"I'm the bait? Well, I guess I have been since the beginning. Did you ever find anything from the camera behind the coffee shop?"

"No, it had been turned off. Lee said that she noticed a pattern for turning the cameras off and alerted the cops. Apparently that alleyway is used for drug deals. So she suspects Grey might have known that or hadn't considered that there would be cameras."

Daphne pulled her notebook closer to her and then jotted down what Kenji was telling her. That really didn't tell her anything else about Grey except she might have bought drugs back there or felt safe because of the staffer she knew.

"Detective Miller has been down to talk to the other shop owners. No one saw or heard anything the night you were shot. We still don't know who the shooter was. But we do know that the caliber of bullet that fired at you was a 9mm which are used in Glocks."

"The same model as the one used to shoot at the car," Daphne said.

"Yes. No one on your staff has weapons training except for Carl and Pam."

"Pam?" she asked. It was hard to imagine Carl or Pam as the one who shot at her in the alleyway. Like it was almost impossible. She couldn't picture either of them holding a weapon.

"Yes. She has a conceal permit and goes to the range on the weekends with her husband."

How did she not know that? She'd had so many conversations with Pam, and none of them had involved that. But to be fair, they only talked about work. Pam kept her personal life very private. "Interesting."

"Yes. Also, she was the most emotional and nervous when I took her photo, and today when Cass was shot. Do you think she's involved? She is your secretary."

"She's my legal secretary. She does a lot more than keep my calendar."

"Does she have access to it?" Kenji asked.

"Yes. Actually, anyone who works at Mitchell and Partners can view my calendar. Though I didn't put the meeting with Grey on there. But I did message my team that I had a lead. So perhaps that was an alert?"

"Probably. A lot of people know where you are all the time. Is your address in the company directory?" Kenji asked.

"Yes. But anyone could type my name into a search engine and find it," Daphne said. Pam had no reason to want to harm her.

"Very true. I'm not accusing her of anything, but it seems to me that someone had to know your team was ordering out today," Kenji said.

"Everyone—"

"I already heard it from Carl's assistant. Many teams order in on Thursdays because of the discount. But someone knew when you ordered and which driver to knock out."

Daphne didn't like the facts that Kenji was presenting, but she couldn't argue with them. He was careful to be logical, and she suspected he was trying to keep her from defending her colleagues. It was working.

Someone had to have passed on the information for their order. "So we have Alan and Janice at my place, maybe Carl. But I think that's a long shot."

"Agreed," Kenji said.

She put her pen down and leaned toward him, taking his hands in hers. "What is it you are suggesting?"

He turned his hands under hers and rubbed his thumb over her knuckles. "That you let everyone on your team know you are meeting with Grey Joy. Then see what happens."

"What if Grey is a whistleblower?" Daphne asked. "Should we warn her?"

But she knew the answer to that before she asked it. They couldn't alert anyone to their plan. Right now the only people she was certain weren't trying to kill her were Kenji, Cass and Gerry.

That was it. Which left too many people at her office and at the museum that she'd spoken to about this case.

"Okay. How would it work?" she asked.

"I'd have to get my entire team involved, but I wanted to discuss this with you first. It will be dangerous," he warned her.

"That's fine. If we are successful, maybe we can revisit going to Madness for your old boss."

"Never. If we are successful, I plan to discuss us dating again."

"You do?"

"Yes."

She licked her lips and smiled over at him. "I'd like that."

"Me too," he said.

Chapter 20

That she was open to dating him again was all he wanted. There was a lot of work to do, but while they were safe at the tower, he wanted this chance to take her into his arms and make love to her. Not because she was reacting to fear and danger but because she wanted him.

He still held her hand in his and turned it over, drawing a shape on her palm. Her fingers curled around his hand.

"Kenji…will you make love to me?"

"Yes," he said, his voice low and guttural. He stood and walked to her side of the table, then put his hands on her waist and lifted her up. She had changed into a skirt with a slit on the side, and he couldn't resist running his hand up it. Her soft skin under his fingers smelled of peaches and another musk that was all Daphne. *Seductive* and *sensual* were the two words he always associated with her. Just being in her presence made him hot and hard.

His fingers shook as he touched her, slowly moving his hand up the inside of her thigh, her legs parting as his caresses traveled up until he felt the heat from her sex. With his hand on her waist, the both of them still fully dressed, he looked down into her wide brown eyes. Her lips were parted and her eyes half-lidded.

How did I ever leave her when I was younger?

He bent until he could kiss her, driving his tongue into her mouth when she wrapped her arms around him. He was so damned horny for her. Seeing her safe in his apartment had made him slip on the leash he normally used to control his base instincts. But it was gone. As her tongue slid along his, he could only suck it deeper as the gnawing ache inside of him grew. He finally had her spread out on the table in front of him.

He tore his mouth from hers, his breath sawing in and out. He groaned and stopped thinking about anything but his thickening erection and how much he wanted her.

She wore a silky blouse that clung to her chest, revealing her erect nipples. She arched her back as he drew the hand on her waist up her body, her breasts thrusting toward him. He palmed her other breast as he leaned down and sucked one nipple into his mouth through her blouse.

She moaned his name. He felt her hands in his hair, tracing the shape of his ear before moving down his neck again, caressing his chest and undoing the buttons of his shirt, then pulling the tie from his neck. Her fingers were cool against the warmth of his skin. He lifted his head from her breast and stepped back, undoing his pants and pushing them down his legs.

She stood, pulled her blouse up over her head and tossed it on the floor. Her bra followed, and Kenji caught his breath as she bent forward to take off the knee-high boots she wore and her breasts swayed forward.

He reached out to fondle her as she undid the waistband of her skirt. With a shimmy, pushed it down her hips and onto the floor.

She shoved her panties down and stepped out of them, totally, gloriously naked in front of him.

Their eyes met, and she smiled. "Remember the first time?"

He groaned. "I wanted you so much I could hardly wait until you were naked."

"That's right. You were in before I finished taking my panties off."

He got even harder when she mentioned that fact. She held her hand out, and he stepped forward. His cock jutted in front of him, and she took him in her hand, grasping his shaft and pulling him closer to her.

There was no hiding his reaction to her. And he didn't want to. For the first time since she'd come back in his life, he felt like he'd found his purpose. Protecting her and everyone in the family he'd created for himself.

Every breath he took was filled with the scent of her. The feel of her under his fingers inflamed every sense in his body. He was compelled by the need to fill her completely. Putting his hands on her waist, he lifted her up and turned until he could set her down on the table. He stepped between her legs, tangling his hands in her long silky hair, tugging lightly on it until her head fell back, exposing the long length of her neck. He kissed it.

Tasting that creamy expanse, he moved his mouth slowly down the elegant length of it. He brushed a strand of her hair aside with his nose, continuing to kiss her skin.

She wrapped her arms around his shoulders and

tightened her legs around his hips. Her response to him was addicting, and he craved more of her reactions.

He put his hands on her legs, caressing her knees and slowly moving his hands down her left leg until he got to her foot. He lifted her foot and placed it in the center of his chest. She wriggled her toes against him, and he caressed the arch of her foot.

He ran his finger along her instep, tickling her, and she squirmed. All thoughts of small feet and tickling dropped away. He glided his fingers up her leg. It was strong, muscled from years of walking in high heels, he suspected.

There was so much strength in all of her. The last few days would have broken the strongest of men, but she just kept powering on. Not looking for a shortcut or an easy way out but putting herself right in the middle of the action. She was willing to do it again, making herself the bait.

It was only his confidence in himself to keep her safe and in her to keep her nerve that had even made him suggest it.

He lowered his mouth, kissing and nibbling his way up her other leg until once again his head was buried between her legs. He mouthed her. Her thighs tightened around his head, and then she let them fall open.

Her hair was neatly trimmed, and he parted her with his fingers. Her flesh was a delicate pink and the little nub at the center swollen with need. He gently caressed her. Her hips shifted a little bit left to right. He touched her in a circular motion, and she moaned. A sound of approval. He continued to move his finger over her before he leaned down closer.

He exhaled hard watching her legs fall wider apart as she lifted her hips toward Kenji, presenting her body to him. She grabbed his head, and her legs undulated next to him, one of them falling over his shoulder as he licked at her delicate flesh. He traced her core with his finger, just teasing the opening, and then slowly pushed one finger up inside of her. Her hips jerked upright, and he continued to eat her. She was delicious.

He added a second finger inside of her and thrust them deep and deeper. This was what he needed. To taste her and feel her passion before they both left this apartment and he put her out there for someone to try to hurt.

He was rock-hard, his cock straining to be inside of her, but he wanted to make this moment last as long as he could. He continued moving his mouth over her until he felt her body start to tighten around his fingers, kept rocking them in and out of her until she arched her back and cried his name.

He lifted his head, pulled his fingers from her body and looked up at her. She was on her elbows, gazing down at him. Her eyes were fiery, passionate. There was a flush to her body, and her breath flowed in and out, causing her breasts to rise and fall rapidly.

He felt her hand rubbing up and down his cock. He jerked forward and realized his control was more slippery than he'd imagined. She traced his length, her fingernail scraping over his skin. He loved the feel of her hand on his naked shaft.

She took his shaft in one hand, stroking him in her fist. Moving it up and down in a slow and sensuous movement that made his balls tighten. She skimmed her finger over the tip of his erection, and his hips jerked forward.

She cupped his sac in one hand and squeezed very softly as she tightened her grip on his shaft. He started to thrust in her hand. She leaned in, and he felt her breath on his erection a moment before her tongue dashed out and traced the tip of him.

Sensation shivered up and down his spine, and he canted his hips forward, feeling her mouth engulf him. He tried to control himself. He'd been lauded for his self-control, but her mouth made a mockery of that. He was thrusting into her mouth, his hands in her hair and her hands on his balls.

He didn't want to come until he was inside of her and pulled her up his body, pushing her back until she was supine on the table. Then he leaned forward over her. He shoved his hand into her hair and brought his mouth down on hers as he shifted his hips and entered in one long thrust. Heat burned between them as they drove themselves harder and harder, until he felt her body tightening around his cock. He held her hips hard against him as he continued to thrust up into her until he felt his balls tighten. And he came, and her along with him. He emptied himself as he continued to thrust into her until he was spent.

He held her in his arms on the table in his living room, resting his head against her breasts and knowing that he would do anything he had to in order to keep Daphne in his life. He needed her more than he'd wanted to admit out loud, but his soul already knew the importance of this woman.

He felt her hand stroking his neck and shoulders and

lifted himself so he could see her face. She gave him that soft, gentle smile, and he knew that whether he wanted to say the words or not, he had more than feelings for Daphne. He loved her.

He had loved this woman probably from the first time he'd seen her back in college. He'd loved her when he left her. He'd loved her when he'd been in the world doing unspeakable things. And he still loved her now.

The only thing he wasn't sure of was if he was worthy of her love. He knew he'd do whatever he had to in order to keep her safe. Not the right or moral thing, the thing that would keep her alive no matter what.

That wasn't a choice Daphne would approve of, but there it was.

"I wanted you from the moment you walked into my conference room," she said.

"Did you?"

"Yes. I was so happy to see you, and I felt like I could finally breathe. I thought, *Kenji's here. I'm safe.*"

He buried his face in her shoulder and hugged her tightly to him. "I will always keep you safe."

That vow was one he'd never allow himself to break. And if he felt himself slipping toward that monster he'd been when he'd worked for the agency, he'd do the right thing and walk away from her. Because Daphne safe and healthy was the only thing that could make him feel okay.

"Kenji?"

I love you, Daphne. He thought it, but didn't allow himself to say it out loud.

Chapter 21

Daphne was still trying to process everything that had happened between her and Kenji when they were called to Lee's office and the conference room area. She wore a pair of ripped jeans and a Christmas sweater that she and Cass had bought together for their Black Friday not-shopping day. She and Cass always went on a hike the day after Thanksgiving, and Gerry came with them if he was able to. Because Gerry was an ER doctor, his schedule wasn't always set. This year it had been just her and Cass.

She sensed that Kenji was having second thoughts about using her as bait. Mainly because he held her hand when they were in the elevator, and that wasn't something he normally would have done.

"We should talk about us," she said.

"After the meeting. Detective Miller got a set of prints from the censer that weren't yours. Van asked Nick if they could see whether there were any prints on the shield he bought at auction, and he agreed."

"Thank you for doing that," she said. "I never thought to ask the cops to dust anything for prints."

"After the poisoning at your office today, Detective Miller mentioned they are ramping up their efforts to try to catch whoever is after you," Kenji said. "Not that they weren't before, but the cops are overworked. It helps that Nick is family so we could easily get the item."

"Will he be at the meeting?"

"Both he and Luna will be. Everyone on the team is going to be there. I think you've met them all except maybe Rick."

She nodded. "You're right, I haven't met Rick. Before we go in there, please know that I'm not going to be swayed from putting myself up as bait."

Kenji put his hand on the back of her neck and brought his mouth down on hers hard and fast. She kissed him back just as fiercely. He might not like her putting herself in danger, but she hated the thought of him doing it as well.

He lifted his head just as the elevator doors opened. "I know."

"Good," she said, squeezing his hand as they walked into the room and found the group waiting along with Detective Miller.

She caught them up on the prints she'd found, which she had a team running through the database. She'd also given Lee a copy, which she was running through the international databases she had access to through her connections. So Lee was at her computer.

"I have a quicker way to find Daphne's attacker," Kenji said as they all sat down.

"We have an idea," Daphne said, not willing to be sidelined. Now that Cass had been poisoned in her place and she realized that winning the case was going to take too long to stop the threat to both herself and those she cared about, she was determined to do whatever she could to stop it herself.

"Let's hear it," Van said, leaning forward and lacing his fingers together.

Daphne cleared her throat. "I think the informant who called me was Grey Joy. Her voice was very familiar, and when I started to question her at the museum, I think she was about to confirm she was the contact before we were attacked."

"I've located Grey Joy with Lee's help, and we'd like to set up a meeting in a public place," Kenji said. "The rest of us would be in position to keep the women safe but also to observe who else is in the area. Daphne doesn't believe anyone on her staff could be complicit in the attacks on her."

"I don't. But Kenji pointed out that one of my paralegals has a permit to carry a concealed weapon, and so does my boss. He's suggested I add the meeting to my calendar so everyone with access will know about it."

"That's a lot to take in. Are you ruling out the museum?" Detective Miller said.

Daphne wasn't. "Detective Miller, I wondered if you could let them know that I found the censer the night I was shot and that I am meeting with my contact to try to find more missing items."

Detective Miller made some notes on the narrow pad in front of her. "I can do that. When is this meeting?"

"I haven't set it up yet," Daphne admitted.

"The police should be there as well," Detective Miller said. "If I can make it, I will. If not, I can ask for someone from the art team."

"That would be great," Daphne said. "I'm hoping to record Grey's statement to use in court. But I need her to trust me. I'm not entirely sure why she didn't stay in the alleyway that night."

"Perhaps she only planned for you to find the item," Rick said from the corner of the table. "When I worked for the DEA, that was a common practice so that you couldn't really identify each other."

Honestly, she'd thought the man was on the verge of falling asleep. Van nodded at Rick.

"I hadn't considered that. But it makes sense," Daphne said. "I guess I need to call Grey first and get her to agree to meet me."

Kenji leaned in. "We need to know where you are going to meet. It needs to be a place busy enough that we all won't stick out but are protected."

"Do you have an idea in mind?" Van asked Kenji.

"Zara's Brew—the coffee shop with the alleyway where Daphne was first meant to meet her. It's in North Hollywood and has a large glass window front but walls on three sides. There is only one small hallway with a unisex bathroom and an exit door. Easy to keep them safe inside."

"Plus lots of vantage points. Bulletproof glass?" Van asked.

"Doubtful," Detective Miller said.

The team started talking about logistics that Daphne didn't need to be a part of. She'd committed to this, and there was no turning back. She could only hope that no one on her team was part of it. She hated to think that she'd been naive or that she'd put others in danger.

Even though this had been his idea, Kenji didn't like it. Daphne had spoken on the phone with Grey, who'd agreed to meet at Zara's Brew in North Hollywood the next morning at ten. He noticed Nick and Daphne talking and knew she wanted to find out more about the provenance that had come with the shield when he purchased it and the illegal auction he'd been invited to attend. But it was just listed as an item from the Hazelton-Measham collection, and the grandson, Thomas, was listed as the one selling it.

"Did anyone on your team speak to Thomas?" Kenji asked.

"I think Pam was meant to call him," Daphne said. "Let me ping her. Should I mention in the chat that I'm speaking to Grey tomorrow?"

"Might as well," Kenji said.

Daphne started typing out the message on her phone, and Nick turned to Kenji. "Regarding the other matter we discussed, I have the time and place for the auction."

"I'll pass the information along," Kenji said.

"Have you reconsidered you and me going?" she asked him.

"No," he said firmly.

Daphne pulled him away from Nick and the others to a corner of the room. "If we are going to be together, then we have to be a part of each other's lives. You've gotten a good glimpse at my job. I want a chance to know your world too."

"I want you safe."

She put her hand on his cheek. "This isn't going to be the last threat to either of us. I'll take another high-profile case. You'll guard someone who is at risk. Our lives aren't going to be safe."

Kenji didn't like her assessment, but he knew that she had a point. "What if you don't like it or get tired—"

"I'm not going to do that. I didn't want to join the agency because I knew we'd be separated and working different missions. Maybe never seeing each other. The fact that we will be able to come home to each other— that is all I need."

"Are you sure?"

"I think so. I mean, I didn't like it when I thought you were shot , but with your team around us…" She trailed off. Kenji realized that she really didn't have any idea of how dangerous this mission she'd agreed to was.

There was a chance that they caught the bad guy and she got hurt. He vowed to himself again that he wouldn't let anything happen to her. He knew he could keep her safe. That was the only thing he wanted to do.

"Sorry to interrupt, but you're needed, Kenji," Xander said, coming over to them.

Kenji nodded and straightened his tie before he walked back over to his boss. Van clapped a hand on his shoulder as he arrived. "You'll be on Daphne. I want someone watching the informant too, but I'm not sure two bodyguards in the coffee shop won't give the game away."

Kenji understood they all carried themselves in a manner that was different from people just getting coffee.

"I can do it," Rick said. "Unless you wanted me on the alley? I blend way better than you lot do."

"Hey, I can blend," Luna argued.

"You can, but you are better at being sociable," he reminded her. "Someone is going to have to be behind the counter with the barista."

"True," Luna agreed.

"So you two will be in the shop. Rick, get there when they open and set up near the front. Luna, the barista has agreed you can shadow her for the day. You're doing research for a book," Van said.

Luna and Rick both nodded. Xander and Lee were still awaiting assignments, and Kenji was sure Van would be close by.

"I'm going to hang with Miller's cops. Lee's on over-watch, and Xander, you take the alleyway," Van said. "Bulletproof vests on everyone including Daphne, and earpieces as well."

He glanced at Daphne and noticed her face seemed a little paler. It was one thing to imagine being bait in a sting. It was something else entirely to get ready to do it. He worried about her reaction, but she just stood up straighter and nodded at him.

His heart beat a little faster. He loved her for her courage and her strength, especially when she was afraid. It was one of the many things he admired about her. She had thrown him when she'd mentioned wanting to see what he did.

He didn't want her anywhere near his world, but he knew she wouldn't be satisfied with anything less. She wasn't going to just be a woman he came home to. He wasn't sure how he felt about that. He might have this found family at Price Security, but there had always been a part of himself he kept hidden from everyone else.

Daphne felt like it was obvious she had the bullet-proof vest on under her clothes. But she had checked herself in the full-length mirror twice and knew it wasn't visible. Today she'd dressed in a one of her A-line skirts, a shirt that she could blouse out a bit and a blazer. She had her favorite Louboutin heels and her bag that she carried everywhere with her.

Kenji was waiting for her when she came out. He was in total bodyguard mode, his face serious, his body tense. But he smiled when he saw her. "Ready?"

No, who in their right mind would be ready for this? "Yes, of course. I'm ready to hear what Grey has to say."

"Good," he said. "Will the judge allow you to submit the recorded conversation?"

"Yes. I'll tell her she's being recorded and have her acknowledge it. It will be fine."

Kenji nodded, and Daphne wondered if he was nervous. "It'll be okay. I trust you to keep us safe."

Kenji gave her a tight smile, and she realized nothing she said to him was going to put him at ease. Her phone pinged as they headed down to the car. Janice was running late to work, and Pam was going to stop by the courthouse to drop off the brief she'd finished the night before.

Daphne asked to approve it first, but Pam had set her status to Not Available in their Slack chat. Kenji drove them to the coffee shop, and they arrived a few minutes early. She glanced around the parking lot but didn't see any of the other Price Security team or the cops.

Which she guessed was a good thing. They were meant to be hidden, and she knew that with Kenji by her side, she'd be fine, or as fine as she could be.

"When we get out, we'll follow the protocols. Inside you just do your job, get the information from Grey you need, and allow me to do my job."

"I will," she said, and stopped him before he could get out of the car. Leaning over, she pulled him close. "Don't forget to keep yourself safe too."

"I won't," he said.

Then he opened the door, and she took a deep breath, knowing this was the moment that she'd get the answers she'd been waiting for. This was it. They walked slowly across the parking lot. When they got inside, the booth that she and Kenji had sat in before was taken, and he frowned as he had to take one in front of the windows. She noticed Rick was slouched in the corner of one of the booths in the middle of the shop, and the booth next to him was available.

"That one. Sit on the left," he said, which put her on the same side as Rick's booth.

She slipped into it. Kenji hesitated, and she knew he was debating if he could leave her to get coffee for them. "It has to look normal. I'll have a peppermint latte."

"Watch me, and if I gesture, you get under that table."

"Of course." She didn't want to be killed, so she was going to take every order that she was given seriously.

The door opened as Kenji got in line, and Daphne noticed Grey's silver bob as she entered. The other woman glanced furtively around before spotting Daphne. She hurried over to her and slid onto the bench across from her.

"Morning," Daphne said. "Thank you for agreeing to meet me. Would you like a drink?"

"Cappuccino," she said.

Kenji, who'd come back for Grey's drink order, nodded. "Be right back. Remember what I said."

"I do."

Daphne had a form for Grey to sign acknowledging that she knew her statement was being taped and that she was telling the truth.

"I need you to sign this form as we discussed last night so I can use your testimony in my filings. You will be called into court to testify that these statements are yours and that they are the truth. Are you still willing to talk to me?" Daphne asked.

"I am," Grey said. "This has been going on for too long."

"Don't start talking yet. Let me get the voice recorder open on my phone," Daphne said. "Would you mind wearing one of my Airpods so I can get a clearer sound of your voice? The ambient noise in here is very loud."

Grey held out her hand, and Daphne put the left pod in it. She put in her right pod so that both of their voices would be recorded.

"This is Daphne Amana, counsel for Marjorie Wyman, representative of the culture office of Amba Mariam in the case regarding the ownership of the Hazelton-Measham collection.

"I am here with…state your name."

"Grey Joy."

"Who works for…"

"The Los Angeles Museum of Foreign Cultures as an archivist."

"For how long?"

"I've worked there for fifteen years."

Daphne wanted to get to the missing items, but she knew she had to build who Grey was so that Judge Mallon would allow the testimony. "What does your job entail?"

Grey sort of scrunched up her nose and shrugged. "Everything really. I catalog all of the items that are brought in and out of the archives."

Kenji was making his way back to them with a tray that had their drinks on it. She noticed he was watching the restaurant and the sidewalk outside.

"Did there come a time when you became aware of the Hazelton-Measham collection?" Daphne asked her.

"Yes—"

Grey broke off talking, slumping forward as Kenji dropped the tray and Rick sprang to life. Daphne was still processing that the other woman had been shot as Kenji reached her side and was hit with a bullet in the shoulder. He fell to the ground, dragging her to the floor with him.

Kenji hugged her close, pushing her under the table, and Rick was at his side as Kenji ordered her to stay there and took off in the direction of the shooter.

Chapter 22

Adrenaline pumping, Kenji ran full out in the direction of the shooter. He didn't let the graze to his shoulder affect him as he pushed through the panicked people in the coffee shop and ran straight across the parking lot. Xander was hot on Kenji's heels, and two undercover cops were behind.

Kenji had been trained as an operative, but he'd also taken extra combat training, and he drew on that now. He and Xander kept each other honed by working out all the time, something he barely acknowledged as he raced full-on to find the shooter.

He wasn't letting this man get away. Unlike the car, where he'd had to keep Daphne safe, this time he knew she'd be taken care of, and there was nothing that would stop him. This time the shot had been too close. In his mind, he saw Daphne lying forward with the blood coming out of her chest instead of Grey Joy.

This ends now.

Scanning the area where he thought the shot had come from, Kenji spotted a man in camo running toward the highway. Days of waiting and investigating were over, giving him an extra burst of speed.

He was gaining quickly on the other man, who was

carrying a rifle case in one hand and had a Glock in the other. The shooter turned and fired wide but still close to Kenji. Kenji used the man's distraction and didn't hesitate.

Gathering his energy, Kenji took a flying kick toward the man, hitting him square in the back and knocking him to the ground. Kenji also hit the ground on the side where he'd been shot and groaned as he rolled and got to his feet. The other man stood up too, throwing his rifle bag to the ground. He hit Kenji with a solid left hook to the arm that was bleeding where he'd been shot.

Kenji hit the man hard in the throat. Then he lifted his leg in a forward front kick and brought it down hard on the shooter's neck, knocking him backward. Kenji followed with a one-two punch to his jaw and then hit him hard in the gut, driving the other man to the ground before kicking him backward. He came down with his full weight on the other man's chest. The man put his hands up by his shoulders and stayed in position.

"I'm here," Xander said, sliding up next to Kenji.

"Search him. He dropped the rifle over there, and I think he had a Glock." A professional would have more weapons on him. Kenji wasn't sure how long he could hold the assailant, but with Xander next to him, he was sure they'd be able to keep him here or knocked out until the cops arrived.

"Who do you work for?" Kenji asked, dropping to his knee next to the man.

The man just shook his head.

"You were the shooter in the car on the freeway?"

"Yes."

"Who was driving?"

"I'm not giving that up," he said with a hard look. "Good luck keeping that woman alive."

"Are there more contracts on her?"

He shrugged, and Kenji drew back to punch him again. But Xander stopped him. "Cops."

Kenji almost didn't let that sway him. This man was baiting him, but he must feel confident that whomever had hired him would keep him safe.

"We'll take it from here," the lead officer said. "Thanks for catching him."

"No problem. Has the ambulance arrived yet?"

"Yes. The victim is being transported to the hospital," the officer said.

Hospital, not morgue.

Daphne would never have forgiven herself if Grey had been killed in a sting that they'd set up.

"She won't be talking for a while," the shooter said.

Kenji stumbled and fell hard on the man's chest, making sure he brought the full weight of his body down when his knee connected with the body. "Sorry. Ground's slippery."

Xander offered Kenji a hand and helped him up. Kenji took more than a little satisfaction out of watching the other man struggle to breathe. As Kenji got to his feet and the cops put the other man in handcuffs, Xander and he were ready in case the shooter tried to make a break for it, but he didn't. The cops collected the dropped weapons, and then they both felt like they could move.

"You okay? That wound on your shoulder is bleeding like a mother."

"Yeah, I'm fine. I knew this would shake something loose, but I don't recognize that guy. He's not from Mitchell and Partners or the museum."

"He looks like a hired gun to me. The cops will find out who's paying him. He's not going to want to go down for this. Grey looks like she might not make it."

"I guess that's been the goal, to keep her from talking," Kenji said. But something still didn't feel right. There was more to this than he'd seen so far.

"Luna's riding with Grey to the hospital, and I'm sure Daphne will want to go with her."

"Not today. Let's get back there before she does something rash," Kenji said.

"Rick's riding herd on her," Xander said with a slight smile.

Kenji couldn't smile about anything at this moment. His shoulder hurt, and his woman had been put in danger. Once again they didn't have the person responsible. When he got back to the coffee shop, Daphne dashed into his arms.

"You scared me," she said, hugging him tightly. "You're bleeding, so I know you were shot this time."

"It's just a graze. The bullet hit the wall behind me. Other than Grey, was anyone else injured?" he asked.

"One lady fainted, but otherwise no," she said.

She called an EMT over to them and didn't let go of his hand while he was examined and had a bandage put on the wound. When they were alone, she turned to him.

"I don't like that Grey was shot before she could really talk to me. Was the shooter anyone we knew?"

"No. Hired gun."

"So all of this was for nothing," she said.

"Someone doesn't want Grey talking to you," Kenji said.

"I already knew that. I shouldn't have set her up like that," Daphne said.

"She knew what she was doing."

"You say that, but I'm pretty sure she was scared too," Daphne said. "I want to get back to my office and go through the notes I have. There must be something I've missed in all of this."

"Okay. Let's go."

"You're not going to try to talk me out of it?"

"Why would I? Like you said, there isn't anything else to find here. The cops will let us know what they find out from the shooter. Maybe it will be a name that you can use," Kenji said.

Daphne was pale, and her hand shook as she looked back at the table where her work bag and phone still sat. He nodded to Rick, and the other man got Daphne's stuff, even cleaning the blood spatter from her phone before bringing it over to them.

"Here you go," Rick said. "Sorry things got hairy."

"Thanks," Daphne said, taking her bag and phone from him. "Sorry I was difficult when Kenji left."

"No problem. I hate not being in the action too," Rick said, winking at her before he turned away.

Kenji looked over at Daphne, who held her phone gingerly. He glanced at it and noticed it was still recording. He took the phone from her and stopped it.

"Did you try to follow?"

"Yes. I told you I don't like seeing you shot at," she said.

Daphne wasn't sure that she'd ever be able to forget seeing the blood spattering from Grey's chest as the other woman slumped forward. Her hands were still shaking. Kenji stood behind her, the scent of blood mingled with his aftershave. He kept her in the shadow of his body as they moved, but she was afraid for him. He'd proved that he was going to put her life ahead of his.

She was angry that she hadn't seen this possibility when they'd set up the sting. She'd believed they'd at least have a chance to find out who was behind the attacks on her and the missing museum pieces.

She turned to say something to Kenji when she saw a black Mercedes driving too fast for the parking lot. Then she realized it was coming straight toward them, not slowing.

"Kenji!"

He saw the car just as it mounted the curb and plowed into them. Kenji wrapped his arms around her as they fell, his body taking the impact of fall to the concrete. He rolled with her until they were away from the car. Her head hurt as they stopped, and she realized she was bleeding…and so was Kenji.

She reached up to touch his face as they both heard the car door open. Kenji was clearly dazed, and Daphne looked beyond him to see Ben Cross get out of the car, holding a gun pointed at her.

The opposing counsel looked angry and not like Daphne had ever seen him before. She got to her feet.

"Ben? What's going on?" she asked, more than a little confused. Why was the lawyer trying to kill her?

"I'm here to make sure you don't ruin everything," Ben said.

"How? We are going to have our day in court, and you are a capable lawyer. I'm sure—"

"I don't want a day in court," Ben said. "I've had an agreement with Dan Jones at the museum for years that worked out just fine until you brought the case. Now everyone is looking into the Maqdala items, and my market has dried up."

"What market?"

"Selling the items back to the country that they belong to," he said, lifting his weapon and pointing it at her chest.

Daphne realized he was going to fire. She had the bulletproof vest on, so she walked a little closer as she heard Kenji curse behind her.

He shoved her to the side as he flew past her, grabbing Ben's arm and forcing it up over his head. Ben's shot went into the air as Kenji tackled him to the ground. The other man was no match for Kenji and the other members of the Price Security team along with Detective Miller, who were all streaming out of the coffee shop.

Miller handcuffed Ben and read him his rights. She also dispatched officers to pick up Dan Jones. Ben admitted that he'd kept tabs on Daphne through her paralegal, Janice, whose kids were at the same school as his sons.

They all went to the police station, where Ben further confessed to working with Dan to sell the objects back to the country they came from. Then Dan would "borrow" them back so they would remain on display. The shield that Nicholas DeVere had bought was meant for a wealthy member of the elite in Amba Mariam. Which had ticked Ben off…

Grey Joy recovered enough to admit she'd been paid to call Daphne and set up the meeting. She told them she was meant to just drop the censer so that Daphne would find it and be injured. It would seem like Daphne had stolen the item and was trying to sell it. They thought the cops would find the item with her. When Grey failed, Dan was angry with her and threatened her, and Grey realized she might be framed instead of Daphne and decided to talk to Daphne.

It was a long day and well past midnight when they left the precinct. Now that the truth was revealed, Pierce was willing to talk to Daphne about settling out of court. He was horrified to learn what Dan had been doing. Daphne was going to take a few days off and would be mediating talks between the museum and Marjorie.

Kenji stood quietly behind her while she was given all the information and their statements were taken. He had somehow had time to change into a clean suit and now leaned against the wall waiting for her. He straightened when he saw her, and her heart beat faster.

How was she going to be able to live with the risks he took? She loved him. She'd known that last night but hadn't wanted to admit it to herself or him. She wondered if she'd fallen in love with him again or if the truth was she'd never really fallen out of love with him.

Maybe the reason she'd poured herself into her work was that no man could measure up to

"You're off the hook. The danger to me is over," she said.

"Great. Where to? Your place or mine?" he asked.

"I'm not sure," she said. She needed time to think and process everything. She needed a few hours to make sure that her emotions were true and not left over from the past or the danger she'd been in.

"Really? Because I am," he said, coming closer to

her and not stopping until there wasn't even an inch of space between them.

"How can you be?" she asked him. This was hard. She was trying to do the smart thing. To prove to herself that she wasn't falling for Kenji again only because he made her feel like she was enough just as she was. That there was nothing missing inside of her.

But she knew it was more than that. He saw her, and he also accepted her. Was she willing to take the risk of loving and living with him?

She just wasn't sure.

How could he be? He didn't blame her for asking. They'd been through a lot the last few days, and it had taken a toll even on him. But for him, it had simply reinforced what he already knew. He wasn't letting go of her again. He'd admitted to himself he loved her, and he knew it was time to tell her as well.

A police station late at night wasn't exactly what he'd had in mind for when he told her he loved her, but he wasn't going to wait another second. They'd been through a lot today. He'd been shot at too many times. His shoulder throbbed from the gunshot, his chest ached from the impact of the fall he'd taken when Ben had hit them with his car. And he just wanted to be back at Price Tower secure in the knowledge that nothing could come for them while he held Daphne in his arms and made love to her and then slept.

That was what he wanted. But he had no idea what her desires were. She'd mentioned dating after her case was over. And he'd thought maybe that would work. But today had shaken her. She'd seen him in action, and she had said she wanted to see what his job was like, but he knew the reality of it was that she might not have liked it.

"Is it my job?" he asked her. That was something he wasn't sure he could change. Being a protector had been ingrained in him since childhood. He'd taken a less dangerous job, but he wasn't sure there were any other options for him.

"No. I mean, I don't love it, but you're so good at what you do, Kenji. When I saw the way you moved today, I realized how important it is that you are out there keeping everyone safe," she said.

He shoved his hand through his hair and saw that he had some dirt under his fingernails. Even Daphne didn't look as sophisticated and put together as she usually did. Her skirt had been torn when they fell to the ground outside the coffee shop, and she had a faint bruise starting on her cheekbone.

He'd done a great job at saving her life, but he wasn't sure he'd done enough to keep her safe. He'd had the idea to set her up as bait and felt so confident in himself and his team that he hadn't considered they might get their man but also allow Daphne to get hurt.

"I am. I won't quit."

"I know. I wouldn't ask you to," she said. "Truth?"

"Always."

"I'm trying to stall for time to make sure that what I feel for you is legit and not just some hangover from all those years ago," she said. "Not a pretty answer, but there it is."

"How do you feel about me?"

She chewed one side of her lip, something he'd never seen her do before, as she took a deep breath. "I love you."

She loved him.

That settled it. Whatever else needed to be sorted would work itself out. "I love you too."

He pulled her into his arms and brought his mouth on hers, kissing her with all the love that he'd kept hidden over the last few hours. There wasn't anything that would keep him from making her his. They'd work out the details of how to live together, but he knew that this time, he couldn't walk away from her.

She hugged him tightly. Turning her head, she broke their kiss, and their eyes met. "I'm not sure what to do now."

"We'll work it out together. You by my side…it's all I've ever wanted," he said.

"Not all," she said.

"I might have thought I wanted excitement and a life of adventure, but these last few days with you have proved to be more excitement, danger and adventure than the others. And loving you, Daphne—I think that will be the greatest adventure of all."

* * * * *

The Price Security team will be back in 2025.

Romantic Suspense

Danger. Passion. Drama.

Available Next Month

Colton's Secret Past Kacy Cross
Protector In Disguise Veronica Forand

Her Sister's Murder Tara Taylor Quinn
Cameron Mountain Refuge Beth Cornelison

LOVE INSPIRED

Tracing A Killer Sharon Dunn
Montana Hidden Deception Amity Steffen

Larger Print

LOVE INSPIRED

K-9 Ranch Protection Darlene L. Turner
Guarded By The Marshal Sharee Stover

Larger Print

LOVE INSPIRED

Deadly Secrets Cathy McDavid
Texas Revenge Target Jill Elizabeth Nelson

Larger Print

6 brand new stories each month

Romantic **Suspense**

Danger. Passion. Drama.

MILLS & BOON

Keep reading for an excerpt of a new title
from the Intrigue series,
CAPTURED AT THE COVE by Carol Ericson

Chapter One

Astrid's breath came in short spurts as her gaze darted among the Dead Falls Spring Fling crowd, searching for Olly's bright blond hair. He'd promised to be back before the fair ended. She'd been giving him too much freedom since his father had entered the Federal Witness Protection Program. Just because she couldn't find Russ didn't mean he couldn't find her...and Olly.

"I'm a sucker for sprinkles."

Astrid's head whipped around to confront her customer, a tall, dark and handsome...cop. Her lips stretched into a smile across her gritted teeth. Pointing at the cupcakes arrayed on the trays, she asked, "Vanilla or chocolate frosting?"

He wedged a finger against his impossibly square jaw and cocked his head. "That depends on what's underneath."

"Excuse me?" She raised her eyebrows. Typical cop—always with the flirty double entendre. Did they teach that at the academy? She hadn't seen this deputy around the island. Must be new.

He had the grace to duck his head as a blush touched his cheeks. "I meant the cake part. If the cake is chocolate, I like a vanilla frosting and vice versa."

"You're in luck." She poked a plastic fork in the direction of a chocolate cupcake with white buttercream frosting and sprinkles. "This one is chocolate. I also have carrot cake with a cream cheese frosting."

"Sprinkles?" He ran a hand through his short, dark hair, as if this were the most important decision of his day.

It might very well be, given he belonged to the crack Dead Falls sheriff's department. The residents of the island had been hopeful the new sheriff would turn things around after the disaster of Sheriff Hopkins, but Astrid wasn't holding her breath. Cops—if they weren't inept, they were probably corrupt. At least in her experience.

She sighed. "I can add sprinkles to a carrot cupcake, if you like."

"That would be great…if it's not too much trouble." He took a step back from the table as a middle-aged couple swarmed him.

The woman beamed. "Just wanted to say welcome to Dead Falls Island, Sheriff Chandler. I'm Lydia Feldman, and this is my husband, David."

As Astrid dipped at the knees to grab the plastic bottle of sprinkles, she kept one eye on the exchange between the new sheriff and the Feldmans. So that's why he was at the Spring Fling—meet and mingle with his constituents.

She screwed off the lid of the multicolored sprinkles and shook the bottle over the cream cheese frosting on one of the carrot cupcakes while she watched the new sheriff's easy banter with the couple. He had them wrapped around his little finger.

"Ah, I think that's good." He nodded at the cupcake in the tray, smothered with sprinkles.

"You're the new sheriff." She narrowed her eyes and thrust the cupcake toward him. "That's one dollar."

He carefully took the cupcake from her, the fingers of his left hand pinching the silver sleeve. He extended his right hand. "That's right. West Chandler."

Placing her hand in his, she said, "Astrid Mitchell. Welcome to Dead Falls."

She'd had sprinkles stuck to her fingers and had transferred them to his hand during the shake. They both eyed the sprinkles for an awkward second, their hands still clasped.

"Nice to meet you, Astrid." He slid his hand from hers, sprinkles and all. "Did you make these?"

"Yeah, I did." She wiped her hand on a napkin as if he had cooties. "The Spring Fling is a fundraiser for Samish Elementary, and my son is a student there."

"I knew that—I mean, that this was a fundraiser for the school. It's great to see parents involved in their kids' education. Do you and your husband do a lot of volunteering for the school?" He retrieved a dollar bill from his pocket and handed it to her. Then he peeled back the paper and took a big bite of the cupcake.

She didn't want to talk about her husband, her ex-husband, and a flash of blond hair in the crowd saved her. She waved her hand in the air. "Olly!"

Her son galloped toward her in the booth, his long, skinny legs almost tangling. "Hey, Mom."

"You were gone so long. Where did you end up going?"

He flung his arm out to the side. "You know, just regular places."

He lunged for a cupcake with chocolate frosting, and she smacked his hand. "You have to pay for those. It's a fundraiser."

"I'll get that for him." Sheriff Chandler handed her a crumpled bill.

"Hey, thanks." Olly sank his teeth into the cupcake and asked with his mouth full, "Are you the new sheriff?"

Even her son had figured it out before she had. "This is Sheriff Chandler. Sheriff, this is my son, Olly."

"Good to meet you, Olly." He raised the half-eaten cupcake in the air as he turned away. "Thank you."

Astrid stared after him, the khaki material of his uniform stretched across his broad back as he reached out to shake another hand. He'd only wanted to hit on her and had decided to hightail it out of here as soon as her son showed up. Jerk.

As Olly stuffed the rest of the treat in his mouth, leaving a smear of chocolate on his chin, Astrid noticed his high color and bright eyes. He still hadn't told her what he'd been up to all afternoon while she'd been slaving away at the cupcake booth. "So, where did you and Logan go?"

"Umm, we took our bikes out and rode around, near the cove and stuff." He jabbed a dirty finger at another cupcake. "Can I have that one if I pay you when we get home?"

"Hold on." She turned to Peyton, skipping up to the booth, followed by her mom, Sam. "Hi, you two. Cupcakes?"

"They look delish." Sam patted her curvy hip. "I know I shouldn't, but hey, it's for the school, right?"

"Exactly." Astrid nudged Olly. "Did you say hi to Peyton?"

Olly dropped his chin to his chest, looking up at Peyton through his lashes. "Yeah, hi."

Astrid and Sam exchanged grins as Sam plucked two cupcakes from the tray. Some of the kids were just getting beyond their shyness with the opposite sex, but Peyton and Olly were not among them. Astrid was fine with that. She didn't need to deal with girl problems just yet, not as a single mother.

Peyton swiped her tongue along some vanilla frosting. "I saw you and Logan on your bikes on the cliff over the cove."

"Did not." Olly kicked the leg of the table with the toe of his sneaker, and the remaining cupcakes trembled. Astrid gave him a sharp look from the corner of her eye.

She'd told Olly plenty of times not to ride his bike on the cliff. The lack of guardrails on the edge would result in a sheer drop to the cove.

As Sam peeled back the paper on her cupcake, she asked, "Did you meet the new sheriff? He's here somewhere."

"I did meet him. He bought a cupcake."

"He *is* a cupcake. Or is that beefcake?" Sam wiggled her eyebrows up and down. "And I heard he's single."

"Yeah, he's all right." Astrid stuffed the bills in the cash tin and closed it with a bang. "Let's hope he's better than the last guy."

"Mom." Peyton tugged on Sam's sleeve. "Can we play the game to get a betta fish before they close the booth?"

"Sure. I'll win one for you." Sam gave Astrid a wink before walking away with her daughter.

Still eyeing one of the last of the cupcakes, Olly said, "Fair's almost over, Mom. Can I have that one for free now?"

"You can have it now and pay me later. I baked these to make money for your school, not so you could gobble them all up."

He snatched it up as if he were afraid she'd change her mind.

As she consolidated the remaining cupcakes on one

tray and stacked the other trays, she asked, "Were you and Logan on the cliff above the cove on your bikes today?"

"Peyton doesn't know anything. We weren't up there. Logan's not allowed to ride on the cliff, either." He pulled his cupcake apart at the middle and stuck the bottom half on top of the frosting to make a little cake with icing in the middle. His uncle had taught him that trick.

She decided not to press him but didn't know whether or not to believe him. Ever since she'd told him his father would be away for a long time for his own safety, Olly had been secretive. Her friend Hannah Maddox, who was a child psychologist, told her it was natural for Olly to close down a bit after that news.

Astrid had been trying to give him a little space to process, but she'd been having a hard time of it since her brother, Tate, had left on a special assignment to DC. He'd followed a woman there, and she had no intention of dragging him back here with her whining about Olly. He was her son, and she'd have to raise him as a single mother.

"These are awesome, Mom." Olly rubbed his belly and nodded. "Good job."

She ruffled his shaggy blond hair. "Thanks. Clean your hands off with this sanitizer. Then take this tray with the last of the cupcakes, walk around and try to sell them while I pack up."

She held her breath, expecting pushback, but he squirted a dollop of the clear gel in his palm and vigorously rubbed his hands together. As he grabbed the tray and spun around, she called after him. "And don't try anything sneaky. I know there are seven cupcakes, and I expect seven bucks if you return with an empty tray."

He waved one hand in the air as he delved into the crowd.

Astrid wiped down the table and crouched to grab the box beneath it. She stacked the empty trays inside the box and put the hand sanitizer on top of them, along with a few items she'd brought from home. Lastly, she dropped the plastic bottle of sprinkles in the box.

The new sheriff sure did like his sprinkles but didn't seem to like kids much, or he didn't like women with kids. Sam had mentioned he was single, so that explained a lot. Not that Astrid was looking to date anyone, but if she did, she always thought going out with a divorced dad with kids might be easier than trying to hit a bachelor over the head with family life right out of the box.

She slipped her phone from the pocket of her denim jacket. It might be spring in Dead Falls, but the winter chill hadn't quite dissipated. She tapped Kelsey Monroe in her contacts. Kelsey was the PTA treasurer and all-around volunteer queen.

"Hi, Kelsey. It's Astrid Mitchell. I'm about ready to close down the cupcake booth. Do you want to pick up the money now, or should I drop it off later?"

Out of breath, as usual, Kelsey said, "I'm just picking up the money from the hot dog booth. I'll be right over."

By the time Astrid finished counting the money, Kelsey scurried up, a large duffel bag over her shoulder, weighing her petite frame down on one side. Kelsey flashed a set of dimples. "Your cupcakes were a smashing success. Everyone was raving about them—even the new sheriff."

Astrid cleared her throat. "Good to hear. I sent Olly out to sell the remaining ones. If he comes back with any more money, I can drop it off in your mailbox."

"Perfect." Kelsey shook out a zippered money pouch and

produced a sticky note and a felt pen. "Just write down the amount here and stuff the money in the bag."

As Astrid began to scribble the total for the cupcakes, Olly ran up to them, panting and waving a ten-dollar bill in the air. "Mom, Mom. Sheriff Chandler bought all the cupcakes left on the tray, gave me ten bucks for them and handed them out to some kids leaving the fair."

"Isn't that nice?" Kelsey's cheeks turned pink. "I like him better than Sheriff Hopkins already."

Astrid crossed out the previous amount she'd written and added ten to it. So, Chandler did like kids—just not hers. "He overpaid. There were only seven left."

"Well, I like him even more then." Kelsey zipped up the money bag and dropped it in the duffel with the others. "I think this was a great success, and even the weather held."

Astrid and Olly finished clearing the booth, and she made him carry the box of supplies to the car. Tate had left his Jeep behind when he went to DC, but she preferred her truck although she knew she'd have to trade up if she wanted to be a successful Realtor on the island. Nobody wanted to see a Realtor pull up in a beat-up old pickup.

Olly loaded the box in the truck bed and joined her in the cab. The sugar from the two cupcakes—maybe three— had made him hyper and he yakked in the seat beside her about the games he'd played and the friends he'd seen at the Spring Fling. She let him chatter on during the ride, enjoying his vivacity after a few months of morose silence.

She pulled the truck in front of Tate's cabin, as he'd insisted on calling it, despite its size, comfort and amenities. Olly had the door open before she even killed the engine.

As she stepped out of the truck, she called him back. "Hey, get the box out of the back."

He scampered past her and dived into the back head-first. He then followed her up the porch to the front door, hopping from one foot to the other. He either had to pee or she was facing a long night ahead getting him down from his sugar rush.

She slid the key into the door lock, and then shoved it into the deadbolt lock. It didn't click over, and she tsked her tongue. Had she forgotten to lock the dead bolt?

Bumping the door with her hip, she reached for the security keypad. Her fingers rested against the display with the red light. Had she forgotten to set the security, too? She must've been in a rush this morning.

She tapped the side of the box in Olly's arms. "Take this to the kitchen, and we'll put away the stuff."

She followed him to the kitchen, where he dropped the box on the floor, the metal trays clanging.

"Hey, be careful with that."

"L-look, Mom."

She raised her head to follow his pointing finger and gasped at the broken glass from the side door. She grabbed Olly, digging her fingers into his bony shoulder. "We need to get out now."

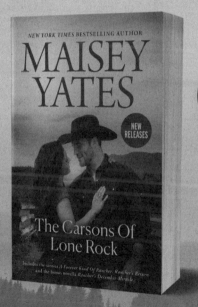

Subscribe and fall in love with a Mills & Boon series today!

You'll be among the first to read stories delivered to your door monthly and enjoy great savings.

WE
SIMPLY
LOVE
ROMANCE